SAUCE FOR THE GANDER

JAYNE DAVIS

Verbena
Books

Development editing: Antonia Maguire

Copyediting & proofreading: Sue Davison

Cover design: SpiffingCovers

ACKNOWLEDGEMENTS

Thanks to my critique partners on Scribophile for comments and suggestions, particularly Alex, Daphne, David, Lynden, and Violetta.

Thanks also to Beta readers Dane, Helen, Marcia, Tina, and Trudy.

CHAPTER 1

Tuesday 17th June, 1777
      William Charlemagne Stanlake, Viscount Wingrave, put the final touches to his neckcloth as he stood before the looking glass in his small bedroom. Getting out of bed before dawn was quite a novelty; he normally only saw a sunrise on the way home from a club or gambling hell. It was shaping up to turn into a glorious summer's day—he should appreciate that, even if it turned out to be his last.

"My lord!"

Will's valet entered, eyes wide and mouth agape. His crooked wig and loosely knotted neckcloth indicated he had dressed in haste.

"What is it, Ferris?"

"You said the duel was tomorrow!"

Will's eyes narrowed, the suspicions he'd harboured for some time surfacing. "What does it matter? As you can see, I'm quite capable of dressing myself."

"But I told—" The valet closed his mouth with a snap.

"Told my father it was tomorrow, did you?"

Ferris paled, his eyes sliding to one side.

"No matter. As you are also in my father's pay, you won't mind that I haven't the blunt for your wages this quarter."

1

Will glanced at the pile of tradesmen's bills on the chest, topped with the list of IOUs he'd written the night before last on his misguided drunken gambling spree. His quarterly allowance from his father was due; if he survived, he'd use it to stake some card games—sober ones this time. With his normal mix of skill and luck, he'd soon have enough to redeem his vowels and pay off most of the bills. He'd managed to supplement his meagre allowance that way for several years.

"But my lord, I—"

"We can discuss this later, if Elberton doesn't kill me. Hand me my waistcoat."

The valet picked up the deep blue waistcoat, its silver buttons glinting even in the indirect light. Will took hold of it, but Ferris did not let go.

"My lord, shiny buttons and... I mean, it's said they make it easier to aim..."

Ferris' voice tailed off at Will's glare, and he mutely held the waistcoat out. Will put it on and fastened the buttons.

"Coat."

The valet handed the garment over without argument.

Will ran his hand through his short hair. "Wig."

"Very smart," a new voice said. "Morning, Wingrave."

Harry Tregarth, Will's friend since their schooldays together, stood in the doorway, his face sober in spite of the cheery greeting. He, too, was dressed smartly but not ostentatiously.

"Tregarth, come in." Will straightened his wig. "I'm ready for a bit of breakfast." He turned to the valet. "Take yourself off, Ferris. I don't want to see your conniving face again today."

"Yes, my lord." Ferris bowed deeply and left the room. Will heard the clatter as the valet took the stairs at a run.

Tregarth raised an eyebrow.

"He's off to send word to my father that the duel is this morning, not tomorrow," Will explained.

"Ah. You knew he'd tattle. Marstone would try to stop it?"

"Undoubtedly. After all, if his heir is too precious to join the army, or even go on a Grand Tour, risking life and limb in an affair of honour is no better."

"Good job he's in Hertfordshire, then."

"Ferris has likely gone to Marstone House to get some brawny footmen to come and restrain me." Will picked up his hat. "Breakfast?"

Tregarth followed him down the stairs and out into the street. "You don't seem worried by the prospect of being stopped?"

"Ferris thinks we're heading to Hyde Park." Will smiled—there was some small amusement in the situation. "I hope he enjoys the morning there."

"Ha!"

They walked on, weaving between delivery carts and street-sellers calling their wares, before pausing outside a chop house. They'd be out of place amongst clerks and traders taking early breakfasts, but food was food. "This do?" Will asked.

Settled at a small table, Will ordered a small meal of ham, eggs, and coffee, surprised to find he had an appetite.

"I tried to present your apology again, via his second," Tregarth said, as he cut up his meat. "Jaston said he'd been instructed not to accept it."

Will shrugged. "I expected that, but thanks for trying."

"I've been asking around," Tregarth went on between mouthfuls. "You're not the first she's convinced that her husband neglects her, and doesn't care what she does."

"She's a good actress, I'll give her that." Will recalled again Hetty's big blue eyes swimming with tears, her lips trembling. He was angry with himself for believing her lies. He'd learnt his lesson with Sally, ten years ago, and had largely abstained while he was at Oxford. Even in Town he'd been sure to only dally with widows or married women whose husbands were complaisant.

He recalled Lord Elberton's expression too, as he walked in on his young wife, half dressed, in Will's arms. His shock and anger had been clear but also, Will thought, his hurt. Hetty had started to cry, sobbing that Will had forced his way into the house, at which point Will had grabbed his discarded coat and wig and left.

3

His lips twisted in wry amusement. It could have been worse; Elberton could have walked in ten minutes later.

"Jaston's found a doctor," Tregarth said. "He'll meet us near the Grey Coat School."

Will nodded, his mouth full of ham.

"He's organised a coach as well, with a driver who knows the way to Dover." Tregarth put down his cutlery, and met Will's eyes with a sober face. "Will, he means to kill you. He refused first blood, although he did not insist on *à l'outrance*."

Not fighting to the death mattered little when a bullet wound could kill you slowly. He'd be just as dead.

"I did cuckold him," Will said. "The fact I thought he wouldn't mind doesn't change that." He pushed his plate away.

Tregarth shook his head. "In truth, I'm amazed you've got this far without duelling someone."

"I've been in plenty of arguments, but the only two that reached the point of a challenge were..." Will's gaze fixed on the far wall of the chop house as his words dried up. "Damn him!" He slammed a fist on the table, making the plates and cutlery jump. "I'll lay money my father bought them off! I'm twenty-five years old and *still* he's treating me—"

"Wingrave!"

Recalling where he was, Will took a deep breath.

"Are you saying that your father paid people to apologise?" Tregarth asked.

"Not apologise, no. But Lathom agreed to settle the affair by target shooting. I did duel with Benhurst, but the seconds negotiated swords and first blood only. Possibly not paid, either, but an earl can bring pressure to bear, or promise patronage." He got to his feet abruptly, tossing enough coins on the table to pay for five such meals. "Come, let's be away."

Outside, he stalked off down the street, Tregarth having to almost trot to catch up with him.

"He may as well just wrap me in wool and suffocate me," Will muttered.

"Not before you've got an heir of your own," Tregarth said, between breaths. "That's why he's doing it, isn't it?"

"Apparently. He was like this even before Alfred died. He wouldn't buy me a commission, nor fund a Grand Tour. I was to take no risks until Alfred had produced a couple of heirs, he said. Although I've never understood why he's so concerned. Even if I get myself killed, there's Uncle Jack to inherit, with three sons of his own."

A mist rising from the Thames added a chill to the air as they neared the meeting point at Tothill Fields, although Will could see blue sky above.

The doctor awaited them by the school, and followed them into the fields. Lord Elberton was already pacing back and forth, his grey wig and coat giving the impression of a ghost. Nearby stood a small table, incongruous in this setting, with another man beside it.

Will stopped twenty paces away, while Tregarth and the doctor went to confer with Elberton's second. Hands in pockets, resisting the impulse to pace like Elberton, Will watched as the two seconds examined the pistols. Tregarth even squinted down the barrels.

He wondered what Uncle Jack—Colonel Jack Stanlake—would say if he were here now. Something short and to the point about keeping his breeches buttoned, no doubt, but reprimands from his uncle had never put his back up the way his father's rantings did. Would things have been different if Uncle Jack hadn't left for India when Will was only nine?

The seconds paced out the requisite distance, sticking swords in the ground to mark each point, and returned to the table. Will's lips twisted at the irony—his father's obsession with the succession had led to this. If Will had had his way he might still have faced death, but death on a battlefield in service to one's country was surely a more honourable end than duelling over an unfaithful wife.

But the past could not be undone, and the future was out of his control.

Tregarth waved Will over, and he and Lord Elberton converged on the little table. Elberton's lips were pressed together in a thin line and he glared as he gestured for Will to choose a weapon.

Will took the nearest, checking there was enough powder in the pan.

"You will take your positions, gentlemen, and turn to face each other," Jaston directed. "On the drop of my handkerchief you will fire. If the matter is not resolved at that point, you will remain in position while we collect the pistols and reload them."

Jaston looked at Will, waiting for his agreement before turning his gaze to his own principal. Elberton nodded, and strode off to his mark.

Will took his place, breathing deeply of the damp air. His heart accelerated, but aside from that he felt remarkably calm. The click of the hammer moving into position as he cocked the pistol was loud in the stillness. Turning sideways, he presented his right side to Elberton, keeping one eye on Jaston's handkerchief. As it fluttered to the ground, he raised his arm and fired well above his opponent's head, the shot ringing in his ears.

He felt nothing; glancing down, there was no blood to be seen. He had only heard one shot, so Elberton must have fired at exactly the same time, however unlikely that seemed.

Elberton's shout of rage gave him the true explanation—his opponent's pistol had misfired.

A feeling of lightness spread through him, making him aware how tense he'd been. Fate was kind, he thought, turning his face up to the warmth of the sun.

Tregarth called him back to the little table as Elberton stalked over to his own second, anger in every line of his body.

"Jaston, what the hell did you—?"

"Both pistols were loaded correctly, Lord Elberton," Jaston said, not reacting to what was, in effect, an accusation of misconduct.

Elberton thrust his pistol towards his second. "Load it again. Now."

Will stood to one side, exchanging a quick glance with Tregarth.

"Lord Wingrave deloped, Lord Elberton. That is normally the end of the matter." Jaston did not take the proffered pistol. "To demand another shot goes against protocol."

"Damme, due to your incompetence, I haven't had my *first* shot!" Elberton thrust his face forward. Jaston took a step back.

"Nonetheless, sir, it will do your reputation—"

"Damn my reputation, sir, I demand satisfaction." He turned and glared at Will. "Do I have to strike you, sir, to make you face up—?"

"Take your shot, Lord Elberton," Will said. He turned to walk back to his point, but Jaston's voice stopped him.

"This will be a second *exchange* of shots, Lord Elberton. I insist upon it. I will not damage *my* honour by agreeing to such an improper proceeding as you suggest."

Will turned back and handed his own pistol to Tregarth to reload.

Tregarth kept his voice low. "Wingrave, you cannot delope again. Let him know you will aim properly this time, else he'll have too much confidence. He *will* kill you if he can."

"No," Will said, loudly enough for Elberton to hear. "I will do as I did for the first exchange. Lord Elberton made a valid challenge, and it was not his fault the pistol misfired." Whatever the rules said, *he* considered it an act of cowardice to rely on a misfire. A stupid opinion, quite possibly, but one he intended to abide by.

"Wingrave, your—"

"Tregarth, do *not* invoke my father!"

His friend sighed, but returned to the table to load the guns. This time Elberton chose; Tregarth brought the remaining gun to Will, and Will walked back to the sword stuck in the ground.

CHAPTER 2

*C*onnie knocked on the half-open door and stepped into her father's study. Beyond the windows, what had once been her mother's rose garden was now merely an expanse of grass, backed by the line of beech trees marking the side boundary of the gardens. Drops of dew glittered in the morning sun; the day would be warm again.

A portrait of the first Mrs Charters and her two daughters hung above the fireplace, the brass plaque on the frame giving as much prominence to her father's rank of baron as it did to her own name. There was no trace of Connie's mother in the room.

Bartholomew Charters sat at his desk, sheets of paper with pressed flowers spread across its surface. He was halfway through writing a letter—to one of his aristocratic acquaintances, no doubt. Connie had always thought he bred new strains of snapdragon only because it gave him an excuse to correspond with earls and dukes keen on plant collecting.

"You asked to see me, Papa?" She smoothed the apron over her skirt. Being summoned to his study invariably meant he had found some fault in her management.

Charters looked up, the usual furrows forming between his brows and beside his down-turned mouth. "Why is there no snuff in my jar?"

Because you only allow me in here once a week to dust and check your supply.

An apology, even if she didn't mean it, could prevent an argument developing. "I'm sorry, Papa, I didn't know—"

"I'm not interested in excuses. It should be a simple enough matter to ensure my snuff jar is not empty. If you cannot even—"

"I will order some, Papa."

"I want it today!"

"Mr Fancott may be able to let you have some, Papa," Connie interjected, before he could work himself up into too much of a temper. "You could write a note to send with Fanny or Charlie."

"Go yourself." His lips thinned. "And make it clear this is your fault." He waved a hand in dismissal.

Connie hid her smile as she left the room—as she'd hoped, he'd chosen the option that involved the least effort for him, and also avoided having to personally ask a favour from someone as lowly as the vicar. Upstairs in her room she untied her apron and donned her hat. She picked up her book of sermons, quickly checking to make sure it was the correct copy before retying the ribbon that held the cover closed.

In the kitchen, the smell of frying bacon, warm bread, and coffee filled the air as Mrs Hepple prepared breakfast.

"I'm to go to the vicarage," Connie said. "Do you need anything while I'm in the village?"

Mrs Hepple looked up from the butter she was shaping into curls. "You're missing your breakfast?"

"He wants me to go now."

The cook's eyes rolled heavenwards.

Connie took a roll from the plate. "I'll eat this on the way. Mrs Fancott will give me something."

"Can't think of anything urgent, Miss. I can send the girl later, if need be."

Leaving the cook to her preparations, Connie walked out through the scullery into the sunlit garden. Their house stood half a mile from the village, along a narrow tree-lined lane with mud dried into ankle-turning ruts by the hot weather. She crossed the lane, and took her habitual path across the fields.

The main street of Nether Minster was almost deserted; the few shops had their doors standing open, and only the clang of the black-smith's hammer broke the sleepy silence. Connie pitied the poor man having to toil over his forge in such weather.

At the vicarage, Martha Fancott was cutting flowers in the front garden, and straightened as Connie came through the gate. "Hello, Connie. I wasn't expecting you today." She tucked one greying curl back under her cap.

"Papa has run out of snuff."

"Ah. And all your fault, I suppose." She shook her head, glancing with a smile at the book beneath Connie's arm. "Come in, I'm sure Joseph can spare some. Have you breakfasted?"

"Not yet."

Ten minutes later the two women sat beneath the shade of a large apple tree, the table before them spread with rolls, butter, jam, and a pot of tea.

"How are things with you?" Martha asked, pouring the tea.

Connie shrugged. "Papa is as irascible as usual." She reached for her book of sermons and undid the ribbon. Opening it, she removed the small novel that had been concealed in a cavity in the pages and set it on the table.

"Did you enjoy it?" Martha asked.

"Very much, yes." Connie smiled. "Although more because Papa would disapprove than due to its own merits. I still prefer Mr Fancott's books, though, they give me more to think about." History and geography and languages—all interesting, but also knowledge she might need if she ever had to earn a living as a governess.

Martha nodded. "It is unfortunate that most of them are too large to hide in your sermons. I've had letters from the girls," she went on.

"If your father will permit you to help me with the church flowers later this week, I can give you all their news, and you can catch up on some reading as well."

"That sounds an acceptable way for a pious daughter to spend her time." Connie smiled as they rose, and she helped to carry the dishes back into the kitchen. "Thank you for breakfast. May I take some flowers?"

"Help yourself." Martha waved a hand at the border full of blooms.

Connie gathered a small handful of cornflowers and columbines, and headed for the churchyard.

Her mother's grave was next to that of the first Mrs Charters and her stillborn son. The headstone was smaller, but at least it *was* next to the other family grave. Connie wondered if that still rankled with her father, but she suspected he had forgotten about both his wives.

She replaced last week's wilted blooms and sat down on the grass, spreading her skirts to cover her legs. Her father would have an apoplexy if he saw her, but she'd never known him pay the slightest attention to this part of the churchyard. It was a long time since Connie had been in the habit of talking out loud to her mother here, but she still enjoyed sitting for a while in peace where her father would not find her.

She traced the lettering on the headstone with her fingers.

Henrietta Charters
1733-1759

That was all, but something like *Beloved wife* would have been an outright lie, from what Martha had told her.

Such a short life.

"Did you just give up?" she asked the headstone. "What you did was a sin, but Mr Fancott says that God would forgive you, even if your husband did not."

She couldn't remember much of Mama, only the scent of roses, and the security of having someone to look after her and love her.

Martha had taken over that role to some extent, but had her own children to care for.

Would she ever have children of her own? She hoped so, but there was little prospect of that at the moment. Her two half-sisters were married to close relatives of titled families but were not, she thought, particularly happy in their marriages. She wasn't interested in rank or wealth in a husband. The Fancotts were happy together, both loving and respecting each other, and helping those around them. That was the kind of marriage she wanted.

If wishes were horses, beggars would ride.

With a sigh, she stood. Her father would be impatient for his snuff, and she had almost forgotten about it.

CHAPTER 3

*T*he mist had cleared, and the sun warmed the side of Will's face. A gentle westerly breeze brought the scent of early hay and the sound of birdsong.

He stood side-on again, the pistol cocked, his right arm ready to raise it and fire. His honour demanded he do this, but there was no need to make it *too* easy for his opponent. The handkerchief fluttered, and he fired above his opponent once more. As before, he felt nothing, and heard only his own shot, but this time there was a different explanation.

Lord Elberton remained in position, his pistol raised; Will could see the small black circle made by the end of the barrel pointing directly at him. He swallowed hard as his opponent squinted along the barrel.

If I'm going to die, I hope it's quick.

The idea of lingering for a week or more while an infected wound gradually killed him was more frightening than death itself. On that thought, he turned to face Lord Elberton directly, providing a larger target. He was tense, but felt only a sense of regret—all he had to show for his twenty-five years on this earth was a string of mistresses and a bastard child.

"Fire, Lord Elberton," Jaston called.

Elberton stood as if frozen, then gradually lowered his arm and started to walk towards Will, his pistol pointed at the ground. He came to a halt a couple of feet away, his mouth turned down. Their seconds hurried across, stopping behind him.

"You said my wife approached you?" Elberton's tone was clipped.

"Yes, sir."

"I thought you lied to try to save your own skin."

"No, sir."

"You were not the first?"

Probably best to be honest.

"I don't know, sir," Will said, "but I doubt that I was."

Elberton's eyes met his, and Will had to suppress a desire to look away. As he watched, Elberton's head drooped until he was looking at the ground, his shoulders slumped. He pointed his pistol to one side and pulled the trigger. Then he looked up, one hand rubbing his face.

"I'm glad it misfired the first time, Wingrave," he said. "It seems your greatest fault, and mine, was believing what my wife said." He handed the pistol to his second, and walked off towards the waiting coach, defeat evident in his dragging pace.

The two seconds glanced at each other, eyebrows raised, and turned to watch him go.

"Better go after him, Jaston," Tregarth said. "I'll tidy up here, and bring the pistols round when I've cleaned them."

"Highly irregular," Jaston muttered, handing over the pistol and setting off after Elberton.

"And no hope of it not being the subject of gossip," Tregarth added, waving his hand towards groups of spectators gathered a safe distance away.

Will shrugged. Ferris would give his father all the details he knew —and by the time the valet had finished asking around the local area and listening to servants' gossip, he'd probably know as much as Will himself.

"Come, I'll help you clean them," he said to Tregarth. "Then we can have a second breakfast. Perhaps go on to Angelo's?"

"Very well."

Good—a practice session with swords would help to dissipate the remaining tension in his body.

Will turned into Pall Mall heading for his club, his brisk pace an attempt to work off his bad mood. He'd returned from his fencing session to find a letter from his father summoning him to Marstone Park immediately, and Ferris already packing. Will had tersely instructed him to unpack again, and left as soon as he'd donned a fresh shirt.

Once inside the club, he was accosted by a group of acquaintances, men he normally only saw across a card table.

"Unscathed, eh, Wingrave?"

"Lucky dog. Was she worth the risk?"

"Did you wing him?"

Will took several paces beyond them before stopping and turning. He'd have to say something, or he'd get no peace. "My apology was accepted, gentlemen."

"Damme, Wingrave, last time I saw Elberton he was after your death. You've the luck of the devil."

You have no idea!

"Indeed. If you will excuse me?" Will headed for the small library, hoping to avoid further inquisition. The usual group were still discussing Meredith's speech in the Commons the month before. Reducing the number of offences for which a man could be hanged was important, no doubt, but he didn't see the sense in endlessly going over the details. He picked up a pile of newspapers and settled himself in a wing chair in one corner, ordering brandy when the waiter came. It was time he caught up with the events of the past week or so.

The war in the colonies—the dispatches from the Americas reported only small, inconclusive actions. It was now summer, and so little achieved this year, what were they doing? Two leaders of a smuggling gang tried, and acquitted for lack of evidence. Announcements—betrothals, marriages, deaths. A new journal about the campaigns in North America in the 1750s—that might be worth reading, with Uncle Jack having fought there. Corn prices, lists of bankruptcies...

He threw the paper down—he'd survived the day unscathed, against all expectation, and wasn't in the mood for such mundane matters. There'd be someone in the card room to give him a game, although conscious of that pile of bills and IOUs in his rooms, he'd do it sober and for small stakes. He'd taken enough risks for one day.

Wednesday 18th June

Will sprawled back against the padded side of the carriage, gazing morosely out of the opposite window as they passed through the grounds of Marston Park. In other circumstances he would have enjoyed the view of gently rolling land, with deer grazing beneath artfully placed clumps of trees and the afternoon sun glittering on the ornamental lake.

The carriage came to a halt by the pillared facade of the building, rocking slightly as his escorts descended from the roof. Will opened the door before one of them could do it for him, and stepped down. Benning waited at the top of the steps, wearing his usual dour expression.

"His lordship will see you in the blue parlour, my lord," the butler announced.

"Very well, Benning." Will was tempted to find some excuse to delay the coming interview, but decided against it. Doing so would only make the situation worse.

Despite the high ceiling and the bright weather, dark blue walls gave the parlour a gloomy air. A small fire burned in the grate, making the room too hot and stuffy for Will's taste. The earl sat in a chair near the fire, his stick leaning against the arm and one bandaged foot resting on a low stool. He did not look up from the book he was reading when Will was announced.

SAUCE FOR THE GANDER

The usual games.

Will crossed to the tray of decanters and glasses and poured himself a large glass of port. Sipping the sweet liquid, he looked up at the portrait of his older brother. Once they reached school age, Alfred had developed the same reverence as their father for family lineage and prestige, not to mention the sense of his own superiority as the older son. The only image of Will in the room was in the family portrait over the fireplace, which had been painted over ten years ago, not long before his mother died.

He passed on to the portraits of previous earls, sipping his port as he gazed at their frozen visages, and finally picked up a book lying on a side table. He flicked through it, grimacing as he noted that it was a book of sermons. One of his sisters must have recently been summoned to read aloud from it, and probably questioned on her obedience to its precepts. Not that his father read such things himself.

"Well, what have you to say for yourself, sir?" The earl's voice was sharp.

Will suppressed a smile—it was petty, no doubt, but he had won the first minor skirmish with his father.

"About what?" He sat in a chair facing his father, slouching to one side with one leg hooked over the arm; he wasn't going to stand before the earl like a small boy awaiting punishment.

Marstone's scowl deepened. "Your idiocy yesterday. Not only fighting a duel, but allowing that cuckold a second shot after a misfire!"

"You appear to be well-informed, sir. Do I have Ferris to thank for that?" Of course he did, but he didn't expect his father to admit to spying on him.

"That is immaterial. The point is that your profligate ways nearly got you killed yesterday. I have had enough of you flouting my authority as the head of this family. You have..."

Will stopped listening as the volume of his father's voice rose. The earl's face, ruddy at the best of times, began to assume an unhealthy darker hue. Was he about to have an apoplexy?

17

"…if your brother were still alive…"

Instead of driving his carriage off the road while drunk.

"… married, with children of his own by now…"

If only he had, perhaps you would leave me alone.

"…arranged several advantageous matches for you…"

Chosen for their lineage, not their personality or looks.

"…managed to alienate *three* separate families enough to withdraw their agreements…"

Flirting with the mother works well, or pretending to admire the son of the house to an inappropriate degree.

"…ignoring my wishes too long. This time you will do as you are bid."

Will brought his attention back. Instead of the anger he expected to see, his father was smiling—no, sneering. That did not bode well.

"You will stay here at the Park until I have arranged your future."

Will took a deep breath, working to keep his own expression neutral as his earlier amusement vanished.

"Am I to have no say in this?" he asked, pleased at how calm his words sounded. He would not give his father the satisfaction of seeing his irritation.

"You have had three years since Alfred died, and several before that. Had you wished to choose your own bride, you could have done so, instead of seducing married women."

"Not seduce, father. I assure you they were all perfectly willing."

"Do not interrupt me, boy!" The earl slammed his hand on the arm of his chair. "You will stay here. I have sent to London to terminate the agreement on your lodgings."

"You had no right to do that," Will protested, sitting up straight, his anger growing.

"The rent was paid with your allowance, provided by *me*." The earl jabbed a finger in his direction. "That gives me the right. If you go to London, you will be returned here as you were this morning. Now get out of my sight!"

"With pleasure." Will placed his glass on a side table with a snap and got to his feet, not even looking in the old man's direction as he left the room.

Exercise, he decided. That might calm him down sufficiently to let him think.

CHAPTER 4

*R*iding attire donned, Will headed for the stables. He'd ordered a horse saddled, and he was pleased to see it was Mercury, one of his father's best hunters and his own favourite mount. What he hadn't expected to see were three more horses saddled and waiting, a groom holding each one. Will took Mercury's reins and mounted; the men holding the other three horses mounted as well.

Will glared—he'd wanted a solitary ride. "I do not require an escort."

"We have orders, my lord." The one who'd spoken looked to be in his forties, signs of grey in his hair and his body running to fat. His eyes met Will's briefly, then slid away. The two behind looked determinedly down at their horses.

"What, precisely, are your orders?" Will asked through stiff lips. While he was changing, he'd toyed with the idea of riding to London and inviting himself to stay with Tregarth. His father—damn him—seemed to have anticipated that.

"Well? Morris, isn't it?"

"Yes, my lord. You're to go no further than five miles." Morris shifted in his saddle.

"You do realise you will be working for me one day, Morris?" Will kept his voice quiet.

"Yes, my lord. But I don't want to lose my job now."

Will glared at him for a moment and, to his credit, Morris met his gaze. This was not the man's fault.

Damn my father!

"If I give you my word I will not exceed that limit, will you ride some distance behind me?" His father would never attempt to bargain with a servant like this, but he was not his father.

The men exchanged glances. "Orders was not to let 'im out of our sight," one of the others said. Will dredged his memory for the men's names. Noakes had just spoken; the youngest was Archer, looking little more than nineteen or twenty.

"I can see a long way," Archer added.

"Very well. If you do happen to, er, mislay me, I will end up at the inn at Over Minster."

He waited for their nods, then wheeled his horse and set off at a canter. Hooves clattered on the cobbled yard as the grooms started after him. Their mounts were capable of keeping up with his own, but were the men? Exercising the earl's horses did not necessarily involve jumping hedges.

He turned south towards the woods, gradually increasing speed. He jumped a hedge, and set the horse to a gallop across the field on the other side. As he spurred his horse on into the trees he spotted the three men entering the field via a gate in the far corner. After that it didn't take him long to lose them in the woods, and he slowed Mercury to a walk. Over Minster was a mile further on.

The Royal Oak stood on the edge of the village green, a sagging half-timbered building with a beady-eyed painted King Charles on its sign. He handed the horse off to an ostler and entered the dim coolness of the taproom. A couple of men played dice in one corner, looking up briefly as he entered before returning to their game.

"What can I get you, sir?" Goodwin, the landlord, was as thin as Will remembered, his head now almost completely bald. "My lord, I should say," he corrected himself, shuffling his feet awkwardly.

"A pint of ale, if you please." Will cast a glance at the two gamblers. "I'll have it outside."

Goodwin gave a small bow and went to pull his pint. Will wandered back out into the sunshine and sat on a bench by the door, leaning against the wall. His ale arrived, and he took out his watch and checked the time, wondering how long it would take the three grooms to stop searching for him and come here to see if he had kept his word. Leaning his head back against the wall, he closed his eyes.

Elberton's defeated look came back to his mind. The man would have discovered his wife's infidelities at some point, but that did nothing to mitigate Will's regret for having caused him hurt.

It *was* time for a change in his life, but he'd prefer it to be of his own choosing.

He turned over options. He could try to take a horse without being seen and go to London, but sponging off his friend didn't appeal. Earning a living from gambling was risky and required stake money he didn't have, and enlisting as an ordinary soldier would probably get him flogged for insubordination within a week. Whatever he did, his father was quite capable of having him tracked down and forcibly brought back to Marstone Park. An undignified process, to say the least.

If only Uncle Jack were in the country, he might be able to counter whatever his father was planning. His aunts would be no help; their husbands wanted Marstone's favour and would send him straight back, like an errant child. He'd just have to wait and see what his father decreed.

Marriage, most likely. His way of life for the past few years had been an attempt to stave off boredom, rather than an expression of his true character. What would he do if his father selected someone like the faithless Hetty as his bride? Or he might get some mouse who couldn't even look him in the face—he'd met some of those at the few society balls he'd attended. Neither prospect was enticing.

It was nearly half an hour, and two tankards of ale, before he heard horses on the road, and the three grooms came to a halt in front of the inn.

"See, I told you he'd be here!" Archer exclaimed. "We could've come straight here, like I said, instead of wandering round the woods like gormless idiots."

The three dismounted. Will raised a brow as Morris came over to where he sat, the groom's face set in a scowl. "You gave me your word, my lord."

"And I kept it."

"But you—" Morris stopped talking as Archer jabbed him in the ribs.

"His lordship only promised not to go more than five miles," Archer said. "And he's here, like he said. This isn't even four miles from the Park."

Morris still wore the scowl.

"Oh, very well," Will said. "Morris, I give my word I'll not give you the slip again if you agree to keep me just in sight."

Morris nodded, mollified.

"Get yourselves some food and drink," Will added. It was peaceful here. He'd sit for a little longer, then go back. It was time to see his sisters.

Back at the Park, he changed out of his riding gear before climbing the stairs to the schoolroom on the top floor. The girls were seated around a large table in the centre of the room, a scatter of books and papers across its surface. With them sat a new governess, much younger than the one Will remembered.

Theresa and Lizzie, at fifteen, were too grown up now to show enthusiasm, but Bella jumped up from her place at the table and dashed towards him. He grabbed her under the arms and lifted her high enough for her to hug him, before setting her on her feet again, her curls bouncing. Gone were the days when she was small enough to swing around.

"I'm glad you've come home to see us, Will!" Bella took his hand and pulled him over to the table. Her bottom lip stuck out a little as he failed to completely suppress a grimace. "You didn't come for us, did you?"

"Papa sent for me," he admitted. He turned his gaze to the governess. "My apologies, Miss…"

"This is Miss Glover, Will," Bella said, as the governess inclined her head.

"I apologise for interrupting the lesson, Miss Glover."

"It is no matter, my lord." She began to collect together the books and papers. "Tea will arrive shortly, in any case."

Will sat down at the table.

"Is Mr Tregarth coming, Will?" Theresa asked, her voice slightly breathless.

Will shook his head.

"Betsy said you fought a duel." Lizzie's eyes were wide.

"Yes, I'm afraid so. But no-one was hurt," he added, seeing Bella's bottom lip come out again. More guilt nudged at his mind—he'd only contemplated the effect his death might have on his father, without giving a thought to his sisters.

"Enough of such things," he added, hoping the heartiness in his voice didn't sound too forced. "Tell me what Miss Glover has been teaching you."

He met the governess' eyes as Bella started to chatter about Queen Elizabeth and the Armada. The governess pursed her lips for a moment, then turned her attention back to tidying her papers.

The notion that duels were affairs of 'honour' began to seem quite ridiculous.

CHAPTER 5

Friday 20th June

Connie's father looked up from a letter he was reading, running his eyes from her head to her toes and back again, his scowl darker than usual. His study was cooler than the scullery, for which Connie was thankful.

"Why on earth are you dressed like that, girl?"

"It's washing day, Papa. Everyone needs to help if the washing is to get done." *As you would know if you took any interest in your household.* "If we had another maid or two, we—"

"You need to manage the household better, as I've explained numerous times."

Connie bit her lip against the sharp retort she longed to make. It was too hot to bother arguing with him today. "What did you want? The laundry won't do itself."

"Never mind that now," her father interrupted, waving a hand. "I have a visitor today who will wish to be introduced to you." A pleased smile spread across his face as his gaze become unfocussed.

It must be someone with a title.

"Go at once and change into a decent gown, and dress your hair properly to look like a lady." He scanned her clothing again. "You are supposed to be the granddaughter of a viscount, do try to look like one for a change."

"Who is the visitor, Papa?"

"Do as you're told, girl, do not question me."

She stood her ground. "I only asked in case Mrs Hepple needs to prepare refreshments." Charters opened his mouth, but she continued to speak. "It would not do, Papa, to serve the best brandy to someone not deserving of such consideration."

"Hmpf. Bring a new bottle of the best brandy and one of port."

Definitely someone with a title.

"And come back when you have changed so I can ensure you have attired yourself correctly."

The visitor must be important indeed, Connie thought as she went up to her room. She regarded the garments hanging on pegs in her closet, and pulled out her best gown. Its fine woollen cloth was a dark green, worn over a sprigged muslin underskirt. It had only enough fullness in the skirts for a small bum roll; if her father wanted a fashionable daughter, he should have given her a much greater clothing allowance.

Her father's eyes narrowed as she entered his study. "That will do, I suppose."

Connie didn't wait for his dismissal. Mrs Hepple and Fanny looked up as she re-entered the kitchen, Fanny's mouth dropping open.

"He's expecting a visitor," Connie explained.

"It'll be his lordship," Mrs Hepple said, with a decisive nod. "Oh, you wasn't here when that footman came yesterday."

"Footman?"

"One of Lord Marstone's."

"I did 'ear that footman say 'is lordship 'ad been duelling," Fanny said, keeping her eyes on the collar she was scrubbing.

"Not him, his son," Mrs Hepple corrected. "Over some woman, I heard."

Connie was torn between her duty to suppress gossip and her

desire to hear more. She settled for listening while she sorted the remaining linens.

"Did 'e win?" Fanny asked. "'E's supposed to be a crack shot, I've 'eard. Be a shame if a good-lookin' young man got 'isself killed."

"How do you know he's good-looking?" Mrs Hepple asked. "When did the likes of you get to see him?"

"Must be," Fanny said. "Else 'ow would 'e get all them women to lie with 'im?"

"That's enough gossip," Connie said firmly, diverting the decidedly improper direction of the conversation.

Mrs Hepple muttered something about young girls thinking they know it all when they don't, then asked, more loudly, if Connie was thinking of picking some lavender for the linens. "For it won't do to stand in this steamy kitchen in your best gown."

The clop of hooves on the hard-baked mud in the lane carried clearly to the back garden. Connie set down her basket and hurried around the side of the house. She recognised the Marstone crest on the carriage that drew to a halt in the lane. The portly gentleman who emerged was clad in a beige velvet coat, elaborately frogged in gold, with froths of lace at his neck and wrists. It must be the earl himself. A footman handed him a walking stick and he hobbled up the front path.

Marstone Park was only a few miles from Nether Minster. As Charters was happy to tell anyone who'd listen, he'd attended Eton with the current earl's cousin. However, as this cousin had never called, Connie thought the vaunted friendship must be mostly in her father's imagination. As far as she could recall, this was the first time the earl himself had deigned to visit.

Why would he want to see her? Did he need a governess for his daughters?

Mrs Hepple called her from the back door. "He wants you in the study," she said, then returned to working the dolly in the soapy water.

Connie knocked on the study door before pushing it open. The earl did not stand as she entered the room, but did make an awkward bow from the waist, one hand gesturing towards the bandaged foot stretched out before him. As he sat back, his paunch strained the buttons on his waistcoat. His gaze swept her from head to foot, as her father's had earlier, but at least she hadn't felt her father was looking through her clothing.

"My lord," Charters said. "This is my daughter, Constance."

Connie dutifully curtsied. "Good day, my lord."

"Miss Charters."

Although she had not been invited to, Connie seated herself in a nearby chair, folding her hands in her lap. If her father wanted her to look like the granddaughter of a viscount, she would not stand before him like a child about to recite her lessons.

"Where were you educated, Miss Charters?" the earl asked.

"The local vicar and his wife taught me with their own daughters, my lord."

His expression remained neutral. "You manage this household?"

"Yes, my lord."

"It is but a small establishment, is it not?"

"Big enough, my lord," her father interjected. "I do apologise that the footman was not—"

"No matter, Charters," the earl said. "Miss Charters, how do you suppose you would go on managing a much larger staff?"

Was she being interviewed for a position as housekeeper? Surely not—not after her father's emphasis on his own father's rank.

"I would take advice from those with more experience, my lord, but I imagine the basic principles are the same."

"The household is well managed, Lord—"

"Do you read, Miss Charters?" The earl's words cut across her father's statement.

That was the first time she'd heard any approval from her father of her management. He must want something from the earl—but what?

"My daughter does not fill her head with nonsense from novels," her father said, before she could make her own answer. "She has been well trained to know her proper place in the natural order of things."

"You read the scriptures then, Miss Charters?"

Connie glanced at her father out of the corner of her eyes. If he suspected her of reading anything other than the books he gave her, his face gave no indication of it.

"Yes, my lord. I am very fond of my copy of Fordyce's *Sermons to Young Women*. It contains some admirable precepts." Admirable from her father's point of view, not her own. Her hollowed out version usually contained far more interesting books.

The earl nodded his head, his eyes narrowing. "So, tell me, Miss Charters, what the Bible has to say about obedience."

Connie's gaze moved between the two men in front of her. Was the earl as hypocritical as her father, forever insisting that she study the Bible and its teachings while rarely bothering to attend church himself? Charters was particularly fond of hearing her recite the verses about obedience and chastity.

"Saint Paul said that children should be obedient to their parents in all things," she said.

"And what about obedience within marriage?"

Connie looked at her father again. Where was all this leading? Were they arranging a marriage for her? Surely an earl would not be interested in any of his connections marrying the supposed daughter of the second son of a viscount. Nevertheless her chest tightened at the idea these two men might be deciding her future, and with no thought for her own wishes.

"Miss Charters?" The earl sounded impatient.

She took a deep breath. "Every man should bear rule in his own house, my lord." That was certainly a precept her father admired.

The earl smiled; it curved his lips but did not reach his eyes. His turned his gaze to the portrait over the fireplace. "Which of those children is you, Miss Charters?"

"It was painted before Constance was born, my lord." Once more, her father spoke before she could reply.

"Hmm. Only three children."

"My wife became ill shortly after Constance was born, otherwise I'm sure there would have been many more."

Her father was talking as if he'd had only one wife. His gaze was on her, his lips compressed. She dropped her eyes. It was no business of hers if her father chose to deceive the earl.

"Do you have any more questions for my daughter, my lord? If not, I'm sure she has duties to attend to."

"I think we can continue this discussion alone." Lord Marstone ran his eyes down Connie's figure again. "Thank you, Miss Charters, I look forward to further acquaintance with you."

She gave a shallow curtsey before leaving the room. Pulling the door to, she was tempted to stand and listen, but the consequences of being caught were not worth any information she might glean.

Half an hour later she heard voices in the hallway. Opening the kitchen door a crack, she saw her father shaking hands with Lord Marstone. Her father turned to go into his study after the earl left. She stepped back, only going upstairs to change when the study door closed behind him.

Her father had looked pleased. That was not a good sign.

CHAPTER 6

The countryside around Marstone Park was pleasant, with pretty villages set amongst fields, woodland, and streams. Will had spent most of the last two days riding, followed at a discreet distance by the three grooms. But he found himself longing for the wilder coastal scenery at Ashton Tracey, the wind in his face on the cliff-tops, and the sun glittering on the sea.

It wasn't just the different scenery that made him want to be there, but the happy memories. He'd spent most of his childhood summers there with his mother and siblings, while his father stayed in Town or at Marstone Park. Even after his mother died, their father had packed the girls off there in the summer with their governess, and he and Alfred had joined them in the school holidays.

Towards the end of the second afternoon, Benning found him to announce that his father wished to see him.

The library was an imposing square room, inadequately lit by a couple of windows on one side. Dark wooden shelves lined the walls, filled with leather-spined books and bound copies of reports and journals. Will had never seen his father reading anything beyond the parliamentary proceedings and newspapers, and suspected that he kept the rest of the library stocked only because that was what an earl was supposed to do. The effect would be impressive to anyone who assumed his father had absorbed the knowledge in all the books.

Marstone sat at his desk, beneath a huge portrait of the second earl. "Sit," he commanded, waving a hand towards a low chair.

Will perched on the arm, knowing from previous experience that if he sat on the chair properly he would be looking up at his father.

"I have arranged a marriage for you," the earl stated.

Already? He'd known this was coming, but so soon? How had his father arranged it so quickly?

"She's the granddaughter of Viscount Charters through her father. Her mother was the daughter of a baron. Not as high as I would like, but I want your heir soon, and you've managed to acquire a reputation that makes it difficult to find a match amongst higher families."

"I'm sure I could mend my reputation, Father, if—"

The earl slammed one hand down on the desk. "You know it's your duty to marry and get an heir, yet you have done nothing but gamble and whore your way through London since your brother died. I will wait no longer."

That was unfair—he'd never had to pay for a lover.

"It's time you learned how to manage an estate, so you can—"

"I *did* take an interest when Alfred died."

"For a few months!"

Will clenched his jaw. He'd tried, but the earl's steward was so set in his methods he couldn't explain why things were done in a particular way. Any suggestions Will made had been met by a blank stare and a refusal to change anything. It was no use saying that to his father, though—the earl was not open to discussion at the best of times, let alone when he was in this mood.

"I need you out of the way, Wingrave, so your reputation doesn't damage the chances of Theresa and Elizabeth making good matches."

Will straightened. "They're only fifteen," he protested.

"It will take three or four years for people to forget your... ah... *exploits*."

Exploits? He'd done nothing worse than most other young men in Town. What, exactly, had Ferris been telling him?

"When do I get to meet this… paragon?" There was a possibility—however remote—that his father had picked a woman he could get along with. Although as he hadn't bothered to even mention her name, it seemed unlikely that he knew anything of her other than her lineage.

"On Monday—three days' time. You will be married in the church in Eversham."

"What?" Will shot to his feet. "You can't seriously expect me to marry a woman I've never even set eyes on?"

The earl leaned back in his chair with the same humourless smile that Will had seen two days before. A cold knot of doom settled in Will's stomach.

"You will do as you are bid." The earl leaned to one side and pulled a drawer open, taking from it a pile of papers.

Will recognised the top one as the list of vowels he'd made two evenings before the duel. If Ferris had brought that along, the rest would be the tradesmen's bills he owed.

"How do you intend to pay these if I do not reinstate your allowance?"

Will didn't bother to reply.

"You could be taken to the Fleet if you don't pay." The earl tapped a finger on the bills.

"You wouldn't damage the family reputation that way," Will stated confidently.

"True."

His father still wore that smug smile. The feeling of doom intensified.

"I will pay them, all the outstanding ones," the earl said.

Will didn't think thanks were appropriate.

"And if you disobey me, I will cut off your allowance and sell Ashton Tracey to repay the Marstone estates for the monies spent."

The earl's smile was triumphant now. Will stared at him, trying to make sense of what he'd said.

"It's part of the estate, you can't sell it." he protested.

"No. It came as part of your mother's dowry. It is not a traditional part of the Marstone holdings, nor is it included in the entail."

"But it's worth far more than any debts I've run up!"

The earl did not answer, but pushed the bills across the desk. Will frowned—there were a lot of papers there, many more than he remembered owing. He turned the top one over, then the next, flinging them to one side. The first few were bills he knew he needed to pay, the rest he didn't recall. Most of them had 'paid by the Marstone estate' written on them in the steward's crabbed hand.

"I don't recognise these," he protested.

The earl reached out and picked up a few of the scattered sheets.

"Blue coat with silver trim," he read out. "Matching waistcoat and breeches."

Will closed his eyes—that sounded remarkably like the suit he'd worn to the duel.

"...crates of port, four of burgundy..."

Ferris must have taken some of his bills, and he'd never noticed. Being under his father's thumb like this seemed a harsh price to pay for not keeping a detailed account of his spending. He rubbed a hand across his face, realising his father had pushed the bills to one side.

"You have incurred some of these expenses by flouting my authority and taking your own lodgings in London, instead of staying at Marstone House."

Where every member of staff would be reporting my activities to you.

"You will wed this woman on Monday. You will live here or at Ashton Tracey until you have two healthy heirs."

It could be worse, he supposed. He could have been made to live here, under Marstone's eye.

"You will not go whoring, or swive anyone other than your wife."

"You were not so nice yourself," Will protested, stung that his father so readily assumed he would not obey his marriage vows. He suppressed the thought that his fidelity might depend on what his future wife was like.

"I'd sired the two of you before I took a mistress—I did not risk getting the French disease, nor being killed duelling over some strumpet before I'd got my heirs." He ran his eyes down Will from his head to his toes, the curl of his lip making it plain what he thought of his remaining heir.

"It's not fair on... what is her name?" The woman was clearly only a brood mare to his father.

"Miss Charters."

"It's not fair on Miss Charters, either, to marry in such circumstances." Unless, of course, she'd take anyone in line to inherit an earldom.

"It is not her place to object; she will obey her father. She knows her duties to man and to God."

Good grief, that sounds almost as bad as being shackled to someone like Hetty!

"...should be grateful I have chosen such an obedient wife."

Obedience—he's obsessed by it.

Will stood and walked over to the window, aware of his father's triumphant gaze on his back. He'd rather see Marstone Park itself go than sell the place that held his happiest memories, but Ashton Tracey was only a house and some land. Meagre though it had been, he'd find it very difficult to manage without the allowance from his father. If he accepted this arrangement, he would at least be able to live away from his father with an estate to manage for himself.

But what would the earl do to keep a hold over him once he was married? Of course—Ashton Tracey would still be held over his head. That estate would not be his own until the old man died, and if that went, so would his independence.

"You will be signing Ashton Tracey over to me, then, if I am to live there." He knew what the answer would be.

"Why would I do that?" The earl's brows rose.

Fairness?

"Then I decline the arrangements you have made."

Will had only taken a few steps towards the door when the earl spoke. "What will you do with no money?"

"Sign on as a deckhand in an East Indiaman." Will turned to face him. "Uncle Jack will see me right if I get to India."

The earl banged his desk. "I will not have a son of mine serving as a common deck hand!"

"Then you know what to do!"

This time his father did not call him back as he left the room.

CHAPTER 7

*L*ate that afternoon Connie was summoned once more to the study, where the lowering sun slanted a pink light through the windows. Her father sat behind his desk, a small pile of papers before him and a rare expression of satisfaction on his face.

"Sit down, Constance. I have good news for you."

That sounded ominous.

"You are about to improve your situation in the world. Lord Marstone came today to agree your marriage arrangements."

Connie stared at him. "Marriage?" *To the fat old man with a gouty foot?*

No.

"Yes, yes. Marriage!" His complacent smirk faded. "You should be thanking me. That is what all young women should aspire to, marrying well."

Nausea rose in her throat. "Papa, he's old enough to be—" She bit her lip against her words, and against rising panic. He was old enough to be her father, yes, but Charters wouldn't see that as an impediment.

"Ha! No, girl. The marriage is to his son. I'll have a viscountess for a daughter, a countess one day."

The son who fights duels over loose women? She closed her eyes for a moment—that could be worse.

"But Papa, I have never even seen him!"

"What difference does that make? It's all arranged, you ungrateful girl." He tapped the papers on his desk. "The contract is signed and witnessed, and irrevocable. You will be married at Eversham on Monday, at eleven..."

Three days?

Her father talked on, his tone gloating, but she was no longer listening. Was she even to meet her future husband before the ceremony? Was it truly irrevocable? What if she told her father—no, told the earl—some fiction about a lover, that she was no longer—

"Constance!"

She started as her father's hand slammed onto the desk. His smile was completely gone now, a vein bulging in one temple.

"Some gratitude would be fitting," he spat. "It's a better match than you could ever have hoped to make. Get your things packed up, and make sure you don't disgrace me on Monday. Now get out of my sight!"

Tears pricking her eyes, Connie got to her feet and left the room. In the hallway she hesitated, clenching her hands into fists so that her nails dug into her palms. She'd be alone in her room, but that wasn't what she needed—instead, she turned the other way and strode out of the house, out of the gate and across the fields.

The brisk walk helped to calm her mind a little, and her panic had settled into a dull weight on her chest by the time she reached the vicarage and walked around to the back garden. The vicar and his wife sat together at their little table beneath the apple tree, glasses of wine before them. The contrast between that picture of domestic happiness and what she might expect from this arranged marriage brought a lump to her throat. She took a deep breath.

Martha must have seen something in her face, or in her bearing, for she stood and came towards her, holding her hands out. Connie ran the last two steps towards her and allowed Martha to hug her close for a moment.

"Do you have time to talk to me? Please." She took another deep breath as her voice verged on a wobble.

"Of course, my dear." Martha led the way back towards the table, and Connie took the seat the vicar had just vacated. "Joseph, can you bring some tea, please?"

Mr Fancott set off for the house.

Martha leaned across the table and patted her hand. "Tell me what your father has done now."

"I'm to be married." Connie told Martha of the earl's visit and the interview she'd just had with her father. Her explanation sounded garbled, even to herself, but Martha nodded as she spoke.

Before Martha could comment, the vicar came back into the garden carrying a tea tray, a couple of shawls draped over one arm.

"It's getting a little cool." He set the tray on the table, and handed the shawls to Martha and Connie. "Enjoy your tea."

Connie watched him go, not feeling a need for the shawl yet, but grateful for the thought.

"What can I do, Martha? I don't want to marry someone I've never met, a libertine." Her voice rose in pitch as she spoke, and she paused to take a ragged breath. "I don't know what my father will do if I refuse—he'll force me in some way, threaten to cast me out. He... it's as if I'm a *thing*, something he owns, to do with as he pleases."

Martha did not contradict this supposition. Connie hadn't expected her to—Martha knew her father as well as she did.

"I can't escape, can I, Martha?" She had no relatives who would take her in, no qualifications or references to be a governess, even if she could find a job. No money of her own. "I won't enjoy being married to such a man!" A profligate, as the earl's son was rumoured to be, could have little respect for women, and a man who resorted to duelling... well, she'd seen in the village the results of husbands being prone to violence.

"Drink some tea," Martha said, pouring two cups and pushing one across the table.

Connie obeyed, the hot liquid welcome in spite of the warm evening. It soothed her a little, although she'd hoped for more sympathy from Martha.

"What am I to do?" Connie asked, when her friend did not speak.

"Make the best—" Martha broke off as Connie jumped up, her tea spilling on the grass. "No, hear me out, Connie." She held Connie's eyes until the younger woman sat back in her chair.

"First, Connie, believe me that if the match had been with the earl himself, as you first assumed, we would do everything in our power to prevent it. But we know something of Lord Wingrave, and I know Fancott considers he is a good man at heart."

"How do you know him?"

"I'm not at liberty to tell you. He may tell you himself if he wishes, but that should be between you and him."

"But he only wants me to... to breed—like buying a mare!"

"That's the earl's view," Martha said, her tone even. "It may not be your future husband's. And knowing what I do of the earl, Wingrave is probably being forced into this as much as you. No, I don't know how," she added, before Connie could interject, "but believe me, if there is a way to enforce his will, the earl would find it."

"But a marriage that neither party wants? How will that turn out?"

"You will have a family of your own, my dear, and more control over your life than you have now." Martha leaned over and patted Connie's hand again. "Men can be trained, you know, as long as you don't let them know you're doing so. But it's not unlike bringing up children—you must set boundaries and start as you mean to go on."

Connie's jaw slackened at this unexpected turn in the conversation.

"Come and see me tomorrow, dear, or stay after church on Sunday, and we can talk some more."

"My father..."

"If he protests, tell him you need me to explain your wifely duties."

Connie did not want to think about that now. She'd find some excuse, or just not bother to ask her father for permission to leave the house. He could hardly lock her in her room for days when she was supposed to be getting married.

"Thank you, Martha."

She didn't understand why Martha thought the marriage would turn out well, but as she tramped back home across the fields in the dusk, she decided she had to trust the wisdom of her friend.

There wasn't anything else she *could* do.

CHAPTER 8

Saturday 21st June

The day after the interview with his father, Will rode into Nether Minster. The maid at the vicarage told him Fancott was at the church, so Will entered the cool dimness and took a seat in one of the rear pews to wait. This church was as plain and practical as the vicar and his wife, with none of the memorial plaques for previous generations of Marstones that cluttered the walls in the small church in Eversham. Will had always considered those, and the stained glass windows paid for by previous earls, as his ancestors' attempts to bribe their way into heaven.

He used a handkerchief to mop his brow. Taking off his wig, he placed it on the bench beside him and ran his hands through his hair. Gradually the cool peace seeped into him, leaving him calmer than he'd been since leaving London three days ago.

"Wingrave?"

Fancott looked as hot as Will had been earlier, a thin sheen of sweat clear on his face even in the dim light.

"Mr Fancott." Will stood as he spoke, and they shook hands. "Do you have a little time to spare?"

"By all means, my boy. Perhaps a glass of ale? There is a shady spot in the garden that might be cool enough."

"So, that's my future," Will finished, leaning forwards with his elbows resting on his knees. "I don't understand why he doesn't marry again himself, if he's so opposed to Uncle Jack being next in line after me. It's ten years since Mama died, three since Alfred—he's had plenty of time to get another heir."

"Have you asked him?"

"I did once, when he first tried to arrange a marriage for me." He'd never seen his father so angry; he'd almost frothed at the mouth as he'd shouted about ungrateful children, the duty of obedience, and other things that Will hadn't bothered to listen to.

"I've wondered that myself," Fancott said, "after hearing of some of his attempts to marry you off. One possibility is the carriage accident, not long after your mother died."

Will sat up. "I didn't know about that."

"You would have been away at school. I don't *know*..." Fancott raised a finger to emphasise his point, "but it is possible he may have been injured in such a way that he couldn't father any more children. He was certainly bedridden for some time, by all accounts."

"I haven't heard of a mistress since then, either," Will said slowly, trying to think. That wasn't proof though—he didn't know what his father did with most of his time. Then he shook his head. "That doesn't matter now. What am I going to do about this woman I'm supposed to marry?"

"Hmm." Fancott settled back in his chair, the dappled light through the branches making his expression difficult to read. The lines beside his eyes looked a little like amusement, but surely the vicar would not laugh at his situation.

"Did you say Miss Charters is the granddaughter of a viscount and of a baron?"

"Yes, according to my father."

"Is her pedigree important to you?"

"Not really," Will replied. Within reason, of course; it wouldn't do to be marrying an uneducated woman. On the other hand, the young women who'd fluttered their eyelashes and fans at him had been of good birth, and all had been more interested in his inheritance than him. And Lady Henrietta Elberton, deceiver of her husband, also had an aristocratic lineage. If they were examples of women of good pedigree, blue blood was no predictor of a good wife.

"What do you want in a wife?" Fancott held up a hand before Will could speak. "A wife can be a friend as well as a lover, if you choose the right woman."

"How can I, now that my father—?"

"It is possible for many women to be the right one, I suspect, but only if you go into the marriage determined to try to make it work. Have you never given the notion any thought?"

Will rubbed his face, then picked up his untouched ale from the table and took a draught. "I wish to marry someone who would be as good a mother as mine was. She loved all her children." She hadn't left them to nurses and nannies, inspecting them once a day as most high-born women did.

"A good mother, then. Biddable? Obedient?"

There were those lines beside his eyes again, and a twitch of the lips this time. Will put his glass of ale on the table, firmly enough to make the liquid splash. "I'm glad you find it amusing, sir." He got to his feet. "I do not."

"Sit down, Will, do."

Reluctantly, he resumed his seat.

"Have you never met a woman you could imagine spending your life with?"

"No." But even as Will spoke, an image of Lady Anne came into his head. He hadn't loved her, but he would never have become bored with her.

Fancott was watching him, one brow raised.

"There was one," Will admitted. "A widow. She was content to remain a widow." In truth, he'd been too young for her, too unsophisticated, too ignorant. She had terminated their arrangement, not him —although she'd done it kindly. "She was a bit of a bluestocking."

"Some intelligence in your wife would be acceptable, then?"

Will recalled Hetty's vapid giggles. "A requirement, even, if I had the choice. But what's the point of discussing…?" Will rubbed his face again. There was no point, really, but he *had* asked Fancott's advice.

"Will, I cannot tell you what to do, but I can give you some things to think about." Fancott paused, one eyebrow raised, until Will gave a nod.

"Firstly, I know… I know of Miss Charters, and I think you will deal well together."

"How—?"

"No, I am not going to tell you more on that head. But do remember that you may not be the only one being coerced here. You need to talk to each other, and remember that sauce for the goose is sauce for the gander."

His parents had *not* talked to each other, so that was probably good advice.

"Do you wish to meet her before the marriage? She attends church here."

Did he? "To what end? It will change nothing."

Fancott gazed at him, reproach in his eyes. "It might help the two of you to adjust to your new circumstances."

The vicar had a point. "Very well," Will said. "But not in public, I think."

"I will see if she can be here tomorrow afternoon. I'll send a note over if so. On a different subject, I had a letter from Sally a month or so ago."

"She is well, I hope?"

"Yes. They now have six children, and Vane's inn is thriving."

"That's good. Alex is doing well, too. I try to see him now and then when I'm in Devonshire. The Westbrooks were a good choice."

Fancott smiled as he felt in his pocket and pulled out a watch. He flipped the case open, then shut it again with a snap. "I'm afraid I have a call to make."

Will rose along with him, and they shook hands again. "Thank you for your advice, sir."

Fancott did not release his hand straight away. "Will, you resent your father's actions—with some justification—but do not take it out on your wife."

That was fair.

"You probably have some notion of revenging yourself on your father." Fancott waited for Will's reluctant nod. "Do consider what Marcus Aurelius has to say on injury and revenge. You have read him, I assume?"

"Some time ago, I'm afraid."

"'The best revenge is to be unlike him who performed the injury.' Think on it, Will."

"I will, thank you, sir."

"I have confidence in you, Will. You can make a success of this marriage, as you can of your life once you decide what you wish to do with it."

Will stared after Fancott as he strode away across the lawn. That had sounded remarkably like praise. It set a warm glow inside him, however unjustified it might be.

CHAPTER 9

onday 23rd June

Connie checked her hair in the mirror, then put the comb and spare hair pins into her small trunk and closed the lid. She looked around the room one last time, making sure she hadn't left any of her possessions behind, and fastened the straps.

Dolland knocked on the open door. "Mrs Hepple says there's breakfast ready for you, miss." He eyed the trunk. "You want me to take that down?"

"Please, Dolland. You can leave it outside the front door. The earl's coach should be calling for us in half an hour."

"Yes, miss."

Connie stood in the doorway. Her room was small, with plain whitewashed walls, but it had been hers for all her life. It looked strangely unwelcoming now, with grubby squares on the walls marking the places where her mother's watercolours had hung, the vase empty of flowers, and the bedside table without her books.

Those watercolours, an inlaid sewing box, and a trunk of outdated gowns were all she had left of her mother, besides memories. It was almost as if Mama had ceased to be a person when she married. All her possessions had belonged to her husband, and he'd sold most of them after she died.

She turned and marched down the stairs, her shoulders squared. It was a new beginning, with far more potential than a life as her father's unpaid housekeeper. Martha hadn't had time to say much yesterday—Connie's father had only allowed her to linger behind for quarter of an hour after church, and had left Dolland to escort her home.

No-one was in the kitchen, but Mrs Hepple had set out a sweet roll and a cup of tea for her. Connie was grateful not to be faced with a plateful of food, but wasn't sure she could manage anything at all with the nervous weight in her stomach.

A murmur of voices and a giggle warned Connie that she was about to have company, and she assumed a more cheerful expression. Mrs Hepple came in through the back door holding a small vial and a length of pink ribbon, followed by Fanny with a handful of roses.

"I've got a present for you," Mrs Hepple said, handing Connie the vial.

Connie removed the stopper and sniffed cautiously. Rather than the sharp tang of hartshorn she'd been expecting, the liquid inside gave off the smell of roses—far stronger than the sweet scent from the real flowers that Fanny spread out across the table. In spite of her trepidation, she smiled. "You know Papa won't have roses in the house."

"Yes, but your mama loved them." Mrs Hepple sat at the table and began to assemble the flowers into a posy, snapping off the thorns and tying the stems together with the ribbon. "I'll give it to one of the footmen on the coach so Mr Charters don't notice until it's too late."

The Earl of Marstone's coach arrived promptly at ten o'clock. Her father walked down the path, dressed in his best embroidered coat and waistcoat, a scowl forming as he waited by the door of the coach for someone to open it for him. Finally one of the men loading her trunks came around and swung the door open.

"Sorry, sir, had to get the luggage loaded." He folded down the step and stood back.

Charters snorted and heaved himself into the coach. "Well, come on, girl!"

Connie ignored him. Mr and Mrs Fancott were approaching over the field, and she went to greet them. Mr Fancott carried a small valise—heavy, from the way he held it. He gave it to the groom to be loaded. She caught sight of Fanny out of the corner of her eye, handing the posy of roses to the groom with a whispered word and a giggle.

"Be happy, my dear," Martha said, giving her a quick hug.

"Constance!" Charters' voice called from the coach.

Connie ignored him, meeting Martha's smile with one of her own. She was escaping from one unpleasant autocrat; she had to hope that her new husband was not too much like her father.

"Write to me, Connie. And remember what I said yesterday," Martha added, before stepping back to allow the vicar space to shake Connie's hand.

"It will be well, Connie," he said. "May God go with you."

Connie blinked back tears. These two, and Mrs Hepple standing by the front door of the house, were her friends. Mrs Hepple met her eyes, and mimed dabbing her neck. Connie recalled the vial of rose perfume in her pocket. She hurriedly applied a liberal amount to her wrists and below her ears, then took a deep breath before entering the coach.

"What kept you, girl? You'll need to show more obedience than this to your husband." Charters' rant paused as the coach lurched into motion. "Do not disgrace me, girl, once you... What's that smell? What have you...?"

His voice faded in Connie's ears as she leaned out of the window to wave to the Fancotts and the small group of servants.

"Pay attention while I'm talking to you! His lordship will expect you to..."

Connie rested her head against the padded wall of the coach, closing her eyes while Charters' voice rose in annoyance. She wondered if he realised that marrying her off would remove her from his power.

~

Will stood at the front of the church, not wanting to wait with the earl and his sisters in the family pew. He was clad in the same blue suit he'd worn to the duel, less than a week ago. It was quite fitting, in a way. He'd been prepared for his life to change that morning, from being alive to being dead, but he hadn't expected to be going from bachelorhood to parson's mousetrap within a week.

The crunch of hooves and wheels on gravel drifted in through the open door. Will turned to get his first look at the woman he was to marry, feeling more nervous than he had before the duel. There'd been no note from Fancott yesterday, and it was too late now to change his mind.

The light blazing through the south door dimmed for a moment before two figures came into view. One was a thin man wearing the kind of wig that had gone out of fashion years ago and a scowl as thunderous as any his father managed.

Miss Charters was tall, only half a head shorter than the man beside her, and clad in a plain green gown opening over a patterned underskirt. A cap beneath a flat bergère hat concealed her hair, only a few escaped tendrils of unpowdered dark brown escaping. Her bowed head and the rim of her hat hid most of her face, but what he could see seemed pretty enough, in spite of her set mouth. She might still be a harridan or a mouse, he reminded himself; nevertheless he felt a slight optimism growing.

That feeling vanished as she approached and an overpowering scent of roses filled his nostrils. He liked roses, as they reminded him of his mother's love of her gardens. But the scent she wore was almost strong enough to make him gag.

He took a deep breath—through his mouth. There was no way out now.

The vicar cleared his throat. "Dearly beloved, we are gathered here in the sight of God…"

Will let the words wash over him, glancing now and then at the bowed head beside him. He made his responses in the right places, his new wife made her own vows in a voice that was low but clear, and finally the heavy Marstone wedding ring was on her finger, the huge ruby glinting in the light.

They signed the register in the vestry, and he offered his arm to escort the new Lady Wingrave to the door, squinting as they emerged into the sunshine. A slight breeze helped to dissipate the smell of roses.

"The housekeeper has arranged a cold collation," he said. "Then we are to set off for Devonshire."

Her hand was light on his arm, but he felt a sudden movement as he spoke. She glanced up, and he caught a glimpse of wide brown eyes before she lowered her head again. She was surprised—had no-one told her where they would be living? Perhaps Fancott was right, and she was no more willing for this match than he had been.

The earl, sweating visibly under his powdered wig, hobbled past them towards the waiting open carriage. Charters followed, bowing towards Will but hardly glancing at his daughter.

"My lady," Will said, leading her over to the carriage and handing her in, her hand clasping his firmly. He toyed with the idea of walking back to the park, but he couldn't abandon his new wife to his father's lecturing so soon.

Rather than sit facing his father's complacent expression, he spent the short journey pointing out various features of the estate as the carriage passed along the boundary wall and through the gates. Lady Wingrave looked where he indicated but said nothing, merely nodding at intervals. She had a clear complexion, dark brows arching above her eyes. Her hands, clasped in her lap, were not the smooth, white hands of an idle lady, but showed a slight tan, as if she spent some time out of doors, and her nails were cut practically short.

In contrast to his daughter's silence, Charters gushed about the elegant design and sweeping vistas. From the earl's faint sneer, Charters' obsequious prattle was doing him little good.

When the carriage drew up in front of the house, Will handed Lady Wingrave down. "If you will excuse me, my lady, I need to check the final travelling arrangements."

She nodded, but still did not speak. The earl's expression darkened, and Will felt a brief pang of remorse at leaving his wife in the company of the two older men. It would not be for long, he told himself.

In the stable yard, Archer was waiting with Mercury, and Will's trunks had been loaded onto the roof of the second-best coach. Will had packed his own things the evening before, including his mother's jewellery box—he didn't want his father to sell off her remaining personal items in a fit of pique. He'd also told Ferris his services were no longer required. No doubt several people at Ashton Tracey would be reporting his doings to his father, but he might at least be able to find a valet who had some sense of discretion.

There didn't seem to be much else on top of the coach.

"Archer, where is Lady Wingrave's luggage?"

Archer jerked his head upwards. "Up there, my lord, there was only two small trunks and a valise."

Only two trunks? Why hadn't she brought all her things?

He put that minor puzzle from his mind, turning back to Archer and Mercury. Keeping up with the coach for three days, with horses changed at frequent intervals, would overwork the animal, so he'd arranged for the groom to take him at a slower pace. Although Will would prefer to ride Mercury himself, it would be too rude to his new bride, at least for today.

"Look after him, Archer," Will said. "You know the way to The Crown at Marlow?"

"Yes, my lord."

Will headed back to the house as Mercury clattered out of the stable yard. He'd say a quick farewell to his sisters before he set off. One unwanted marriage in the family was enough—preventing their father from forcing them to wed men they did not care for might be easier now he had a wife.

CHAPTER 10

$\mathcal{C}$onnie looked after Lord Wingrave as he walked away around the front of the building, feeling suddenly alone. She turned and gazed up at the pale stone, glaring bright in the sunshine. A wide flight of steps led up to the front door. Half columns picked out the front of the building; two rows of huge windows were topped by a stone balustrade.

She would be mistress of this one day? It did not seem real.

She twisted the large ring on her left hand. It was a loose fit, and she clenched her fingers, suddenly afraid of losing it. The ring felt like a symbol of possession, of a commercial contract, not something to mark the joining of two people for 'the mutual society, help and comfort' suggested by the marriage service.

Taking a deep breath, she followed her father and father-in-law up the two flights of steps and into the house. There would be plenty of time—too much—for such thoughts later.

"Excuse me, my lady."

Connie took a couple more steps across the black and white tiled entrance hall before she realised that she was the lady being addressed. The woman who had spoken wore a black dress and plain cap, the bunch of keys hanging from her waist proclaiming her the housekeeper.

"You will wish to refresh yourself before your journey, my lady," the housekeeper said, with a small curtsey. "I can take you to a room where you may do so."

She set off up the stairs without waiting for a response, and Connie followed. She *did* want to wash off the overpowering scent of roses, but irritation rose at the housekeeper's assumption that she would automatically follow.

The stairs turned two corners before reaching a galleried landing. The housekeeper led the way along a corridor, and opened a door into a small bedroom. A pitcher of water and a bowl stood on a chest of drawers, together with some towels.

"Could you have some food packed for the journey, Mrs...?"

"Williamson, my lady. I will see that a basket is prepared for you. I will send a maid to assist you."

"No, thank you, I do not require help. But send for me, please, when my... when Lord Wingrave is ready to depart."

Mrs Williamson curtseyed and left, closing the door behind her.

A maid? She supposed that all ladies had a personal maid. Would her husband expect her to have brought one?

Shrugging, she rested the posy of roses on the chest and poured water into the bowl. Pulling off her fichu, she used a wet towel to wash her face and neck, the moisture refreshingly cool against her skin. It was going to be stuffy cooped up in a coach for several days.

With her new husband.

Although she was relieved not to be living in this huge house under the eye of the earl, Devonshire was also far from her only friends. What would Lord Wingrave be like as a husband?

Tall—she had noted that—with broad shoulders, and not fat like his father. Although his expression had not been welcoming, he *had* offered her his arm, and his talk during the short carriage ride could have been intended to set her at ease. There was politeness there, at least, and possibly some consideration for her feelings. And he didn't seem to look through her clothes as the earl had. Things could have been a lot worse.

But he was still a stranger, and the idea of intimate relations, possibly tonight, made her shiver. Could she ask for that to be delayed?

She gave her neck a last wipe with the damp towel and tucked her fichu back into her gown. There would be plenty of time to think about that in the coach. Picking up the bunch of roses, she made her way back along the corridor.

A dour-faced man awaited her at the bottom of the stairs, and made a small bow as she descended the last few steps. "His lordship and Mr Charters are in the front parlour, my lady, if you will step this way?" He turned and walked off, heading for a door on one side of the hall.

Connie stood still—the butler had made no mention of Lord Wingrave, and she had no wish to see her father or the earl again. Remembering Martha's admonishment not to be intimidated by servants, she walked towards the front entrance. As she approached, a footman dressed in ornate livery bowed and opened the door for her, his eyes sliding sideways as hurried footsteps sounded behind her.

"My lady!" It was the butler, his face even more severe.

"I will wait outside," she stated. "Please show me to a shaded part of the garden." She raised an eyebrow when he made no immediate move, and finally he gave a little bow.

"My apologies, my lady. I was instructed to show you to the parlour, but if you wish to wait elsewhere, there are some shaded seats in the parterre. Trent, show her ladyship the way."

The footman bowed again, and Connie followed him down the steps and along a gravelled path. The seat he indicated was set in an alcove cut into the hedge, blessedly cool. The parterre was laid out in a cross pattern, the beds bordered by neatly clipped box hedges, with a statue of a Greek muse in each one. The flowers filling the beds were not yet in bloom, and the dark, regimented hedging gave the garden a gloomy and forbidding air in spite of the sunshine. She much preferred the look of the vicarage garden, the grass usually over-long and the roses rambling through everything in a disordered riot. It must take an army of gardeners to keep all these hedges so neatly trimmed and the gravel raked. Perhaps the point was to demonstrate the earl's wealth.

Nevertheless, it was a pleasant place to sit, with no-one trying to tell her what to do.

～

Will found his father seated at the table in the dining room, a plate of food before him containing only crumbs. Charters, with a glass of port in one hand, was inspecting the ormolu clock on the mantelpiece.

"Where is Lady Wingrave?"

Charters looked around. "Has she not returned?" He bowed towards the earl. "No doubt she will soon be here to pay her proper respects to you, my lord."

Will was hard-pressed to avoid a sneer as Charters continued. "I look forward to visiting my daughter here, my—"

"She will be living in Devonshire," Marstone interrupted, his tone bored.

Will suppressed his amusement as dismay crossed Charters' face. His father seemed as little impressed with the man as he was. But he didn't want to spend time with these two—the sooner he was away from here, the better.

"If you'll excuse me..." Will said, and left the room before either man could reply.

The butler stood in the hall, awaiting Marstone's next command.

"Benning, do you know where Lady Wingrave is?"

"I believe she is waiting outside, my lord."

So she had declined to join their fathers—that showed some spirit, at least.

Gravel scrunched as the coach drew up before the house. Noakes sat beside the coachman on the box; a woman in servants' clothing occupied the seat behind them.

"Who's the woman?"

"Milsom, my lord," Benning said. "Lady Wingrave's maid. Shall I inform her ladyship that the coach is ready?"

"If you please."

"Trent, fetch Lady Wingrave. My lord, I will inform his lordship that you are about to depart."

Will descended the steps and stood looking over the park while he waited. The deer that normally roamed the grounds were, very sensibly, resting in the shade of the oak trees.

His new wife appeared first, casting an uncertain gaze at him as he moved forward to hand her into the coach. There was still no sign of her father, or his, although Benning had reappeared.

"Benning, inform Mr Charters that his—"

"No, please. Don't bother on my account." Her face, looking up at his, held a crease between her brows. "I'm sorry, my lord." She cast her eyes down. "You will wish to take leave of your own father."

"No more than you do yours, my lady." He had a packet of letters for the solicitor in Exeter. That was all he wanted from his father, as the deeds to Ashton Tracey would not be forthcoming.

She took his outstretched hand hesitantly, although she did not lean on it as she stepped up into the coach. He followed her in and took the rear-facing seat, relieved to find the smell of her perfume had faded. A basket on the floor showed someone had had the sense to provide some food for the journey. Trent closed the door and stood back as the coach began to move.

Will gazed out of the window as the familiar parkland gave way to country lanes, the feeling of unreality returning. Last week he'd been single and free—or as free as his father had let him be. Now he was leg-shackled to... to what?

His wife sat upright, back rigid, head turned towards a window. The hands clenched in her lap made him wonder if she was actually seeing the scenery. She turned her head, but looked away again when she caught his eyes.

Feeling the need to do something, he pushed the window down, then slid along the seat to open the other.

"I trust you have no objection, my lady?"

"No, thank you. The air will be welcome." She managed to hold his gaze this time, although her anxious expression remained. "May I ask where we are going, my lord?"

"Devonshire, as I told you." Had she not been listening earlier?

"Yes, my lord, I remember you saying so. But Devonshire is a large county, is it not?"

Connie watched Lord Wingrave's face as he described the house and grounds at Ashton Tracey, paying more attention to his expression than his words. He had appeared forbidding earlier, but his impatience had given way to something almost resembling enthusiasm, and his face was now lightened by his smile and the lines that appeared at the corners of his eyes. Blue eyes, she noted, and a square face with a firm chin.

Although relieved that his mood seemed to be improving, she was also dismayed at the confirmation that their destination was so far away.

"We will be several days on the road, then," she said, when he finished talking.

"Yes—we stop at Marlow tonight, then, all being well, at Salisbury tomorrow."

Salisbury—would she have a chance to look at the cathedral there? Mr Fancott had told her how much he admired it. But the journey pushed thoughts of the cathedral away. Salisbury was some way from Exeter. She would be cooped up in a coach with a man she didn't know for two more full days.

She loosened her fichu, wishing she could remove it and feel a little cooler, but that would be improper. She'd never travelled more than a few miles by coach; in this heat the journey would seem long indeed, even without her worries about her life to come.

A sudden movement made her look up. Lord Wingrave pulled his wig off and dropped it on the seat beside him, then peeled his coat off. What was he doing? Her father frequently removed his wig, and even his coat on a day such as this, but not in public. Her stomach knotted as she realised this was *not* in public. She belonged to this man now, whether she liked it or not.

And whether he liked it or not.

He looked more approachable without his wig and coat—less like his father, and younger than he'd appeared at first. Her father shaved his head; Lord Wingrave did not, but wore his brown hair cropped fairly short.

She averted her gaze as he unbuttoned his waistcoat. Was he going to remove that, too? Here, in the coach? Surely he did not intend to consummate—?

"I beg your pardon, my lady, but it is insufferably hot in here."

Not now, then. The knot in her stomach eased, but only a little. There was still later.

She took a deep breath. The topic had to be broached at some point—it might as well be now.

"My lord, may we have separate rooms at the inn tonight?"

His hands paused on the last buttons of his waistcoat, and he raised an eyebrow. "I am told I do not snore, my lady."

Connie felt her cheeks glow.

"I mean..." She swallowed hard. "Is it possible... er, may we delay our... our marital relations for a while, my lord?" She stared at her hands, only looking up again when he spoke.

"And if I demand my marital rights, my lady?"

Thankfully, he didn't appear angry. "You can force me, there is little doubt about that." He would have no difficulty overpowering her.

"You have just made a vow to obey me." Neither his tone nor his expression gave any indication of his feelings.

"And you vowed to love and cherish me, my lord. Is it cherishing to force a woman to have intimate relations with a stranger? No decent woman would wish for that."

She swallowed again, impressed that she had got all that out without stumbling. He had one brow raised again, but she could not make out anything but mild surprise on his face.

59

"Arranged marriages may be common amongst people of your rank, my lord, but even then, do not the two people get to know each other before meeting in the church?"

Not if they've been forced into marriage.

As Will watched, a muscle tensed in her jaw and her eyes dropped to her hands again. She did have a point.

"How long would you like, my lady? A week? A month, perhaps?"

"A month should be adequate," she said, with a small nod. "Thank you, my lord."

With that, she reached to pull loose the ribbon holding her hat, and placed it on the seat next to her posy. Resting her head back against the squabs, she closed her eyes.

Will realised he was gaping, and closed his mouth with a snap. His response had not been intended as an offer. Amusement crept in. She had bested him—temporarily, at least. He could explain that he hadn't meant it, but he thought he would not. The little mouse had some backbone and, more importantly, had not reverted to tears and pleading to get her way. Forcing her before she was ready was no way to start their life together.

She couldn't really be asleep—no-one could sleep in that position without their mouth falling open—but feigning sleep had been an effective way of terminating their discussion before he could retract.

His smile widened into a grin. His father would be livid if he knew what Will had just agreed to.

What had her life been before today? He'd initially assumed she'd agreed to the match for his title and future wealth. That might still be the case but, from what he'd seen, her father cared as little for her as his own did for him. Could he really blame her for agreeing to the match, whatever her reason?

In spite of the open windows, the air in the coach was close. He rested his head on the padded side of the coach, closed his eyes and attempted to sleep.

CHAPTER 11

*W*ill opened the basket of food after they stopped to change horses. There was a selection of cold meats and cheeses, fresh rolls, and pastries. Lady Wingrave accepted a few slices of cold chicken and a roll, but only picked slowly at the food. Nervous, he supposed, making a good meal himself.

"Thank you, my lord," she said, finally handing her empty plate back. She wiped her fingers on a handkerchief and regarded him for a moment. He thought she was about to speak, but she turned her gaze to the window instead.

Will packed the food away, and sat back against the squabs. He ought to make some kind of conversation, but what should he talk about? His address was not usually so lacking, but this was not a normal situation.

"Have you travelled often, my lady?"

She turned her head towards him. "No, my lord. I've never been more than a few miles from home."

So much for that topic. She clearly wasn't about to start a conversation herself. Complimenting a woman's appearance was his usual opening move, but she might take that as an indication that he'd changed his mind about waiting a month. He'd agreed, and he'd stick to it.

Giving up, he watched the passing scenery instead. Better a silent spouse than a chatterbox, he thought, turning his mind to the things he needed to do when they reached Ashton Tracey.

∼

Connie alighted with relief when the coach finally stopped in Marlow, glad to be out of the awkward silence.

A short, plump woman climbed down from the coach, demanding that Noakes take care with her own bag before turning to Connie. "I'm Milsom, my lady. My lord employed me as your personal maid."

"I only need those…" Connie found herself talking to the maid's back, as she had turned to give more orders about luggage, her sharp voice cutting through the noise in the yard.

Lord Wingrave had vanished into the building, so she stood waiting, feeling more lonely in this crowd than ever before. Martha had warned that her new status would require a personal maid, but she'd hoped to be able to choose someone she could get along with.

Look on the bright side, she told herself sternly. Staff can be changed. 'Be firm from the start,' Martha had said. 'There'll be some servants who'll spot your inexperience and take advantage.'

Straightening her shoulders, she walked across the yard and into the inn. No-one took any notice of her—which was to be expected, she supposed, as her clothing wasn't ornate or rich enough to denote anything more than a respectable woman.

"Ah, there you are." Lord Wingrave emerged from a door in the passageway, then turned his head and called to someone behind him. A woman as plump as Milsom emerged, but this one wore a smile.

"If you'll follow me, my lady, I'll show you to your room, and get your trunks sent up. You'll want to change before dinner. This way."

She waddled up the stairs. The room she ushered Connie into was small but clean; the bed looked comfortable and a large jug of water and clean towels rested on a washstand. A table stood beneath the window, open to allow in a gentle breeze from the fields behind the inn.

"Your maid can ask for anything else you need when she comes up, my lady."

She slipped out of the room as heavy footsteps and terse orders in the corridor heralded Milsom's entry. Two men followed her in, carrying Connie's luggage. Connie retreated to the window, and sat at the small table. The two trunks took up much of the floor space in the room, and Noakes deposited Mr Fancott's valise on the bed.

"One moment," Connie said, before the men could leave. "I only need that trunk and the valise. You may store the other one elsewhere."

The two men glanced in her direction, their mouths tight with annoyance.

"If you had deigned to listen, Milsom, you would have heard when I told you that in the yard. See to it."

The corners of Milsom's mouth turned down even further, but the inn porter rolled his eyes and shrugged. At least the men knew who to blame for their wasted effort.

When the men had taken the trunk away, Connie went over to the washstand and poured some water into a bowl. Milsom opened the trunk and lifted Connie's old muslin gown from it.

"Milsom, you may leave me. I do not need your assistance."

"But my lady, you must change for dinner. There must be something better than these gowns. If you hadn't sent that other trunk—"

"I will dine in here." It would be a chance to look at what the Fancotts had given her, as well as avoiding further strained silences.

"My lady, his lordship—"

"Milsom, I said leave them, and leave me." Connie tried to keep her voice calm. "I will have tea sent up in ten minutes, dinner in an hour, and you will arrange for my breakfast to be sent up one hour before we are due to leave in the morning."

Milsom stared at her.

"Is that clear?" Connie held her gaze until Milsom looked away.

"Very well, my lady." Milsom closed the lid of the trunk, bobbed a small curtsey and left the room, her stiff back showing her offence.

Connie sighed. If she hadn't been before, the maid was an enemy now. She walked over to the door—there was a bolt, and she shot it home. With relief, she removed the green gown and her underskirt and washed. Her second-best gown would do for now, and she quickly donned it.

A knock sounded, and she hurried over to unbolt the door. To her relief, it was the friendly woman from the inn with a tea tray.

"Here you are, my lady. That maid of yours said you'd be wanting dinner here, is that right?"

"Yes. Is that a problem?"

"No, indeed, my lady. I was wanting to know if you want a hot meal, or we have some cold meats and salad greens, and a jelly and cream."

"The cold meal, please, Mrs..."

"Mrs Farthing, my lady."

"Thank you, Mrs Farthing. You may remove the tea things when you bring the meal." That should give her a little time without interruptions.

She poured a cup of tea, then sat on the bed next to the valise. Lifting the lid, she took out a cloth bag. It contained a small embroidery hoop, a selection of coloured silks, squares of fabric, and needles. She took a deep breath, tears pricking her eyes. She had learned to embroider with Martha's daughters in their parlour in the winter, and under the apple tree when the weather was fine, enjoying the way beautiful patterns of flowers and leaves formed beneath her fingers. Once her father turned over the housekeeping to her, she'd had no time to indulge in embroidery.

Beneath the bag were books. Lifting them out, she turned them to read the titles on the spines. Several were novels, while the rest were essays and other books belonging to Mr Fancott that she'd expressed an interest in reading.

She still had friends, even if they were not here.

~

Will brushed a speck of dust off his jacket and went downstairs to meet his wife for dinner. The private parlour he'd arranged was empty, so he went into the taproom and bought a pint of ale, wishing he'd made clear arrangements for their meal. Women did seem to take longer to change their clothing than men, so he spent half an hour exchanging tedious remarks with other customers about the hot weather before going back to the parlour.

It was still empty.

"You ready for your dinner, my lord?" Mrs Farthing stood in the doorway behind him.

"I will wait for Lady Wingrave."

"My lady is dining in her room, my lord."

Damn. He needn't have bothered getting changed to eat in splendid isolation. How could he get to know her if she wouldn't even dine with him?

On the other hand, at least his meal wouldn't be ruined by the strains of polite conversation. They'd had hours together in the coach today, with hardly a word spoken. He had a month; there was no great rush.

"...bit of game pie left, or the beef..."

He'd missed Mrs Farthing's recital of the dishes on offer. "Game pie," he said, latching onto the first words he'd registered. "And a bottle of burgundy, if you have it."

"I'll send Farthing in to sort out the wine, my lord."

A decent bottle of wine, and perhaps a game of cards in the taproom afterwards, might enliven the evening sufficiently.

Perhaps.

CHAPTER 12

Tuesday 24th June

Will groaned as the banging on the door continued, his head pounding in time to the knocking. The bottle of wine had relaxed him enough to enjoy playing cards in the taproom, and he'd ordered another bottle. Or was it two?

Stupid.

"Come in," he called. He had a vague recollection of telling Noakes to wake him up at seven, so they could get an early start. *What a stupid idea!*

"Mornin' my lord."

"Archer?"

"Yes, my lord. Noakes sent me up."

"Damned coward," Will muttered as he sat up.

A muffled snort from Archer seemed to indicate his agreement.

"What time did you get here last night?" Will remembered seeing Noakes and the coachman drinking in the taproom, but not Archer.

"Quite late, my lord, went straight to bed. Mercury's fine, though. I reckon it'll take me a couple of days longer than you to get there without tiring him too much."

Will hadn't given much thought to the staff he'd need at Ashton

Tracey, but he recalled that Archer had been the quickest thinking of the three grooms who'd been following him around for days. This man might be worth having. "Get some coffee sent up, will you? And tell Noakes he's to take Mercury down. You can go on the coach."

"Yes, my lord."

When Archer had gone, Will checked his pockets, spreading the coins out on the bed. He was relieved to find he had a little more money than he'd started with. They'd been playing for small stakes and, surprisingly, he'd enjoyed the game as much as the higher-stakes ones he was used to in London.

That would have to be the last gambling for a while. He had only the money his father had given him to run Ashton Tracey, and he wasn't going to risk losing that.

~

Used to rising early, Connie was already awake and dressed when Milsom knocked on the door, bearing a breakfast tray.

"Leave it on the table," Connie said, ignoring the way the maid's gaze swept over the old muslin gown she'd donned. The prospect of remaining cooler had won over looking well turned out.

Connie poured coffee from the jug and broke a piece from one of the sweet rolls. Unlike her wedding day, she had an appetite this morning. She'd spent the first part of the night wondering if Lord Wingrave would come to her room, in spite of what he'd said in the coach, but had slept well when it became clear he would not.

Milsom fussed about brushing down the green gown and folding it into the trunk. When she fastened the lid, Connie dismissed her. She'd pack the books up herself.

Half an hour later she stood in the inn yard, the air still pleasantly cool. Lord Wingrave was the last of their party to appear, squinting against the morning sunlight. Had he over-indulged the evening before?

Martha and her husband thought it would be well, she reminded herself. One evening's drinking did not make a man a drunkard.

She wasn't sure whether to be pleased or sorry when the groom closed the door behind her. With any luck, riding on top of the coach would give Lord Wingrave a taste of Milsom's sour temper and make him more likely to allow her to be replaced.

She'd chosen a book from the selection the Fancotts had given her. When she opened Volume I of *Tristram Shandy* she found a note written in Mr Fancott's hand, saying that if she liked it, she should be able to buy the complete set quite easily as there was a good bookshop in Exeter.

Connie paused as that idea sank in. If her husband gave her an allowance, as Martha thought he would, she would be able to buy books whenever she wished.

It was only much later that she wondered how Mr Fancott knew she would be living near Exeter.

Will clambered up to the roof of the coach, the effort making his head pound. Lady Wingrave's pinch-faced maid was already sitting on the bench behind the driver, and had the temerity to look down her nose at him.

"Sit with the driver," he ordered, and sat in her place with his hat tipped forward to block out the sun.

Archer sat next to him, but twisted himself around to look behind. Following his gaze, Will saw he was watching Noakes riding out of the inn yard on Mercury.

"You're not happy to be on the coach?" Will asked, suspecting what the answer would be.

"I do what you say, my lord," Archer said, now staring straight ahead.

As he thought—he'd offended the groom. *Damn.* Best get this over with now, then, before Archer's resentment built up any further.

"Noakes will be going back to Marstone Park with the coach," he said, keeping his voice low. "I was hoping you wouldn't mind staying on in Devonshire."

Archer's head turned towards him, eyes widening.

"You don't want to?" Will asked. "Got a girl in Hertfordshire?"

"No, my lord. I mean…no girl."

"Just say it, Archer," Will said, when the groom hesitated before speaking.

"You're asking me what I want?"

"Don't worry, I won't make a habit of it." He was pleased to see that this raised a brief smile. "I will be paying the staff at Ashton Tracey, not my father. I want some people there who will be working for *me*, not for him. That means people who want to be there, not ones who've been made to move to Devonshire against their will."

If his head didn't hurt, he'd have been quite amused by the changing expressions on Archer's face. The groom's initial smile was followed by a frown as he worked out the implications, then a stare into the distance.

"You've got a brain, Archer, you're wasted as an under-groom. But you'd have to be loyal to me. Think on it."

Will closed his eyes, wishing the bench had a higher rail at the back so he could doze without risking falling off the coach.

"My lord?"

"What?" He opened an eye to see Archer holding a stone bottle.

"Mrs Farthing gave us some elderflower cordial. Might help your head."

Will took the bottle and pulled out the cork. The stuff smelled sweet, but that could be a good thing.

"Thank you, Archer. Is that a 'yes'?"

"I reckon."

The coach made good time on the sun-baked roads and Will's head had cleared by the time they stopped for refreshments. He'd ride inside when they resumed the journey—he'd had enough of his eyes and mouth filling with dust.

His wife descended from the coach before he could offer his arm. Her gown today was even less fashionable than the green one she'd worn the day before, the pattern on the muslin faded. He knew a dowry hadn't been his father's priority when he chose the next Countess of Marstone, but he was surprised she seemed to have so little in the way of decent clothing.

How many people had his father approached? Surely not many; he'd only had a couple of days, unless he'd been planning this for some time. Had he needed to find someone desperate for money to get anyone to accept?

Connie asked to use a private room at the inn, then joined Lord Wingrave in a parlour where the landlord had provided a cold collation of sliced beef and a raised pie, with a lemon syllabub. She took food from the dishes he offered with a word of thanks, but did not eat much. It was too hot.

Lord Wingrave ate sparingly too, his brow creased—in thought or annoyance, she couldn't tell. Her father, on the rare occasions she ate with him and guests, had not wished to hear anything she had to say. Lord Wingrave seemed little like her father, from what she'd seen so far, but she didn't want to risk irritating him when they had another day and a half to travel together.

When they were ready to set off, he followed her into the coach. She sat gazing out of the window for a while, fascinated by the changing scenery. Glancing at his face now and then, she could see that he seemed to be lost in thought.

"What is this town?" she asked, as they slowed to pass market stalls in a wide street between tall buildings.

"Andover."

She had hoped for a little more information, but it was clear Lord Wingrave still did not wish to talk. With an inaudible sigh, she picked up *Tristram Shandy* again and found her place. Better to pretend she did not wish to converse at all than to be ignored, so for the rest of the journey she divided her attention between the window and her book.

They arrived in Salisbury late in the afternoon. Connie caught a glimpse of the cathedral spire from a turn in the road, but as the coach rumbled on through the streets it passed out of view behind them.

"Did you say we were stopping here?" she asked, trying to keep the disappointment from her voice.

Lord Wingrave turned his head. "The Rose and Crown is just over the river." As he spoke, the coach began to slow.

"I trust you will dine with me this evening, madam," Lord Wingrave said as he handed her out of the coach.

"If you wish it, my lord."

"How else are we going to get to know each other, my lady, if you always eat in your room?" He didn't smile, but neither was he frowning.

You had the whole afternoon to talk to me in the coach.

"Excuse me, my lady." The new groom interrupted before Connie could reply.

Lord Wingrave nodded and headed into the inn.

"My name's Archer, my lady. I was wondering which of your trunks you need this evening?"

Connie's eyebrows rose and she smiled. "Has Milsom not told you? The small valise, and that one, if you please." She pointed to the trunk that held her own clothes. Archer climbed up to the coach roof.

The maid waited by the door.

"Milsom, please find out what time my lord intends to dine."

The woman pursed her lips. "Very well, my lady."

In her room, Connie washed her face and hands, and tidied her hair. They would be moving on in the morning and, in spite of feeling weary from the heat, she wanted to see the cathedral.

"He hasn't said, my lady." Milsom entered the room behind her. "I'll get your gown out. You'll be wanting to—"

"Milsom, knock before you enter a room." Connie finished pinning her hair and turned to see Milsom's expression turn from a scowl to merely sour.

"I'll just brush off your green gown, my lady, then you'll—"

"I intend to walk to the cathedral, so I will need you to accompany me. The gown can wait."

Milsom's lips tightened. "It's not proper for you to go about the town on your own, my lady."

"I know. That is why you will be with me."

"I can't walk far, miss. My lady, I should say. My feet hurt." She turned to the trunk and began to lift out the green gown, as if that were the end of the matter.

Connie sighed. She knew she should address Milsom's truculence, but they might not pass this way again and she didn't want to waste time arguing now.

Downstairs, she asked the landlord if someone could accompany her to the cathedral. He scratched his head, then his face brightened. "I reckon our Jen wouldn't mind a break. Save her nag—" He cleared his throat. "I'll fetch her, my lady."

Jen proved to be a stout girl with a distinct resemblance to the landlord. She was also a girl of few words. "Quickest way or by the river, my lady?"

Connie chose the river and Jen set off at a brisk pace. It wasn't far to the riverbank, and Connie paused to admire the sight of the cathedral across the water meadows, its stone walls glowing warmly in the early evening light. She hurried to catch up with Jen as they crossed a footbridge. Seen from so close, the spire seemed to touch the sky. With the tall windows and carved stonework, the building was a far cry from the small parish church in Nether Minster.

"I would like to look inside, Jen."

"This way, my lady." Jen stopped outside the porch. "I'll wait here, my lady." She grinned, lightening her face. "Nice to have a rest here in the cool instead of working in the kitchen."

The interior was a contrast of dark corners and bright patches where the sun streamed in through the stained glass. Connie was still gazing in awe at the tall pillars and vaulted roof when she was interrupted by a small cough.

"Can I help you, miss?" The man wore the black gown of a verger, bulging out over a slight paunch. He straightened his wig as he spoke.

"Thank you, but I have come only to admire the building. I have never seen anything so magnificent as this."

The verger seemed to stand taller. "I can tell you a little of the history, if you wish, miss."

Connie recognised the gleam of enthusiasm in his eyes, and hesitated a moment. But Mr Fancott always said that knowledge only enhanced awe, so she accepted with thanks.

"The cathedral was completed in the thirteenth century, after the land it stands on..."

The verger moved off down the aisle as he spoke. Connie missed parts of the history as carvings or tombs took her interest, but the verger seemed to need nothing more than an occasional murmur of appreciation to keep him going.

CHAPTER 13

$\mathcal{W}$ ill set the empty tankard back on the table. The ale had revived him a little; now he needed some exercise to ease the stiffness in his limbs from a full day on the road. Perhaps his wife might like to accompany him.

His comment about getting to know her had been a little unfair. She had asked him about the places they passed through, but he knew little more than the names of some of the major towns. Then she'd started to read and it had seemed churlish to interrupt. He laughed— he hadn't wanted a chattering, giggling wife, so he shouldn't complain.

He was about to find the landlord to ask if there was a path beside the river when he noticed his wife's prune-featured maid sitting at a table in conversation with the coachman.

"Why aren't you attending Lady Wingrave?"

The maid hurriedly got to her feet. "My lady said she did not need my assistance, my lord."

"Very well. Go and ask if she wishes to accompany me on a short walk before dinner."

The maid pursed her mouth and left the taproom. What possessed his wife to keep such a person about her?

Milsom's expression was more worried than ill-tempered when

she returned. "I thought she was in your private parlour, my lord, but she's not there, nor in her room."

"Well, don't just stand there, woman, find out where she's gone!"

"My lady..." Milsom stopped and cleared her throat. "Er, my lady did express a desire to see the cathedral, my lord. I reminded her it was unseemly for her to walk about unaccompanied."

Will's eyebrows rose. Hopefully his wife was not wandering around Salisbury alone, but it might be worth going to the cathedral to check.

Several people sat or knelt in the nave, but none of them was Lady Wingrave. A murmur of voices came from a side aisle; he recognised her voice, then a man spoke in reply.

An assignation?

He shook his head. That was impossible; she hadn't known until yesterday that they would come to Salisbury. He would turn into his father if he wasn't careful, assuming the worst of everyone.

Approaching quietly, he rounded a pillar to see his wife standing by a stone knight on a tomb, her face intent as a man who must be the verger pointed out features of the armour and sword.

He cleared his throat.

"Oh!" She spun round to face him, one hand flying to her mouth. "I'm sorry, my lord, I forgot to leave word for you."

"You came here alone?" He tried to keep censure from his voice—if a reprimand was due at all, it should be given in private.

"No, one of the women from the inn came with me. She should be waiting in the porch." She dropped her eyes. "Do you wish me to return?" Her tone was resigned.

"Not if you wish to continue your tour," he replied. It was cool in here, and they had the whole evening to get through together.

Her smile was hesitant, as if she couldn't quite believe she was not being summoned back.

"Do carry on, sir," Will said to the verger.

"Er, yes, my lord. I was saying that we have an older tomb,

showing chain mail armour." The verger moved off down the aisle, listing names, dates, and battles as he went. Will caught snatches of information as they walked, but he was more interested in the way his wife was listening and responding to the torrent of details. She clearly had some knowledge of the period the verger was discussing.

Before Will could get bored, Lady Wingrave thanked the verger for his time, and promised that she would try to return to learn more about the cathedral.

"My lord, do you have any coins on you?" Her voice was too low for the verger to hear.

Will patted a pocket. "Some, yes."

"Could you put something in the poor box for me? I should do something for the time this gentleman has given up for my education."

"If you wish, my lady." Will suspected that the verger would rather have the money for himself, but the man nodded in approval as the coins clinked into the box near the door. Another misjudgement?

A stout young woman stood as they left via the porch.

"You accompanied Lady Wingrave here?"

"Yes, my lord."

Will handed her a coin. "I will escort Lady Wingrave back to the inn."

The girl smiled, gave a brief curtsey and walked off. His wife stood by the door, hands folded in front of her.

"I'm sorry for not leaving a message, my lord, I would not have inconvenienced—"

"I wished for a walk in any case, so it is no matter. Shall we return for supper?"

She took the arm he offered, resting one hand lightly on his sleeve. They crossed the grassy area towards the river without speaking, and she released his arm before they reached the bridge, stopping to look back. It was a lovely scene, he had to admit. The low sun cast long shadows and warmed the colours of the cathedral. He breathed the air, cooling now as dusk approached, and glanced at his wife's face. She was smiling, but he thought she had a wistful air, gazing at the scene as if she would never return.

"Why were you not accompanied by your maid?" he asked as she finally turned back towards the river.

"She said her feet hurt. It was easier to ask for someone from the inn to accompany me. Jen knew the way."

And doesn't scowl, Will added to himself. "Why do you employ such a woman?"

Her head tipped to one side. "I thought you had employed her. She said you had."

Either the maid was lying, or his wife was. He'd lay money on it being the maid—unless it was a misunderstanding.

"What exactly did she say, can you recall?"

She thought for a moment. "She said 'My lord employed me as your personal maid'."

"She must have been referring to my father." Milsom would be another spy in his household. "Did he know you were to leave your own maid at home?"

"I've never had a personal maid, my lord." She took his arm again, and they continued along the river path.

No maid? What gently bred lady managed without a maid? "I'm sure we can find someone better," he said, and was rewarded with a smile mostly concealed by the brim of her hat.

To his relief, talk over dinner proved easy. He knew something about Salisbury, and he mentioned that they'd often stopped at Stonehenge on his boyhood journeys to or from Ashton Tracey.

"Oh, may we see that too?" Then her face fell. "I suppose we have no time. It is a long journey tomorrow, is it not?"

"I'm afraid so; we need to make a very early start. Are you interested in antiquities?"

"I am interested in anything, my lord. I have never been above three or four miles from Nether Minster in my life. It is a pretty enough place, but there are so many fascinating things to see in other parts of the country."

"Have you not had a season in Town?"

"No. What is Stonehenge like?"

Any other woman of his acquaintance would have been asking him

77

when they would remove to London, not enquiring about some ancient stones. This new wife of his was certainly a puzzle.

Connie sent Milsom away that evening as soon as the maid brought in her washing water, preferring to manage herself, as she always had. She stood before the mirror on the chest, combing out her hair, the events of the evening passing through her mind again.

Lord Wingrave hadn't minded her going to see the cathedral, and had proved surprisingly knowledgeable about Stonehenge. She'd even got the impression that he imagined they would visit it together at some point.

There was more to him than the image of a womanising duellist that rumour had painted. From Stonehenge, he'd gone on to talk about the stone circle at Avebury, and an ancient hill fort at Old Sarum, showing a breadth of knowledge she hadn't expected. Their conversation had remained fairly impersonal, but she was pleased that he had been happy to discuss such things; her father would have told her to stick to women's business.

His acceptance of her interest might not extend to other areas, but there was at least a possibility that Martha could be proved right in the end.

CHAPTER 14

ednesday 25th June

Will watched as Archer loaded their luggage. Should he ride on the roof for the morning or join Lady Wingrave inside the coach? Inside, he decided. He'd enjoyed last night's conversation with his wife, her face animated as she asked questions.

Their route that morning led across rolling chalk downland. Lady Wingrave peered out of the windows. "Did you say there were forts here?"

"Ancient ones—with only circular mounds and ditches left," he replied. "Nothing like the one near Salisbury."

"But still, think of the people who lived there long ago…" Her face took on a dreamy expression. "Could I see one sometime, do you think?"

"Not today, I'm afraid; we have too far to go."

Her eager look faded, but she nodded. "Of course."

"We can certainly see such things some other time. Later this year, perhaps, when you have settled in."

Her smile was the widest he'd seen yet, and he felt a warm glow somewhere inside at being able to please her.

"Thank you, that would be wonderful." She shifted on the seat, rolling her shoulders.

"Are you uncomfortable, my lady?"

"No, I am perfectly..." Her voice tailed off as he raised an eyebrow. "Well, yes, then. I am not used to sitting still for so long. At home I was used to running the house, and there was always much to do."

"Did you have many servants?"

"No. It was only a small household. Are there many at Ashton Tracey?"

Connie awaited his answer with some trepidation. Although he'd referred to the house as small when he'd been describing it on the first day of their journey, he might only have been comparing it with Marstone Park. Something half the size of that would still feel enormous.

"Not many," he said. "I do not go there often, and my father never, but there is a skeleton staff on board wages. A butler, housekeeper and cook, a footman, and maids."

That didn't sound too bad.

"There are plenty of walks in the gardens and grounds," he went on.

Walks? Oh, he was referring to her discomfort again.

"Did you say it was near the sea?" She had never seen the sea.

"Yes, it's a mile or so to the cliffs from the house. Mama would take us there for picnics when we were young. My brother and I used to watch for smugglers." A wry smile lifted one side of his mouth. "In broad daylight—it was no wonder we never saw any."

"Smugglers?" Connie shook her head. "I should not be surprised. I suppose smuggling is common along much of the coast."

"And is just a business," Lord Wingrave said. "Not the romantic adventure that young lads dream of."

A criminal enterprise, Mr Fancott had called it. He'd shown her stories of intimidation and even murder of riding officers and informers. The Hawkhurst gang had been dealt with more than thirty years ago, but their brutality was still notorious today.

It was a little worrying that Lord Wingrave did not seem to regard smuggling in the same light. That was not something she felt she could discuss with him now, though. Instead she asked him about Exeter and the area around Ashton Tracey.

After they stopped for refreshments, Lord Wingrave produced some newspapers. "I've got behind on the news," he said, indicating them. "Do you mind if I read?"

"Not at all," Connie replied. When she opened *Tristram Shandy*, the silence did not feel as awkward as it had the day before.

Connie gave up on her reading as the shadows lengthened. When Lord Wingrave turned his attention to the scenery, she guessed they must be nearly there.

"We've made good time," he said as they passed a row of cottages with a squat church beyond. "This is Ashton St Andrew. Ashton Tracey is only a couple of miles further, at the top of the valley leading down to Ashmouth."

"A bit of a theme in the place names," Connie said, under her breath.

"Indeed." He turned to her, smiling. "The River Ash flows down the valley."

The land was hillier here than at home, the lanes narrow with the hedges atop steep banks almost brushing the sides of the coach. More hilly than Hertfordshire, Connie corrected herself as she peered out of the window. Her home was to be here now.

Finally they turned off the road in a patch of woodland. A few minutes later they emerged into open ground, the house coming into view ahead on a slight rise. When Lord Wingrave had described the house two days ago, she had been too nervous about the consummation of their marriage to pay attention properly. Looking at it now, she could understand some of his enthusiasm.

The house at Ashton Tracey was built of red brick, its corners picked out with quoins of some pale stone. A low terrace spanned the width of the building, with steps up to it from the gravelled drive. Formal gardens below the terrace were blocks of shadow at this late hour. It was small in comparison to Marstone Park, having only nine windows across the first floor. Her lips turned up at the corners.

"You like it?"

"It looks lovely. Not too big." Would he see that as a criticism?

He held her gaze for a moment, then smiled himself. "I've always liked it far better than Marstone Park."

Two servants stood at the top of the steps as the coach drew to a halt. The man was lanky and thin-faced, dressed neatly in brown coat and breeches, with a grey wig perched on his head. The woman was a little shorter but just as spare, her gown dark with a lacy white fichu and cap.

"Butler and housekeeper," Will explained, as they mounted the steps. "My lady, this is Warren, and Mrs Strickland."

"Welcome to Ashton Tracey, my lady." Warren's voice was unexpectedly deep for such a slender frame. His smile, although small, did look like a genuine welcome, and some of his many wrinkles might turn out to be laughter lines.

"My lady." Mrs Strickland curtseyed, her eyes flicking to something behind Connie, then back to her face. "Do you wish to see the house first, or have supper? Mrs Curnow can have dinner on the table within half an hour."

Will caught Mrs Strickland's sideways glance, and looked around himself. Milsom stood by the coach, giving orders to Archer—Will could see the man's scowl from here. Then he caught the droop of his wife's shoulders as the housekeeper spoke. If she'd never been more than a few miles from home before, she must be exhausted by three days of jolting on the rutted roads. He put out a hand, touching her elbow.

"It's late, and you look tired. There will be plenty of time to see the house tomorrow, and you may have something to eat in your room if you wish."

"Thank you, I *am* weary. Is... can someone other than Milsom attend me?"

"Mrs Strickland will arrange it," he promised. And he would arrange for Milsom to be on the coach when it returned to Marstone Park in a few days' time. "Do you wish for a meal?"

"Just tea and toast would be lovely, if possible." Her eyes met his, and she smiled. "Thank you for your consideration, my lord."

"It's a pleasure, my lady."

Strangely, it was. Grateful smiles from young ladies had previously been bought with gifts—never had he been thanked so prettily for toast.

He ordered a light meal for himself in the library, and arranged for Lady Wingrave's repast. Then he walked around the outside of the house, looking out over the gardens and park in the gathering dusk.

He was fond of the place because of its memories—playing hide and seek in the formal gardens when he and Alfred had been small enough to hide behind the low hedges, then later chasing Lizzie and Theresa through them. By the time Bella could toddle he'd thought himself too old, at fifteen, to play with his younger siblings, and had spent his summers trying to persuade the men in Ashmouth to take him on a smuggling run. They had, naturally, denied all knowledge of such activities. It was just as well they'd refused—if his father had found out he'd even attempted such a thing, it would have been his last visit here.

He came to the stables where Archer was rubbing the horses down alongside Stubbs, the old groom who had been at Ashton Tracey since Will's childhood. Archer was putting in considerably more effort than Stubbs, who appeared to be as lazy as Will remembered, and probably as incurious: most men would be questioning Archer about the new Lady Wingrave. He made a mental note to put Archer in charge of the stables.

From what she'd said, his wife's life until now had been quite restricted; he should make an effort to take her around the countryside, even if they didn't yet have the finances to entertain the local gentry. She'd need some kind of carriage to take her about if she didn't ride, or for the two of them to use together. The old one-horse open chaise stood in a corner of the stables and Will went over to inspect it. It needed cleaning, but seemed in good repair otherwise. He'd get a horse for the chaise, and another for her if she rode.

He entered through the back of the house, hearing a clatter of pots from the kitchen. As he went through the hall to the library, he tried to look at the place as a stranger might. It must be thirty years since anything other than cleaning or basic repairs had been done, and it showed. The rug on the library floor was worn, the curtains were fading, and the leather on the chairs and desktop showed signs of cracking with age. He didn't mind for himself; he was used to it, and it was all comfortingly familiar.

What would Lady Wingrave think, though? She seemed to approve of Ashton Tracey's modest size. He realised that he wanted her to like the place—not only because she was going to live here, but because *he* liked it.

CHAPTER 15

Thursday 26th June

Connie awoke at her usual early hour, and stretched luxuriously. Sunlight entered the room in flashes as the curtains fluttered in the breeze through the open windows. For the first time in as long as she could remember, she did not have to get out of bed if she did not wish to. But there would be more such mornings, and at the moment she was curious about her new home.

Last night she had taken in only a sizeable room furnished with a small table and chair, and an armchair near the fireplace. In the lamplight, the wood panelling on the walls had made the room seem gloomy.

Now, sitting up in bed, she inspected her surroundings properly. She had a corner room, with windows on two walls. The silk damask bed hangings and coverlet were embroidered with swags of ivy on a cream background, the same cream colour used on the chairs and window seat. Although the hangings were faded, and the chairs appeared worn in places, everything was spotless and the wooden floor and wainscoting had a warm glow from much polishing. Perhaps she could replace the fabric at some point, but she rather liked it as it was. It looked lived in—much friendlier than the cold splendour of Marstone Park.

The door opened quietly, and the same young maid who had brought her food last night crept in, strands of black hair curling out from under her cap. She was angular, skinny wrists protruding from her sleeves. Connie found it difficult to guess her age. Fifteen, perhaps?

"Oh, my lady," the girl gasped, seeing Connie sitting up in bed. "I didn't think you'd be awake yet. I come for the slops."

"What is your name?"

"Sukey Trasker, my lady." The girl curtseyed awkwardly.

"Sukey—who else is up and about?"

"Mrs Curnow's making the bread, my lady. And Mary and Katie."

Other maids, Connie guessed. Her stomach rumbled at the idea of fresh bread. "When you've taken the slops, please come back and show me the way to the kitchens."

The girl's eyes went round. "You want to go to the kitch—?" One hand flew up to cover her mouth. "I mean, yes, my lady. Shall I wake Mrs Strickland?"

"No, I think not." She wanted to get to know the staff, and that would be easier without the housekeeper's presence. Sukey bobbed another curtsey and quietly let herself out of the room.

Connie explored the room once she had dressed. The door Sukey had used opened onto the main landing. The other door in that wall led to a small chamber that must be her dressing room. A whole room for her clothing, when she only had enough to fill a small trunk! Well, two, if she could alter her mother's old dresses. She smoothed the gown she wore, aware of the faded pattern and the contrast with the heavy and ornate Marstone wedding ring. Such clothing was adequate for Miss Charters; Lady Wingrave probably required a better wardrobe.

Back in the bedroom, she had her hand on the latch of a third door before it occurred to her that this must be the connecting door to Lord Wingrave's room. There was a keyhole, but no key.

That didn't matter, she told herself. Lord Wingrave would keep his word.

Connie followed Sukey onto the landing. It looked down over the entrance hall, which was open to the second floor. An oak staircase descended around two sides of the hall to reach the ground floor near the front door. She was pleased to see the banisters were well polished, and the black and white tiles on the hall floor were clean and shiny.

The kitchens, below the back of the house, were lit by windows high in the walls. Mrs Curnow glanced at Connie, reaching for a cloth to wipe floury hands. She was plump, as most cooks were, with a face as red and cheery as a ripe apple and grey hair scraped back into a tight knot.

Martha had warned Connie that she could not be familiar with the staff of a large house in the way she had been at home, but that did not exclude getting to know them.

"Don't worry, Mrs Curnow, I don't intend to make a habit of interrupting you at your work." Connie pulled up a chair and took a seat at the kitchen table, away from the dusting of flour where the cook was filling loaf tins with dough. "Please carry on."

The cook hesitated, then filled the last tin and set it aside before wiping her hands again. "There's some of yesterday's bread left, my lady." As she spoke, she lifted a tray containing balls of risen dough and crossed to the range. The oven door squealed as she pulled it open. "These'll be about half an hour, ready for Lord Wingrave's breakfast."

"I'll wait, thank you. But a cup of tea would be lovely."

Sukey, still at the kitchen door, dashed in and took down a kettle, then disappeared through another doorway. Connie heard the sound of a pump.

"Good girl, that," Mrs Curnow said. "Not been here long. Father lost at sea."

"Will you take tea with me, Mrs Curnow? And tell me about the kitchens. Do the gardens here provide enough vegetables?"

By the time the smell of warm bread filled the kitchen, Connie had gained the impression of a household run well enough for its limited number of staff, although it appeared that several of the servants took advantage of the absence of permanent residents to idle away their time. That was to be expected, but as this was her home now, she should do something about it.

"Mrs Curnow, what are—?" Mrs Strickland's voice came from the kitchen door, behind Connie. "Oh, my lady."

Connie turned her head, and saw Milsom standing behind the housekeeper. "Mrs Strickland," she said, rising to her feet. "Perhaps you could show me the way to the dining room. And, after breakfast, the rest of the house."

She'd need to find out Lord Wingrave's plans for the day before making firm arrangements.

The formal dining room opened off the main entrance hall, its dark green walls giving it an air of gloom even after Mrs Strickland opened the curtains. Connie didn't care for the pictures of dead game on the walls—she would far rather look at landscapes while eating. A long table of polished wood must seat at least twenty people. The demands of her new role knotted her stomach; could she entertain so many people of her new class without making a faux pas?

There was only one place set, at the far end of the table. Connie turned to Mrs Strickland. "Is Lord Wingrave not taking his breakfast?"

"Lady Marstone used to take her breakfast in bed, my lady," Mrs Strickland said. "I will send Barton to lay another place." She inclined her head and left. A few minutes later a footman arrived with steaming pots of tea and coffee, along with the extra cutlery and plates.

"Ah, just in time!"

Connie jumped as Lord Wingrave's voice sounded behind her.

Will was surprised, and pleased, to see his wife already up. The women of his recent acquaintance had rarely shown their faces before noon, if then. But then he hadn't either; that was but one change in this new life.

"I trust you slept well, my lady?" She did look better than she had last night.

"Yes, thank you, my lord." A tentative smile appeared.

He pulled out a chair for her, dismissing the footman as soon as he'd served them.

"I normally breakfast around ten when I stay here," Will explained. "I'm eating early this morning as I need to go into Exeter."

She nodded. "You said you might have to."

"I may not be back until tomorrow," he added. "It is possible that the people I need to see will not be free today. Is there anything you wish me to get for you while I'm there?"

She seemed surprised by his offer, then shook her head. "I will look around the house today, my lord. There may be things wanted, but as yet I don't know."

"No matter, there will be other opportunities. Mrs Strickland can tell you all you wish to know about the house."

Her forehead wrinkled, and he recalled her comment that the house wasn't too big. Was she worried about taking charge?

"The place has been running well under Mrs Strickland's direction, there is no great hurry for you to take over."

"Thank you." She took a deep breath. "It is just that there have been a great many changes in the last week. It can be a little overwhelming."

"I'm sure you will manage." She'd shown intelligence and interest; she'd soon learn what she needed to.

That seemed to have reassured her, as she smiled and reached for another roll.

They finished their breakfast in companionable silence, and when

Barton came to say the coach was ready, she accompanied him to the front door.

Connie stood and watched the coach roll down the drive, disappearing where the gravel curved into the belt of woodland that bordered the road. She felt suddenly alone, even though there were at least half a dozen other people in the house. It was probably nerves at being left in charge—although she wasn't really. Warren and Mrs Strickland ran the place between them.

She squared her shoulders. It was just a house and its servants. Larger than she was used to, but as she had told the Earl of Marstone, the basics were the same. She turned back into the house, and asked Warren to send Mrs Strickland to her.

"I would like a tour of the house, if you please," she said, when the housekeeper appeared.

"Very well, my lady. If you would step this way?" Mrs Strickland opened a door near the bottom of the staircase and stood to one side so Connie could enter.

The drawing room was as large as the dining room. Sofas stood in a formal rectangle around a fireplace, with several clusters of chairs and small tables filling the rest of the space. The walls above the wainscoting were dark red, blending with the heavy curtains. The room felt cool—pleasant in this hot weather. Connie turned to ask the housekeeper how warm the room was in winter, but Mrs Strickland was already waiting by the door, ready to move on.

The next room was the library. Connie breathed the scent of leather bindings and wood polish. She would enjoy browsing the books here at her leisure, as long as Lord Wingrave did not regard the room as his exclusive domain, as her father had.

Back in the passageway, Mrs Strickland walked past a door. "That is a billiards room, my lady. Lord Wingrave rarely uses it." She indicated the next two doors. "My office, my lady, and an estate office, although there hasn't been a steward in residence for some years."

Back in the main entrance hall, Mrs Strickland opened the final door. This parlour was much smaller than the first. Light filtering through the curtains revealed furniture shrouded in holland covers; Connie made out the shapes of a round table with six chairs, and several armchairs arranged around the fireplace. Crossing to the windows, she pulled back a curtain to reveal a view down the drive. The sunlight illuminated pale green walls above the wainscoting, and a carpet with a delicate pattern of yellow flowers and green leaves. There was another door beside one of the windows.

"That's only Lady Marstone's private parlour," the housekeeper said as Connie moved towards it.

The room beyond the door was much smaller, but being on the corner of the house it had windows on two walls, facing south and west. It would be a splendid room for needlework, with plenty of light during the day and in summer evenings. The few pieces of furniture were swathed in holland covers here, too.

Connie hadn't been sure what to expect of the housekeeper—some more detail, perhaps, about how the rooms had been used, or on repairs or refurbishments that might be needed. She had not antici-pated blank silence while inspecting each room. Any housekeeper would be wary at having a new mistress, but Connie had made no mention of replacing her. She sighed; life would be more pleasant if Mrs Strickland were more like Mrs Curnow.

She'd started the tour, though, so she may as well continue. "The bedrooms?" she prompted.

There were several guest bedrooms, of varying sizes, all with furniture covered. Dust stirred as she crossed the carpets, and the rooms had a faint musty smell, as if Mrs Strickland hadn't bothered to keep them aired regularly.

They did not enter two of the bedrooms: her own, and Lord Wingrave's. A blush rose to her cheeks as she realised the housekeeper would assume she had already seen them both.

"Is that is all, my lady?" Mrs Strickland stood on the landing with hands demurely folded in front of her.

"Thank you, yes."

The housekeeper inclined her head and descended the stairs.

It was not all—there were several other doors they had not looked behind, and the house had another floor. Servants' quarters, most likely, and she wanted to see those too, but she didn't need Mrs Strickland's disapproving presence.

She sighed, and went to investigate the top floor.

CHAPTER 16

On the way to Exeter, Will occupied himself reading the papers his father had given him. He had a letter of introduction to Snell and Cowper, his father's legal representatives for the Ashton Tracey estate. But if it were only a letter of introduction, why did it need to be sealed?

There was also a draft on his father's bank. He'd told the earl that Ashton Tracey was no use to him without the money to run it, so he may as well run away to India or perish in the attempt. He didn't think his father had quite believed this threat, but he'd not called Will's bluff. The draft was the first instalment of an allowance to be paid quarterly.

His father had assumed he would use Snell and Cowper, but Will had his own connections in Exeter who could help him find a different firm. His father hadn't taken enough interest in his doings ten years ago to know that.

Leaving the coach and driver at an inn, he walked the rest of the way to Pendrick's warehouse by the river. As he had no appointment, he had to wait until Mr Pendrick was free, but it was pleasant to spend an hour on a bench watching the boats come and go, and goods being loaded and unloaded. He was struck by the fact that in his previous life he would barely have risen at this hour, but found that he didn't mind the change.

"How can I help, my lord?" Pendrick came around his desk to shake Will's hand. His weathered face was more lined than before, but otherwise he looked well. "Westbrook is away for several days, and I wasn't aware that my sister was expecting you."

"I haven't come to see the boy," Will said. He would have liked to, but it was best for Alex if he didn't see him too often. "I have a small favour to ask of you."

Pendrick waved Will to a chair. "How may I help you, then?"

Will briefly described his circumstances. "I meant to explain my more permanent presence in the area to Westbrook after seeing you, but as he is away…"

"I will let him know, my lord. Is that all?"

"No. I came to ask if you could recommend a man of business who might act for me. Snell normally handles matters affecting Ashton Tracey, but he would be my father's agent, not mine."

"Not Westbrook? His firm is quite busy, but I think he would oblige you."

"Better not, I think, don't you?"

"Hmm, yes." Pendrick stuck a finger under his wig to scratch his head, gazing into the distance. "Samuel Kellet acts for one of the manufacturers I have dealings with, and I have found him trustworthy and reliable." He looked back at Will. "I will write a note of introduction, if you care to wait for a few minutes."

"Thank you," Will said. Pendrick took a piece of paper from a drawer in his desk.

The solicitor's office was on Fore Street, at the end nearest the cathedral. Kellet, not unexpectedly, was also busy when Will arrived, and likely to be so for the rest of the day. However, the clerk gave Will an appointment for first thing the following morning, and also recommended a stable where he could buy a horse for the chaise. Leaving Kellet's office, Will made his way to the suggested livery to inspect their stock.

He bought a mare—a mediocre specimen that was the best on offer—and arranged to collect the animal the next morning. After arranging for a room at an inn, he set off to look around the shops. He didn't need anything at the moment, but it would be as well to work out what he could find in Exeter, and what might have to be sent for from London.

And Lady Wingrave would be interested to hear about the cathedral.

After inspecting the top floor, Connie was tempted by the sunshine. She rang the bell and asked Warren to send someone to show her to the gardener's office.

Yatton was hoeing a row of carrots but stopped work as Connie approached. He was in his middle years, with a tanned and lined face and spare frame. He was also a man of as few words as Mrs Strickland, but in pleasant contrast to the housekeeper, his silences as they toured the kitchen garden did not feel unfriendly. He answered all Connie's queries politely, and even offered some information without being asked.

The garden was enclosed by a brick wall, providing shelter and support for the fruit trees trained against them. Only part of the area was cultivated, the rest being covered in grass.

"It's been like that all my time here, my lady," Yatton explained. "Lady Marstone, God bless her, used to come in the summer for a month or two, but there weren't no call to keep the whole lot planted. The bit we got planted feeds the staff."

"How many under-gardeners would you need to clear and plant it?"

Yatton scratched his head. "Depends what you want to grow, my lady. Some things take more work than others. There's only me, and a lad from the village now and then when there be fruit to pick or it be sowing time."

"You seem to be managing it very well, Yatton." Connie was pleased to see an answering smile, and left him to his weeding. She'd have to talk to Lord Wingrave about their plans before she considered any changes here.

She headed back to her bedroom, stopping in the kitchen to ask for a drink and a cold plate to be sent up. She'd done enough talking and thinking for now, and wanted to enjoy the luxury of being able to sit quietly for a while.

When Sukey brought the food, she was followed into the room by Mrs Strickland. Sukey set the tray on a table, casting a wary glance at the housekeeper before leaving.

"Mrs Strickland?"

"Might I have a word, my lady?"

Connie suppressed a sigh, recognising the standard prelude to a complaint. "By all means." She sat at the table as she spoke, but with little hope that Mrs Strickland would take the hint to be quick.

"Mrs Curnow reports to me, my lady."

"Naturally."

"You—" Mrs Strickland bit her lip and took a deep breath. "It would be helpful, my lady, if enquiries about the running of the household were addressed to me."

Connie inclined her head. She already had the information she wanted, and didn't feel like arguing the point now. "While you are here, Mrs Strickland, please arrange for me to have a cup of tea in bed at seven. I will breakfast with Lord Wingrave at ten when he is at home."

"Very well, my lady."

"Good. I also wish the small parlour and the adjoining room to be opened up. I will use that parlour for dining, and the smaller room as my own private sitting room."

"Lord Wingrave never uses those rooms, my lady." Mrs Strickland had a stubborn set to her jaw.

"Yes, I recall you saying that earlier." Connie made an effort to stop her irritation showing in her voice.

"There aren't enough staff to keep all the rooms open."

"We can see about getting more." She should check with Lord Wingrave about that, but they could always put the large dining room back under holland covers in the meantime. "Thank you, Mrs Strickland."

She nodded dismissal and turned to the plate of rolls and cold meat Mrs Curnow had sent up, hoping to head off any more comments from the housekeeper.

There was a pause before Mrs Strickland's final "my lady," and the woman left the room.

Connie let out a breath and leaned back in her chair. She would not have put up with such manners from a servant at home, but there her father had left her in complete charge of the staff, as long as she didn't bother him. She hoped that was the case here, but she was not yet sure.

Another thing to talk to Lord Wingrave about.

Will enjoyed a pint of ale in the taproom of the Queen's Head. It was a small place, not far from the dock, and appeared to be frequented mostly by merchants and traders. Just the kind of men his father would despise. He leaned back in his chair as he observed the conversations at the tables around him. A few groups were clearly having a sociable evening, calling for more ale and food, but others looked to be discussing serious matters—business, perhaps.

Useful things—things his father considered were beneath him. He wondered how Lady Wingrave was getting on at Ashton Tracey, and half wished he'd asked her to accompany him. She would have liked to see the city. And he would have enjoyed showing her around.

Will looked up as one of the waiters came to stand beside his table.

"Be you wanting some dinner, sir?"

"Not yet, thank you." The evening would be long without anyone to talk to; no need to eat yet.

The waiter hesitated, then cleared his throat. "It's just that we've more folk wanting to eat, sir, but no space."

Three men stood by the bar, looking hopefully in his direction. Will sighed and prepared to move, then changed his mind. "They are welcome to take these places, if they wish."

The waiter's eyebrows rose, but he went over to the waiting men. The three looked at each other, then came over to Will's table.

"Good of you, sir," one said. "Would you care to join us in a meal? I'm Potterton."

"Stanlake." On impulse, he gave his family name rather than his title. "Thank you, I will."

They ordered their food, and the men resumed a conversation about the weather at sea and the effects of shipwrecks on the prices of goods. They soon drew Will into their talk, asking him his business in the area.

"I've recently acquired a small estate," he said, but admitted to not knowing much of farming, as yet. That led to a discussion on the price of meat and wool, the iniquitous duties on imports of wine, tea and tobacco, wool exports, and the effects of smuggling on the profits of honest traders. Will listened more than he talked, only asking a question now and then, and was surprised how much time had passed when the men finally rose and took their leave.

He called for a final pint and sat with it in the emptying taproom, feeling vaguely envious of the three men and their busy lives. It had been a more interesting evening than any he'd spent gambling.

CHAPTER 17

Friday 27th June

Connie sat in the window seat in her bedroom, her morning tea in one hand. The window looked south, to where the sea must lie beyond the small stretch of parkland and the woodland. She had seen pictures, of course, but it was difficult to imagine there was nothing but water stretching all the way to France. Later today, perhaps, she could go and see it, after she'd inspected the kitchens and the rest of the lower level.

Noises from the dressing room reminded her that Milsom was not far away—doing what, she had no idea. Connie set the cup back on its saucer. The sooner she completed her tour of the house, the sooner she could go for a walk.

She found Mrs Curnow in one of the smaller rooms off the kitchen, its walls lined with mostly bare shelves above a row of cupboards. A few jars of preserves occupied one shelf, and some bunches of herbs hung from the ceiling. Connie smiled as she saw the cook tying flowering stems of lavender into small bunches. Mrs Curnow put aside the stems she was holding.

"This must be the stillroom," Connie said.

"Yes, my lady." Mrs Curnow glanced at the bare shelving. "There's some bandages and the like in the cupboards, but there didn't seem much point in keeping it fully stocked when there was only servants living here permanently. Lord Wingrave never came for more than a few days at a time."

Connie picked up a bunch of the lavender and began tying it together.

"My lady, you shouldn't—"

"I know. But I would like you to show me round the kitchens and cellars, without putting you behind with your work. I had a look at the gardens yesterday. I don't think we can restock the stillroom from there."

Mrs Curnow shook her head. "No, my lady. But it would be good to have more of our own herbs and the like. That Yatton spends half his time dreaming and smoking his pipe."

Connie finished tying the lavender. "I'll see what I can do."

As they toured the service rooms, Connie learned that there never had been a Mr Curnow. Mrs Curnow had worked here for thirty years, since the estate had been transferred to Lord Marstone's ownership, while Mrs Strickland had only arrived a short time before Lady Marstone's death, ten years ago now.

"How many staff would a house this size normally have, do you know?"

"Mrs Strickland could answer that better than me, my lady."

"I could ask her, but I do not wish to be told I should leave all such matters to her." That earned a chuckle from the cook, and Connie wondered if she might have found her first ally. "No matter, Mrs Curnow. I should settle in before I think about any changes. Now, please show me the cellars."

Mrs Curnow lit a lantern, then opened a door. To Connie's surprise, there were no steps, only a long corridor with storerooms.

"They're not really cellars, my lady. We're under the front terrace here. The ground outside's lower at the back of the house where the kitchens are, so those rooms have windows."

Most of the rooms they looked into were empty; one had a wall lined with racks, the few dozen bottles of wine looking lost in the midst of the bare surroundings. The door at the end of the passage was locked.

"I don't have a key, my lady," Mrs Curnow said. "If that's all, my lady, I've some baking to get on with."

Odd. The wine store hadn't been locked; what could be in this room? But Mrs Curnow had already gone—she'd ask some other time.

After breakfast, Connie spent an hour discussing garden plans with Yatton before going in search of Warren.

"Cellar, my lady? I only look after the section where the wine and brandy are stored. You would have to ask Mrs Strickland about the other rooms."

The butler met her gaze with a steady eye—so steady that Connie had the feeling he knew more than he was saying. That might be unfair—one unpleasant lady's maid and an uncooperative house-keeper should not make her regard all the other staff with suspicion.

Mrs Strickland should have been busy opening up the parlour, but there was no-one there and the furniture was still shrouded. Her irritation rising, Connie stalked over to the bell-rope and pulled it, then opened the curtains.

"Send Mrs Strickland to me," she ordered, when Barton answered the summons.

A few minutes later, Connie heard the door open again, but did not move.

"My lady?"

Connie turned. Mrs Strickland stood by the open door, her hands clasped.

"Did you misunderstand, Mrs Strickland, when I asked you to open up this room?"

"But my lady, the maids—"

"If the maids cannot keep all the rooms clean, we will put some of the others back under holland covers."

"Lord Wingrave—"

"Lord Wingrave leaves the running of the house to me, Mrs Strickland. Is that clear?"

The housekeeper pursed her lips. "Yes, my lady."

"You will see to it, then. And you may give me the keys to the cellars, too."

"The… the cellars, my lady?" Mrs Strickland swallowed visibly. "Why would you wish to see those? They're not used, in any case, and some of the keys are lost." Her eyes slid sideways as she spoke.

They would be used once there was more food to be stored. Connie opened her mouth to explain, then closed it again. She did not need to justify herself to the housekeeper. Nor did she believe in the lost keys, but arguing with her would be pointless. "Very well. I'm sure we can break the door down if necessary."

"Break…" Mrs Strickland stared at Connie for a moment, then inclined her head.

Why did the housekeeper think she could ignore her orders? None of the other staff had proved so uncooperative. If Mrs Strickland was worried about keeping her job, her behaviour wasn't helping.

Connie rubbed her forehead. She'd have a cup of tea, change into her old gown, and get one of the grooms to show her the path to the cliff top that Lord Wingrave had mentioned.

Will gazed across the parkland ahead with pleasure as the carriage emerged from the trees. Kellet, the solicitor recommended by Pendrick, had been happy to take on a new client, and would open a bank account for Will and pay in the earl's bank draft. Now that was arranged, Will could start managing the estate properly. He would get Warren to send a message to the steward.

A flash of movement caught his eye. A woman in a white dress was walking across the parkland south of the house, accompanied by two men. His wife? They were heading towards the path through the woods.

Warren came out to greet him as the coach pulled to a halt in front of the steps. "Noakes has arrived with your horse, my lord, and is settling him in to the stables."

That was good; the coach could take Noakes home tomorrow. And Lady Wingrave's maid, if his wife could manage without her.

"Was that Lady Wingrave I saw walking to the woods?"

"I believe so, my lord. She expressed a wish to see the sea. Your man Archer accompanied her, and Stubbs went to show them the way."

"To Lion Rocks?"

"Yes, my lord."

"I will join them." She should come to no harm with Archer, but he needed the exercise. The afternoon was sunny, although dark clouds were gathering in the west. "Go and ask Mrs Curnow to put up a little food and drink, will you?" These clothes were too heavy for walking in this weather, and too fine for sitting on the ground.

In his room, he abandoned his wig as well as his coat, and pulled on an older pair of breeches. Back downstairs, Mrs Curnow had a small satchel ready, and he slung it over his shoulder. Leaving the house, he jumped lightly down from the top of the ha-ha and set a fast pace across the park.

The Lion Rocks were nothing more than a collection of boulders at a high point on the edge of the cliffs. As children, he and Alfred had found the silhouette of a lion in the arrangement, and the name had stuck. The place had been a favourite spot of his mother's.

The weather was muggy today, and he was soon far too warm. He slowed, unbuttoning his waistcoat and slinging it over one shoulder, and found the cool shade welcome as he entered the woods. The trees grew thicker than he remembered, the twisting path littered with fallen branches. He heard the murmur of voices ahead; a dead branch cracked beneath his foot, and the conversation stopped immediately. Pressing on, he rounded a bend in the path to see Archer stepping in front of Lady Wingrave, the groom's tense stance only slackening when he saw who was approaching.

"I wished to see the sea, my lord," Lady Wingrave said, her chin lifting.

"By all means, my lady. May I escort you?"

She nodded without speaking, her posture relaxing.

"You two may return," Will said to Archer and Stubbs. He turned to his wife as the two men left. "Shall we continue?"

She lifted her eyes to his, then smiled, following him in silence until they eventually came out of the woods. The grass-covered ground rose ahead of them, hiding the sea, and Will took the path leading directly to the rocks. He reached them first, and paused to take in the expanse of glittering blue before looking at his wife. Her wide smile as she gazed at the sea reminded him of Bella when he surprised her with a present.

"It's wonderful!"

She turned the smile on him, and his breath caught for a moment. He'd thought her face reasonably attractive before, but her smile and the way her eyes sparkled with pleasure...

With an effort of will he turned away and opened the satchel, pulling out two stone bottles and a cloth-wrapped packet.

"Sit," he invited, spreading his waistcoat on one of the rocks. He pulled the cork out of one bottle and sniffed—lemonade. Handing that to his wife, he unwrapped the cloth to find slabs of seed cake and ginger cake. Mrs Curnow had remembered two of his favourites.

The second bottle contained ale. He lowered himself to the grass, resting his back against a rock. As he sat down beside her an unexpected feeling of content spread through him. The taste of the ginger cake in his mouth and the sun's warmth on his face took him back to his childhood, playing here with his mother and siblings. Now here he was again, in the company of a beautiful woman—his wife. She was nothing like the women he'd known in London, and that could only be good. Was happiness a possibility again, in this place, with her?

He glanced at her again. The seed cake she'd accepted was ignored in one hand, the other shading her eyes as she looked out to sea, the smile still on her face. Such pleasure from a sea view!

Why did I agree to give her a month?

He forced his eyes seawards, trying to turn his mind to more prosaic subjects. To the west, fishing boats were heading towards

Ashmouth, the outflow of the river itself hidden behind a curve in the cliffs. Beyond the boats, approaching clouds loomed.

"We should return, my lady." He gestured towards the west. The misty grey of rain above the sea and dark cloud-shadows on the water made plain just how quickly the storm was approaching.

"Must we?" She took a bite of the cake.

"We risk a soaking if we do not go now."

"And would cooling down be a bad thing?" Her smile looked mischievous now.

He laughed. "No, but there could be lightning. This is an exposed position."

She finished the piece of cake and dusted her fingers as he put the bottles back into the satchel. "Very well." With one last, wistful glance at the sea, she walked with him towards the woods.

"You may come here any time you wish, my lady."

She bestowed that smile on him again, and hurried into the trees. He followed, watching the sway of her hips as she walked, aware of the air becoming damp and the first patter of raindrops on the leaves above them. When they reached the edge of the woodland their heads and shoulders were wet, and the house was half-hidden beyond sheets of heavy rain.

"Race you," she said, hitching up her skirts and setting off across the grass at a run.

He stood and gaped for a moment, then sprinted after her with a laugh. He caught up easily, hampered as she was by her skirts. Taking one hand, he pulled her on until they reached the edge of the gardens.

He'd aimed directly for the house as he usually did, forgetting that she would not be able to clamber up the ha-ha wall . Running ahead, he leaned with his back against the bricks and made a stirrup of his hands. *Will she use it?*

She did, hardly pausing before placing a muddy shoe on his linked hands, one hand on his shoulder, her knee landing on top of the wall when he boosted her upwards. She scrambled to her feet and waited for him to vault up too, her hair plastered to her laughing face and her skirts to her legs.

Why do women wear so many damned layers?

Her smile faded when he did not speak, and he brought his mind back to practicalities. He offered his arm, and they walked through the gardens towards the front door as if the heavens had not opened.

"Will you take refreshment with me, my lady? It is a long time until dinner."

"Connie." She met his eyes with a shy smile. "Please would you call me Connie, my lord? It is what I am used to from my... my friends."

"Very well. Will you drink tea with me, Connie? In an hour?"

"Half an hour will be enough for me, my lord. Unless you need longer?"

Warren opened the door as they approached, and they stepped into the shelter of the hall.

"Half an hour then."

She smiled, then walked up the stairs. He dragged his eyes away from her retreating form, and went to ask Mrs Curnow for more cake.

CHAPTER 18

*C*onnie sat before the mirror as Milsom combed out her wet hair. The maid's glance flicked to the pile of wet clothing visible through the dressing room door, and she gave a particularly hard tug at Connie's hair. Wincing, Connie put up a hand and took hold of the comb.

"I will do it myself, Milsom. I won't need you again today."

"You need your hair dressed prop—"

"I *said* that will be all. You may deal with those wet clothes, then leave."

"My lady." The maid let go of the comb, and went into the dressing room, her feet making more noise on the floor than was necessary.

Connie turned on the stool as she continued working at the tangles, reminding herself that Lord Wingrave had said they could find someone better. Glancing at the clock on the mantelpiece, she hurriedly twisted her hair up into a knot. She'd said half an hour was plenty; if she didn't hurry she'd be late.

In spite of that thought, her hands stilled as she pulled the green gown on, recalling Lord Wingrave's form sprawled on the grass on the cliff top.

Forcing herself to concentrate, she fastened the front of her gown.

He had looked happy eating cake and drinking ale on the cliff-top. Was that why she'd challenged him to race her back? That was the kind of thing she'd done with the Fancott children when they were all younger, not something a future countess should be doing. But he hadn't minded—there had been laughter in his blue eyes as they faced each other in the rain. She'd seen the way his wet shirt clung to his chest, glimpsing intriguing contours and shadows before she'd averted her eyes. Like the drawing of a Greek god in one of Mr Fancott's books.

Heat rose to her face. What would he look like without his clothing? She'd never wondered that about a man before, but surely it was not improper to think in that way about her husband?

That look in his eyes after he'd helped her up the ha-ha wall—had he been thinking the same thing about her?

She stood abruptly, checking her appearance in the mirror. She was tidy enough, and hopefully her blush would have faded by the time she reached the parlour.

Connie stopped in the parlour doorway—not only was the tea not set out there, but the furniture was still shrouded in dust sheets. Connie rubbed her face. She *had* told Mrs Strickland to remove the covers, hadn't she?

Yes, she had. That was why she'd come in here. The tea must be set out in the large drawing room.

That room looked even more depressing now. Although the rain had eased, thick clouds still obscured the sky to the west. The only bright spot was made by the plates of sandwiches and small cakes on a table by the window.

She took a seat as Barton carried in the tea tray, followed by Lord Wingrave. Dry and fully clothed in his formal coat and waistcoat, his expression serious again, he seemed very different from the wet and laughing man who had boosted her up the wall. She lowered her eyes.

"Thank you Barton," he said. "We will serve ourselves."

"Very good, my lord." The door shut behind the footman.

"I've never been comfortable with servants overhearing my conversation," Lord Wingrave said. "Not to mention the formality of it."

Connie's lips twitched. That sounded more like the friendly man from earlier.

"Is that amusing, Connie?"

It felt strange hearing her name on his lips. "No, my lord, but I was thinking the same thing."

"Will. My name is Will."

"William Charlemagne Stanlake; I remember." It felt even stranger saying *his* name.

Will grimaced. "My father had—has—a rather inflated view of our family's importance. I was the second son, my late brother's name was Alfred. I also have three sisters."

Her lips curved. "Is one of them called Elizabeth?"

"Indeed." She had wit, then, this wife of his. "There is also Isabella..."

She thought for a moment. "Queen of Castille?"

"Yes. And Theresa." What would she make of that?

"Maria Theresa," she exclaimed, after only a moment's thought. "There are a number of them to choose from."

"Theresa would be named after whichever of them was the most powerful, I imagine." He handed her the plate of sandwiches, took one himself, and then became aware that she was regarding him with that wary look in her eyes.

"My lord, do—?"

"Will."

"Er, Will, do you share your father's reverence for rank?"

"No. That's not to say I'd give up the earldom, but rank alone stands for little. Some of the best men I know have no titles, nor any connection to the aristocracy, as far as I know."

That seemed to reassure her; he wasn't sure why. They ate in companionable silence for a while, although she seemed to be doing little more than nibbling at her food.

"How did you spend your time while I was away?" he asked.

She set her half-eaten sandwich down. "I toured the house with Mrs Strickland yesterday," she said. "Then the gardens, and this morning Mrs Curnow showed me the kitchen level."

"Then you wanted to see the sea."

"Yes, but..."

"If you have a question, Connie, please just ask."

"My lord... Will... I asked Mrs Strickland to open up the small parlour on the other side of the hall. It would be more cheerful than the dining room. Those pictures..." She made a small moue of distaste.

"You're right," he said. Game was good to eat, but he wasn't fond of looking at paintings of dead birds while dining. "I'm sure my mother used to use that parlour, and the smaller room next to it was her own private place."

"So you wouldn't mind if we close up the dining room again, for a while at least? Mrs Strickland said there are not enough maids to have all the rooms open properly."

"Not at all. You may make what arrangements you like, Connie. I will send to ask the steward to call here on Monday, and after that I will have a better idea of how many new servants we can afford."

Her earlier smiles had not returned.

"Is there anything else bothering you?"

She took a deep breath. "I asked Mrs Strickland to open up the other parlour yesterday afternoon, and again this morning when I found it had not been done."

"And we are taking tea here because she still has not done it?"

Connie nodded.

"Do you wish me to speak to Mrs Strickland?" he asked.

"I think the... the question as to why it has not been done needs to come from me, or I will find it too difficult to deal with her in the future." She looked down, fiddling with her tea cup, then met his eyes. "Could you be there to support me, if I need it?"

"Of course, if you wish it." It must be difficult to take over a house this size if she had only managed somewhere much smaller.

"Thank you."

She looked a little more cheerful. Good.

"There is one more thing. There is a locked door in the cellar, and Mrs Strickland claims the key is lost."

"Do I hear a 'but' to follow?"

She smiled. "Indeed you do. I don't think she's telling the truth. She was... worried when I said we could break the door down if necessary."

Strickland again.

"Shall we sort this out now?" he asked. If Mrs Strickland was going to cause Connie worry like this, she would have to be replaced. He'd never had any problems with her before, but he'd not been here often in recent years.

"Please, if you don't mind."

He rang for Barton, and asked for Mrs Strickland to be sent in.

"Did you have a successful trip to Exeter?" Connie asked, when the footman had gone.

"Yes. It was mainly dealing with some financial matters, but I had a look at the cathedral as well."

"Oh." Her face lit up. "Is it as fine as Salisbury? May I see it?"

Will laughed, pleased at her interest. "By all means. It has a tower, not a tall spire, but the inside is as impressive." He gave a rueful smile. "I'm afraid I excused myself from the guided tour." He described what he could recall, but wasn't sorry when Barton finally reappeared. Connie asked too many questions he couldn't answer.

"I couldn't find her, my lord."

"Have you looked?"

"Yes, my lord. Even got Sukey and Mary to help. She's not in the house."

"When she does reappear, tell her to report to me after dinner."

"Yes, my lord." Barton bowed and left.

"Perhaps she went for a walk," Connie said, doubt clear in her voice.

"We can ask her when she returns." Will eyed the table—there was little food left, although he had probably eaten most of it himself. "Do you wish for more tea?"

"Thank you, but no."

"Then if you don't mind, I will see you at dinner. I want to take a look through the accounts."

"Very well." She glanced at the table, and back at him. "I enjoyed having tea together." She blushed as she spoke, and hurried out of the room.

He had enjoyed it too, but duty called. In the library he took one of the account books from a drawer. His hand paused as he opened it, part of their earlier conversation coming back to him.

Cellars.

At the time he'd been concentrating on Connie's worry about the housekeeper, but why would the woman lie about a locked cellar?

A question for later, he told himself firmly, and turned to the columns of figures.

❧

Barton was standing outside the door of the dining room when Connie descended the stairs for dinner. He was dressed not in his normal blue coat and grey breeches, but in the same ornate livery she'd seen on the footmen at Marstone Park.

He bowed, and ushered her to a seat at one end of the long table. She couldn't see another place setting until she leaned to one side to peer around the huge epergne adorning the centre of the table. Her husband's place—Will's place—was set at the far end.

So much formality?

Will's voice behind her made Connie start and look around. "Barton, why on earth have you laid the places like that?"

"Mrs Strickland said—"

"Well, move it, man."

Will took a seat next to Connie as Barton gathered up plates, cutlery, and glasses and set them out, then brought dishes and decanters over from the sideboard.

"Barton, the livery—is that Mrs Strickland's idea too?"

A quick grimace crossed Barton's face. "Yes, my lord."

"Well, unless you enjoy getting dressed up, don't bother in the future. I'll let you know if I want you tricked out like that. If you've brought in all the dishes, you may go."

Barton unbent enough to smile. "Thank you, my lord."

"May I help you to something, Connie?" Will asked, when the footman had gone.

Connie regarded the array of dishes in front of her. A game pie stood next to a dressed salmon, a roast capon was surrounded by five dishes of vegetables, and there were several choices of jellies, tarts, and fruit. "It seems rather a lot for two of us."

"I suspect Mrs Curnow was pleased to be cooking for more than the staff," Will said. "I assure you I do not normally require such a display."

Connie felt her face heat. "I meant no criticism, my lord—Will."

"I know. Do try the pie. Mrs Curnow makes excellent pastry." He added slices of pie and a variety of vegetables to her plate and his own.

Mrs Curnow *did* make excellent pastry. Connie took small portions of all the other dishes as well, sparing a thought that the cook was one of the members of staff she need not worry about.

Will offered her more wine when they had emptied their plates. "I intend to look over the estate tomorrow. Would you care to accompany me?"

Yes, she would, if she could—this was to be her home, after all. "I'm afraid I do not ride."

"No matter. There is currently no mount suitable for a lady here in any case. There is an open chaise; I brought a mare for it back from Exeter." He picked up his glass, gazing at the wine as he twirled the stem. "In future, there will only be the chaise, should you need to go to Exeter, or elsewhere. The coach will be returning to Marstone Park tomorrow."

"Oh." That seemed strange.

"Milsom will be on it, unless you need her until we can find a suitable replacement."

Fanny had helped with her hair at home, on occasion, but Sukey could probably do that here. "I don't need her, no." She let out a breath. "That will make things a little more pleasant."

"Indeed." He glanced at her plate. "Shall we retire? I find the library more comfortable than the drawing room. We can see Mrs Strickland in there."

He didn't move until she nodded, then he rose and pulled her chair back for her. He really had been consulting her wishes—a novel experience.

Lamplight in the library reflected softly from the spines of the books. Connie settled into an armchair, placing her glass on the table beside it. Will poured himself some port from a decanter and took a nearby chair.

The door stood open. Mrs Strickland knocked and walked into the room, her gaze flicking from Will to Connie and back. "You wished to speak with me, my lord?"

Will turned, glass in hand. "No, Lady Wingrave wishes to speak to you."

"My lady?" The housekeeper faced her, brows raised in what could pass for polite enquiry. The thinned lips belied that impression, although Connie was sure Will couldn't see her face from his position.

"Several things, Mrs Strickland. You are aware that the coach is returning to Marstone Park tomorrow." Connie waited until the housekeeper acknowledged her words with a nod. "Milsom will be returning with it. Ensure she is ready."

Mrs Strickland pressed her lips together, and Connie saw her take a deep breath. "My lady, who is to be your maid if Milsom leaves?"

"I'm sure you can find someone, Mrs Strickland. In the meantime, Sukey can do whatever is necessary."

"She's an under-housemaid, she won't know how to keep your clothing properly, when it arrives."

Connie kept her expression neutral. "You *do* know such things, I assume."

"Of course."

"Then you may instruct her as necessary."

The housekeeper's lips tightened, and Connie felt a brief pang for subjecting Sukey to Mrs Strickland's tutelage. But being a personal maid would be a better position for Sukey if she was a quick learner.

"I also wish the two parlours I saw this morning to be opened up and cleaned. I gave you explicit instructions to do so yesterday after-noon, and again this morning, yet you have done nothing."

"My apologies, miss. I had other—"

"*What* did you say?" Will's voice was quiet, but forceful.

The housekeeper's face paled. "My lady, I should say."

"You should indeed. And Lady Wingrave runs this household, not you."

"Begging your pardon, my lord, but she does't know—"

"Mrs Strickland, how is it you think you know *anything* about Lady Wingrave's experience of running a home?"

That was a good point; Connie didn't believe her manner had been too timid with either Milsom or Mrs Strickland, but both had attempted to dictate to her. Even a young woman trained in the ways of large houses might feel intimidated only a few days into her marriage.

Mrs Strickland did not answer.

"There is one other matter," Will went on. "It appears you have mislaid the key to one of the cellar rooms."

"Unfortunately, yes, sir. I will have a search made for it now." The woman's voice sounded calm.

"I suggest you look for it very carefully, Mrs Strickland. I wish to inspect the cellars—all of them—tomorrow, and if we have to break the door down, the cost of repairing it will come from your wages."

"Yes, my lord. Is that all, my lord?"

Will looked at Connie, one brow raised.

"Yes. You may go," she said.

Will went to the door and closed it behind the housekeeper, then turned to face Connie.

"Thank you for... for supporting me, Will," she said, before he could speak.

"Connie, I'm sorry you've had to deal with her... her insolence and insubordination. That behaviour is not normal."

"It's not your fault. I don't suppose you ever needed to say much to her when you visited."

"No, indeed."

"She didn't seem as worried about the cellars as she was earlier."

Will's brows rose. "Odd. Well, we'll see tomorrow what the fuss was about."

He said nothing more, but Connie didn't feel she could discuss the matter further. As he said, they would find out more tomorrow. He'd already had to intervene in her dealings with the servants, and that was not a good start to her life here.

"If you don't mind, I will retire to my room now."

Connie hung her gown in the dressing room, thankful Milsom had not been waiting for her. As she brushed out her hair, her thoughts turned again to the set of contrasts that was her husband: a womaniser who had promised not to bed her for a month, a man knowledgeable about pagan monuments who could race through the rain, a man about town who enjoyed eating ginger cake on the cliffs.

She knew some things about him. He did consult her wishes, although there were likely to be limits to that. He had supported her against the obnoxious Milsom and Strickland, and without any indication that he thought she should have been able to handle them herself.

Should she have stayed in the library? Even if she still felt too shy to ask him about his childhood, they could have talked about books.

She'd used the excuse that they didn't know each other to extract that promise of a month; it was only fair that they should try to get to know each other. That would take some effort from both of them.

Tomorrow, she thought, putting the brush down and climbing into bed.

CHAPTER 19

*L*eft alone in the library, Will poured himself another glass of port and crossed to the windows. The earlier clouds had partly cleared, leaving orange streaks to the north west. He watched as the sky darkened, the first bright star showing above the trees.

Connie. The image of her racing through the rain came back to his mind, her laugh, and her sparkling eyes. How long was it since he'd had such simple fun? Perhaps not so simple, he thought, trying to ignore the flush of heat as he remembered the way her wet skirts had clung to her legs.

She was still unsure of herself—hardly surprising for one thrust into a new life so abruptly. But she'd handled Mrs Strickland well, being both reasonable and firm.

The housekeeper's behaviour had been odd indeed. Which room was locked—had Connie said? Childhood memories crowded in as he frowned at his reflection in the window. That last summer, the one before his mother had fallen ill, he and Alfred had been obsessed with the servants' tales of priest holes and secret passages in the house. They'd even gone so far as to measure all the rooms in the cellars. Unless their calculations had been wrong, the cellars extended beyond the north wall of the house. They hadn't found a passage to the outside, but that didn't mean there wasn't one.

The connection flashed into his mind—obvious as soon as he'd thought about it. He and Alfred had been avid listeners to stories of trains of pack animals at the dark of the moon, carrying loads of brandy, tea, and silks up from the beach at Ashmouth, goods hidden in barns and outhouses until they could be taken to their final destination. What better place to store smuggled goods than the cellars of an unused mansion, only a couple of miles from the village?

Mrs Strickland had been absent that afternoon and was now much less worried about their threat to break the door down than she had been earlier. There was an obvious explanation.

The only way to see if his supposition was correct was to watch— even if that meant sneaking around in the dark, as they'd wanted to as boys. Was he being over-dramatic and indulging his childhood fantasies? Perhaps, but he couldn't dismiss his suspicions now that they had taken root.

He stood at the window for some time, turning over plans in his head, until the sky had was dark and stars were visible. Warren was locking the front door when he passed through the hall. Upstairs, Will looked through the garments in his dressing room, pulling out his black breeches. His riding coats were dark, devoid of trim or embroidery, and he selected one that buttoned up to the neck to help hide his white shirt. A dark neckerchief hid his collar.

If his suspicions were correct, someone might come to check he was still in his room. Leaving the clothing he'd removed flung over the back of a chair, he looked through the chests and cupboards in the room until he found some spare blankets. He rolled up two of them and positioned them beneath the bedclothes. Standing back, he thought it would look sufficiently like a sleeping form to fool anyone who didn't approach too closely.

Will put a loaded pistol into each coat pocket and, as an afterthought, added a sheathed knife. Picking up his boots, he lifted the latch on the door leading to the corridor and opened it a short way.

He could hear nothing so he stepped out, closing the door quietly behind him. Another pause, then he crept along the corridor to a guest room at the far end of the house, which had windows looking north. One of the shutters was open, and the faint starlight made ghostly shadows of furniture under holland covers. He crossed the room, taking care not to make a noise, and eased the shutter open further.

Nothing moved outside. Even if someone *was* there, he may not be able to see much from here; looking downwards, men would be dark shapes against the dark ground. Returning to the door, he took up a position just inside the room, from where he could see the entrance to the servants' stairs and the top of the main staircase.

If he was wrong about this evening's activities, he was going to have an uncomfortable spell waiting, not to mention feeling an utter fool.

A couple of hours passed before someone moved across his line of sight, a dark shape only just visible against the unlit corridor. He couldn't even make out if it was a man or woman.

Opening the door wider, he saw little more than a thin bar of light —someone was opening the door to his room. The figure took a step into the room, but no further, then retreated and moved along the corridor towards Connie's door, out of sight. Will picked up his boots and hurried across the landing and down the stairs, his stockinged feet making no sound. He ducked into the small parlour to pull his boots on, struck by a sudden doubt. Should he have first made sure the person was not intent on harming Connie? Even as he hesitated, he heard quiet steps on the stairs, and made out the shadowy figure heading for the kitchens.

A door from this parlour opened into the dining room, at the south end of the house—the opposite end to where he suspected the cellars had been extended. That would be the best place to leave.

Sliding up a window sash with the faintest of squeaks, he climbed over the sill and dropped into the flower bed below. Something prickly scratched his hands, and he swore beneath his breath.

The half moon hung low in the sky to the east, providing just enough light to see. Debating which way to go around the house, he settled on the back, through the orchard towards the stables—there was more grass to muffle his steps that way, less crunchy gravel. He moved slowly, sticking to the shadows until he could see beyond the north end of the building. Leaning against a tree, he resigned himself to waiting again. If he kept still and silent, no-one would notice him.

Connie gazed up at the canopy above her bed, lit by the moonlight shining in through the open windows. The earlier rain had cleared the air, but she had woken feeling uncomfortably warm. Thirsty, too, with a dry mouth. Those two glasses of wine with dinner, perhaps. She liked the taste, but she very rarely drank wine.

The glass of water beside her bed was almost empty. She filled it from the jug on the washstand and walked over to a window. A gentle breeze through the open sash helped to cool her, and she sat on the window seat while she sipped her drink.

This window looked over the orchard to the east, the tops of the trees merely black shapes in the pale light. The stables and coach house lay beyond, near the north end of the house. She sat for some time, dreamily comparing this view to the small patch of back garden that was all she'd been able to see from her old bedroom in Nether Minster. As she watched, she gradually became aware that something—or someone—was moving beyond the solid shadow that was the stable block.

Setting the glass down, she put her head out of the window. Several people, each leading a horse, were visible only as they passed through a patch of moonlight. Thieves, perhaps? Whatever they were doing, Will needed to know about this.

She moved over to the connecting door, but paused with her hand on the latch. Might he misinterpret her entry into his bedroom? That thought was no longer as frightening as it had been, but she didn't feel ready yet.

She must tell him. She pulled a robe on over her chemise, then cautiously lifted the latch. "Will?"

There was no reply. He'd left his curtains open, and the moonlight showed his discarded clothing over the back of a chair, and a lump beneath the bedclothes.

She swallowed. She didn't want to raise her voice, for fear of alerting someone else, so she'd have to shake his shoulder. But when she put her hand down it met only softness. Pulling the covers back revealed folded blankets.

Was *Will* involved in whatever was happening outside? Or had he expected something to happen tonight? The blankets could not have been intended to fool her, so he must suspect some of the servants were involved. If that were the case, it would be unwise for her to venture out of her room.

Will's comments about smugglers came to her mind. The cellars, of course. That would explain Mrs Strickland's nervousness when asked about the key. Something was hidden there, and was being removed now they had threatened to break the door down.

There was nothing she could do now, other than wait for Will to return. Going back to the window in her own room, she peered out again. There was no movement beyond the stables. She wrapped her arms around her body, feeling very alone. The idea of people—strangers—creeping around the house was frightening, but at least they had been outside, and at the far end of the building from her.

Eventually her eyes drooped in spite of her wish to stay awake. Telling herself firmly that if they were going to harm her they would have done it by now, she returned to bed. Whatever it was, it seemed Will had it in hand.

Finally, Will heard the jingle of harnesses, and low voices from the north. He had no intention of confronting them, or even trying to identify them—that was far too dangerous. He'd only wanted to see if his suspicions were correct.

How big is the operation?

He cautiously stepped forward, moving towards a tree that would disguise him while he got a better look. The one ahead, with a nice, thick trunk.

The trunk changed shape, and part of the shadow turned into someone else, watching as Will had been.

Will froze. If this was one of the smugglers, Will might get some information from him without endangering himself. If he wasn't, Will wanted to know who he was.

He pulled a pistol out of his pocket. He didn't cock it—the last thing he wanted to do was to attract attention by firing. The other watcher was intent on the happenings nearer the house, and Will crept to within two feet of him before he started to turn. Too late—Will pushed the muzzle of his pistol into the back of the man's neck, reaching round with his left hand to cover his mouth.

"Not a sound," he breathed. "Understand?"

He felt the man's head move—a nod? He moved his hand a couple of inches from the man's face.

"My lord?"

"Archer?" The tension left his body, and he put the pistol away.

"I was locked in, my lord." Archer's words were so faint Will could hardly hear them. "Climbed out of a window to find out what's going on." The sleeping quarters above the stables were much closer to the ground than Will's own bedroom windows.

They stood together in silence. A few sounds and shifts in the shadows to the north of the house indicated that something was happening, but they could not see any details without moving close enough to risk being seen.

"Time to go back," Will breathed. "Best if no-one knows we've seen them. I'll talk to you tomorrow."

Archer moved off with only a faint rustle, and Will began to pick his own way back around the house.

CHAPTER 20

Saturday 28th June

Connie was woken by Sukey bringing her morning tea. She sat up to drink it, surprised she'd not heard Will return in the night. He was there now—she could hear movement and a low murmur of voices.

There was a knock on the connecting door. Setting the cup down, she pulled the sheet up to her shoulders before calling him to come in.

Will appeared—fully dressed, she was relieved to see.

"Good morning. I trust you slept well?"

"I... er, yes, well enough thank you. But I wanted to tell—"

"Excellent. I came to ask if you would be happy to leave soon for our tour of the estate? It will be cooler in the morning. Mrs Curnow can pack some provisions for a picnic breakfast."

Irritated by the way he'd cut across her words, Connie stared at him for a moment. The sound of drawers opening and closing came from the next room; Will tilted his head in the direction of the open door, then shook it.

Ah—he doesn't want Warren to hear.

"Very well," Connie said. "Half an hour?"

"Thank you." He left her to finish her tea.

Will was waiting when Connie emerged from the house, the chaise ready on the drive with Archer holding the horse's head. She accepted his help to climb into the vehicle with a small smile. Will gathered the reins, and Archer jumped onto the narrow seat at the back as they set off.

They turned right at the end of the drive onto a road that led along the side of the valley towards Ashton St Andrew. It road rose gently, flanked by woodland, and it wasn't long before Connie spotted the church tower surrounded by rooftops. They slowed, then Will turned off the road into a patch of trees.

He must have caught her surprise.

"I wanted to talk in private," he said. "Archer, bring the blanket, will you? This concerns you, too."

He tethered the horse loosely to a tree, and walked a few yards to an area of flat ground. Archer spread the blanket on a fallen log for Connie to sit on and sat on the grass nearby.

"I brought you both here because I don't know who else in the house to trust," Will began.

Connie listened carefully as he described how he'd crept out of the house the previous night.

"Archer—was anything said to you this morning?" Will went on, before Connie could tell him what she'd seen.

"No, my lord. I pretended I'd slept through."

"Mrs Strickland couldn't be found yesterday afternoon," Connie reminded him. "Do you think she was making arrangements?"

"That was my supposition, yes. She may not be the only one, though. Archer, you haven't heard any talk at all about such things?"

"No, my lord."

"Very well. Listen, will you? To any gossip, or other talk, at Ashton Tracey or in the villages. I'll give you some drinking money. I imagine most of the staff know what is going on, even if they are not directly involved. You could also see if you can locate the exit from the cellars beyond the north end of the house—but do not put yourself in danger."

Connie felt a sense of unreality. Whatever she'd expected of her marriage, it certainly wasn't this.

"There's another matter," Will went on, glancing at Connie. She nodded to show she was listening. "It's almost certain that at least one person will be sending regular reports to my father—not only household affairs, but about my actions as well."

Spying on him? She shouldn't be surprised, really, from what she'd heard about Will's relationship with his father. Archer merely grunted, as if this was nothing new to him.

"I suspect that it is Mrs Strickland. It is probably why she appears to think she has more authority than her position warrants. What I don't know is whether she is the only one. Milsom, most likely, although she's now safely on her way back to Marstone Park with the coach. See if you can find out about anyone else, Archer."

"Yes, my lord." The groom sat a little straighter.

"Now, Archer, I wish to talk to Lady Wingrave in private, without the chance of anyone overhearing. Can you think of an errand that would take you into the village?"

Archer's face screwed up in thought. "Is there a farrier there?"

"There certainly used to be."

"Right—I reckon I need the shoes checking on this new mare," he said. "And to see if the man's good enough for shoeing Mercury."

"Good idea. Take the chaise. We'll walk up when we've finished—leave us the basket before you go." Will handed over some coins. "There's an inn, too. Good place to start listening."

A big grin spread across Archer's face as he got to his feet. "Right you are, my lord."

"Will, I saw something last night." Connie spoke before Will had worked out where to start his explanations.

"What? Where were you?" She hadn't put herself in danger, had she?

He relaxed as she explained what she'd seen and why she'd stayed in her room.

"You did the right thing," he confirmed.

"Will, why does your father have people spying on you?"

"And you—that's almost certainly why he employed Milsom."

"Me?" Her voice was almost a squeak. "Why should I—? That is, why does he feel the need to spy on either of us?"

"To ensure the next heir is truly of his blood." He spoke without thinking, realising too late what his words could imply.

Her mouth fell open for a moment, eyes wide. "If that's what he thinks of me, why force me into this marriage? Is that what *you* think?"

"Connie, *I* am not suspecting you of anything." He reached one hand towards her, but let it drop. "My father has to be in control of *everything*. He doesn't trust me. He doesn't trust anyone, and they are watching me as much as you. More than you, probably."

She drew a deep breath, and nodded.

"He even wrote to his solicitors in Exeter, instructing them to send on copies of the Ashton Tracey accounts, and details of any of my activities they knew about." That letter had gone in the kitchen fire when Mrs Curnow wasn't looking.

He kept his eyes on her face until she relaxed and managed a weak smile. "I think you'd better explain," she said. "You clearly didn't want this marriage any more than I did. Why did you agree?"

Fancott had been right, then. He was not the only one being coerced.

He stood, pacing back and forth across the small clearing as he related his story. He felt again the resentment at his father's unexplained determination to exclude Uncle Jack from the succession, and his frustration at being prevented from doing anything useful with his life.

"So I've spent the last few years in London," he finished. "With most of the staff spying on me. Father arranged several marriages, solely for me to produce an heir, but I managed to avoid them."

He stopped pacing, turning to face her, and was surprised to see her eyes narrowed. She was angry—with Marstone?

"You find it onerous to have your activities restricted?" Her calm voice belied her expression.

"Well, yes," he said. "Who wouldn't?"

"Half the human race, apparently. I, like most women, must belong to a man. A father or a husband, it makes little difference; we are *property*. We are supposed to be obedient and accept this situation without complaint, as the natural order of things."

"Connie—"

"My father is just as bad as yours," she went on as if he hadn't spoken. "Only with less money and status. *You* could live as you please in London, fighting duels over... over..."

Loose women, he filled in mentally, feeling dazed. She hadn't raised her voice, but the way she spoke left him in no doubt that she was angry. And with him, not with his father as he'd expected.

"I was forced into this marriage on pain of being cast off with no money, and the only people who might have helped me would have lost their living had they done so." She dropped her eyes for a moment, taking a deep breath before going on. "Would *you* have been destitute if your father had turned you off? Heaven forfend you might have to work for a living. Without references, what could I have done?"

She held his gaze, her face now flushed.

"Nothing," he admitted. Shame washed through him as he realised she'd spoken no more than the truth. "Connie, I'm sorry. You are perfectly right, I had far more choice than you did."

Her eyes widened. Had no man ever admitted he was wrong to her?

"Let me finish my story, Connie. Reluctance to work for a living was not why I agreed to this. Although, naturally, I *was* reluctant to do the only kinds of jobs that would have been open to me at short notice."

"Go on."

He explained about his debts, and the threat of selling Ashton Tracey. "It *was* time I settled down," he admitted. "Many of my aff— er, misdeeds in London were... well, I had to fill my time somehow.

Here, I can learn to manage an estate properly, without my father's hidebound steward vetoing every idea."

Will waited for a reaction, surprised how much her acceptance of his explanation mattered. Her gaze moved from the trees down to the blanket, before finally rising to meet his own. Much of the tension had left her face.

"So your father is still attempting to control you, by having the staff report on you."

He nodded.

"Why don't you replace Mrs Strickland with someone you trust?"

"I will, at some point, but if I get rid of her now, he'll either bribe someone else, or threaten to sell the place if I don't employ some staff of his choosing."

She seemed to accept that, but her gaze was focused somewhere in the distance again.

"Connie?"

"I was thinking. How do you feel about deceiving your father? Sauce for the goose is sauce for the gander, after all."

"He's deceived... What did you say?"

"Sauce for the goose. It's a common saying, is it not?"

And one that Fancott used often. She'd referred to 'Martha' a couple of times—Fancott's wife was called Martha. "Connie, where did you live before we married?"

"Nether Minster. It's only a few miles from—"

"I know where it is." Fancott had said he knew 'of' Miss Charters... ha! "The old devil!"

"Who?"

"Fancott. He helped me with... with a problem I had some years ago, so when my father told me of the marriage arrangements, I went to him again. He advised me not to resist, and that all would be well."

Connie's eyes widened. "Martha was—is—a mother to me," she said. "She told me it would be well, too. But I never wanted to be a countess, or have wealth. I just wanted a proper family, with..." She shook her head.

"That can still happen," he said, keeping his voice gentle.

"There is something else." Her voice was hesitant.

"Tell me." A previous lover? Was that why she didn't want…

Stop thinking like Father!

"Connie?"

"When you said you didn't care for rank, did you mean it?"

Rank? "It matters little to me."

She looked into his face and took a deep breath. "My father lied to yours. He implied I was the daughter of his first wife, who was a baron's daughter."

"You are not?" He couldn't help feeling amusement at his father being deceived, but he was careful not to show it. He would not make light of her concerns.

"My mother was his second wife. Her father was in trade, and Charters married her for her dowry." She looked away. "I was too young to ask about it while she was still alive, but Martha said she was in love with someone else when she was made to marry Charters."

"Connie, that—"

"That's not all. Charters isn't my father either, so I'm not a viscount's granddaughter. Martha thinks Mama's former suitor came to see her after she'd been married for a year or so. Charters knew I wasn't his. Mr Fancott made Charters accept me as his own by convincing him he'd be ridiculed as a cuckold and earn the enmity of my mother's relatives."

She was back in control now, her voice steady, but he could see the tension in her neck, and in her closed fists.

"So now you know. I'm nothing. A bastard."

"Not a bastard," Will said, saying the first thing that came into his head to try to reassure her. "Not in the eyes of the law, and not in my eyes either. Good grief, Connie—the fact you're not related by blood to Charters is a good thing if he's anything like my father."

Her eyes widened. "Really?"

"Trust me, it's who *you* are that counts."

"You don't know me very well."

"No," he said. "But I'm learning."

CHAPTER 21

They walked slowly up the road together, neither of them wanting to hurry in the heat of the sun. They had made a late breakfast out of the bread and ham Mrs Curnow had provided, sitting in companionable silence.

Connie felt light, floating—happy even. Until she'd told Will about her true parentage, she hadn't realised how much the secret had been weighing on her mind. Did he really think it was a good thing? He had sounded sincere.

She bit her lip against a smile at the memory of her scold. She'd meant every word, but now she had calmed down she could see how galling it must be for a man, used to being in charge of his own life, to have his hand forced in such a way. Reassuring, too, that his only resentment of this forced match seemed to be directed against his father, not her.

Ashton St Andrew was little more than a cluster of houses around a green, dwarfed by the church. Connie spotted the chaise in the shade of a huge oak tree, the mare cropping the grass nearby. Archer was nowhere in sight.

"Would you care to wait in the chaise while I turf Archer out of the inn?" Will indicated a small, tumbledown building half-hidden by the oak. "I'm afraid the place isn't really suitable for a lady."

"Very well." It would be cool, at least.

Will was only a few minutes. "We have an appointment for Mrs Strickland to show us the cellars," he said, as Archer backed the mare between the shafts. "Then, if you wish, we can drive around the estates as I promised last night."

On their return to Ashton Tracey, Connie headed for the parlour. The dust sheets had finally been removed, the room looking bright and cheerful with the curtains open. The furniture was pushed to the walls, leaving bare floorboards where the carpet had been.

Good—Mrs Strickland appeared to be doing a proper job, having the carpet beaten. Connie ran a finger over the tables and the mantelpiece. It had all been dusted, although the woodwork needed a good polish to make it gleam.

She could hear Warren's voice in the hall. "...gave me a key this morning, my lord. Do you wish to see the cellars now?

"Yes." Will turned, meeting her eyes as she stood in the parlour doorway. "Shall you accompany me, my lady?"

Why not? She followed the two men down to the kitchen level, where Warren collected a couple of lanterns.

"There didn't seem much point in cleaning these rooms, my lord, while no-one was in residence," the butler said, showing Will the smaller rooms that Connie had seen the day before. "They can be cleaned now, if you are wishing to restock the cellars."

"I need to find a supplier first, Warren. Prices in the merchants in Exeter were rather high."

"I will see what I can do more locally, my lord."

"Thank you. Lead on, if you please."

Connie puzzled over this exchange as the two men looked into more storerooms. Had Will just asked Warren to find a source of smuggled goods—while they were looking for traces of smugglers?

132

They finally came to the door at the end of the corridor. Entering behind the two men, Connie peered around Will with interest, but there was nothing to be seen, only walls and the stone-flagged floor.

A very clean floor.

"It's—" Connie closed her mouth again; Will might not want her to say anything in front of Warren.

"Thank you, Warren, you may return above stairs," Will said. When the sound of the butler's footsteps had faded he spoke again, keeping his voice low. "What were you were about to say?"

"It's much cleaner than the other rooms down here."

"Hmm. It's either in regular use, or they cleaned it when they took the goods away." As he spoke, he walked towards the end of the room, holding the lantern high. The far wall was obscured by another set of empty wine racks. Will lowered the lantern with a sigh.

Are those scratch marks? "Will, shine the light on the floor."

He moved the lantern, as she requested. "Ah, someone's moved these racks. Hold this, will you?" Will handed her the lantern, then dragged one of the racks a little way from the wall. Connie held the lantern higher, making out lines on the wall.

"A door? Is that where they took things out?" Connie asked, her voice a whisper even though Warren had gone.

"It must be. Let me put the shelves back."

"So no-one could get in from the outside unless someone in the house moved the racks?" Connie asked, as he dragged the rack back into place.

"That's possible. But it's also possible that this rack was only put here to stop us finding the door."

"Does Warren know?"

"I'm not sure; we have to assume he does. However he doesn't know that we know, so we will express disappointment at the fact there was nothing interesting to be found in the locked room."

"What about on the outside?" Connie tried to imagine the ground beyond the walls, but she didn't know the place well enough yet.

"There may be a trapdoor, covered in earth or plants."

"So some of the gardeners must know, too."

"Not necessarily, but we should assume that they do. It may just be a case of them turning a blind eye. But again, it would be best if none of them suspect that we have found anything."

Connie had routinely deceived Charters over small things for many years, but he had been the only one. Keeping track of who knew what here could become very complicated.

When they emerged from the cellars, they sat on the terrace and Barton brought out a tray of refreshments.

"We have not had our tour of the estate, Connie," Will said. "Do you still wish to join me?"

It would be hot, but she didn't want to turn down the chance to find out more about her new home—and her new husband.

"I would enjoy that, yes. Thank you."

"Excellent. I don't intend to go far, just to drive around some of the tenant farms, to become more familiar with the area."

Didn't he spend time here as a child?

"I know my way to the nearest villages," he went on. "But as a boy I was more interested in exploring the woods and the cliff tops." Her lips twitched and he paused, his cup halfway to his mouth. "Let me guess," he said, his lips curving up at the corners. "You were about to ask me why I don't know the farms. Is that right?"

She nodded, returning his smile.

Once in the chaise, Connie took the map Will handed her. It was more of a sketch than a properly surveyed map, but she identified Ashton Tracey and the two nearby villages. "Where are we going?"

Will leaned towards her, pointing out a couple of nearby farms, his arm warm against her own. "Up through Ashton St Andrew again, then past Low Hill Farm and Quarry Farm." His finger traced a path through the maze of lanes. "It doesn't matter exactly."

Will let the mare amble along. The roads were quiet, and he could give much of his attention to the scenery, and to the woman beside him.

Although he'd come out to re-acquaint himself with the area, he found himself more interested in her reactions than in the countryside: her smile of delight as a buzzard swooped down and flew along the lane ahead of them, the sudden turn of her head as a blackbird flew chattering out of a hedge.

"Do you like watching birds?" he asked, when she twisted in her seat to watch a kestrel hover.

"I used to put food out for garden birds," she replied. "I didn't have much time for watching once I started keeping house for Papa. I'd never seen seagulls until I came here."

"There's a lot more than gulls to be seen," he said. "Wait until you see a flock of gannets diving into the sea."

"Gannets?"

"I'm sure there's a book in the library with bird illustrations. I'll look it out when we get home."

"Thank you. And will you take me to the cliffs again to see them?"

"With pleasure." He'd watched birds as a boy with his brother; he would enjoy it again with her, he was sure. "Did the Fancotts encourage you to study nature?"

"Yes, Martha loved birds. She even trained some to eat out of her hand."

As she talked about the lessons she'd shared with the Fancott children, her affection for the vicar and his wife was clear. It seemed that parts of her childhood had been happy, in spite of her father. He responded with tales of his own adventures as a boy, and almost ended up lost in the maze of lanes through lack of attention. In the end he had to consult the map to work out the shortest route home to avoid being late for dinner and upsetting Mrs Curnow.

Connie peered at her face in the mirror as Sukey pinned her hair up. Her complexion normally had some colour from walking to the village in all weathers—her recent excursions in the sunshine were adding to that.

Fine ladies were supposed to have white skin; perhaps she should ask Will to buy her a parasol. She smiled, imagining trying to control a parasol on a breezy cliff top.

"You look lovely, my lady," Sukey said, fastening a few final curls in place. "Have I done it right?"

Connie turned her head from side to side—the knot wasn't quite as neat as Fanny would have managed, but it was very good for the girl's first attempt.

"Very good, thank you Sukey."

Her eye caught the row of books on the chest. Before her marriage, she'd wondered if Will would restrict her reading as her father had tried to do, but now she was sure he would not.

"Sukey, please take those books to the library. Leave them on one of the tables."

"Yes, my lady."

Connie adjusted the position of a few of the pins. Sukey seemed bright enough—she'd soon learn.

Downstairs, dinner had been laid in the small parlour, now thoroughly cleaned, dusted, and polished. Light from the lowering sun sparkled on wineglasses and cutlery, and someone had placed a bowl of flowers in the middle of the table. Connie breathed the scent of beeswax and sweet peas.

She heard Barton directing Will to this parlour, and turned as her husband entered the room. He looked around, a smile spreading across his face as he moved over to the table to hold her chair.

"This is much better than the formal room," he said. They waited while Barton laid out the meal, and then Will dismissed the footman.

"I intend to open up the little parlour next door," Connie said, once they had served themselves. "Is that is all right?"

"You don't need to ask, Connie."

He had said so yesterday, but she still wasn't used to the degree of freedom she had here. "Thank you. I found an escritoire in one of the guest bedrooms. I thought I could have it moved here, or next door."

"Take some paper and ink from the library," Will suggested. "I can get more next time I'm in Exeter."

That reminded her of an idea she'd had while dressing. "Will, how do letters get to the post from here?"

"Someone will take them—the inn up the hill is the local office, I think. Who do you wish to write to... not to your father?"

"No, to Martha." That wasn't why she'd asked. "But I was thinking about Mrs Strickland. Anything she writes to your father would be taken by... by a groom, I suppose."

"Indeed. I could get Archer assigned—is that what you were thinking? He could retrieve the letters before they are sent."

"Yes, but as you said before, if the letters stop, your father will get someone else to do it. If her letters can be intercepted, we could at least see what is in them."

"She would still be reporting on our actions, though," Will countered.

"If you copied out the letters, you could omit anything you did not want him to know. The first time you do it, you could explain that Mrs Strickland has sprained her wrist, and you are writing at her dictation. You could be...Mrs Curnow, perhaps. Or Warren?"

"Lady Wingrave, you have a devious mind!" He raised his glass in a toast to her with a smile.

Connie felt a flush of pleasure at the praise.

"I think you had better write, though," Will went on. "My father might recognise my handwriting."

"Does he write to her, do you think?"

"His secretary might. That shouldn't be a problem—Archer can fetch the post, too. We can't keep it up forever, but it's a good plan for now." He smiled. "My father told me you knew your duties to man and to God, and that you would be an obedient wife."

Obedient? Was that what he wanted?

"That wasn't a criticism, Connie. I was only thinking that the description seems inconsistent with your devious—and totally admirable—ability to work out such schemes. More lies from your father to mine, I suppose."

She let out a breath. "Oh, no, my father believed it himself. He only allowed me to read the Bible and books of sermons." She smiled. "I have something to show you after dinner."

When they retired to the library, Will saw a stack of unfamiliar books on one end of his desk.

"Those are my books," Connie began, "and some that Mr Fancott lent me. You might be interested in the sermons; the black book with the ribbon around it."

Will picked up the book she'd indicated. Why did she think he was interested in sermons?

"Open it," Connie directed.

Pulling the ribbon loose, he tried to open the book in the middle but the pages appeared to be stuck. Starting at the front, he found that after the first couple of dozen pages, the rest had been glued together, with a large rectangular hole cut in them.

"Mr and Mrs Fancott used to lend me their books," she explained. "If the one I was reading was small enough to fit in there, I could take it home without my father finding out."

His lips curved, then his smile turned into a laugh—his father really had no idea who he'd chosen for the next Countess of Marstone.

"Mr Fancott gave me those others on the morning I set off for the... for Marstone Park."

"When it was too late for your father to find out." He'd never thought of Fancott as devious—although unlike his father, Fancott was doing it for someone else's benefit.

"Yes. Am I... May I buy some books myself? I would like to read these, but it would not do to deprive Mr Fancott of his volumes for too long."

She should not need to ask such a thing. Of course, he chided himself, he'd said nothing about pin money or a clothing allowance. He would remedy that soon—on Monday, after he'd talked to the steward.

"Of course you may."

She smiled. He liked making her smile.

He caught her gaze shifting to her pile of books. "Do sit and read, if you wish."

"Thank you."

He recognised the book she chose as the one she had been reading in the coach—or at least, it was one with a similar binding. He picked another from her pile, but sat with it in his lap. She was a far more interesting object of study.

She wore the green gown again, and looked well in it, but it was as sober in colouring as her other gowns. What would she look like dressed in something brighter? Hopefully when the rest of her things arrived she'd have more to choose from.

Not that she needed adornment, he thought, glad of the book resting in his lap. Seen like this, with her attention on what she was reading, she was not much out of the ordinary, but he knew that her face could show enthusiasm and joy. She could laugh with him; she would probably laugh *at* him as well, and he thought he wouldn't mind.

He'd been married five days, only another twenty five to wait.

Only?

CHAPTER 22

Sunday 29th June

It felt strange to Connie to spend a Sunday without attending church. When she'd asked, Warren had said a visiting curate only held a service once every month or so at Ashton St Andrew, or when weddings, baptisms, or funerals were required.

Will made no mention of it at breakfast, instead asking her if she would care to go out in the chaise again.

"We can go down to Ashmouth, if you wish."

"I would like that, thank you." The view of the sea from the cliff top had been wonderful; now she wanted to see the waves up close. Talking to Will about the church could wait. In truth, she had enjoyed church mostly for the familiar rituals, and being able to escape from the house for a while with the chance to talk to Martha afterwards.

They took Archer with them, on the back seat of the chaise. Connie enjoyed the journey down the hill, through dappled shade with only the sounds of birdsong and the clop of hooves.

There was no reason for Will to *need* her company; he must have invited her because he thought she'd enjoy the outing. Or because he wanted her with him. She stole a glance at his face just as he turned towards her with a smile. Something in his eyes made her breath catch and heat rise to her face; she managed a smile in return before giving her attention to the road again.

The bottom of the valley broadened and the woodland gave way to small stone houses lining the road, birdsong changing to the mournful cries of seagulls. Shading her eyes as the land opened out into a small bay, happiness rose in her as she made out the glitter of sun on the water and fishing boats bobbing at anchor.

The buildings along the sea front were a little larger than others in the village. The inn here looked more prosperous than the one in Ashton St Andrew, a brightly painted sign portraying a smiling dolphin with huge teeth. A couple of men lounged against its wall, their unsmiling gaze following the chaise as Will brought it to a halt at the edge of the beach. Others scraped at the bottom of a boat propped up on the sand, or mended nets.

"There isn't a lot to look at." Will sounded apologetic.

"There's the sea." Connie smiled at him.

Leaving Archer to look after the mare, they walked towards the water. Wavelets made a rhythmic hushing noise as they surged up the beach and retreated again, the salt air mingling with a faint odour of rotting fish. Connie gazed with delight at gulls wheeling overhead, fighting over scraps thrown from a table outside the inn where women were gutting fish.

"Shall we walk?" Will offered his arm.

They picked their way along the water's edge, around piles of lobster pots and tangles of old rope. She met his eyes, laughing with the joy of it all, and was warmed again by his answering smile.

"My lord!"

Connie released Will's arm, and they both turned to see Archer running towards them.

"You'd better come, my lord. It's Mrs Strickland."

"What's wrong?"

"Says she took a fall, my lord."

Archer led the way into the inn. Mrs Strickland was slumped in a chair in an empty corner of the taproom, hunched over with her arms wrapped around her chest. Connie gasped in horror when the woman raised her head. One eye was swollen shut, blood smeared her chin from a cut lip, and other patches of red marred her face. From the way she was sitting, her ribs hurt, and likely many other places as well.

"Good grief. Who did this to you?" Will's sharp voice indicated that he was as horrified as Connie.

Mrs Strickland shook her head. "No-one did it, my lord. *No-one.*" She kept her eyes on the floor. "I fell down some steps."

She was lying. Nobody received injuries like that from falling down stairs.

Connie could tell from the tight expression on Will's face that he didn't believe it either. She glanced around the room—the two men she'd noticed earlier sat in one corner with mugs of ale. The larger one had a bent nose, possibly the result of a fight; the other was nondescript, although better dressed than most of the drinkers. Both stared, stony faced, at a group of card-players at another table. Those men kept their attention on their cards.

At least a few people in the taproom should have been watching them—it was human nature to be curious.

Something is very wrong here.

"We'd better get you back to Ashton Tracey," Will said. "The chaise is outside—can you walk?"

"Yes, my lord."

Archer stepped forward and offered his arm. Connie could see that movement was hurting the woman, but Mrs Strickland said nothing as she hobbled outside. Getting her up into the chaise caused even more pain; in spite of Connie's dislike of the housekeeper, she had to admire her stoicism.

"The seat is not wide enough for three," Connie said, as Will offered his hand. "I can walk up the hill with Archer."

"No, definitely not."

Surprised by the vehemence in his tone, Connie looked at the chaise again. "I can ride on the seat behind. There's room for me as well as Archer."

Will drew a deep breath. "No. Archer, you drive. *I* will sit on the back with Lady Wingrave."

"Right you are, my lord."

Connie gasped as Will lifted her onto the back seat. It felt odd, facing backwards with her legs dangling. The seat was not as wide as the one in the chaise itself, and when Will climbed up his arm and shoulder pressed against hers. She was conscious of the warmth of him where their thighs touched, the feel of his hands around her waist still lingering. His solid presence was comforting—someone had attacked Mrs Strickland, but she knew Will would protect her. She glanced sideways, before returning her gaze to the road rolling away beneath their feet. Was he as aware of her as she was of him?

It was just as well she hadn't shared the seat with Archer.

Warren came down the front steps to help Mrs Strickland out of the chaise. There was concern on his face, but Connie could detect no sign of surprise. He knew something, even if he was not directly involved.

The first priority was to assess Mrs Strickland's injuries, and call a doctor. Warren offered to get Barton to help carry her, but she declined, leaning heavily on the butler's arm instead. Connie and Will followed them in. Mrs Curnow came out of the kitchen as they passed the door, gasping as she saw the damage to Mrs Strickland's face.

"We'll need water, Mrs Curnow," Connie said. "Hot and cold, please, and clean cloths. Then you can make some willow bark tea and prepare comfrey poultices. I'll get her into her bed."

"Begging your pardon, my lady, but it might be better if I undressed her. There's not much in the stillroom, but I can take a look afterwards."

Connie realised that this was right—the housekeeper would be less embarrassed if Mrs Curnow helped her. She added restocking the stillroom with medicines to her mental list of things to be done.

"Can you deal with this?" Will asked in a low voice.

"Yes."

"Good, thank you. Connie, I need to talk to you afterwards."

"Very well. Can you send to the gardener to bring comfrey leaves, if he has any?"

Will nodded, and went off with Archer. In the kitchen, Connie set Mary to heating water, and asked Sukey to bring bandages from the stillroom.

~

Will sat at his desk in the library, toying with a penknife. Mrs Strickland had failed the smugglers in some way, that was clear. No rational person would blame her for Will wanting to look in the cellars, but she'd had several days' notice by letter of his arrival. The gang could have moved the goods out before Will arrived, instead of risking them being found.

Those injuries were hours old, too—he recalled the progression of his own injuries from fist fights in his youth. That meant she'd sat in the inn for hours, nursing her injuries with no-one helping.

What would Connie make of it all? She'd work it out quickly, he was sure, if she hadn't already. He wondered what Mrs Strickland had told her masters about Connie. Could they resent her for her request to inspect *all* the cellars?

Connie entered the library, interrupting his thoughts. Concern filled him at her appearance—she looked tired, with tendrils of hair clinging in damp wisps to her face and neck and her apron damp and streaked with blood and dirt.

"Come, sit down." He moved to a pair of chairs near an open window. "Wine? Or cordial?"

She spoke before he could ring. "Mrs Curnow is still busy with Mrs Strickland. I'm just tired." She unfastened the apron, bundling it up and dropping it on the floor, and then sat with her eyes closed, one hand massaging the back of her neck.

Will opened the door wide, letting in a cool breeze. "How is she?"

"Her face, you saw. Bruises on her arms and back, and it's possible she may have broken ribs. A sprained ankle—possibly even broken, but that is beyond my skill. Bruises and broken skin there, too." She swallowed hard and rubbed her forehead. "She insists we don't summon a doctor."

"We may ignore her wishes if you think that best."

Connie glanced at the door.

"If the door is open, no-one can listen behind it," Will explained, keeping his voice low.

She nodded. "Will, those injuries were not new."

"What makes you say that?" He wanted to hear her reasoning.

"It takes time for eyes to swell up like that. The cuts on her face didn't bleed again when they were washed. I helped Martha sometimes in the village," she added.

"Should I send for the doctor, then?" From what she'd said, her medical judgement would be more sound than his own.

"I don't know. Perhaps, if she doesn't start to improve by tomorrow." She took a deep breath, and sat up straighter in her chair. "Those injuries were *not* all from falling down steps. She refused to say how long she'd been sitting there, but Mrs Curnow says she went down to the village this morning, quite early."

"Why would she do that, and on a Sunday?"

"Mrs Curnow doesn't know. She seems to make a point of *not* being observant or asking questions. I'll feel like screaming if she says 'I really couldn't say, my lady' once more."

Will, having had a similar conversation with Warren, sympathised.

"Sukey knows," Connie continued. "I wondered out loud who could have done such a thing. She started to say something, then stopped. She was frightened about what she'd nearly said. I think the other staff know, too, but are better at hiding it. And all the people in the inn—they must know who did it."

"The smugglers." Will said.

"Yes, but why? They didn't lose their goods." Connie massaged her neck again. "I suppose they had to move things at short notice. Silly woman—if she had any sense she'd have shown me the cellars herself that first morning and passed off the last door as being stuck. It was only her manner that made me suspicious."

Will smiled; he couldn't help it.

145

"I don't see anything funny in that." Her words were sharp.

"My apologies. It was just that you came to exactly the same conclusions as I did." However, Mrs Strickland's failings weren't important now. He had to keep Connie safe, but after their discussion this morning, he wasn't sure she would like what he was about to say.

"Connie, will you agree never to go about the estate alone? Take Archer with you, at the very least."

Her eyes widened. "Do you think someone will attack me?"

"No, but it is not worth taking any risk. It would also be wise to continue to pretend we don't know that the cellars here have been used."

She sighed. "Very well."

His shoulders relaxed. He'd wanted her willing agreement; after her complaint yesterday about women being treated as possessions, ordering her to comply would not go down well. "Thank you."

"For how long? Not for ever?"

"Not if I can help it. I don't know what to do yet, but I'll think of something."

"Very well." She hesitated for a moment. "Will, in the cellars yesterday, you asked Warren to find a supplier."

"The cellars need restocking."

"Yes, but… Will, were you asking Warren to find a source of smuggled goods for you?"

He shrugged. "Most people buy smuggled goods. I suspect that the majority of the people in Ashmouth, and probably many of the surrounding villages, are involved, to supplement their income."

"I see." She met his eyes, her mouth turned down at the corners, then stood. "If you will excuse me, I need a wash and a clean shift." She left the room without waiting for him to reply.

She didn't approve of him buying smuggled goods, it seemed. She did have a point, after what they'd done to the housekeeper.

He shook his head—he'd think about that later. If the smugglers had removed goods from his cellars, what would they do with them? If they were destined for places inland, why were they still so close to the coast? The discussion in the Queen's Head in Exeter came back to him. Duty on exports—could the goods be going *to* France? They would get a better price for wool in France, while still selling more cheaply than official exports. If that were the case, they'd want to move them on soon from their interim store.

He could ignore the whole situation, of course, but that could result in the gang continuing to use his house. Connie wouldn't be safe. Or he could inform the preventatives, but they were notoriously poor at getting convictions. The last thing he wanted was the smuggling gang still free *and* wanting revenge on him.

He recalled a steep hillside above Ashmouth from his days playing in the woods, and a clearing with a good view of the bay. If he went there tonight, he might see if anything was happening. The more he could find out about the smugglers the better, as long as the servants didn't know what he was doing.

Sighing, he took the estate accounts from their drawer.

Connie stripped off her gown and washed her face and hands, the cool water welcome on her skin.

Accompanied at all times? It made sense, she knew, although she didn't care for the idea. She was used to walking the fields around Nether Minster alone. Then she shook her head—she was better off now than she had been then. Here, she wouldn't have to scheme and manipulate her father to be allowed out; having a groom accompany her was a small price to pay for that freedom. And Will had asked rather than ordering her.

Will's attitude towards the smugglers concerned her, though. The attack on Mrs Strickland had been vicious. Will could allow them to continue using the cellars, but would they trust him not to inform on them? Perhaps, if he bought enough contraband goods from them, but then he'd be even more complicit. And any criminal activity could easily result in potential witnesses being threatened or harmed.

She rubbed her temples. Will was clearly not the controlling type of man her father was, but how would he react if she told him she wasn't happy with his casual acceptance of smuggling? She didn't really know him well enough yet.

The gown lying over the back of a chair caught her eye, and she gladly turned her thoughts to her wardrobe. The gown badly needed a wash, and the pattern was faded. She'd never really minded what her gowns looked like, but now she wanted to dress in something brighter. Something more attractive.

Her only other light gown was well past its best. The remaining gowns were all of fabric too thick for this weather, and too dark and drab for her taste.

In her dressing room, she sorted through her mother's gowns, pulling out one made of a cheerful yellow brocade, embroidered with butterflies and exotic birds. It was made to be worn over panniers, not the bum roll she used, but she could deal with that. Tomorrow she would get the second small parlour opened up, and start to make herself a new gown.

Will cursed in the dark as he dodged a branch—again. He swung the lantern upwards before moving on. It was shuttered to only provide light ahead, allowing him to follow the faint traces of the footpath, but it didn't illuminate the branches above him.

Not for the first time this night, he marvelled at how much harder it was to sneak out than it had been when he and Alfred were boys, trying to re-enact Uncle Jack's stories of fighting in the forests of British America. Back then, a friendly Warren had left a lantern for them behind a hedge in the formal garden, together with a tinder box. This evening, Will had had to find one himself, and without anyone knowing.

Better planning, he told himself. If he was going to discover what the smugglers were doing, he needed to think things through properly first.

Relying on his childhood memories was the second mistake. Paths changed, trees fell, sometimes the land even slipped a little. He should look for the path in daylight.

Go on or go back?

He took out his watch, squinting at it in the flickering lantern light. Two o'clock. The sun would be rising in a couple of hours, and he needed to be back in his room before dawn, with no indication he'd been out. He turned with a sigh, hoping he wasn't going to run into the same branches again on the way back.

CHAPTER 23

Monday 30th June

Will awaited the steward's arrival in the library, drinking his way through a second pot of coffee while he reviewed his map of the estate. Nancarrow presented himself at eleven o'clock precisely. Around twenty years older than Will, he was running to fat, and his boots and breeches showed the signs of a ride on dusty roads. He deposited a pair of saddlebags on the floor to return Will's handshake.

"Welcome, Mr Nancarrow." Will waved him to a seat at one end of his desk. "Have you had far to come?"

"Ottery St Mary, my lord. A pleasant enough ride, in this weather." He pulled out a handkerchief to mop his forehead. "I normally only report annually, with my recommendations and so forth, but the accounts are up to date as far as the last quarter day. Do you wish to start with those?"

"If you please."

Nancarrow extracted a couple of ledgers from his bags. "These should be the same as the ones you have, my lord. First, the wages for the staff here at Ashton Tracey."

Nancarrow ran through the amounts. Will compared them against his own ledger, noticing one omission. "Where are your own wages recorded?"

"Bless me, sir. My lord, I mean. I'm not a regular steward." He laughed, setting his jowls wobbling. "I receive an annual retainer from Lord Marstone to pay wages, collect the rents, authorise essential repairs, and make any other recommendations as I see fit. I do the same for several other local estates."

Will felt his face reddening; he should have known. "I do beg your pardon, sir."

Nancarrow laughed again. "No matter. To speak plain, my lord, I'm pleased you take enough interest to see me. Since your esteemed mother died, my recommendations for improvements have invariably been ignored. I am hoping that will change—you have some good land here, and it could be more productive. It just about supports itself, but some investment should recoup the cost within a few years."

"I intend to do what I can, yes," Will said, warming to the man. He was certainly different from the steward at Marstone Park. "Tell me about the farms, if you please." He unrolled his map, weighing the corners down with books. On his drive with Connie, he'd been more interested in her reactions than in the state of the fields they'd driven past.

"I made some notes, my lord." Nancarrow put a folded sheaf of papers on the desk. "Best you go to see for yourself, but I can quickly run through things."

"Please do."

"Home Farm." Nancarrow pointed. "That's Abel Stevens. Doing a good job, but the barns..."

That was almost on the way to the cliff tops; he could walk over there later.

"...Dennison, at Quarry Farm. Poor soil, but he does his..."

Visiting the farms would keep him busy for a few days.

"...definitely visit Knap Hill Farm. Mrs Goodman makes splendid squab pies." Nancarrow patted his ample stomach. "Don't drink more than a small glass of her cider, though, or they'll be carrying you home."

Will laughed. He liked this man, and his comments sounded sensible and to the point. He paid close attention as the steward discussed the other tenants, and at the end of the meeting Will had a detailed set of his own notes.

Sorting out the estate would take some time, and money. He wasn't sure how far his quarterly allowance would stretch, so he'd have to prioritise Nancarrow's recommendations. First, he'd talk to all the farmers himself, then compare what they said with Nancarrow's conclusions and the account books. After that he would need to work out what funds he had, what income to expect, and how best to allocate it all. It should, eventually, provide a comfortable income.

He rubbed a hand through his hair. A long process, and too much of it involving poring over ledgers. He sighed and started to sort his notes into better order.

"Ate a small breakfast," Mrs Curnow replied, when Connie asked her how Mrs Strickland was faring.

"Let me know how she's getting on, please," Connie said. "You're more likely to get a true report from her than I am."

"I will, my lady."

Connie spent the rest of her morning with duster and beeswax polish in hand, helping Sukey and the other maids to clean her new small parlour while Barton took the carpet outside to beat it. Then she had Barton and Warren move in the writing desk and another table from one of the bedrooms. It would be a lovely little room to sit in for sewing, looking out over the lawns.

She sent the two maids off to the kitchen for a drink, and to ask Mrs Curnow to provide refreshments in the parlour. Will joined her there shortly afterwards.

"I've seen Nancarrow," he began, helping himself to a slice of pigeon pie. "I need to visit the various farms to check his recommendations. It seems there is much to be done. Repairs to buildings, some land to be drained..."

Connie watched his face as he talked. He seemed to be reciting the improvements from memory, with more enthusiasm than she expected for such a list of mundane tasks.

Finally he broke off, looking embarrassed. "My apologies for boring you with the details."

"I wasn't bored." She was pleased he'd shared the information with her. "Are you to visit them today?"

"I was intending to start, yes. Would you care to come with me?"

"I'd love to."

Will took the chaise, with Connie beside him and Archer on the seat at the back. He was going to need Archer as an ally, so he'd need to learn his way around the area.

They went to Home Farm first. As they approached, Will took in the barn roof patched up with tarpaulin and rope, which contrasted with the spick and span farmhouse, its step and front path swept and the windows clean. Mrs Stevens answered his knock, and he introduced himself.

"Stevens is in the end fields, my lord," she said, folding her arms. "He's not like to be back until evening. About our barn at last, is it? If you be wanting to fix a time, I'll tell him you want to see him."

"Thank you, Mrs Stevens." He'd planned on going to Exeter again the following day. "The day after tomorrow, if that is convenient?" Will gave her his most charming smile, to no avail; Mrs Stevens gave him a curt nod, then looked beyond him to where Connie still sat in the chaise.

"Is that Lady Wingrave, my lord? I heard there was a new mistress at the big house."

Connie must have heard, or seen the woman's look, for she jumped down and joined Will.

"You have a lovely neat farm, Mrs Stevens," she said, her gaze moving from the windows to the step. "I hope it's not been too difficult these past few years, without a proper steward?"

Mrs Stevens' face softened a little. "We gets by, my lady."

153

"Lord Wingrave is keen to make the estates prosper," Connie went on. "But I can see you are busy—perhaps I could accompany Lord Wingrave when he comes again? Mr Stevens can tell Lord Wingrave what needs doing on the land, and you can show me any problems with the house."

"That'll be fine, my lady." Mrs Stevens made a passable attempt at a curtsey.

Will nodded at her, and held his arm out for Connie. He didn't speak until the chaise was bowling down the road, well out of earshot of the farmhouse.

"Thank you," he said. "You turned her up sweet very nicely."

She chuckled. "There are ways of making it clear the state of their barn isn't your fault without actually saying so. That, and the promise to get it mended, should do the trick with Mr Stevens, if he's anything like his wife."

"Do you mind having to come back again?"

She turned to face him. "No, not at all. No more than you will mind talking to Stevens."

That was a fair point. They would make a good team, he hoped.

"Do you think it might be better to send a message to the other farms?" she asked, her tone diffident. "Then they can think about what they want to say before you get there. Some of them might not find it easy to talk to you instead of Mr Nancarrow."

"Good idea. I don't think Mrs Stevens would be shy about it, though."

She chuckled. "No, not from what I saw."

He wondered if she was laughing at him, a little. If she was, he didn't mind. He pulled the chaise to a halt.

"If we are not to visit other farms now, would you care for a walk instead? We could go to Lion Rocks, and come back through the woods above Ashmouth. It would be about three miles."

"Yes, please. It would be good to get some exercise."

"It's not too far for you?"

"No. I was used to walking a lot at home. I mean, at Nether Minster."

Will sent Archer back with the chaise and offered Connie his arm. They walked across the fields together, then along the familiar path up to the rocks, until they were on the cliff top with the sound of the waves below them.

"I'll bring the bird book with me next time," Connie said, seating herself on the grass at the top of the cliff.

He wished he'd brought it this time, as he failed to identify most of the birds she spotted. She'd keep him on his toes with her thirst for knowledge; he found himself looking forward to the challenge. "You can often see seals from here," he said, in an attempt to distract her from his ignorance. "Dolphins and porpoises, too, sometimes."

"Really?" Connie's eyes sparkled as she smiled, then she turned seawards to scan the water below. While she watched, he examined the view from the perspective of a smuggler.

Did they use the spot for a lookout? It was possible—there was a clear view along the coast to the east, but the sea beyond the mouth of the River Ash was hidden, and a lookout would have to walk a mile or so before being able to signal down to the village.

He wanted to find the path he'd failed to follow last night, so when Connie finally gave up hoping for seals, he led the way along the cliff top. As they neared Ashmouth, a worn track in the scrubby grass appeared, eventually turning into a stony path zig zagging down the final steep hillside.

Will paused at the top. "I don't want to go right down to the village. I think I remember a path back to Ashton Tracey from half way down, but if I'm wrong we'll have to climb back up here again."

"That's all right." Connie moved slowly on the steep path, bunching her skirts and peering down as she placed her feet.

Nice ankles, slim.

About half-way down, a small level area near a bend in the path afforded a clear view into the cove and a little way up the road. This was the place he'd remembered, about fifty feet above the sand, with the path home branching off a few yards further down.

A fishing boat was hoisting its sails in the bay below. They watched until it cleared the far headland, then Will led the way back,

Connie keeping up with him easily on the flatter terrain. He made a note of where the path emerged from the woods so he could find it in the dark tonight.

Connie headed straight for the library when they got back, taking the bird book away to her parlour and leaving Will to his ledgers. He'd have to steal the book back if he was to keep up with her.

~

Sukey made a quicker and tidier job of Connie's hair this time, and then stood back to consider her work.

"I hope that's all right. Are you wanting that gown, my lady?"

Sukey pointed at the yellow gown draped across the bed. Connie had laid it there to help her decide how to rework it.

"No. That was my mother's, I'm going to alter it to fit me."

"It's beautiful material, my lady." Sukey stroked one hand down the skirts. "Ma would like to…" She bit her lip and looked away.

"Do you think your mother would like a gown like that?" Connie asked, wondering why Sukey hadn't said that *she* would like such a garment.

"No, my lady. Well, she would, but I was meaning Ma used to do sewing before… She'd have liked to work with something like that." Sukey gave the brocade one last stroke. "Is there anything else, my lady?"

"No, thank you."

She would ask Will if she could take on someone to help with the sewing.

~

"I discussed household expenses with Nancarrow today, as well as the farms," Will said, passing her a dish of vegetables.

Connie looked up sharply, then let out a breath. This was not her father, who only mentioned expenses to complain.

"Overall, there is sufficient money to take on more staff," Will continued.

"Oh, good." That meant she needed to make some decisions. "More gardeners, I think, if Yatton is to grow enough for our use."

"And indoor staff? Mrs Strickland would know." He paused. "How is she, by the way?"

"Still in need of rest. I think her ankle is broken, so it will be some time before she's about again." She smiled. "I'm hoping she takes a long convalescence."

"Ha, yes. Can you manage without her? This house must be larger than you're used to."

"It's not so different." People had the same mixture of faults and strengths no matter the size of house they worked in. "I'll ask her about staff." She could always check with Mrs Curnow and Warren if the housekeeper wasn't well enough—or wasn't sufficiently helpful. Mrs Trasker could be taken on, too, but Connie knew she would have to take all their needs into account. Getting the kitchen garden ready for autumn planting was more important than her gowns.

"A couple more maids would be useful." She wouldn't need to consult Mrs Strickland about that. "We would need more kitchen staff as well if you are thinking of entertaining."

"Not at present. I'm about to send a letter to my friend, Harry Tregarth, saying he can visit whenever he pleases, but he will not need any special treatment." Will paused, raising one brow. "Unless you wish to entertain. We should have some contact with nearby families."

"I would rather settle in properly first." The prospect of entertaining other people of rank worried her more than managing servants.

"So would I." He smiled. "Once I'm more familiar with the area, I might be able to manage polite conversation with the local gentry. I need to go to Exeter tomorrow," he added. "Do you wish to accompany me?"

She would love to, but she also wanted to start remaking that gown. "Thank you, but no. I should keep an eye on Mrs Strickland, and think about new staff. But would you buy some other things?"

She'd already been given permission to take on new servants, but this would be for the household as well. "The stillroom needs restocking."

"Of course. List anything you need—if there is too much for the chaise, I'm sure I can get a carrier to deliver the rest."

He was *not* her father.

"Why is that amusing?" Will was looking enquiringly at her.

She must have smiled at her thought. "It is so refreshing to be able to buy things without having to use endless persuasion."

He smiled. "We should not be extravagant, Connie, but there is no need for penny pinching."

Perhaps, when she knew how much she needed to spend on wages for the new staff, she might ask if she could buy some new gowns.

Will glanced at her plate. "If you have finished, shall we retire to the library?"

Connie tried to keep her eyes on her book, even remembering to turn a page now and then to make it appear she was reading. Will had not opened the volume he had chosen; when she glanced his way, his gaze was fixed on her. There was something in his eyes that made her feel uneasy. No, not uneasy, exactly: a slight breathlessness, and a strange feeling in her stomach that wasn't fear.

After turning a few more pages, with her eyes running across the words but her mind not absorbing them, she finally gave up. She closed the book and rose to her feet.

"If you will excuse me, I need to make a list for tomorrow."

There was no reason he should object, but she was relieved to see him smile as he spoke. "Do rejoin me later, if you wish."

"I... perhaps." She left *Tristram Shandy* on the table, taking with her instead the book of household receipts that Martha had loaned. She should get Will to buy a copy of the book for her to keep.

In the kitchen, Mrs Curnow gave her paper and a pencil. As she drew up her list of essentials, the task gradually removed that odd feeling. Some remedies she could make herself, given time and the cooperation of the gardener, but for now it was best to buy salves and tinctures, and enough dried herbs to make poultices and tisanes.

In the stillroom, Connie could tick off only a few of the items on her list. She made a fresh copy of the things to be bought and, as an afterthought, added the details of the household receipts book and the thread and pins she would need for altering her mother's dresses.

Tired, but not sleepy, she sat by an open window in her chemise, enjoying the cool air on her body and emptying her mind of the events of the day as birdsong quietened with the fading light.

Sounds from the connecting door told her that Will was in his room. That look earlier—did he want to join her tonight? She couldn't tell from the sounds where he was in the room, whether he was standing by the door, his hand hovering over the handle. Would he be wearing only a nightshirt? The thought made her feel slightly breath-less, that strange feeling again.

Would she mind if he came in? He would be kind to her, she knew that now.

Did she *want* him to? That was a better question.

CHAPTER 24

Tuesday 1st July

"Lady Wingrave asked me to give you this, my lord."

Will took the list of things she wanted him to buy and placed it with the letter ready to be posted to Tregarth. Why hadn't Connie come down to give it to him herself? Perhaps he should have told her he was going to make an early start. Why did he mind? He was only going to Exeter, but he didn't like the idea that she might be avoiding him. She hadn't rejoined him last night.

You've only been married a week, you idiot. Give her time.

He poured another cup of coffee. Last night's excursion, with Archer this time, had been as futile as the first. There had been nothing to see in Ashmouth, and all he'd done was lose more sleep. He'd give some thought to sending Archer on his own some nights.

Once they were on their way, Will asked Archer if anyone had seen him return from their nocturnal excursion.

"Yes, my lord. I didn't try to sneak out—told them I was seeing a girl in the top village. My old man always used to say better get your lie in first, not have to make it up when you're found out."

"Your old man?"

"He's dead now, my lord. Was a successful thief in London, before my mum married him and sorted him out."

"Good grief. Did you feel any desire to... er... follow in his footsteps?"

"Wasn't worth the risk of getting my neck stretched, my lord. Or being sent to the Americas."

Time for a change of subject.

"Have you managed to hear anything interesting in the village?"

"Dunno how much is of use, my lord. Went down the hill last night for a few pints. Not a one mentioned Mrs Strickland to me, but they knew I was the one what found her."

"Hmm. That might not mean anything. Someone else from Ashton Tracey could have told them how she is getting on."

"Funny thing, though," Archer went on. "I said I didn't know why the old bat..."

Will suppressed a smile.

"...had come to the village when she had servants below her she could order around, and they all shut up sharpish."

"So?"

"If they didn't know either, wouldn't they have made a guess? We was all drinking by now, and they was loose enough mouthed about everyone else. Looked to me like they all knew why she'd come, and were too frightened to say anything at all in case they got the same treatment."

"You're sure about that?"

"No, my lord. Just an impression."

"Anything else?"

"Lots of talk, but I dunno how much is useful. I could tell you who might be doing what she shouldn't while her husband was at sea, but you don't want that. Joss Trelick nearly wrecked his boat last month while he was drunk."

"He's not likely to be running things then."

"Ha, no, my lord. Surprised he can find his own arse. Davy Nance seems to have a second sight for where the fish are, but..."

Will glanced sideways, to see Archer's eyes narrowed.

"What is it?"

"Most of the folks in Ashmouth do the fishing, apart from Coaker at the inn, and Bill Roberts. He does carpentering."

"Go on."

"There's a couple, three maybe, they've got a boat, but no-one ever mentions them when they're talking about catches and prices."

"Ah. Another source of income, perhaps?"

"Might be, my lord. Tom Kelly—right big bloke, he is. Sam Hall, Joss Sandow—they're nothing much to look at. Don't say much, either."

"Plenty of money in the village?"

"Not so's you'd notice." Archer described houses in need of repair, boats patched up, skinny children—an overall impression of people barely making ends meet. Will wondered how much of their income came from the smuggling. The *need* for money, not merely the liking for a bit more, would be a powerful inducement to risk hanging.

That was something to address in his plans for the estate. If there was more paid work on the land, would fewer of them get involved in smuggling? Possibly not—labouring was harder work than carrying tubs a few times a month. It would be worth trying to find out how much money was involved. Pendrick might be able to help him there.

Archer finally wound down. Will thanked him and turned his thoughts to his tasks for the day. A quick glance at Connie's list had shown him that he could get Archer to buy most of it while he saw Kellet and then Pendrick. The household management book he would get himself. He'd looked through her books again last night, after she'd left him. The titles Fancott had sent were mostly works on economics and geography, rather than the novels he'd expected. Fancott was a sensible man, and he wouldn't have sent things she had no interest in.

Picking up *The Wealth of Nations* after she had retired, he'd become unexpectedly engrossed in it. It had brought back memories of wrestling with philosophy at Oxford, when getting a good degree had been a purpose of sorts, even though he wasn't going to use the knowledge for anything. He wondered what Connie would make of the ideas in it.

He'd also found Fancott's note about the remaining volumes of *Tristram Shandy* and remembered being entertained by it himself. Perhaps he would buy the set for her; the notion of wooing his wife with books rather than jewellery brought a smile to his face.

Rather to Will's surprise, Pendrick accepted his invitation to take a drink with him, and they sat with mugs of ale in front of the warehouse. Sunlight glittered on the river, and their bench was a little spot of calm amongst the men carrying bales, barrels, and crates onto the moored ships.

"We're waiting on the *Sally May*." Pendrick pointed down the river. "I can keep a lookout for her from here." He glanced at Will. "I take it this isn't a social call."

Will shook his head. "I wanted to thank you for recommending Kellet, but I also wanted to ask if you have any idea how much the locals might receive from smuggling."

Pendrick's brows drew together. "Why?"

"A gang has been using my house to store goods. It has come to my notice that they readily resort to violence to protect their interests. Hardly surprising, but I would like to know more before deciding what action to take."

Will didn't want to admit his acceptance of free trading as a local way of life, or the fact that he'd asked Warren to find a source of smuggled goods for him. Something else to think about—later.

"You could report it to the local excise men," Pendrick suggested, without much conviction. "Most of them try to do their job, but they're too thinly spread, with not enough funding. Even if they do make an arrest, sympathetic juries rarely hand down a guilty verdict."

"Why the need for violence then?" Will wondered if he was missing something. He already knew all that.

"Over half the price of dry tea sold to the public is duty, so you can see that smuggling gangs can undercut legitimate traders and still turn a healthy profit. Even if they're sure they won't be convicted, they'll still protect their goods—and their profit."

That much duty? Will was beginning to feel like a schoolboy who hadn't paid attention in his lessons. "So just how much might the Ashmouth gang be making?"

"That would depend on what they are selling and the quantities involved." Pendrick gave him a quizzical look. "If you really need to know, I can let you have a list of estimated purchase and sale prices, although the latter will also depend on how much they water down the spirits or adulterate the tea."

"Thank you," Will said meekly. He might be able to estimate quantities of goods if he could watch a run being landed.

Pendrick sighed. "In some places free trading is a community activity. They all put a little money into buying the cargo, and all take some of the profit. That could well be the case in Ashmouth; it might make it harder to stop it, if you choose to try."

They chatted a little longer before Pendrick took his leave. Will had time before his appointment with Kellet, so he had another mug of ale. The sizeable profits that Pendrick had implied didn't tally with Archer's report of general poverty in the village. Even so, calling in the preventatives and getting the smuggling stopped would worsen their situation.

He had a lot to think about.

Mrs Strickland was still abed, although her bruises were beginning to fade. She attempted to sit up when Connie entered, a groan escaping her. Connie had intended to ask her about the number of people needed to run the house properly, but it didn't seem the time to have a detailed discussion.

"I'm sorry to disturb you, Mrs Strickland," Connie said. "I just came to check you have everything you need. Do ask Mrs Curnow if you require anything."

Mrs Strickland muttered thanks.

Connie exchanged a few more words with the housekeeper and then went down to the kitchen. Mrs Curnow would have to be her adviser, so she asked the cook to join her for a cup of tea at the kitchen table.

"I only wish to ask you how the house used to be run, Mrs Curnow," she began, noting the cook's rather wary expression. "What was it like when Lady Marstone was in residence?"

"This was a happy house when she was alive, my lady." Mrs Curnow's plump cheeks wobbled as she nodded. "Her ladyship spent several months here each summer, with the children. Lord Marstone only came but once or twice."

"I don't think he has any intention of changing that," Connie said, hoping it was true. "How many maids and footmen were there?"

"Oh, now you're asking, my lady. Let's see..." Her gaze became distant and her lips moved, as if she was recalling past staff by name. "Nurse, nursery maid, governess..."

Connie felt a blush rising as she wondered how soon *she* would need a nurse and nursery maid.

"...several upstairs maids, them lads were forever coming into the house muddy—"

The cook broke off, her face becoming even redder than usual. Connie guessed that Will was one of 'them lads', and suppressed a smile.

"The old account books should say, my lady. Might be in Mrs Strickland's office or his lordship's library."

Why hadn't she thought of that?

"An excellent idea, Mrs Curnow. We will naturally need more servants now that Lord Wingrave and I are in residence. I suppose we can employ women from the village."

"Yes, my lady, if they're willing."

Connie opened her mouth to ask why local women might not want a job here, but Will's words about possible danger came back to her. Her questioning might give away the fact that they knew the house was being used. She would have to talk to Will again—it might not be wise to bring more people here who might be in league with the smuggling gang.

"Mrs Strickland normally decides who to take on, my lady."

"Mrs Strickland answers to me, Mrs Curnow."

The cook met her eye and, to Connie's surprise, smiled. "Yes, my lady. Will that be all?"

"Yes, thank you."

Leaving Mrs Curnow, Connie asked Warren to get the old household account books for her, then went to her room to fetch the yellow dress. Her mind was still on employing new people. They could find some from further away, of course, who would not have any links with the gang. But then, willing or not, they might be recruited. If Will did not mind having only a few rooms open, they could manage for now with the staff they had. She'd talk to him about it when he got home.

That decision made, she settled down to spend the rest of the morning in her new parlour. With looking over the accounts, and adjusting the yellow gown, she had plenty to keep her occupied.

"Lady Wingrave is sewing in the south parlour, my lord," Warren said. He held his hand out for the parcel Will carried, but Will held onto it.

"Show Archer where to put the stillroom supplies, will you?" He went on into the parlour, appreciating again the light and airy feel to the room. Leaving the parcel on the table, he crossed to the door of the smaller room.

He expected to see Connie with a frippery piece of embroidery in her hands; instead she sat in the middle of the sofa, her lap covered in a vast mound of pale yellow fabric. She was picking at a seam with a tiny pair of scissors, apparently concentrating so hard she hadn't heard him approach.

"Good afternoon."

"Oh!" She looked up with a start and then gave a wide smile. "Did you have a good trip?" She lifted the mass of fabric, depositing it on the sofa beside her, and brushed wisps of thread from the front of her gown.

"Yes, thank you." He examined the material more closely. It appeared to be a gown. "Is this why you wanted thread? Isn't there someone to mend that for you?"

"I'm not mending it, I'm altering it to fit me. It's one of my mother's old dresses. I'm making it more fashionable, too; skirts are not as wide as when Mama wore it."

"I thought your father was sending on the rest of your clothing?"

Her face reddened. "I brought all I had with me, and a trunk of Mama's gowns. There was no time to get new gowns, even if my father would have agreed to buy them."

The memory of the two small trunks on the roof of the coach flashed through his mind. "Those trunks contained *all* your clothing?" Disbelief, and rising ire, made his voice louder than he intended, ringing in this small room. He clamped his teeth together as he saw Connie's reaction, her gaze dropping to her lap.

He took a deep breath. "I'm sorry, I'm angry with your father, not you."

"He doesn't have much of an income. Only a small legacy from his mother."

"Even so..." Will broke off—in his position, who was he to complain about a second son not wanting to work for a living? He rubbed his forehead—he *had* wanted to, if he'd been allowed to join the army, to do something useful for the country. "You don't need to spend your time altering old clothing," he said. "Come into Exeter with me next week, you can order some new clothing then."

Perhaps some lacy nightwear...

"I enjoy doing it," she said, smoothing a hand across the fabric. "I've little left from my mother, only these and a couple of water-colours. I'd like to remake a couple of her gowns, at least."

"Of course, if you want to. Take on someone to help you, if you wish."

"I was thinking about that. Sukey said her mother used to do sewing, I could ask her. I think the family could use the extra income, as well."

"That sounds like a good idea."

"I've had second thoughts about taking on other servants, though," she added.

Will nodded as Connie explained; what she said made sense. "As long as you can manage with the people we have."

"I think so, yes."

"Good. Now, if you can leave your sewing for a few minutes, I've bought you a present."

Her face lit up with the sparkle in her eyes that he liked to see. He felt a sudden qualm—he hoped she wasn't thinking of jewellery.

"It's in the next room." He led the way through, and gestured to the parcel on the table.

She unfastened the string, pulling the paper apart. "Oh, books!" She lifted them out, reading the titles in turn, and her smile broadened. "All for me?"

"For us, really. I found Fancott's note about the other volumes of *Tristram Shandy*, and I'd like to read that myself, when you've finished." He picked up *The Wealth of Nations*. "I started on your copy of this last night. I hope you don't mind."

She looked surprised for a moment, then her smile returned. "Of course not. As long as you don't mind my reading such things."

"Why...? Oh, your father, I suppose."

"It is not women's place to pretend to men's knowledge," she quoted, lips pursed.

Will laughed at her portentous tone. "What rot. In fact, I was hoping to hear what you think of it when you have read it too."

"Really?"

"Yes, why not?"

"I... yes, I would enjoy that. The Fancotts used to talk about such things together. With me, as well, sometimes."

He glanced at the clock. "We have a couple of hours before Mrs Curnow will have dinner ready. I wish to go for a short ride, but would you care to walk with me in the gardens first?"

They walked out onto the terrace, arm in arm, and down to the formal gardens. Low hedges in geometric patterns outlined flower beds, with yews clipped into pyramids and cones at the corners. It reminded Connie of the garden where she had waited at Marstone Park, but this one had lower hedges and larger beds, filled with a ragged collection of geraniums, snapdragons and phlox. She'd enjoy dead-heading them herself.

"We used to play hide and seek here when we were still small enough to hide behind the hedges," Will said, a faraway look on his face. "We probably annoyed the gardener by trampling his flowers."

"I used to play like that with the Fancott children sometimes. My father thought Martha was teaching me."

As he smiled, an attractive dimple appeared beside his mouth. She hadn't noticed that before.

"How old were you when your mother died?" he asked.

"Five or six. I don't remember details." She looked away. "I was happy when she was alive. My mother was not, from what others have said to me since, but she made sure I didn't know it." She ran her hand along the top of a hedge. "She had a little garden like this, filled with roses. That's one of my memories of her, the scent, and the beautiful flowers. My father had all her roses dug up after she died." Connie had occasionally wondered if his action had been a wish not to be reminded of past mistakes rather than a futile act of revenge. She didn't feel the usual sadness at its loss. It didn't matter now; it was past, and she was beyond his power.

Will stood close, his eyes intent on her face. "Was that why you wore that rose perfume at our wedding?"

"Yes. It was rather overpowering, I'm afraid."

"Indeed." He leaned towards her, breathing in. "You are wearing it now."

Her breath caught, her gaze on his lips. What would it feel like if he kissed her?

"Connie?"

What had he said? Oh, the perfume. "Yes, but not *quite* so much of it. It wasn't my idea; a woman in the village who knew Mama sent it. A small act of revenge."

He surprised her by laughing out loud, genuine amusement on his face. They strolled on, and her breathing gradually returned to normal.

"My mother loved the flowers," Will said, after a few paces. "This is well enough, considering how few staff are here, but I'd like to see it restored when we have the funds to spare. You could plant roses between the hedges, if you wish. Turn this into a rose garden. It wouldn't be the same as your mother's, of course."

"That would be lovely, thank you. The shapes don't matter, but the sight and the smell..." She closed her eyes, the faint scent rising from her own perfume bringing back happy memories.

"You could even invite your father to come once it is established."

She smiled, but knew she would not. If she managed to be happy, that would be revenge enough—that, and *not* inviting him to the home of the future Earl of Marstone.

"Shall we walk on? To the orchard, perhaps, for some shade."

They turned, his hand warm on the small of her back, its gentle pressure comforting—and something else. When they left the formal gardens and he offered her his arm instead, she was sorry.

Was a month too long to wait?

CHAPTER 25

ednesday 2nd July
        Will flicked the reins and the chaise drew away
from Home Farm. It had been a productive visit, if longer than he'd
anticipated.

"Stevens kept you talking a long time," Connie said. "Are there a lot
of problems?"

"Not really, mainly the barn roof. He was telling me his plans for
improving the fields. I certainly know a lot more about farming than I
did this morning." Stevens' explanation had been very detailed, and
for the second time in two days Will had felt like a schoolboy.

"That's a good thing, surely." Connie looked at him, her lips
curving in amusement. "Is it just that you don't care for being
lectured?"

He laughed. "I think you might be right there. I hope you didn't
mind waiting so long."

"Not at all. I had a nice long chat with Mrs Stevens. You'll be
pleased to know that the house is in good repair." She patted her
stomach. "She also makes excellent apple pies."

"Hmm. I must stop in at the farmhouse next time I'm here. And we should go to Knap Hill for our next visit. Nancarrow tells me there are excellent pies to be had there, too."

"Are we going there now, Will? I sent Sukey with a message to ask her mother to call later today."

"No. It's best if I make some notes about what Stevens told me."

"Before you get lectured by someone else."

"Indeed."

That amused smile lit up her face, and he didn't mind in the slightest that she was poking gentle fun at him.

Sukey clearly got her looks from her mother, Connie thought, as Warren showed Mrs Trasker into the sewing parlour. The same curling black hair showing beneath her cap, the same slightly tilted nose and grey eyes. From Sukey's chatter, Connie had learned that she was the oldest in the family, so that would put Mrs Trasker in her mid thirties, at least. She looked older than that, her face gaunt and dark shadows under her eyes. A young girl clung to her faded skirts.

"My lady, thank you for asking me to come." She glanced down at the child. "I hope you don't mind me bringing Bessie, my lady. There be no-one else to keep an eye on her."

Connie kept the surprise from her face. In Nether Minster, the women of the village regularly helped each other out.

"That's all right, Mrs Trasker. Sukey, please take Bessie to the kitchen and tell Mrs Curnow you are both to have some milk and a piece of cake."

"Ooh, thank you, my lady."

Connie smiled at Sukey's enthusiasm as the girl led her little sister out of the room. "Do sit down, please, Mrs Trasker."

Mrs Trasker hesitated, then brushed non-existent dust from her skirts before sitting on the edge of a chair.

"Sukey tells me you have made dresses in the past?" Connie said.

"Yes, my lady. I done a little work for the late Lady Marstone the last couple of summers she was here, and I do... used to do some sewing in the village. I can do other work as well, if you..."

"We may need some more staff in the house soon, yes," Connie said, wondering why Mrs Trasker was so hesitant. Examining her more closely, Connie thought her dress fitted rather loosely; was the family so short of money that the mother was starving herself to feed the children? She got up and rang the bell. "Tell me about Lady Marstone," she went on, wanting to put the woman at her ease.

"She was a lovely lady. Treated the servants with respect, she did. She—" Mrs Trasker stopped talking as Warren appeared in the doorway.

"Warren, please ask Mrs Curnow to provide tea, sandwiches, and cake. For two."

He glanced towards Mrs Trasker with a tiny lift of one eyebrow. "Yes, my lady." He bowed and left.

She let out a small breath of relief; Mrs Strickland would have queried her order, she was sure.

"My lady..."

"I prefer not to eat alone," Connie said. That was a plausible motivation; enough, she hoped, to allow Mrs Trasker to accept what she might regard as charity. "Now tell me, if you please, what work you did for Lady Marstone."

Connie listened as Mrs Trasker described gowns altered to cope with pregnancy, then taken in again afterwards, the stitching of baby clothes, and the mending of tears in breeches and coats caused by overenthusiastic play.

"Lord Wingrave?" Connie asked, trying to imagine Will as a small boy.

"That was the older brother then, my lady. But yes, this Lord Wingrave and his brother. Right little hellions—" She broke off abruptly, putting a hand over her mouth in a gesture so like Sukey's that Connie had to laugh.

Warren brought the refreshments, and Connie explained what she needed doing as Mrs Trasker ate and drank. When the food was gone, she showed Mrs Trasker what she'd done with the yellow gown, and then they went up to her room to look over her other clothing.

Will let himself out of the house at eleven, moving as quietly as he could. Although more than an hour had passed since sunset, the western horizon still showed as a paler streak of sky beneath the ominous clouds that had been building up in the western sky all evening. Archer waited by one of the clipped yews at the bottom of the steps and they set off together.

This night was little different from the previous times he'd gone to watch. The western cliff rose in a dark mass beyond the village, its top visible only as a change from black to grey. The village itself was no more than a few faint patches of light in windows—not many, for most people would be in bed at this hour. The breeze made enough noise in the bushes to mask any sounds from below.

It would be a new moon in a couple of days, making it more likely that a smuggling run would be made. Surely something would happen soon.

Over the next few hours Will struggled to keep awake, seeing only an occasional glimpse of light in the village as a cottage door opened.

Finally, Archer nudged him, and pointed. The cliff top opposite was no longer straight. A moving shape—a man on horseback?

"Riding officer?" Archer asked.

"Could be."

The breeze freshened as they lost sight of the man on the far cliff. Large drops of rain began to patter on the leaves around them.

"In for a storm, I reckon," Archer said.

It must be only a couple of hours before dawn by now. Nothing would happen tonight. "Time to go back," Will decided.

The rain turned to a downpour as they climbed back up through the woods, and by the time they reached the house they were both soaked to the skin.

"Hope she was worth it," Will said, as Archer headed for the stables. He heard only an answering chuckle.

Will stood by the front door in the shelter of the porch and considered his options. Entering through the window in the dining room after this rain would mean leaving muddy footprints on the floor. Taking his boots off between the flowerbed and the windowsill was likely to end up with him falling in the bushes. His coat would drip water wherever he went anyway.

He shrugged. The front door was still unbolted, and the tiles in the hall would be easier to clean than the polished floor in the dining room. He would not skulk around hiding from his staff any longer. If Mrs Strickland, or anyone else, couldn't keep a still tongue in their head about his movements, they were welcome to find another job.

Connie awoke to the sound of rain and flapping as gusts of wind blew the curtains about the open windows. Throwing back the sheet, she carefully made her way across the room in the dark, and closed the windows far enough to stop the rain coming in. Properly awake now, she sat on the window seat. There was nothing to see outside, but she'd always enjoyed listening to rain when she was dry indoors and it wasn't spoiling her plans for the day.

After a while she wondered if Will had woken to close his own windows against the rain. Crossing to the connecting door, she put her ear close to it. Yes, that was the sound of the sashes sliding—but why had he left it so long? Was he a sound sleeper?

About to return to her bed, Connie paused when she heard a muffled thud, then another, sounding remarkably like boots being removed and dropped on the floor. A drawer scraped open, accompanied by a muttered curse.

Had he been outside in the night?

Last week, on the night the smugglers had emptied their cellars, he'd left the house to see what was happening. But nothing had occurred since then—had it? She thought he would have told her if he had found anything out. Many men would not, but she'd come to believe Will was different.

They were dangerous men. What would happen to her if Will was killed? Her father hadn't mentioned any kind of settlement, nor had Will, and she'd been too concerned with other aspects of her new life to ask about it.

Don't think the worst.

There could be a different explanation. Perhaps Mercury was unwell and he'd been to the stables.

Has he been seeing another woman?

Mrs Hepple and Fanny had been talking about him duelling over a woman on the day Lord Marstone's footman called. It was not unusual for men of his class to have relations with other women, she knew. In fact, it was almost expected.

Connie went back to the window seat, sitting at one end with her feet tucked up under her chemise, her pleasure in the sounds of the night gone. She'd thought things were progressing well between them, but if he was already seeing someone else, her dream of having a marriage like the Fancotts' was just that—a dream.

She took a deep breath. There could be other explanations for what she'd heard—she'd thought of two others herself. She should at least ask him before making assumptions.

Whatever it turned out to be, her situation was still far better than it had been only a couple of weeks ago.

CHAPTER 26

Thursday 3rd July

Barton knocked on the door with the morning coffee. Will sat up, catching the footman glancing at the wet clothing on the floor as he placed the tray on a table. No doubt by now someone had also spotted whatever traces of mud he'd left in the hall.

"Barton." Will waited until he had the footman's full attention. "You will instruct Warren that no-one is to leave the house until I have spoken with you all later this morning."

"Yes, my lord."

"You may go. I will join Lady Wingrave for breakfast at ten."

Although he'd not spent much time in his bed, the cooler air following the storm had allowed him to sleep better. Well enough, certainly, to manage an hour or so with the estate ledgers again, and then conversation over the breakfast table.

Will smiled as he entered the breakfast parlour. Connie was already there, sitting with her back to him and gazing out of the window at the puffy white clouds scudding across the sky. The haze of the last week was gone, washed out of the air.

"Good morning," he said, taking his seat at the table. His good mood diminished as she looked at him with no answering smile.

"You must have got very wet last night," she said, taking a roll and breaking it in half. She was buttering the roll and spreading jam as if nothing was wrong. But the set of her lips and the tension in her jaw belied that calm demeanour.

"Yes, I have been going out in the night. Why does...?"

Ah, of course. The usual reason for sneaking in and out of houses at night was not to look for smugglers. How could she think that of him?

Easily. If she'd heard talk of his life in London, it wasn't surprising she'd jumped to that conclusion.

"Connie, I intend to keep my marriage vows, and I *have* done so. It is not what you are thinking." He was surprised to find how much he wanted her to believe him.

She put down the knife. "I was trying *not* to make assumptions."

"I wanted to see if there was any more smuggling activity going on. The dark of the moon is the usual time for smuggling runs." He realised as he spoke how little thought he'd given to what he was doing. He'd treated it like some kind of boys' adventure—spying on smugglers, creeping around at night with no-one knowing.

Keeping secrets from my wife.

"Connie, I'm sorry. I should have told you what I was doing."

She was still not happy, although her expression did relax a little. "*Why* are you watching, Will? Are you going to report them to the authorities?"

"I... no, not right away, at least. I wanted to know more before deciding what to do. I wasn't going to try to stop them myself."

That didn't seem to have reassured her. "I came to no harm," he added, venturing a smile. "You needn't worry about me."

Connie looked away again, concerned by the way he seemed to be treating the whole thing as a game, and irritated by the satisfied smile on his face. Was he pleased that she was worried? Worried about *him.*

"I'm not," she said, pushing away the thought that she had been. "I am worried about *myself*."

Good. That had wiped the smile off his face.

"What will happen to me if you get yourself killed? I'll be returned to my father ready to be sold to someone else."

He hesitated. "You'll be a widow, independent."

"Oh, yes. Free to starve. Unless you know what provision was made for me in the marriage settlements."

He didn't know; she could see that from the way his face reddened.

"You did sign some kind of settlement, I suppose." She took a deep breath, and calmed her voice. If anyone was at fault here, it was their fathers, not Will. "Do you think that my father, or yours, would give any consideration to what would happen to me if you died?"

"No, I don't suppose they would. Or did. Unless you'd... we'd already had a son."

"But then your father would be the legal guardian of our children, with the right to dictate how they are brought up and educated, and the right to forbid me to see them if he wishes to."

She was angry, and rightly so. When he accepted this marriage, he'd promised himself that he wouldn't turn into his father, yet he'd not given a moment's thought to how his actions might affect Connie.

Finding out more about the smugglers was justified, but he should have considered all the implications. He didn't recall signing a settlement—no property was being transferred and, as she'd said, neither of their fathers would have been concerned with her possible future. In fact, it would be like Marstone to deliberately *not* make provision for her being widowed; she and any children would then be completely in his power.

What could he do? He had no money of his own; the income from Ashton Tracey would revert to his father as long as Marstone owned the place.

Guardian. He latched onto that thought. Uncle Jack, possibly, but what use was a guardian in India?

A rattle of cup against saucer roused him from his thoughts. He pushed back his chair and stood. "You are quite right, Connie. I apologise for my thoughtlessness." He took a deep breath. "I... we... need to talk, but I'm too angry to think at the moment. With myself, not you."

Her expression softened, but he spoke before she could reply. He didn't want her to apologise to him. "I'm going to see Mercury. We will talk when I return, if that is convenient."

She nodded, and smiled. It didn't quite reach her eyes, but it *was* a smile.

Mercury, at least, was pleased to see him this morning, whickering gently before turning back to his hay.

Seeing the animal was just an excuse. Will leaned on the edge of the stall, mentally berating himself for his lack of thought. And telling Connie where he'd been off to in the night would have spared her this morning's upset, so why hadn't he?

You knew she wouldn't like it.

It was possible that Connie might agree with his wish to know more before deciding how to act, but by keeping his activities secret he'd avoided having to persuade her that his choice was right.

It was time he grew up. They'd been getting on so well, and he could have ruined the progress they'd made.

"My lord?"

Will turned. "Archer."

"Excuse me, my lord, but how long are the...? I mean, Mrs Curnow wants someone to go down the hill for some fish."

Damn—he'd forgotten about that.

"Tell them all to be in the entrance hall in an hour, Archer. I need to talk to Lady Wingrave, then I will explain matters to them."

He'd intended to say that anyone who passed information on would be out of a position, but he needed to start thinking things through properly before rushing into action.

"Archer—whatever I say in there, our arrangement about Mrs Strickland's letters will still stand."

"Right, my lord. I'll let Mr Warren know it's an hour's time." Archer went off.

Total honesty. It was the only way. He'd take Connie for a walk around the gardens, or the orchard, where they could not be overheard. *They* would decide, together, what was best to be done.

Connie greeted him with a tentative smile, and they strolled in the formal gardens, as they had a couple of days ago.

Will started with the easier topic. "This morning, I sent orders for Warren not to let anyone leave Ashton Tracey until I'd spoken to them. Someone is bound to know by now that I've been going out in the night, and I didn't want word of that getting to my father or to the village." In considering what to say to Connie, he found that he was thinking more clearly himself. "But I think I've reasoned myself out of saying anything at all."

"Oh."

"Your idea about Archer intercepting letters solves the problem of people reporting to my father. I wanted to find out if anyone else was doing so, but either they report to Mrs Strickland, or they write their own letters."

"In either case, Archer will intercept them."

"Indeed." And how would he have found out if anyone else was spying on him? They were hardly likely to admit it. "The other problem is finding out whether or not Mrs Strickland is the only one in league with the smugglers. However, even if the staff are loyal to me, it would be unfair to expect them not to pass on information if they're threatened with a beating."

"Are you going to continue watching?"

"I cannot allow someone to injure and threaten my staff without trying to do something about it."

She didn't argue this time, but he could see a crease of anxiety on her brow. Was she still worried about his safety?

"I promise to observe, and not get involved. I *did* take Archer with me last night. Will that do?"

She bit her lip, but nodded.

"Archer has been letting Stubbs think—" *Damn.* He shouldn't have mentioned Archer's excuse for being out, not after this morning.

"He has a girl in the village," she suggested.

"That was his excuse, yes."

"It seems the obvious excuse." She cleared her throat. "I'm sorry I thought that of you, but if it will help, Archer may spread the idea that…" She waved a hand, clearly embarrassed to be discussing such things.

"I could not let people think—"

"*I* know it is not true, and no-one is likely to mention it to me."

She *did* trust him then. In that, at least.

"Thank you. I will ensure he only does so if talk arises."

There were still her worries about a possible future without him. "I will give the matter of a guardian some thought," he promised. "But in the meantime, I have left myself in the position of addressing my staff but having nothing to say."

Her laugh lifted his spirits. "If you don't want to say you've changed your mind?"

He shook his head.

"You could say you wanted to tell them all formally that you will be living here for the foreseeable future, and you might be taking on more staff. And that *you* are now paying them, not your father."

That was an excellent plan. "Yes. And that you'll be acting as housekeeper while Mrs Strickland is indisposed. Do you wish to listen to my non-announcement?"

"I wouldn't miss it for the world."

CHAPTER 27

*M*rs Trasker arrived not long after Will set out for his next farm visit, and Connie spent a couple of hours with her, working on the yellow gown.

They were interrupted by Warren. "A Lady Elberton has called, my lady."

"Who is Lady Elberton—one of our neighbours?"

"I have not heard the name before, my lady. She asked for Lord Wingrave."

"I'd better see her, I suppose. Can you carry on, Mrs Trasker?"

"Yes, my lady."

Connie stepped out into the hall, pulling the door to behind her. She glanced at her gown. Her old, comfortable muslin was not the most impressive of garments.

"You may inform Lady Elberton that I will be with her in twenty minutes. Ask Mrs Curnow to provide some refreshments."

"Yes, my lady. I put her in the formal parlour." Warren cleared his throat, his eyes fixed on some point beyond her shoulder.

"Yes, Warren?"

"I... er... Lady Elberton did not seem... pleased, when I said I would see if the lady of the house was at home to visitors."

Connie stared at him, trying to work out what he was hinting at. Why wouldn't a visitor wish to see…

One of Will's mistresses? *Former* mistresses?

Will had promised he would keep his marriage vows this morning, and she believed him. He would not—could not—have said such a thing if he'd invited one of his paramours to visit. No, Lady Elberton had come of her own volition.

She must change—a pity the yellow dress wasn't finished. Connie hurried up to her dressing room, already pulling pins from the edges of her stomacher. The muslin gown was left in a heap on the floor as she hurriedly lifted and tied the underskirt of her best gown. She pushed her arms into the sleeves and pinned the front. A fichu… where was the fichu? If this *was* one of Will's old lovers, she was going to present a respectable image.

Her hair—all she could do was to tidy it into a loose knot. There was no time to dress it fashionably high, even if she knew how.

She had the satisfaction of seeing the butler's eyes widen as she descended the stairs. "You may announce me, Warren."

Lady Elberton sat in the parlour, a full cup of tea on the table beside her, delicate white hands clasped in her lap. Connie was glad she'd changed, although she still felt dowdy next to Lady Elberton's lace-trimmed silk gown and elaborately dressed and powdered hair. Still, being seen in the old muslin dress would have been far worse.

The woman's lips, surely redder than nature made them, turned from a hard line to a pout as Connie entered, and her blue eyes scanned from Connie's face to her feet.

Not a normal social call, then. Her supposition may well be correct.

"Good afternoon, Lady Elberton," Connie said, keeping her voice calm. This was *her* home, after all. She took a seat and poured herself a cup of tea, although she had no wish to drink. "To what do I owe the pleasure of this visit?"

"I came to see Lord Wingrave."

No pretence at politeness—that made things easier. "Such a shame you missed him. Perhaps I can help you instead. Have you come far?"

"From London." Lady Elberton's eyes focused on Connie's waist. "Your marriage was very sudden. I don't recall it being announced beforehand."

Connie shaped her lips into a smile. "The betrothal announcement was only made to his friends." She was pleased to see Lady Elberton's mouth twist in anger. "Can I give him a message from you?"

"I understand he will return this afternoon. I can wait here and speak to him myself."

"Oh, I think not," Connie stated. No reasonable person would expect her to entertain her husband's former lover.

Lady Elberton looked down at her hands, still clenched in her lap, then back up at Connie. Now her blue eyes swam with tears, one drop welling over and trickling down her cheek. Her hands showed that she really was worried, but the change from spite to pathos was too sudden to be convincing.

"I must see him, Lady Wingrave. It is of the utmost importance. Please, *please*, do not make me leave before he returns." She gave a delicate sniff, and dabbed her eyes with a lacy handkerchief.

"Oh dear, my lady, whatever is the matter? Surely your husband—"

"My husband is divorcing me."

Connie lifted her cup and took a mouthful of tea. "I fail to see how this is relevant to your visit here."

"Lord Wingrave..."

"Is he named as co-respondent? Is there a child that your husband will refuse to support?" It was Connie's turn to inspect Lady Elberton's waistline, trying to keep her face mildly enquiring even as a weight settled in her stomach. An illegitimate child would be a scandal that would sour Will's relationship with his father even further.

"I... no."

Connie let out a breath. "Then why have you come?"

"I... Wingrave..." Lady Elberton looked down again, sniffing delicately and dabbing at her nose with a lacy handkerchief. She was facing social ostracism and likely poverty, if neither her husband nor her male relatives would support her. Connie would have felt some sympathy had it not been for the brief, assessing glance the woman darted her way.

"Go on." Connie took another, unwanted, sip of tea.

"He fought a duel over me, you know!"

That rumour was true then. But what he had done before their marriage did not matter now.

"Yet he did not kill your husband. I thought he was a better shot than that." Or so she had gathered from Fanny's gossip.

Lady Elberton looked away.

"Was Lord Elberton badly injured?" Connie asked.

"No." Lady Elberton looked at her. "He was not hurt at all."

"I'm pleased to hear it." Connie nodded, as if her concern was for Lord Elberton. "What, exactly, do you want of my husband, Lady Elberton? You cannot expect him to divorce me and marry you— someone who has already demonstrated that she cannot keep her marriage vows."

Lady Elberton looked away, delicate teeth biting her bottom lip. "I... I will need... I mean, my husband will only give me a small allowance. A pittance."

Connie waited. Lady Elberton was about to ask for money.

"Lord Wingrave will want to help me, I'm sure."

Connie made an effort to keep her expression neutral as Lady Elberton's hand went up to the neckline of her gown, toying with the lacy trim. It looked as if she was proposing that she become Will's mistress in return for financial support. To his *wife*?

She suppressed her anger. "It is a long way for you to come, Lady Elberton. Have all your previous lovers declined to aid you?"

The red flush spreading up Lady Elberton's face told Connie that she'd hit the mark. She stood and rang the bell.

"My lady?"

"Warren, Lady Elberton is leaving."

Lady Elberton made no move to rise from her chair.

"Warren, if Lady Elberton does not leave of her own accord, get Barton, and one of the grooms if necessary, to assist you."

Connie turned her back on her unwelcome guest and walked out of the room, taking refuge in her parlour. Mrs Trasker took one look at her face and bent over her stitches again.

Connie stood by the south window, taking deep breaths. She was still astounded at the bare-faced cheek of Lady Elberton. Or stupidity —what would-be mistress thought that telling the wife of her target was a good idea?

The waiting coach moved off down the drive. Connie turned back to the room and picked up her sewing, unable to dismiss the interview from her mind.

The duel—that was odd. Will had not been harmed, as far as she knew. And by all accounts, Will was a crack shot, so why hadn't Lord Elberton been injured? Will must have missed deliberately, but she couldn't work out why he would do such a thing.

She would have to ask him.

Will took Mercury straight to the stables before heading into the house through the kitchens. Warren awaited him in the hall.

"A Lady Elberton called," the butler said, as he took Will's hat.

Will cursed under his breath. "You sent her away, of course," he said, with more hope than expectation.

"I told her you were not at home, my lord, but Lady Wingrave saw her."

Damn. "Where is Lady Wingrave now?"

"In her sewing parlour, I believe, my lord."

Will hurried to Connie's parlour. Hetty might have fed her with all manner of lies.

He pushed open the door. Connie stood on a stool in the centre of the room, facing away from him, clad in the yellow brocade he'd seen her working on the previous day. Her green gown was draped across the back of a chair, and Mrs Trasker knelt at her feet, her mouth full of pins.

"What is it, Warren?" Connie did not turn as she spoke.

Mrs Trasker hurriedly took the pins from her mouth. "My lady—"

"Connie, you mustn't believe what that woman told you!"

Connie's shoulders stiffened, then she turned her head. "Oh, Will. Did your visit go well?"

Will gaped for a moment. Whatever he'd expected her to say, it wasn't that.

"I… er… yes. It did."

She smiled, but it wasn't the usual, unrestrained smile with which she normally greeted him. It didn't reach her eyes. What had Hetty told her?

"Er, would you take tea with me, my lady?" What else could he say, with Mrs Trasker still kneeling there on the floor, regarding him with interest? Of course, the whole household would be speculating about the visitor.

"That would be nice. In about half an hour. Do carry on, please, Mrs Trasker." Connie looked down and pointed. "Do you think the hem is a little uneven just there?"

He'd been dismissed.

Will gazed at Connie's back for a moment but her attention was fixed on Mrs Trasker and her pins, so he headed to his room. He was covered in dust from the lanes and it would be only polite, as well as politic, to change.

As he washed and tied a fresh neck cloth, he had the uneasy feeling that tea in the parlour might not be the pleasant interlude he'd grown accustomed to lately.

Will entered the parlour to find Connie pouring tea.

"Connie, I didn't know Lady Elberton was going to visit, I swear it. What did she say to you?"

She raised a brow. "It was an interesting visit. Have some cake, Will."

Will ignored the plate she held. Her greeting earlier had been strained, but now she was acting as if nothing had happened. Something was wrong. They'd been getting on so well—was it all about to unravel?

"What did she want?"

"Perhaps it was a social call," Connie said, as if entertaining one of her husband's past lovers was nothing out of the ordinary.

"It cannot have been."

Connie took a sip of tea, then set the cup back in its saucer. "I think she wanted to resume her position as your mistress."

"She..." *What?* Hetty had said that to *Connie?*

"In return for financial support, of course," Connie went on calmly. "This is very good seed cake, do have some." She was wearing that odd smile again, the one that did not reach her eyes.

"I don't want cake!" He pushed his chair back and strode over to the window, a sick feeling settling in his stomach. He turned to face her. "Connie, you don't think I asked her to come, do you?"

Her expression softened. "Come and sit down, Will."

"Connie, I'm sorry you had to deal with her. I had no idea she would come here."

She met his eyes, her expression serious now. "I know you did not. I'm sorry for provoking you, Will, but I was..." She took a breath. "You seemed to think I would believe whatever she told me rather than trusting you."

Did I? He thought back—yes, he probably had given that impression.

"You said you would keep your marriage vows, Will. I *do* trust you."

Some of his tension dissipated. "Thank you. I meant it, Connie."

She smiled again—a proper smile this time, that lightened his heart.

"Who is she, Will?"

The truth—nothing less would do.

"Her husband caught me with her, and that led to a duel and to my father's ultimatum." That they hadn't made it into bed wasn't a mitigating factor—they would have done if Elberton hadn't returned when he did. "Connie, what did she tell you?" He'd freely admit to his own errors, but not to any of Hetty's fabrications.

"She said her husband was divorcing her, and told me about the duel." She paused, fiddling with the tea cup. "I did ask if there... if there was a child, but she said not."

At least Hetty wasn't trying to lie about that.

"There *was* a duel, Connie, but not quite for the reason she thinks. She persuaded me that her husband neglected her, and didn't care what she did. When he caught us, it was obvious that she'd lied. I accepted his challenge because I'd been stupid enough to believe her."

"That doesn't make standing in a field firing pistols at each other any more sensible." She sighed. "I suppose it's a male notion of honour."

"Yes." And if he'd been killed, Elberton would have had a murder charge against him, and still be saddled with an unfaithful wife. "As you say, if you examine the idea rationally, it is nonsensical."

"And they say women cannot think logically." She raised one brow.

"Touché, my lady." Some women could not, but he was not going to point that out.

She smiled—a proper smile this time, the kind that warmed him inside. The sense of relief left him feeling drained.

"Tell me, Will, have you any other past lovers who might come calling?"

Past lovers, yes, but all with complaisant husbands, and other lovers since. "No, Connie, no-one else will come."

He should tell her about the boy, though. Not now, but soon.

CHAPTER 28

Friday 4th July

Connie examined the finished yellow gown with satisfaction, twisting around to see her back view in the dressing room mirror. It was a vast improvement on anything else she had—hopefully Will would think so, too, when he returned from his farm visits.

Yesterday, she'd felt a flash of hurt at his assumption she wouldn't trust him, and hadn't been able to resist making him squirm a little. He hadn't held it against her, she reflected, starting to unpin the stomacher. They'd talked about his plans for some of the farms over dinner, and then spent a companionable evening reading together in the library.

"Do you wish me to adjust another gown, my lady?" Mrs Trasker asked, pulling Connie from her reverie.

"Yes, of course. There's half a dozen more, at least." Although Mrs Trasker needed the work more than Connie really needed the gowns. "That one." She pointed to a gown laid over the back of a chair—pale, creamy muslin, printed with a delicate pattern of leaves. She started to unpin the yellow gown. Beautiful though it was, it was too fine for everyday use.

"That'll be lovely, my—"

"Ma!" Sukey burst into the room, her face screwed up and eyes red with tears. "Ma, come quick. It's Danny."

Mrs Trasker cast a quick glance of apology at Connie, and dashed out after her daughter.

Only half-dressed, Connie removed the yellow gown as quickly as she could, pulling on the muslin she'd been wearing earlier and hurrying downstairs.

In the kitchen, Mrs Trasker, Mrs Curnow and Warren were gathered around a boy sitting at the table. Across the room, Sukey had her arm around her little sister, tears running down both their faces.

From the back, Danny had the same black hair as the rest of the family, but Connie sucked in her breath as the boy turned his head. One side of his face was swollen and streaked with blood and tears, the eye closed. His nose, too, ran with blood, and bruises were already forming on his forearms, visible below rolled up sleeves.

"Who did this?"

The faces around the table showed the same shuttered looks as when Mrs Strickland had been attacked.

"Ma has to go back down to the village," Danny said, mumbling as if it pained him to speak. His glance met hers for only a moment. "She has to go back."

The look on Mrs Trasker's face was as horrifying as Danny's injuries—white, and wide eyed. The look of someone about to face execution.

"How old are you, Danny?" Connie asked. With all the damage to his face, she couldn't tell.

"Twelve," Mrs Trasker said. "He's been going out on the boats since my man drowned, but he's still a child."

Connie took a deep breath—everyone was looking to her for guidance. The first thing was to try to make Danny more comfortable.

"Mrs Curnow, you helped me with the poultices for Mrs Strickland, please prepare the same for Danny." She glanced across the room. "Sukey and Bessie can help you."

"Yes, my lady." The cook bustled off, looking pleased at the excuse to be out of the way.

"Warren, fetch water and clean cloths, then you may wait outside. Make sure no-one else comes in."

"Yes, my lady."

"Mary, Katie, Barton." The other two maids and the footman were still gawping at Danny. "I'm sure you all have something to do elsewhere."

They mumbled something and shuffled out. Warren returned with the water, and Connie stood back while Mrs Trasker gave her son a cloth wrung out in cold water to hold over his eye, cleaned his other cuts, and checked the rest of him for damage.

"Nothing broken then?" she asked at last. Danny mumbled a 'no'.

Mrs Trasker didn't ask who'd done it. She knew.

Mrs Curnow returned with the poultices, and Connie helped Mrs Trasker fasten them over the worst of Danny's bruises.

"Where is the nearest bed?"

"My room is just down there." Mrs Curnow pointed to a door to one side.

"Help him to lie down there. Could you sit with him? I will call if I need you."

"Yes, my lady."

Danny flinched away as Mrs Curnow reached out a hand to help him up.

"Ma, he said he'd do the same to Bessie if you wouldn't do it with him." Tears began trickling down his face again. "Then he said Sukey was old enough to take your place."

Mrs Trasker sank onto a chair, covering her face with her hands.

Connie looked at Mrs Curnow, a sick feeling settling in her stomach as the implications of Danny's last words dawned on her. The cook looked as horrified as she felt.

"Take him to rest, Mrs Curnow. Then get someone to find Archer and send him here."

Archer arrived a few minutes later, but did not know which farms

Lord Wingrave was visiting. "Said he might not be back until six or so, my lady."

Hours away. She'd have to deal with this herself.

"Who did this, Mrs Trasker? We cannot help if we don't know what the threat is." Although she had a very good idea.

"I can't tell you," Mrs Trasker said. "It won't happen again if I give him what he wants."

"Tom Kelly," Archer said. "Or Joss Sandow, maybe, or Sam Hall."

Mrs Trasker's face drained of its remaining colour. Connie feared the woman was about to faint.

"Who told you that?" Mrs Trasker whispered.

Archer glanced at Connie, who nodded.

"No-one told me," Archer said. "It was a guess. I've been drinking in the village, and I've seen the way people act around them."

"Sandow. He's the one in charge of the smuggling. He's been after me since my Bobby died." Mrs Trasker rubbed the tears from her cheeks. "I know I don't look much now, but that's not why he wants me anyway. He likes power, my lady. I won't do it with him, and that's enough for him to do that to my Danny."

"Why now?" Connie asked, suspecting she already knew.

"He made sure I got no help from the other villagers," Mrs Trasker explained. "They'd sell me food, but no-one was allowed to give me work. Danny took stuff to be sold elsewhere when he wasn't on the boats, but it's all gone now. I'd nearly given up, then Sukey said I could work here."

So now Mrs Trasker had a source of money, the man had resorted to other means. Connie felt sick—she had to do something.

"Archer, how long will it take you to find Lord Wingrave?"

"I don't know my way around yet, my lady. He could get back before me, even."

"Where could they go?" She was talking to herself, really. She knew no-one in the area, and the only person she knew *of* was the steward.

"Get Warren in here." He must be in contact with Nancarrow about household wages, so he would know where the man lived. "No, tell him to find paper and pen, then look out Mr Nancarrow's address."

Money—she would have to look in Will's desk. Had Will taken the chaise?

"He's doing it, my lady," Archer said, when he returned. "It'll take a while for a message… Oh, are you going to send the Traskers to him?"

Connie nodded. "Unless you can think of a better idea."

Archer shook his head.

"Is the chaise the only carriage we have? Is it here?"

"Yes, my lady. Lord Wingrave took Mercury. It'll be a tight fit in the chaise, but we'll manage."

"I'll write a letter for you to take. Warren can give you directions, and I'll send Lord Wingrave after you as soon as he returns."

"Yes, my lady."

Now all she had to do was to persuade Mrs Trasker to abandon any possessions she still had in her house in Ashmouth.

Will watched until the chaise drew out of sight, before turning Mercury back towards Ashton Tracey. Archer's explanation had been hurried but, together with the state of the young lad's face, had been enough to show him that Connie had just helped to thwart a violent and vindictive man. Quick thinking on her part, and he was thankful she had enough confidence to take matters into her own hands. But once Sandow realised his victims were out of his reach, Connie would likely be a target for his vengeance.

He could *not* let anything happen to her.

In the stable yard, he was relieved to find Stubbs mucking out a stall. That was one member of staff, at least, who was not out carrying tales to Ashmouth.

Both Warren and Connie were waiting for him in the entrance hall.

"I met Archer on the road," Will told them as he came through the door. "Warren, it would be better if it got about that Mrs Trasker left here immediately when Danny came for her." They couldn't keep Connie's actions secret for very long, but there was no need to give Sandow any help in finding out.

Warren did not meet Will's eyes. "I don't know what you mean, my lord."

"Really?" Will kept his voice calm with an effort. "Then let me explain. Sandow—"

Warren's eyes shifted to his own, then away again.

"I see you *do* know what I mean. This Sandow will not be pleased that *all* the staff here helped Mrs Trasker to escape him."

Warren swallowed. "No, my lord. But I… they…"

"It doesn't matter which of you did or didn't help, it only matters that if word gets about, I will make it clear that everyone did."

Will took a step closer, thrusting his face close to the butler's. "You, and the rest of the staff, know about the smuggling, and about the methods Sandow uses. It's not your responsibility to try to stop him, but it *is* your responsibility to keep the staff from actively helping him."

"Yes, my lord."

"If not, I—"

"My lord?" Connie put a hand on his arm as she spoke, then turned to the butler. "Warren, I'm sure you understand what Lord Wingrave means."

Will felt her hand tighten on his arm, and bit back the words he was about to say. "You may tell the other staff," he finished.

"Now, Warren, if you please." Connie kept her eyes on the butler until he bowed and headed for the kitchens. Then she released Will's arm and walked into the parlour.

Will followed, closing the door behind him.

"Will, I'm sorry for interrupting you."

He threw his wig onto a chair and ran a hand through his hair. "Why *did* you stop me?"

"I thought you were about to threaten him with losing his job."

"I was, my staff should not…" He stopped, drawing a deep breath.

"He already knows his job depends on your whim," she explained. "We don't know what... I mean, this Sandow might have..."

"Might have threatened any of the staff," Will said. "You're right, of course."

Connie sat down, and he saw some of the tension leave her. "You don't mind that I sent them off with Archer?" she asked.

"No, I would have done the same." At least, he hoped he would have done so.

"Will Mr Nancarrow help them? I sent a letter with Archer, but he doesn't know me."

"Archer showed me the letter. I added my signature to it as well."

"Thank you."

Will took the chair facing hers, leaning forward to help make his point. "Connie, this man *will* find out eventually that you helped the Traskers. Quite soon, if anyone in Ashton St Andrew saw Archer go through with the chaise."

"Will he be able to find them?"

"That wasn't..." He sighed—trust Connie not to think of herself first. "No, hopefully not. I added to the note that Nancarrow should send them as far away as he could, and not let anyone else know where they go. I authorised him to charge as much as he needed to the estate."

He had to trust that Nancarrow wasn't in league with the smugglers; unlikely, he hoped, beyond the purchase of an occasional tub of spirits. He would go and see the man tomorrow.

"I wasn't thinking about the Traskers, Connie. Once Sandow finds out what you've done, he could want revenge on you. Or me, I suppose."

"Oh."

"Did that not occur to you?"

"Not at the time, no. Not that I would have done anything differently." Her chin rose.

"It does mean that you are confined to the house, however, unless you have me or Archer with you. Preferably both of us."

He had no idea how many men Sandow could call on to do something as drastic as harming Connie, but he had to assume the threat was greater than one man. Archer would be back later tonight; he'd have to ask what else he'd found out.

After dinner, Will retired to the library. He needed to plan what to do about Sandow, and the image of Danny Trasker's battered face kept intruding, along with the fear in Mrs Trasker's eyes. Mrs Strickland had failed the man paying her, although even that twisted version of logic did not warrant the retribution meted out to her. What Sandow was doing to the Traskers, however, went far beyond protecting a money-making enterprise.

Sandow was bound to find out that Connie had helped take the Traskers out of his reach, and he was certain she *would* be a target at some point. A magistrate would do nothing—there had, as yet, been no direct threat to himself or Connie.

Whatever doubts he'd had before about interfering in the village smuggling were gone. Sandow had to be stopped.

CHAPTER 29

aturday 5th July

Will hurried down the stairs and into the parlour, relieved to see he hadn't missed breakfast with Connie.

"Another fruitless night?" she asked, greeting him with a smile.

"I'm afraid so." He poured himself a cup of coffee.

Warren entered. "Archer asked if he could speak to you, my lord."

"I'll be at the stables in any—"

Warren coughed. "He's waiting in the hall, my lord."

"Send him in, then." It must be important if Archer had insisted.

"I've been to the village, my lord," Archer said when he entered the room. "There's a letter for you."

Will took it; it was addressed to his father. "Thank you, Archer. I'll give you a reply in an hour. Have Mercury ready then, please."

"Right you are, my lord."

Mindful of Warren in the hall, Connie didn't ask Will who the letter was from. But he held it towards her so she could read the direction.

"Archer managed that well," she said, keeping her voice low.

Will nodded, opening the letter and scanning the lines. He read one side of the sheet and turned it over. His lips thinned, one hand curling into a fist.

"What is it?"

He took a deep breath. "Connie, we said you would be the one to rewrite that woman's letters to my father."

"Yes. What of it?"

He passed the letter over.

Connie skimmed over Mrs Strickland's descriptions of Connie's own activities, given in tedious detail, although she noted the absence of any comment about the cellars. Will's trips to Exeter and his farm visits were covered briefly, then the crabbed writing mentioned his lordship leaving the house at night, with an apology for not knowing any more.

Connie looked up. "She doesn't say where she thinks you've been at night." She didn't understand why he was angry.

"Turn over."

She read on. Mrs Strickland described Lady Elberton's visit, and then apologised again, but this time for not being able to reassure his lordship on the other matter, but she was incapacitated and did not trust the maids to inspect Lady Wingrave's room.

Heat rose to her face as she worked out the implications. "She's reporting on whether you... we..."

"She's leaving," Will said, his voice rising. "I will *not—*"

"Will!" Connie hissed. "Warren."

"Connie, I'm sorry—"

"No." It wasn't his fault. "You are not your father, you are not responsible." She waved the letter. "In any case, no-one *has* spied on us yet."

He nodded, his fist uncurling. "Unfortunately that woman has to stay here for now—if I turn her off, she'll go straight to my father."

That made sense. "Will she report to Sandow, do you think? About what happened with Mrs Trasker?"

Will shook his head. "I doubt it. She might get the blame for allowing you to send them off."

"Oh, yes, of course." She held up the letter. "Do you want me to rewrite this? What do you want to change?"

"Add a bit at the beginning, saying you're Mrs Curnow, writing it at Mrs Strickland's dictation because she had a fall. Omit Lady Elberton. I'll just have to hope that *she* doesn't let it be known she's been here."

Connie chuckled. "Being seen off by your new wife isn't exactly a flattering story."

"Ha, no. Also omit the part about my being out of the house at night, and the end."

"I could say the other matter is satisfactory," Connie suggested, not meeting his gaze.

His hand tensed where it rested on the table. "Yes," he said, after a brief pause.

"I'll do it now, so you can give it to Archer." She stood to get paper and pen from the escritoire.

"Connie." He said nothing more until she turned to face him. "Connie, I keep my word once I give it."

Of course he did, but why did he feel the need to tell her now?

"If *you* change your mind, will you let me know?"

Oh, his promise to give her a month. Her blush before was nothing to this one. She *had* been wondering if she had been right to ask for so long, but it didn't feel right to discuss it at the breakfast table. She muttered something incoherent and went to sit at the escritoire, making herself concentrate on producing a consistent hand, and spelling, that could belong to the cook.

When he left to go to see Nancarrow, she relived that last request from him. There'd been intensity in his blue eyes, an odd note in his voice.

They'd been married nearly two weeks now, and she no longer had the excuse of not knowing him. Did she still want to wait another fortnight?

Will urged Mercury to a trot as he left Ottery St Mary behind.

Nancarrow had reassured him that the Traskers were safely ensconced in a cottage on an estate beyond Honiton, and said that he was also making enquiries about renting rooms in Taunton, should it become necessary. That was all well and good, but the Traskers couldn't live like that forever.

Which brought his thoughts back again to the smugglers. He'd taken Connie's rewritten letter to Ashton St Andrew on his way through, and there'd been a letter from Pendrick awaiting him with details of estimated purchase prices for smuggled goods. Will had wondered about the number of tubs of spirits or bales of silk the village fishing boats could carry, but they probably used a larger vessel than the ones he'd seen. Then there was possibly wool leaving the country as well.

He'd asked Nancarrow what he knew, but the steward had only been able to confirm the price he paid for diluted spirits. Nancarrow hadn't been surprised to be asked, either—smuggling really was part of everyday life in this part of the country, in a way Will hadn't realised when living in London.

It was a lovely day to be riding, with enough of a breeze to keep him cool, and Will's thoughts turned to that morning's discussion. Connie had been more embarrassed by his comment about changing her mind than the idea of Mrs Strickland spying on their bedroom activities. Did that mean she'd been thinking about it?

He hoped so; he was finding it increasingly difficult to keep away from that connecting door each night. Her confusion was attractive in itself—a complete contrast to the bold 'come hither' looks that had initiated his other amorous encounters. Would she blush like that as he unlaced her gown? Her stays? What about—?

"Oy!"

Mercury snorted and side-stepped at his sudden jerk on the reins, and Will glimpsed the cart behind him.

"Bin follering you for near on a mile!" The carter whipped his horse into a trot to go past. "Coming to something when Dolly here can go faster than that fancy prad."

Damn it; he'd let Mercury slow almost to a stop while his mind had been on other things.

He started counting; thirteen days since they married, seventeen days to go.

It doesn't matter.

He wanted her to *want* him to make love with her, not just allow him. If that took longer than the promised month, so be it.

Concentrate on what to do about Sandow, and making sure Connie is provided for.

"I've been giving the matter of a possible guardian some thought," Will said, when they'd settled into the library after dinner. "Someone who will help you as well, if... if something happens before we have any children." His gaze moved from her face down to the neckline of her gown as he imagined how such children—

Concentrate!

Connie put her book aside. "Who have you chosen? Mr Nancarrow, or your solicitor, I suppose."

"No. If it is going to be a matter of standing up to my father, it has to be someone with more influence. There are only two men I can think of. One is my Uncle Jack, but I haven't seen him since I was a child, and he's in India."

"It could take months, a year even, for letters to be exchanged."

"Exactly." And if Uncle Jack *had* been in England, Will might not now be married to Connie and that would be a shame. "The other is my friend, Harry Tregarth," he went on, bringing his mind back to the business on hand.

"Is he...?" Connie's voice tailed off, and she pressed her lips together.

"Is he like me?"

She nodded.

Will wasn't sure if he should be offended at the doubt on her face. "He's more sensible, Connie, truly. And I *am* trying to think more about things rather than just rushing in."

A blush rose to her cheeks. "I'm sorry, I didn't mean... You *are* taking care of things."

Not as much as he might be. "You are quite right to question me. It's your future, after all."

"Possible future. I'd rather not have to test his abilities as a guardian."

Because she didn't want to lose *him*, or because she would be less protected? He hoped it was the former. "He's a good man, Connie," Will continued, bringing his thoughts back to the matter at hand. "And Sir John—Harry's father—is in the government, so he has some influence and can also provide sensible advice."

She bit her lip against a question, but he answered it anyway. "Sometimes Harry even listens to it."

She chuckled. "May I meet Mr Tregarth?"

"Of course. I've already invited him to come and visit us, but I'll write again tomorrow about this guardianship idea." He would write to his sisters as well, to tell them how he was getting on, but he'd have to word the letters carefully—his father was certain to read them first.

"If the weather holds fine tomorrow, Connie, would you care to come for another drive with me? We could go to the sea, if you wish."

"Not Ashmouth?"

"No, not after what happened to Mrs Strickland. We'll go the other way, take some food."

They would have privacy for his final confession. One that she wouldn't be upset about, he hoped.

"I'd like that, thank you." She smiled, and picked up her book. She'd abandoned *Tristram Shandy*, he noted. *Wealth of Nations*? He could see she hadn't got very far into it, so he'd wait a while to see what she thought of Dr Smith's arguments.

A month ago, he would have scoffed at the suggestion he could enjoy just sitting in the same room as a beautiful woman while she read a book. There were other things he'd enjoy more, obviously, but this would do for now. Best to get tomorrow's confession out of the way first, in any case.

CHAPTER 30

Sunday 6th July

Will drove the chaise, dispensing with Archer's services for the afternoon. They turned east, meandering along narrow lanes until finally the track descended gently towards a little fishing village. Connie looked around, her wide smile and sparkling eyes showing her appreciation of the waves beyond a sweep of pebbled beach.

"Will this do?" Will asked, pulling the chaise to a halt.

"Very nicely, thank you." She took his hand as she stepped down from the chaise, and he handed her a blanket.

"Look after your horse, mister?"

A grubby boy stood at the mare's head, stroking her nose. From his size, he would be about the same age as Danny Trasker.

"Very well. Can you loosen the harness and give her some water? There'll be some pennies for you if she's kept comfortable."

The boy's mouth widened in a happy grin, and he bobbed his head before turning back to the mare.

Will's lips pressed together in a determined line. That was what lads like Danny Trasker should look like, not battered and worried sick. The number of people he felt responsible for seemed to be increasing daily.

Connie had spread the blanket on a stretch of grass and crossed the pebbled beach down to the water's edge. Will deposited the picnic basket, then sprawled on the blanket. Connie was playing the age-old game of dodging the waves, laughing as she almost got her feet wet, then advancing again to follow the water running back down the slope.

She'd hitched up her skirts, showing slim ankles, shapely calves. He tried to keep his imagination from wandering further up her legs —he'd brought her here for a purpose.

Connie breathed the smells of salt and seaweed, the cries of gulls almost drowning out the rush of the waves on the pebbles. They had only walked for a few minutes by the sea when he'd taken her to Ashmouth, before Archer had summoned them to the injured house-keeper. This was much better. There were so few people around, perhaps it would not be too improper later to remove her shoes and stockings and paddle in the sea.

She saw that Will was unpacking the basket, and returned to sit beside him. "Thank you for this, Will. It's lovely."

Will returned her smile, but briefly.

"Is something wrong?"

"I have something more to tell you," he said. "I don't want there to be any secrets between us."

Former lovers?

"It's not another woman, Connie. At least, not exactly." He ran one hand through his hair.

"Tell me, Will." Whatever it was, he was worried about her reaction to it.

"I have a son."

She hadn't expected that. Although it wasn't so surprising, really— he hadn't been a saint when he lived in London.

"An illegitimate son?" It had to be.

"Yes. I was fifteen, it was not long after my mother died. Sally was the blacksmith's daughter, in Over Minster."

Fifteen? She stared out to sea as thoughts spun through her head. That seemed very young to her, but she knew little about men of that age. It must be ten years ago now; well in the past.

Then the final part of what he'd said came back to her. Over Minster—the next parish to Nether Minster, where the Fancotts would help anyone in trouble.

She turned towards him to find his eyes searching her face, his expression anxious.

"Is that how you know Mr Fancott?" she asked.

"Yes. My father thought I was stupid to try to help her. I didn't know what to do."

How would he, at fifteen?

"Our own vicar was of the same mind as my father, said it was the girl's fault, so I went to see the vicar in the next parish. Fancott sent her here, without my father's knowledge, until the child was born. I used all my allowance for several years to give her a bit of a dowry. According to Fancott she's happily married with half a dozen more children. He writes to her now and then."

So Will hadn't seen the woman for ten years, and nothing in his demeanour said he wanted to. His actions showed another facet to his character, and one she liked. He'd been thoughtless, yes, but at fifteen that was almost to be expected. More importantly, he'd done what he could to make sure the girl had not suffered for it in the end. From what Martha had said, many men of his class wouldn't think twice about getting a village girl in trouble.

"And your son. Did her new husband accept—?"

"According to Fancott, he knew of the child, but Fancott thought the lad would have a better life with someone who really wanted him. He found a couple in Exeter, the Westbrooks, who were happy to take him in and raise him as their own."

That made sense. Connie's half-sisters had never complained about the way her mother had treated them, but not all step-parents were as fair.

"Is that why you visit here? To see him?"

"I do see him occasionally," he said. "Although most of my news is indirect, via Pendrick, in Exeter. Mrs Westbrook is Pendrick's sister. Westbrook is a solicitor, so the boy's getting a respectable upbringing. The Westbrooks have never made a secret of the fact they are not his natural parents, but it's Westbrook he thinks of as his real father, not me."

"That's good, isn't it? Best for him, at least. Do you mind?"

He had picked a daisy, and was pulling the petals off one by one. She thought he did mind, but he had done what was best for the boy. She looked away, swallowing hard. He would make a good father one day, to *their* children.

"I… I think it would be selfish of me to intrude, Connie. When he's older, it might be all right." He flicked the remains of the daisy away. "He's very much wanted there. You can imagine the kind of life an illegitimate son would have if he'd grown up anywhere near my father."

"Thank you for telling me, Will. It's in the past; you can't change what happened, but you did the right thing afterwards. You're still doing the right thing."

The sudden relaxation of his features revealed how tense he'd been.

"No other secrets?" Perhaps she should trust him and not ask, but she wanted to hear him say no. "I told you all of mine—about my mother, and my true father."

He reached out and took her hand. "No other secrets, Connie, I swear it."

He looked so earnest that her heart turned over. "I believe you."

"Thank you." He lifted her hand and kissed it, his lips warm on her skin. The warmth spread to the rest of her, but he released her hand and turned to the picnic basket.

"Shall we see what Mrs Curnow has given us?" Will opened the basket and brought out ginger cake and lemonade.

Connie gazed out to sea again as she ate, still feeling the print of his lips on her hand, but her mind was on his revelations. Will had loved his mother, that was clear from everything he'd said about her. What must it have been like for a young lad when his mother died, living with such a father? She'd had the Fancotts to comfort her—had there been anyone for Will?

She slid a glance towards him—he, too, was gazing at the waves. As she looked he turned to her and smiled, that dimple showing again. The expression in his eyes made her heart beat faster.

He was a grown man now, not that lonely boy, but men needed love too. She could very easily come to love him—she suspected she was halfway there already.

"Shall I teach you to skim stones?" Will's voice brought her back to the present.

Stones?

Will was sorting through the pebbles near their patch of grass, selecting thin, flat ones.

"Yes, like this." He stood and walked down to the water's edge, waiting for a flat bit of water between waves then leaning sideways to throw the stone. It skipped once, twice, three times before disappearing into the water on the fourth bounce.

"I must be losing my touch," he said, looking back at her with a grin. "My record was seven when I was a lad."

He held out a stone. "Would you like to try?"

Why not?

Will showed her how to hold the stone, with one finger hooked around its edge. "Flick your wrist when you let it go."

He watched her face as she took the stone, not her hands. He had shown more of himself to her today than he had before, and it hadn't been easy to tell—because of both his own regrets and his anxiety about how she might react. He'd needed to move, to *do* something, so now they were skimming stones.

She seemed to have taken it well, although her face had lost the happy sparkle of their arrival. But she looked thoughtful, not sad, and produced a rueful smile when her first stone sank without trace.

"It takes practice." He held out another, but it went the same way as the first. "Keep trying—like this." He stood behind her and folded her hand over the next stone, making sure her fingers were in the right place. Her skin felt smooth on his palm, silky.

"Flick your wrist, like this." He moved her hand to show the action needed, standing close so their arms could move together. He could no longer smell the salt air, just the scent of her skin; the breeze became strands of her hair tickling his face.

He took a deep breath. "Bend your knees a little," he added, stepping back from her abruptly and hoping that his racing pulse would slow. He had to keep his distance if he was to keep his word.

Connie felt Will's absence as he moved away. It wasn't coolness from the breeze that reached her back, but the feeling of a loss of something within her. What would it have felt like if he'd stepped forwards instead of backwards, pressing his body against her and encircling her with his arms? If he had turned her to face him and—

"Connie?"

Oh, yes. Throw the stone.

It sank as the first two had.

Pebbles scraped as he moved, but he held her next stone at almost arm's length, his fingers at one end of it.

This time it skipped. Only once, but she turned to him with a happy smile. "Another!"

She'd half hoped for him to step closer again, to wind his arms around her to show her how to do it better, but he only smiled, a little stiffly. "I'll find some more stones for you."

She threw a dozen stones, managing several skips with most of them. Without his presence so close behind her, she could concentrate on flicking them as he had shown her.

Will sat on one end of the blanket with his knees drawn up, the basket now planted firmly in the middle. Connie hesitated before sitting down at the other end. Was something wrong?

He was gazing at the sea. He'd kissed her hand before—what would his lips feel like on her own? What would those broad shoulders feel like beneath her hands? That warmth inside had little to do with the sunshine. Perhaps tonight she would—

"Connie, I'll be going out to watch for smugglers again this evening."

Not tonight, then.

A bucket of cold water would have been less dampening. She would wait up for him, but he might not be back until the early hours.

"I'll only be observing, Connie, as I promised. Nothing happened last night, and they'll need to move those goods soon."

She nodded as his eyes met hers, but then he turned back to the basket, bringing out two small pie dishes. "Squab pie," he said, handing her a plate and a fork.

Connie wasn't hungry, but it was something to do with her hands while she tried to decide whether to tell him she was changing her mind about waiting. He wasn't looking at her, and he'd moved the basket to place it between them. Something was wrong—she wasn't sure what. Was he feeling regretful about the son he hardly saw?

She could not discuss consummating their marriage now. Not here on the beach, with the ride home to come and nowhere to retreat to if she made a complete fool of herself.

She stuck her fork into the pie, looking doubtfully at the filling. "Squab is young pigeon, is it not?" Was she really babbling about food?

"At this end of the country, squab pies are mutton and apple." He took a mouthful, his gaze fixed on his plate.

So be it. Discussing Mrs Curnow's cooking could distract her for a little while.

"No more, thank you," Connie said, as Will offered her a plate of fruit. She smiled, but her face felt stiff. She'd wanted to ask more about his life after his mother had died, for some reason wanting to know there'd been someone for him, even if only an old nurse or governess. But Will's dinner conversation had stuck to the estate, the farms, books they had read—seemingly anything to keep to impersonal topics. At any other time, Connie would have enjoyed it, but not tonight.

"If you will excuse me, then, I have some urgent letters to write." He stood as he spoke, his smile looking forced.

Letters? He'd not mentioned anything urgent earlier. Although he hadn't said so, it was also clear he didn't want her to join him in the library, as she had done almost every evening so far.

Is he deliberately avoiding me?

She toyed with her wine glass as the door closed behind him, remembering the ride back in the chaise that afternoon. Until today, she hadn't realised how often their bodies had touched as they drove around together—shoulders, elbows or hips. Today, those touches were noticeable for their almost complete absence.

With a sigh, she rang the bell for Barton to clear the table, and retreated to her parlour with a book. She might be able to summon up the courage to talk to him about it tonight, when he returned from watching, or perhaps in the morning.

Will set off across the fields in the gathering dusk, feeling a miserable wretch. Standing behind Connie on the beach had almost undone him; moving away from her had done little to reduce his body's awareness of her, its want.

He'd given his word, and would not try to seduce her into changing her mind.

Keeping their conversation on impersonal topics had helped a little, but the hurt in her eyes when he left her after dinner showed she knew his excuse to be the lie it was. But he knew that if he was to keep his word, he would need to be somewhere away from her.

She knew him much better now, after today's revelations. That had been her reason for wanting to wait. Perhaps he should ask her directly—it might not be easy for a woman brought up as she had been to raise such a subject, particularly if he was keeping his distance. He could not avoid her this way for the rest of the month he'd promised.

"Been talking in the village, my lord." Archer's voice interrupted his thoughts.

"What more do you know?" This, at least, was something he *did* need to concentrate on.

"Quite a bit, after I talked to Mrs Trasker on the way to Ottery." Archer stopped. "My lord, that Nancarrow *will* keep them safe, won't he? It was bad enough before, but after what she told me, Sandow'll be even worse."

"I'll do my best to make sure they are safe, Archer." He didn't like to imagine what Sandow might do.

"That's good, my lord."

They set off again, risking unshuttering the lantern briefly as they entered the woodland. A breeze ruffled the leaves above them, but Will hardly felt it at ground level.

"This Sandow and his mates organise the smuggling," Archer went on, keeping his voice low. "Sandow takes money from all the villagers to pay for the cargo, pays them back with a little profit."

"I've heard of that, yes."

"Thing is, my lord, they don't get no choice about contributing. If they don't pay, they get what Mrs Strickland got, or their kids get it like young Danny. If they do pay, they get their money back, and a little extra. It's not much extra, by the sound of it, but that ain't the point, to me."

"It makes sure they won't want to give evidence if anyone gets—"

A noise—what was it?

It came again, a metallic jingle, hardly audible above the other sounds of the night. Below them, through the trees.

"Someone on the road?" Archer muttered. They waited a little longer, but heard nothing more.

"Come on," Will breathed, and led the way to the little clearing, shuttering the lamp before they emerged from the trees.

There was no moonlight, but the skies were clear and the stars bright.

The land below was black against the faint glow of the sky, but there was enough light to reflect from the foam where waves ran up the beach, turning the fishing boats into darker shapes cutting across the pale lines.

Nothing happened for some time, then Will spotted a flash from the sea. Someone in the village below must have been keeping watch, for doors opened, spilling light onto the streets. More patches of light moving towards the beach must be from shuttered lanterns.

A dark shape came closer, nosing into the bay until it must surely be almost aground. Will heard the rattle of an anchor chain.

The crack of a shot echoed between the valley walls. Shouts and a clatter of hooves came from below, followed by more shots. With the noise of a small army, half a dozen or so mounted men emerged onto the beach. Someone from the revenue had managed to bring in a troop of dragoons.

Will's instinct was to run down to the village, but he recalled his promise to Connie not to get involved. There was nothing he could do, he realised, even if he decided to break that promise. The dragoons would assume he was a smuggler; the smugglers would think he was on the side of the law. He'd be a target for both sides.

The scene on the beach was a confusing mass of shadows, shouts, and shots. In the midst of it all, a rowing boat was lowered from the ship, oars making pale splashes as the crew struggled to tug the vessel back out to sea.

"Them dragoons are brave, or bloody fools," Archer muttered, as the horsemen retreated to the road.

"Bloody fools, I think," Will said, watching as the dragoons clustered in a group, surrounded by villagers, then started moving slowly inland. "They didn't bring enough men to defeat a whole village full of smugglers. All they've done is warn them off." A couple of riders slumped forwards over their horses' necks; the others pointed muskets at the villagers.

"Do you think we can intercept them?" Will asked. The soldiers might be able to give him some information about the smuggling, even if they'd achieved nothing else this night.

"We can try."

There might be a path through the woods to bring them out on the road above the village, but Will didn't know it. Best to head for the house, and then to the road from there. They hurried back the way they'd come, moving as fast as they could in the darkness. Will prayed he wouldn't delay things by tripping over a root or putting his foot in a rabbit hole.

They hadn't needed to rush—once they came in sight of the house, Will heard hooves on gravel. The preventatives had come for help.

CHAPTER 31

onnie awoke to banging on the door. Not her door... Will's door? There was silence for a minute, then the banging resumed, heard clearly through the open connecting door. She must have fallen asleep while waiting for him—that was why she was still wearing a robe over her chemise.

She stepped out onto the landing, a knot of dread forming in her stomach. Something was wrong—if Will was in his room, he would have opened his door by now.

"It's soldiers, my lady," Warren said, his tone urgent. "Lord Wingrave needs to come."

"He'll be there shortly," Connie said. She hoped so, at least; he'd promised to only watch. It was up to her to see what the soldiers wanted. "I will be there directly." She pulled her muslin gown on and hurriedly pinned the front.

Two men lay in the entrance hall, both in the scarlet jackets of dragoons. An officer and a man in civilian clothing knelt by them, two more soldiers standing beyond. The officer rose to his feet as Connie approached.

"Captain Burke, my lady," he introduced himself. "We heard Lord Wingrave was in residence. I hoped he might be able to help with my men."

"What—?"

"One has been shot in the leg, my lady, the other has a slashed arm."

"Of course. Warren, rouse Mrs Curnow and the maids." She turned back to the officer. "Has someone gone for a doctor, Captain?"

"Yes, but he could be some time."

A gunshot wound. She knew nothing about treating such a thing; all she could do was to stem the bleeding, and to make the man as comfortable as possible.

"Ah, you are the cause of the shots we heard. I went out to see what was happening."

That was Will's voice, thank goodness. Connie turned, and let out a breath of relief when she saw him at the front door, apparently unhurt.

"Lord Wingrave?" Captain Burke bowed. "Captain Burke. This is Mr Sullivan, of the Revenue Service. I apologise for bursting in on your home like this, but these men need urgent assistance."

Connie moved closer, trying to see the men's injuries more clearly.

The officer came to stand next to her. "Dennison's arm only needs bandaging, I think, enough to get him home. Vance..." He shook his head.

"Get him to a bed," Will said. "Warren, where's the best place?"

"My room's the closest, my lord."

"Thank you. See to it, please. Burke's men will help you."

Connie stood to one side, watching as two soldiers lifted Vance and carried him through the servants' door, followed by Warren and the captain.

"Can you help him out of his coat?" she asked, turning her attention to the soldier still lying on the floor.

Between them, Sullivan and Will eased Dennison's injured arm from his coat, to the accompaniment of a stifled groan. His shirt sleeve was red with blood, but the gash beneath was only oozing.

Connie put a hand on his forehead; although pale, he didn't have the clammy feel of someone seriously ill.

"I can deal with that, my lady," Mrs Curnow said, hurrying in with a basin and cloth.

"Thank you, Mrs Curnow," Connie replied. "I must take a look at the other man."

Will followed her into Warren's room, where the bed had been stripped to the bottom sheet. Vance lay on it, his face grey. Blood soaked one leg of his breeches, beneath a sodden bandage.

"That bandage needs to come off, and his breeches," Connie said, taking a deep breath. "Cutting them might be best. Warren, more water—boiled water, if possible—and cloths, please." She pulled off her wedding ring and put it into the pocket beneath her skirts; it would only get in the way.

The captain produced a knife and cut through the bandage, then around the wounded man's breeches.

"Turn him over, Burke," Will said from behind her. "He might be lucky."

Lucky?

She saw what Will meant when they rolled the man onto his side. There was a wound on the back of his thigh as well, still oozing blood, but that might only be because they'd pulled off the bandage stuck to it.

"Bullet went right through," Will said, "and missed the arteries."

"We can wash it out," Connie said, regarding the wounds doubtfully. She'd never dealt with such a deep injury before, but the principles must be the same as for shallower cuts.

"If you would, my lady," Captain Burke said. "Hopefully there's no bits of his breeches dragged in, but the doctor can look for that."

Connie swallowed hard. She'd do that as well if she had to, but poking around inside a man's leg was well beyond her experience. She felt a hand on her shoulder, squeezing gently.

"One of us can do it if you wish," Will said.

She shook her head, his touch helping to steady her.

"Washing with wine or spirits is supposed to help, too," she said.

"Captain, you might need to hold him down."

Warren returned with steaming water, only to be sent off again for wine. Vance hardly stirred when she washed the wound with water, and only moved restlessly and moaned when she poured the wine in. That was worrying in itself, she thought as she applied a clean bandage.

"Should we give him some laudanum?" Will asked.

"I... I'm not sure. He doesn't seem to need it at the moment. If he wakes up, then yes."

"Very well. Warren, you sit with him. Captain, please find Sullivan and meet me in my library. I'd like a word with you."

The captain nodded and left.

"You too, Connie," Will said. Once outside Warren's room he put one arm around her shoulders.

"Well done," he whispered, his breath tickling her ear. "And thank you."

"That's all right." He no longer seemed to be distancing himself from her, and some of the tension within her relaxed.

In the library, Will offered everyone a glass of wine. Sullivan and the captain accepted with thanks, but Connie declined. She wanted to keep her wits about her.

"I was watching from above the village," Will began, his gaze on her face.

Connie acknowledged his look with a smile. He *had* kept his word to her.

"They are determined men, Sullivan, to fight off mounted dragoons," Will continued.

Sullivan grimaced, taking a large swallow of his drink. "As are most such criminals in these parts, my lord. We should be grateful none of us are dead, although that's not from the kindness of their hearts." He shook his head. "I'd be able to get a bigger force if we were facing murder."

"How did you know there'd be a run tonight?" Will asked.

Sullivan pressed his lips together, glancing towards Connie as he did so.

"I assure you, Mr Sullivan, nothing you say here will go any further," Connie said, irritated that he didn't want to speak in front of her.

Sullivan shrugged. "A revenue cruiser spotted a boat waiting offshore a few days ago. Last night, a watcher saw a light signalling from Ashmouth. We weren't certain, but a run seemed likely. I hope I can rely on you, my lord, to pass on any information you may come across concerning these criminals."

"Indeed I will, Mr Sullivan. Captain Burke, someone will stay with Vance until the doctor arrives. You may leave the other—Dennison, was it? You can leave him here tonight if you wish. Warren or Mrs Curnow will show him where to sleep."

Both men bowed and took their leave. Connie yawned, feeling sleepy again now there was nothing more to do.

"You can return to bed, Connie. I'll make sure everything's locked up and someone is keeping watch."

He was preoccupied with the wounded men and the night's events, and she was tired after the... excitement was the wrong word. This was not the time to tell him she'd changed her mind.

"I'll take a hot drink up," she said.

Will went with Connie down to the kitchen. There was no-one there — surely it didn't take both Warren and Mrs Curnow to find Dennison a bed? Then he noticed the door to the cellar standing ajar.

"What's in the cellar that they might need?" he asked, keeping his voice low. "Your new medicines?"

She met his eyes, shaking her head.

"Stay here," he whispered, and cautiously pushed the door open further. The corridor beyond was dimly lit by lantern glow from one of the storerooms along the corridor. The only sound was a murmur of voices.

He stepped into the corridor. The cool air smelled fresh, earthy, not the musty smell there had been last time he was down here.

"The secret door must be open," Connie breathed behind him.

Damn. He should have known she would follow him. He turned his head, a finger to his lips, and caught the nod of her head in the gloom.

The light faded for a moment, blocked by someone standing in the doorway of the storeroom. Two men came out and walked away from them, silhouetted by the lantern they carried. They were going towards the end room with the concealed exit.

"Wait," Will murmured. He was aware of Connie's silent presence, a warmth against his back even though they were not touching.

The men, concentrate on them.

The lantern light vanished as the men entered the end room and closed the door behind them. The only light now was from the nearer storeroom.

Will moved forward, treading noiselessly. He wasn't sure what he'd expected, but it certainly wasn't the sight that met his eyes when he reached the doorway. Warren and Mrs Curnow stood over a man lying on a blanket spread on the floor. Not a villager; the fabric of his suit was more costly than the villagers' drab homespun. Blood coated one side of his face, soaking into his neckcloth and the collar of his coat. It was difficult to make out much else in the lantern light.

"Another visitor," he said. Warren and Mrs Curnow swung round to face him, both wide-eyed with fear.

Connie pushed past him to kneel at the man's side. She put a hand to his forehead, then to the side of his neck. "He needs a doctor."

"No!"

The denial came from both the butler and the housekeeper. Connie sat back on her heels, gazing from one to the other. "He may well die without proper attention," she stated, her voice firm.

Will had seen unconscious men before, had even been knocked out himself once or twice while sparring, and in each case had come around of his own accord with little worse than a violent headache and a bit of dizziness. But he trusted that Connie knew enough to give that verdict.

Warren licked his lips and cast a glance at the man on the floor. "He... he's one of the villagers, my lord."

"A doctor'd report him," Mrs Curnow added. "Might arrest him."

And you've been threatened with something dire if he is found or if he dies.

Connie stood, brushing dust from her gown. "He should be in a proper bed, not lying on a cold floor."

She was looking to him to make a decision.

There was little to be gained by handing the man over to Captain Burke or Sullivan now, and possibly more information to be had if they did not. At the very least they might gain some goodwill from the villagers.

"There must be spare beds in the servants' quarters," he said. "Bring one down, or bring a pallet. Ask Archer to help you, it's best if as few other people know about this as possible." He looked from one to the other. "In fact, it would be best if no-one else knows of my involvement or Lady Wingrave's. Particularly Sandow."

Warren and Mrs Curnow both nodded, their faces still taut with worry.

He scrubbed a hand through his hair; they now had two dangerously ill men to look after, and not many people to do it.

"Mrs Curnow, remain with this man while Warren sorts out a bed."

"Yes, my lord."

Connie followed him back through the kitchens. "I'll just check on the soldier," she said. She was gone only a minute before joining him in the library.

"That man isn't a villager," she stated, as soon as the door closed behind them.

"No."

"Are you going to tell the captain, or Sullivan, about him when they return tomorrow? And tell them who runs the smuggling around here?"

"I should, I know."

She nodded, her expression showing no surprise.

"But they would need evidence against Sandow to arrest him, and then people willing to testify at a trial. I've only got hearsay, no direct evidence myself. As for our extra guest—there is something more here than smuggling, Connie. That man could be the organiser, or someone with a particular cargo to see off or collect. I'd like the chance to question him before handing him over."

"You could leave all that to the authorities," she suggested, one eyebrow raised.

"I could," he admitted.

"But then *you* probably wouldn't find out what is going on." That was exasperation in her voice. "Handing him over would mean losing our cook and butler, as well."

"You think they'd run away?"

She stared at him for a moment. "No, I mean you'd have to find them another position far enough away so that Sandow couldn't take his revenge."

Oh. Of course.

She crossed to the door. "I'll wait in the kitchen until the doctor arrives."

"You don't need to stay up," he said, as she put her hand to the door handle.

She gave him that stare again. "I was going to find out how to treat our second guest, without letting him guess why I am asking about head injuries."

"Oh, good idea. I was only thinking you would be tired."

Her expression softened, and he followed her back to the kitchen.

The soldier who had been sent for help returned two hours later—without a doctor. He'd had to go as far as Ottery St Mary, and then had only managed to find an apothecary willing to turn out in the middle of the night. Connie's sleepiness vanished now she had something to do again.

Middleton was a nervous young man of Connie's own age, and not even the apothecary, but his senior apprentice. Connie helped him to ease the bandage from the soldier's thigh.

"Nicely cleaned," Middleton said, his shy smile boosting Connie's confidence. She watched carefully as he examined both wounds, then dusted powder on them and applied a new bandage. "All you can do is keep him warm," he said. "Give him a drink—water, not wine—if he asks for it."

"Laudanum?"

"A few drops in water, if he needs it."

Holding the lantern close, Connie observed little change in the man's face, the greyish tinge still there.

"You must stay until daybreak, at least, Mr Middleton," Connie said. At this time of year, that wouldn't be long. "Do have a cup of tea, or something stronger, if you wish, then we'll find you somewhere to lie down. You can check on him again before you leave."

Mrs Curnow made tea while Connie chattered to Middleton, relating injuries she'd helped to tend in the past. The poor man's eyes were beginning to glaze over with boredom, but she made him listen by plying him with questions about the treatments she'd used. Finally she worked around to the time when the imaginary Jacky Smith had fallen off a roof and hit his head, but the only advice she gleaned was to keep the patient in bed, warm, but not too hot, and to give him something to drink if he came round enough to be able to swallow. That wasn't much help.

Will and Connie left Mrs Curnow to see to Middleton's comfort, and stepped out into the hallway.

"Go to bed, Connie." Will put his arm around her as he had earlier. She leaned back, enjoying the solid feel of him, and the comforting pressure of his hand on her arm. "There'll be much to do tomorrow," he went on. "I'm going to let Archer know about our man in the cellars, then I'm for my bed, too."

"Very well." She'd need to be alert if she was not to let fall any hints about their second patient when the Captain returned. "Goodnight."

CHAPTER 32

*M*onday 7th July

Will knocked on the door to Connie's room, hoping she was awake. He didn't want to disturb her, but she needed to know why he was leaving her alone in the house this morning.

"Come in."

He pushed the door open. Not only was she awake, but she was dressed and sitting in the window seat with her feet tucked up.

She looked up as he came in. "Is something wrong?"

"No. No more than was wrong last night, that is. Are you all right?"

She looked well. No, lovely, with a tentative smile on her lips and her hair spilling down her back. It was longer than he'd thought, a gentle wave to it. It would feel silky—

He dragged his thoughts back to the matter at hand. "Er, I came to let you know I'm going to see Nancarrow. We need a few more men about the place."

She nodded. "And best not recruited locally?"

"Exactly. Will you be all right here? I've told Archer to keep a close eye on things."

"You *do* trust him?"

"Yes, I do."

"I'll be fine, Will. I won't go out of the house unless I have Archer with me."

"And not beyond the gardens, even with Archer?"

"No."

"I'll be back as soon as I can." It was tempting, so very tempting, to lean down and kiss her. But he didn't think he could stop at just a kiss, and he had to get more protection for her.

Connie remained on the window seat for a while after Will left. He'd gone back to being distant again, avoiding her touch. Last night he'd put his arm around her, touched her shoulder—reassuring, but warming too. She wanted more of that, more of the closeness she'd felt when they were dealing with problems together.

She swung her feet off the seat. Time to finish getting dressed—she had wounded men to see to.

"Who is that for?" Connie asked. The tray of ham, eggs, and tea Mrs Curnow was preparing looked too substantial for either of their patients.

"Mrs Strickland, still wanting waiting on." The cook rolled her eyes and picked up the tray.

The housekeeper should be able to get around by now, Connie thought, even if she needed a stick. But she was quite happy not to have to confront the woman's superior attitude.

"What about the soldiers?"

"The one with the cut arm, I sent him to sleep over the stables last night. He's been in for his breakfast, was looking all right to me. A little pale, maybe. Haven't looked in on the others." She gave a quick nod to Connie and carried the tray out.

To Connie's inexperienced eye, the wounded soldier in Warren's room seemed to be improving. He was still pale, and could hardly lift his head off the pillow, but he agreed that he would try to eat a little gruel if someone could help him to sit up.

Warren could deal with that, and help the man to use a chamber pot if he needed it.

She found the butler sitting with the injured smuggler and sent him off, saying she would sit with the patient for a while. Warren had undressed him down to his shirt, and he lay on a pallet covered by a blanket. He was restless, his hands plucking at the covers and his mouth working a little as if he was trying to speak. A tray with a jug of water and a glass stood ready near his head; his outer clothes lay neatly folded next to it, together with a leather satchel.

"Water?" Connie asked.

His mouth moved, as if he was answering. She knelt on the floor, bending closer to him, and repeated the question.

"Mes lettres."

His letters? Was he French?

She sat back on her heels. That shouldn't be surprising—the smugglers would have many dealings with Frenchmen. What were the letters—orders for the next shipment, perhaps, or payment details?

"I'm sure your letters are safe," she said, making her voice sound as reassuring as possible. He must understand English, surely, if he was here.

"Laissez-moi les voir."

Laissez... let... let me see them?

"Where are they?"

"Manteau."

Connie turned to the pile of clothing; his coat lay on the top. She felt through the pockets, finding coins, a handkerchief, a card case, and a folded sheet of paper.

"Here you are," she said, holding out the paper. The man turned his head towards her, then away again.

"Non. Mes lettres!"

Had she misunderstood 'manteau'? She picked up the satchel and opened it, but all it contained was a clean shirt, stockings, and a couple of neckcloths.

"Mes lettres!" he muttered again. "Manteau!"

Sighing, she picked up the coat again, this time laying the contents of the pockets on the floor. She'd checked the inside pockets. A hidden pocket?

She couldn't see any signs of one, but the lantern light was dim. Patting the coat and the seams revealed a section of the front, beneath the buttons, that felt stiffer than the rest of it.

Ah, there was a small slit in the lining, just wide enough for her to stick two fingers into. The stiffness was a long, thin packet with the feel of oiled silk, not paper.

"Is this what you wanted?"

He reached a hand up to touch it. "Oui. Personne ne doit savoir…"

No-one must know?

"All right," Connie said. She put the packet on the floor. No-one *would* know, down here.

The 'letters' surely could not just be details of smuggling runs. She could see the need to keep such things dry, to ensure they survived a trip across the Channel in a small boat, but why hide them inside a coat?

Curious, she turned to one side so he couldn't see what she was doing, and unfolded the paper she'd first shown him. Tilting it towards the lamp, she made out a letter from an attorney in Cornwall, introducing Mr Jonathan Devizes as his business representative. The card case held cards with the same name on them.

She looked again at the man lying on the pallet. It was possible that someone who spoke French as their native language would have an English name, but it didn't seem likely. But if he wasn't a smuggler, what was he doing here?

"Elles sont cachées?"

She held up the coat, patting the hiding place. "Well hidden," she said. "You must sleep now."

The packet had been well hidden—not even the smugglers would know about it. It was important, then. Waiting until he closed his eyes, she slipped the packet up her sleeve. She should show the packet to Will. Or perhaps open it herself?

Footsteps approached, and Warren entered. "How is he, my lady?"

"He was talking a little," Connie said. Why hadn't he asked Warren about his letters?

"He was before, but I couldn't make out what he wanted."

That explained it. She needn't worry about the man asking Warren again. Not until he'd recovered enough to realise he needed to speak in English, at least.

"The captain is here, my lady, with the doctor. He's going to take away the one with the wounded arm, but wants to leave the other here."

Captain Burke—she should show him the packet, but she knew Will would want to see it. Handing it over was a tempting idea; telling the captain what they knew about Sandow would end Will's involvement with the business. Unfortunately, it would also destroy all the trust she felt had built up between them.

"I'll see him," Connie said, standing and smoothing her skirts, moving her hands cautiously to avoid letting the little packet slip from her sleeve. "I'll come down again in a couple of hours. Fetch me if there is any change in his condition."

"Yes, my lady."

Connie pushed the packet further up her sleeve as she ascended to the entrance hall. She must remember to keep that arm bent.

"Good day, Captain."

"My lady." He bowed. "Doctor Harris says that Vance will do better if he is not moved for a couple of days. Would it be possible for him to remain here?"

"By all means, Captain." She'd feel safer with a soldier in the house, even a wounded one—it might help deter the smugglers from coming to check on their comrade.

She turned to the other man. "Doctor Harris, could you give me some reassurance? Our gardener fell off a ladder last week and hit his head. I made him rest, but I wasn't sure what else to do. He seems to have recovered, but is there anything else I should have done?"

"It is difficult to tell without seeing the man himself," Harris said.

"But the main principle is to keep the patient calm and rested, and allow them a little drink and easily digestible food if they request it. Bleeding, too, may help to reduce any pressure on the brain."

"Thank you, doctor."

"I do recommend, my lady, that you always send for a physician. I would be happy to attend should you require my services in the future."

Connie inclined her head graciously. "Thank you sir, I will bear it in mind."

She waited in the hallway until she saw them ride away down the drive. The man in the cellar would have to manage without being bled. That was *not* something she was prepared to attempt.

In her small parlour, Connie sat out of sight of the open door, and spread out the patterned muslin gown she'd picked as the next one to remake. Then she pulled the packet from her sleeve. She would hear anyone approaching in time to hide the packet beneath the fabric of the gown.

The oiled silk wrapping was held closed with a line of stitches. Connie inspected it carefully, deciding that she could re-sew it so no-one would know it had been opened. She hesitated before reaching for her scissors—what if Will did decide to just take the packet to the authorities? Would it matter if it had been opened?

She reached for her embroidery scissors. Of course Will would want to know what was in it.

The sheets of paper inside were thin, the writing on them small. They weren't letters, but lists. One was a set of names and amounts of money—that looked like a wages bill. Another had what looked like dates, next to numbers and sets of initials. A third was just row after row of numbers—was it possible that it was a code of some kind?

They *could* be details of payments for goods bought or sold, or bribes to revenue men, but she didn't quite believe it. A French courier using a false name, with the papers hidden. This was something more. She'd been right to take them for Will to see.

Refolding the papers carefully, she put them in the bottom of her sewing box and replaced the reels of thread. Then she took them out again. The man might not be content to have seen the packet once, in his semi-conscious state. If he asked for the papers again before Will returned, and made Warren understand him, it would not do to have him find nothing. She could copy them, and show Will the copies, but copying lists of numbers correctly would require care. She could not do it quickly.

The man in the cellar had shown no inclination to open the packet. She folded a couple of pieces of her writing paper until they formed the right bulk, and wrapped the oiled silk around them, carefully stitching the seam using the needle holes already made in the fabric. Examining it when she'd finished, she thought it would pass muster in the dim light in the cellar, and probably in daylight, too.

Warren might get suspicious if she returned too soon, but she could pass on the news that Vance would be staying for a few days and find some excuse to get him out of the room while she replaced the packet.

CHAPTER 33

*W*ill's mind was busy as he rode home from Ottery. Nancarrow had promised to send some outdoor staff as soon as possible—within a week, if he could—and had confirmed that the Traskers were still safe. He'd also provided a list of prices paid locally for smuggled goods. Will would need to compare that with Pendrick's estimates of the cost of the goods in France, but from the details he remembered there must be a huge profit involved. There would be other costs, but if they used the fishing boats they owned anyway...

No, he needed to sit down with paper and pen to make a list of all the factors. The profit made was immaterial; the real problem was the way Sandow ran the operation. The man must be got rid of somehow, he knew that. But with Sandow gone, someone else would take over—the profit to be made from smuggling was too great to be abandoned if their leader was killed or imprisoned.

He turned Mercury into the drive, slowing to a walk to allow the horse time to cool off. Sandow's replacement could be as bad, in which case the only way to solve the problem was to stop the smuggling altogether. Archer had said that some of the villagers were forced to contribute to the funding, but that didn't mean they all were. And it did seem as if they made a little extra from it, even if not a fair amount. Trying to close the whole operation down would earn the enmity of the villagers—not a good way to start his life in the area.

Those thoughts fled as he emerged from the woods and saw Connie waiting for him on the terrace, one hand shading her eyes from the sun. A warm glow started somewhere inside.

His pleasure dimmed a little as he drew closer and swung down off his horse. Her expression was strained, and her smile of greeting as she came down the steps towards him was a mere movement of her lips.

"I need to talk to you," she said, her voice low. Glancing up, he saw Warren appear behind her in the doorway.

"Walk with me to the stables." He offered her his arm as he led Mercury around the house. "What is it?"

"I have something to show you." Her voice was only just audible. "But no-one else must know, or see."

His brows rose, but Stubbs approached them to take the horse so he could ask nothing further.

"Would you care for some refreshment after your ride, my lord?" Connie continued in a louder voice. "Perhaps you will join me in my parlour when you are ready?"

Will's curiosity grew while they waited for Barton to finish setting out the tea things on a small table in Connie's parlour. Finally the footman left them alone.

Connie opened her sewing box and handed him several thin sheets of paper. "Our injured smuggler had these on him," she said. "In a hidden pocket, sewn up in oiled silk." She explained how she had found them as Will opened out the sheets.

A man who appeared to be using a false identity, with hidden documents written in code. It could be some criminal enterprise more involved than free trading. Or could it be more serious than that.

"He could be a spy, Connie."

233

"A spy? But why would a Frenchman be spying on Britain?" Connie asked. "We're not at war with them."

Will shrugged. "We have been in the past, and doubtless will be again. We *are* at war with the colonies, and the French sympathise with them. It's possibly easier to get information from France to the Americas than it is to send it directly from England."

"*Is* this going to France, or could he have come from there?"

Good point—why had he been so sure the spy was on his way out of the country? "The boat last night... the dragoons attacked before they landed anyone, or anything. Our spy must have been waiting there to meet the boat. They'd take him back to France once they'd unloaded their cargo."

"Do you think Sandow is spying as well?"

That was a good question. "He lives here—Archer said nothing about him going away from the area, so what could he be spying on?"

"So Sandow's gang are only being paid to take the letters?"

"Yes... I mean..." Will stopped. There was a difference between transporting the letters and transporting the messenger. "No. If Sandow's being paid to transport the letters, he wouldn't have needed to bring the spy here to be looked after. He could have just sent the letters to France."

"So Sandow *doesn't* know about the letters," Connie said. "He may not even know the man is a spy."

"He probably suspects—he's not stupid. But a man like him won't care what the information is as long as he gets paid."

"So what are we going to do, Will?"

Will threw his wig onto a chair and ran one hand through his hair. "He may not be a spy, but I think we have to assume that he is. What if he's only a messenger, though? Arresting him would stop *this* information getting through, but they could easily find someone else to take it."

If they were right, the decision about what to do with the spy would be beyond the local magistrates. Who could advise him on this?

"It would be better to take him to London," he said. "This information may well have come from there." Sir John Tregarth, Harry's father, might be able to help him find the right person to deliver the man to.

"I don't think you should do that."

Will looked up in surprise. "Why ever not? Oh, is he too unwell?" It would not do for him to die before he could be questioned.

Connie shook her head. "No. I mean, he *is* too unwell at present, but I was thinking about what Sandow will do if his... his cargo disappears."

"Oh, yes." Revenge of some sort, naturally, and aimed at himself and Connie. Will was *not* going to let anything happen to Connie. "I'd like to kill the bastard."

"You can't do that!"

Will thought that he could, very easily. "After what he threatened to do to Sukey? And has doubtless done to many others?"

Connie looked away, then down at her hands. "Killing is wrong, I know that, but in this case..." She raised her eyes to his, her expression troubled. "In this case, I cannot help thinking the world would be better without him. I was thinking of your father. If you are arrested for murder—"

"He wouldn't let me hang." Not before Will had sired an heir, at least.

"You're here because you put your life at risk fighting a duel. Won't he sell this place?"

"Damn it." Of course he would, and with it would go Will's independence.

"We can't just let the spy go when he is well enough, can we?" Connie asked.

"No." That would be betraying their country. He tried to read Connie's expression; her words had sounded doubtful, as if she knew it would be an easy way out, but not one they should take.

What if he took the letters? They might provide a clue about the source of the information. He tried to recall what time the stage coach left Exeter; some God-forsaken hour before dawn, he thought, which would mean not arriving in London until the day after tomorrow. Then another whole day to come back, at least, plus the time he needed in London to find the right person to tell his story to.

"Connie, I could take the letters to London, but I'd be away at least three days, probably longer. I might be able to bring back someone who can arrest Sandow and the spy, and to protect the people here until Sandow is dealt with. Sullivan may have some evidence against him to add to whatever we can persuade the spy to say."

"Three days... Can you send Archer with the letters? You trust him."

He rubbed his fingers through his hair. "I thought Tregarth's father might know who I should show them to. But if he's not there, Archer wouldn't know who else to try."

"And probably wouldn't be able to get to see them in any case." Connie sighed. "You need to go, then, but the spy must still be here when you return. I suppose Sandow will not want the man dying on the way to France, so I can impress upon Warren and Mrs Curnow how ill he is, and how dangerous it would be to move him."

That could work. "Will they believe you?"

"If it's really necessary, I can give him laudanum to keep him here. I don't like to do that, but I will if I have to."

"Right, in that case, the sooner I go the better." He could ride until he found somewhere to hire a post-chaise—or another riding horse if necessary. Either of those options would be quicker than the stage. He could be in London tomorrow night.

"They might take him anyway," Connie said. "What then?"

"Did you say he still has a packet, but with blank paper in it?"

"Yes. Should I copy the letters then put the originals back?"

A good question. "That would mean possibly allowing the information to leave the country before we know what harm it might do."

She bit her lip. "He... the spy... didn't want to undo the packet, he just wanted to see it. If he doesn't open it, no-one will find out until he is in France."

"The blank paper he's already got will do then, but it would still be best if you can keep him here until my return." He stood and strode to the door, shouting for Warren.

"My lord?"

"Warren, Nancarrow had an urgent letter for me from my father. I have to go to Marstone Park right away. I'll ride, but put up a couple of clean shirts and my shaving gear, will you?"

Closing the door behind the butler, Will went to stand in front of his wife. "Connie, I will tell Archer to be vigilant." He'd give Archer his pistols as well. "If there's a chance that Sandow, or anyone else, might be a danger to you, Archer will take you to Nancarrow. He'll arrange for you to stay somewhere safe until I return." The extra men he'd asked Nancarrow to send would not be here for a few days, and he wouldn't be here to brief them, in any case.

She blinked, then nodded, wide-eyed.

"In fact, if that soldier is still too ill to be moved, you could let Captain Burke know you are worried in case some of the villagers try to get their revenge on him. He could send a couple of men to stand guard."

"That's a good idea." She put a hand on his arm. "Will, please eat something before you go. An extra half-hour won't make any difference."

"Take care, Will," Connie said, low voiced, as they stood on the terrace waiting for Archer to bring Mercury round. She'd be in charge here for days—a daunting task, but she would manage.

Will met her eyes, his hands on her shoulders. "Connie, you did well today. Very well."

His praise warmed her, bolstered her confidence. They had worked it out together.

Then he put his arms around her and pulled her close. "*You* look after yourself," he said in her ear, giving a quick squeeze before stepping back.

Connie watched as he mounted and rode down the drive, still feeling his closeness and warmth. His words to her hadn't masked his relish in having something active to do. She could understand his father's reluctance to let his heir join the army, but Will would have enjoyed the life.

Would he take care? If he really intended to be in London tomorrow night, he would have no time to rest on the way. A fall from a horse when tired…

No. He had more sense than that. She should concentrate her worries on the spy.

She sat with a book, but gave up after her eyes had passed over the same page several times without any recollection of what she had read. Instead, she continued working on her new gown, trying to focus on her stitching and not on wondering how far Will had got, or if Sandow might come to see his passenger.

Mrs Curnow reported that the injured soldier had taken more gruel during the evening, and now seemed to be sleeping naturally. The spy, by contrast, was still restless, muttering in his sleep. Warren had brought another pallet in, and proposed to sleep there himself.

"If I can, with him mumbling on all night," the butler said. "Still can't make out a word he's saying."

"He's probably dreaming," Connie said. She would check first thing, and if the spy showed signs of talking coherently in English, she might have to resort to dosing him with laudanum.

Tuesday 8th July

The sun was already warm on his back when Will caught sight of the spire of Salisbury Cathedral rising above the trees. His rear ached from riding all night, and he had at least another twelve hours to go, possibly more if he had trouble changing horses.

It was time to take a short break. They knew him at the Rose and Crown, so he stopped there to ask for a quick breakfast and a fresh horse.

While he ate, he checked the coin in his pocket, trying to work out if it would stretch to a post-chaise for part of the way. Normally, he'd have provided himself with more cash before a journey, but he'd had little in the house.

It would pay for a post-chaise, he reckoned, but only if he could guarantee getting more money in London. If Tregarth was out of town, he wasn't sure who else he could ask—not without risking someone gossiping and his father finding out he'd already broken the terms of their agreement.

Not yet three weeks since he was last here, he thought as he rode out of the city half an hour later. Then, he'd still been resenting his forced marriage; now, he couldn't imagine wanting to be without Connie.

Was she changing her mind? She hadn't flinched from his touch or his closeness when they were skimming stones, or when he'd said goodbye the day before.

Was she still safe? That was a more important question. He shook his head—thinking about that now was futile. Pray God that she would do as he'd said, and go to Nancarrow if there was the least sign of danger. In the longer term, everything came back to getting rid of Sandow.

What if he could take over the smuggling himself?

The hired horse skittered as he jerked on the reins, and he patted its neck in apology. His counting of coins must have prompted that idea, but it was worth considering. And something to think about during the miles yet to go.

Connie checked on the wounded soldier first. Mrs Curnow reported that he'd eaten a dish of coddled eggs before going back to sleep again. "Reckon that captain can take him away if he comes today," Mrs Curnow said.

That wasn't really what Connie wanted to hear, not with Will absent. She'd have a quiet word with the captain about the dangers of wounds reopening in a jolting carriage.

In the cellar, the spy was much the same. "Still can't understand a word," Warren said. "Is he a Frenchie, do you think?"

"I suppose he could be," Connie said. "The smugglers buy in France, after all."

Unlike Warren, she could make out a few words. Papiers, urgent, important—words that differed only in pronunciation from their English equivalents. It was time to start dosing him with laudanum.

"He's not making any sense to me either," she lied. "I hope he's not getting worse. It wouldn't do for him to die here, but if they try to move him he's likely to."

"No, my lady." Warren's widened eyes showed much more than the concern due to a stranger. "What will we do if he gets worse?"

"I'm not a physician, Warren, I don't know. My... my mother used to make an infusion that helped me to sleep. We could try that, I suppose."

Warren nodded eagerly.

In the stillroom, she made a tea with valerian, then added a few drops of laudanum. She wasn't sure of the dose, and it wouldn't do to give him too much, but she would see how well this amount worked first. She stirred in some sugar to mask the taste, and carried the cup to the cellar room.

"Help me sit him up, Warren."

Warren lifted the man's shoulders, and Connie persuaded him to take the warm liquid. As before, he seemed to respond to words in English, and obediently sipped until half the liquid was gone.

"I'll sit with him for a while, Warren."

"Thank you, my lady."

"Warren—if someone comes to see how he is doing, it might be unwise for them to find me here."

She could see this idea had not occurred to him.

"The outside entrance to the end room needs to be blocked up, or locked from the inside," she added. "You may explain, if you need to, that Lord Wingrave remembered using it in his youth and ordered it locked." Hopefully that would not make plain to anyone else—Sandow —that she and Will knew their cellars had been used.

"I'll see to it, my lady."

"And Warren, if you cannot stop someone coming for him, make sure there's enough time for me to get out of the way first."

Warren swallowed visibly. "Yes, my lady."

She rubbed a hand across her face as Warren left. Keeping track of who knew what—who they *thought* knew what—was getting too complicated. She'd spent too long deceiving her father; she hadn't thought she'd have to continue in her new life.

The sick man's eyes had closed as soon as he lay down, his breathing quickly becoming slow and even. She wasn't sure if the laudanum had made his sleep deeper, or only helped to ease his anxieties. Not that it mattered; the main thing was that he was no longer muttering.

CHAPTER 34

ednesday 9th July

A night watchman called two o'clock as Harry Tregarth banged on the door of his father's house in Wimpole Street. Will leaned on the railings, bone weary. He desperately needed sleep, and his legs hurt from spending too long in the saddle. The walk from the inn where he'd left the last hired horse had barely relieved his stiff muscles.

A footman let them in, and went to wake Sir John. Will collapsed onto a chair.

"What is it, Harry?" Sir John descended to the entrance hall, swathed in a banyan, a nightcap covering his head and a candle in one hand. "It's gone midnight. It's just as well your mother's with Sarah for her lying in, you'd have terrified her knocking the house up like this. It had better be important."

"It is, Papa. Will—"

"Wingrave?" Sir John's scowl deepened. "I might have known you were involved. I thought Marstone had banished you to the country."

Will flushed. "I apologise for disturbing you so late, sir, but I assure you it is of the utmost importance."

Sir John glared at him for a moment, before relenting. "Oh, very well. We'll go into the library." He turned to the footman who had answered the door. "Jenkins, you may retire."

In the library, Sir John lit more candles. Will told his tale again, giving a few more details than he had to Harry. At the end of his recital, Sir John held his hand out and Will gave him the lists.

Sir John's brows rose as he scanned them. When he looked back at Will, his expression seemed thoughtful rather than censorious.

"You did right to come to me, Wingrave. I don't know what these are, although I have my suspicions."

"Do you know who I should take them to, Sir John?"

"I have a very good idea. However *I* will take them. You will stay here for what is left of the night."

"Sir John, I must—"

"Wingrave, the person I am taking these to may well wish to talk to you, but not necessarily immediately. Your... contribution to the discussion is likely to be more valuable if you have had some sleep."

He was right, of course.

"Harry, you'd better stay here too. I'll leave it to you to sort out somewhere for the pair of you to sleep." Sir John left without waiting for a reply.

Jenkins woke them at nine the following morning, knocking until Tregarth called out for him to go away. Instead, he opened the door, bringing in two jugs of steaming water and setting them on the wash stand. "Breakfast will be served in half an hour, Lord Wingrave, Mr Tregarth. Lord Wingrave, I am asked to inform you that you will have a visitor shortly thereafter."

Will groaned and swung his legs to the floor. "We'll be there."

Jenkins bowed himself out. Will caught sight of his saddle bags resting on the floor by a chair. The one's he'd left at Tregarth's lodgings.

"How did they—?"

"Dickson." Tregarth pointed to a set of clothing draped across the foot of the second bed. "Brought a change for me, too. A most efficient valet."

"I'd tempt him away if I had the money," Will said. If he'd had a man as reliable as Dickson, instead of the weaselly Ferris, he'd not be in this situation now. But then he wouldn't have Connie either.

He splashed water on his face and washed away the sweat and grime of more than twenty-four hours on the road. A bath would have been better, but a shave helped, as did a fresh shirt and neckcloth. However, there was little he could do about the road dust that seemed to have worked its way into the fabric of his coat and breeches.

Sir John was already in the dining room, and greeted them with a nod. Will tucked into breakfast eagerly, finishing off a large helping of ham, eggs, and sausage with several cups of coffee.

"Mr Talbot." The butler announced their guest and withdrew.

Talbot was a slight man, half a head shorter than Will, with uncomfortably piercing eyes. Will took in his ornately embroidered coat, powdered wig, and the jewelled pin in his neck cloth. He looked dressed for a social engagement, not a discussion on national security, but Will had to trust that Sir John knew what he was doing.

"You are excused, Harry," Sir John said.

Tregarth looked from his father to Will, then shrugged. "Father, Mr Talbot." He nodded at the two men, and left the room.

Talbot pulled out a chair and sat opposite Will, pouring himself a cup of coffee. "Your tale, Wingrave?"

They listened carefully as Will related the story yet again. Talbot's face remained expressionless, his eyes on Will's face. He asked Will to describe his other encounters with the smugglers. Will told of his efforts to watch them, and what he had observed on the night the dragoons attempted to arrest them.

"I understand you originally wished to join the army," Talbot said, when Will finished his recital.

"My father forbade it." Talbot already knew that, he was sure. Sir John certainly did.

"So instead you gambled, fornicated, and duelled the years away."

"I... yes." It was true, after all. "How is that relevant?"

"Such activities, if you continue, could leave you open to blackmail." Talbot leaned back in his chair and looked down his nose.

"What are you implying?" Will glanced at Sir John, but his expression gave nothing away. "Are you saying I'm—?"

"I'm saying nothing at all," Talbot replied. "Merely stating a fact. Are you sorry to be giving up that way of life now you are married?"

"That's none of your business." Will managed to keep his voice calm, in spite of his rising temper.

"Hmm." Talbot tapped his fingers on the table. Finally, he rose to his feet. "Later today I will inform you what is to happen."

Will stood too. He hadn't expected to be given a reward, but a word of thanks would have been gratifying.

"Your father is in town," Talbot went on. "You would be well advised to remain here and catch up on your sleep. Good day."

"You are welcome to remain, Wingrave," Sir John said. "Ask for anything you need." He followed Talbot out of the room.

Tregarth slipped back in as his father left.

"Well? What did they say?"

"Not a lot," Will said sourly. He couldn't work out why Talbot had asked him about his way of life, but he was too tired to think about that now. "Fancy a game of cards?"

"Sergeant Potter, my lady."

Connie looked up from her sewing as Warren ushered the visitor into the parlour. The sergeant stood by the door, hat under one arm, his red uniform spick and span.

He bowed. "Captain Burke sent me to collect Vance, my lady, and to give his thanks for looking after him."

Connie's heart sank. If the captain had come she might have been able to persuade him that she was nervous while Lord Wingrave was away, and was worried for herself in case the smugglers resented the fact that they had offered help to the wounded soldiers. Sergeant Potter would not have the authority to leave a man or two here. Should she write to the captain? No, she wouldn't be able to convey her worries convincingly in a letter, particularly as there had been no sign of trouble so far.

"Very well. You may tell Captain Burke that we were pleased to be able to help."

Potter bowed, and Warren showed him out.

She debated asking Archer to be more alert, now there was no clear reason for smugglers to stay away, but the groom was intelligent. He'd work out the implications of the removal of Vance quickly enough.

Picking up the muslin gown, she tried to concentrate on her stitches and ignore the continual questions—had Will found someone to talk to, had he been believed, when would he return?

$$\sim$$

"So how's this marriage business going?" Tregarth asked, dealing the cards.

"Well enough." Will wasn't going to admit to that promise of a month.

"Come on, Wingrave. You hated the idea, now you just say 'well enough'. Is she bracket-faced? A giggler? A bluestock—?"

"For God's sake, Tregarth. I've left her possibly at the mercy of a vicious criminal, and you—"

"Sorry, old man. Seriously, though—if you're so worried you must at least *like* her?"

"Yes, I do." More than like. "That matter I wrote…" He broke off and rubbed his forehead. What day was it today? Wednesday. It was only two days since he'd posted the letter to Tregarth about being a guardian. It probably hadn't arrived yet.

"Tregarth, how do you feel about being made guardian of any children I might have?"

"You don't need… Are you serious?"

"I am." He explained Connie's—and his—worries.

Tregarth nodded when Will's explanation came to an end. "Of course I will do it, if you wish it. Do I need to sign anything?"

"I don't know," Will admitted. "I'll get my man in Exeter to sort out the documents."

"Just don't get yourself killed before then." Tregarth laughed, and picked up his cards, sorting them out in his hand. "Your exchange."

Will closed his eyes. The guardianship didn't matter yet, nor his will—he didn't have anything of his own to leave her.

"Harry—if anything *does* happen to me, you'll make sure she's all right? Her father's as bad as mine. Either of them would use her for their own ends."

Tregarth laid his cards down. "You don't think anything *is* going to happen, do you?"

"No, not if I can help it. But I want to know she'll be safe, have someone to look after *her* interests."

"You have my word," Tregarth said.

Will let out a breath of relief. He knew he could rely on his friend, but it was good to have it confirmed all the same. "Thank you." He picked up his cards.

"That's three guineas you owe me," Tregarth said an hour later, sweeping the cards together and shuffling them again. "I can see why you decided not to top up your funds by gambling."

"I'm distracted." Will's usual ability to concentrate on the odds seemed to have deserted him; visions of Mrs Strickland's battered face, and young Danny Trasker's bruises, kept intruding. Deciding to leave Connie behind could be the most reckless thing he'd done, but it was too late to change that. "Besides, I've no stake money, and if I had there are better things to spend it on."

"Good grief, Will, marriage *has* changed you."

"Are we going to play or not?" Will did not want to start this discussion again, even though he knew his friend was only baiting him.

"Not," Tregarth said, glancing at his watch. "I said I'd meet Jolyon at his club. I'll see you later."

Left to his own devices once Tregarth had gone, Will browsed the books in Sir John's library, but nothing appealed. His comment about lack of money brought to mind his musings during the ride here about taking over the smuggling. If he did so, he could also make sure that no further treasonous transport of spies went on.

He found paper and pen, and sat down at Sir John's desk. The income would be useful, very useful, but taking over wouldn't be a simple matter. He made a list of the problems: Connie, the villagers, learning the business.

He added Marstone as an afterthought—his father would sell Ashton Tracey if it ever came out that Will had involved himself in smuggling. But he'd need to keep his involvement as secret as possible anyway; any scandal would affect Connie and their children.

Connie—she wouldn't like the idea, but he might be able to persuade her it was the only way of stopping someone else with Sandow's methods from taking over.

He leaned back in the chair. Getting the villagers to agree would have to be a matter of persuasion, too, and also tied in with learning the business. It was only Sandow and his lieutenants he needed to get rid of; there must be others who knew enough to carry on the trade.

Rubbing his face, he gave up and folded the paper into a pocket. He needed to give the matter more thought, but not when he was this tired.

What was Connie doing? Was she having problems with the injured men in the house?

Worrying would get him nowhere. He rang the bell and asked Jenkins to find him something to eat. He needed to keep his strength up for the journey home.

By mid-afternoon, with no word from Talbot or Sir John, Will had reached the stage of pacing up and down in the library. Another half hour, he told himself, glancing yet again at the clock on the mantelpiece. If they hadn't returned by then to tell him what he should do, he'd set off for home.

He paused at the sound of voices in the hall.

Sir John entered. "Were you about to leave?" he asked, eyeing the saddle bags that Will had left ready on a chair.

"Soon, if I'd had no word. I've left my wife in a dangerous situation, and I'm not going to kick my heels here much longer."

"Wait another couple of hours, Wingrave. I'm told your instructions will be here by seven."

Another couple of hours? "I could be well on my way by then, damn it."

"Riding?"

Will nodded, reluctant to admit he didn't have enough ready money for a post-chaise. He couldn't ask...

Yes, he could. It was Connie's safety he was concerned about.

"I've only enough ready cash to hire horses," he confessed. "Could I trouble you, if Tregarth doesn't return, to lend me enough—?"

"You can have a post-chaise and four, if you wait for Talbot to send word," Sir John countered. "Calm down, Wingrave. By the time I've got you the money, and you've managed to find a carriage to hire at short notice—not easy, I can tell you—Talbot's vehicle will be here."

Will took a deep breath; he hadn't thought about that. "Very well."

"Good." Sir John took some papers from a cabinet by the window. "I only returned to get these, but I'll be back with your instructions." He gazed at Will, eyes intent. "You *will* wait, won't you?"

"I give you my word, sir." He'd rather be *doing* something, but Sir John's suggestion made sense. And it would have been a wasted journey if he left before Talbot had decided what to do.

Sir John returned not long after six, bringing with him a set of folded papers.

"You are to replace the blank papers with these," he said, handing the packet to Will. "Send the man on his way as soon as you are satisfied he will survive the journey."

"Aren't you going to send someone to arrest him? And Sandow, the leader of—"

"It appears not," Sir John said, still holding out the papers. "You will have to deal with the local criminals yourself."

Will glared at Sir John, who merely lifted an eyebrow. Then he sighed—he'd spent years feeling bitter at his father for not allowing him any responsibilities; he should not now be annoyed at being given this obligation.

He took the papers and, after receiving a nod from Sir John, opened them out. They looked the same as before, as far as he could tell. Small handwriting, lists of numbers and names.

"Why are you sending—?"

"You don't need to know, Wingrave," Sir John replied.

Will's brows drew together. "I'm to trust that these are not giving away vital information, am I?"

"Yes. If it's any consolation, I have no idea whether or not those are the same papers. I trust Talbot to be acting as a patriot."

Will took a deep breath. He'd trusted Sir John by confiding in him; he had to trust his judgement about Talbot.

"The post-chaise is waiting," Sir John added.

CHAPTER 35

Thursday 10th July

Connie continued to prepare valerian tea for the spy every few hours, adding sufficient laudanum to keep him drowsy. She needed to keep Warren from realising that the man was more than a mere smuggler, but also ensure that the spy remained unaware of who *she* was. He must not realise that anyone knew about the packet he was carrying.

She longed to talk to Will about it.

No, what she really wanted was to feel the comforting pressure of his arms around her shoulders, and the relief of sharing the responsibility. But he was not here, and she was capable of managing alone.

Between visits to the spy, she tried to concentrate on her sewing.

How long would he be away? At least three days, he'd said, so she couldn't expect him back until tonight, at the earliest. It could well be longer, if he'd had trouble changing horses.

Finally she flung the fabric down. Exercise. She hadn't had any exercise for the last couple of days. She could at least walk around the house, even if Archer wasn't available to escort her further. Or she could go to the stables and find out if there was a lady's saddle in case she wanted to learn to ride once this business was over. Surely the stables were close enough to the house to be safe.

Anything but sitting here waiting.

Connie greeted the mare Will used for the chaise, rubbing her nose.

"She's called Dolly, my lady." Archer spoke from behind her. "I wanted to speak to you, but I didn't want Warren sticking his long nose in."

"Is something wrong, Archer?"

Archer glanced behind him. Stubbs was doing something with a harness on the other side of the stable yard, well out of earshot.

"It's Danny Trasker, my lady. He's here."

"Here?" Connie cleared her throat. "I mean, how did he get here?"

"Walked from Honiton. I caught him hiding in the woods, said he was keeping watch in case Sandow came. You helped his ma, he wanted to make sure nothing happened to you."

"But he's only twelve, what...?"

Well, even twenty-five-year-old husbands didn't always think things through first, but that was better not said.

"Got to admire his courage, if not his sense," Archer said.

Yes, indeed. "Sandow mustn't find out he's here. He'll get the family's whereabouts from him."

Archer shook his head. "No, my lady. He said someone's been asking about the family in Honiton, and Mr Nancarrow moved them on."

Good, Nancarrow was doing his best for them.

"Danny doesn't know where they were going," Archer added.

"Sandow might still *try*." She didn't like to imagine what he might do to the lad—Danny had already flouted him once. "Danny himself will be in danger. Can't you persuade him to go back?"

"I did try, my lady. He could be useful, though. Seems happy enough staying in the woods. I give him a tarpaulin against the rain, and some food. He'll keep an eye out for anyone coming to the house round the back."

"Thank you, Archer." The more allies they had the better, even if the latest was only a boy.

She asked about a side saddle, and waited while Stubbs and Archer hunted in the tack room and eventually unearthed one. That passed half an hour. She'd visit the spy again and then try to read for a while.

Friday 11th July

Will dismounted in the stable yard with relief. Home at last, even if it was the early hours of the morning and everyone had gone to bed hours ago. He'd left the post-chaise at the inn where Mercury had been stabled for the last few days, as he had to get his mount back to Ashton Tracey in any case. Sir John had been right to make him wait —the journey had been a couple of hours faster. He'd managed to doze a little on the way, but he still felt deathly tired.

Archer appeared as Will led Mercury into a stall, fully dressed and apparently wide awake.

"Keeping watch, Archer? Is everything all right?"

"Yes, my lord." He lowered his voice. "Soldier's gone, spy's still there, sleeping. My lady seems worried, but is safe."

"Good man."

"I'll see to Mercury, my lord."

Will thanked him, picked up his saddle bags and headed for the back of the house. He knocked on the kitchen door, pleased to find it was locked. It was several minutes before he got a response.

"Who's there?" It sounded like Mrs Curnow.

"Wingrave."

Bolts grated, and the door swung open. Will slipped in, bolting the door behind him.

"Welcome back, my lord. Was you wanting anything to eat?" Mrs Curnow was swathed in a voluminous robe.

"Some ale, if you please, then you may retire again."

Best not to surprise anyone sitting with the spy. He lit a candle, picked up the mug of ale, and went through the servants' door into the hall, sensing rather than seeing a flash of movement on the stairs.

Connie?

All he could make out in the gloom was the pale shape of her robe, waiting on the landing. His pulse accelerated as he drew closer, taking in the hair tumbling down her back, her night clothes, and her welcoming smile.

Don't read too much into it.

"Sorry to wake you," he said, resisting the impulse to drop the candle and the ale and pull her into his arms.

"I was already awake. I'm glad you're back safely, Will."

He sucked in a breath as her hand came up to touch his cheek, feeling bereft when she withdrew it again.

"What are we to do?" she asked.

"Give me a few minutes to change, and I'll tell you."

She nodded, and headed for her room. His eyes followed the sway of her hips until she closed her door, then he shook his head abruptly.

She only wants to know what's happened.

He took a pull of the ale before removing his coat, neckcloth, and boots, and splashed some water on his face. Rubbing a hand across his jaw he felt more than a day's worth of stubble, but there was nothing he could do about that now. He would make himself more presentable in the morning.

The connecting door was already open, revealing Connie sitting on her window seat, her legs tucked up under her robe. A lamp gave the room a warm glow.

Will pulled a chair over and sank into it. He should be tired, but the sight of his wife in her night clothes was taking his mind off his weariness.

"How is our spy?" he asked.

He listened carefully while Connie related the happenings of the last few days.

"You did well." *Very well.* He'd known she would cope—his worries while he'd been away had been about the threat from someone outside, not her ability to cope with the wounded men and the servants.

. . .

SAUCE FOR THE GANDER

"Thank you," Connie said. Looking back now, it didn't seem that she had done much, but his appreciation warmed her. He had done well too—riding all that way in such a short time. He must be exhausted.

"I told my story," he said. "They gave me these for the spy to take." He held out some folded papers.

She opened them out and tilted them towards the lamp light. "Are they the same?"

"They wouldn't tell me." He grimaced as he spoke.

"I suppose we don't *need* to know." She turned her attention back to the papers. "It will take me a couple of hours to replace these," she said, thinking as she spoke. "I'll have to take the packet away, and return it. I'll need to leave some time between, in case Warren gets suspicious."

"Will you stop the laudanum? We need to get rid of him as soon as we can."

"When I've put these back, I think," she replied. "Must we leave it to Warren to tell the smugglers he's ready to be moved?"

"I'll think about that in the morning." Sitting up in the chair, he rolled his shoulders.

Connie stood, crossing to the chest and placing the folded papers between the pages of one of her books. She felt his gaze following her; even in this dim light it sent a delicious shiver down her spine.

She leaned on the chest for a moment, taking in his long legs stretched out in front of him, his broad shoulders, and the shadow in the open neck of his shirt, but also the lines of fatigue on his face. She'd been tired herself, before he returned, but the pleasure of seeing him, the anticipation of what could happen between them, had dispelled that.

Would it be the same for him?

What was she thinking? The light wasn't bright, but even so Will had seen the way her eyes had moved from his face, down his body and back again. His fatigue began to drop away.

"You look as if you should be in bed," Connie said. "You must

255

be tired."

Disappointment stabbed him. He'd hoped she'd been as happy to see him as he was to see her.

He pushed himself out of the chair. She was right, of course. He did need his rest, and now was not the time to ask if she'd changed her mind. "I'll see you in the—"

"This bed, if you wish."

He was halfway through the connecting door before her softly spoken words sank in. He spun on his heel, almost losing his balance.

"Connie?"

She was between him and the lamp, its light shining through the thin fabric of her chemise and showing the outline of her body, the curve of her hips.

Chemise? She'd been wearing a robe over it.

His body came to full attention, the last traces of tiredness vanishing.

"Connie?" he said again, taking a step towards her. "What did you say?"

"I..."

He heard her indrawn breath as she wrapped her arms around her body.

"I'm sorry," she whispered. "You must be tired."

God, no. Not any more.

He took another step forwards and put one hand on her shoulder. "I'm not tired, Connie. Tell me what you want."

The lamp light no longer made her a silhouette. He resolutely kept his eyes on her face, not on the effect her deep breaths were having beneath her chemise.

"A month is a long time," she said.

"Have you changed your mind?" Hope warred with caution; he wanted her, of course, but only if she truly was willing. If she, too, *wanted* their joining.

"Yes. I mean... yes, but..." She shook her head. "I'm sorry, I'm not making sense."

He couldn't help it—he touched his hand to her hair, stroking gently, the silken feel of it making his breath catch. She closed her eyes, and he felt the tension in her relax.

"Just a kiss, if you wish?" That would take some self-control on his part, but he mustn't frighten her, not when she'd had the courage to approach him.

She stood still, then took a small step towards him, putting her hands on his shoulders and tilting her face up. He bent and brushed her lips with his own, then ran his tongue along her bottom lip.

"Open?" he requested, his voice barely a whisper.

The touch of his lips was so light it almost tickled; his breath, when he spoke, was warm on her face. She let her lips part.

The feel of his tongue in her mouth made her stiffen in surprise, even as it sent a jolt of warmth right down to her belly, and he instantly drew back.

No—she wanted more of the way he'd made her feel, more of the warmth spreading through her. She moved one hand from his shoulder to the back of his neck, then the other, pulling him closer until their bodies touched.

This time their kiss was deeper, longer, leaving her breathless and holding onto him for support as her knees threatened to buckle beneath her. He lifted his head, releasing her then taking a step back.

"Connie, if you only want a kiss, we have to stop now." His eyes glittered in the lamplight, lids half-closed. His voice sounded hoarse, his breathing as ragged as her own.

"I don't want to stop." She put her hand out, laying it on one cheek, feeling the slight scratchiness of his stubble. His throat moved as he swallowed, and she slid her hand down his neck, then to his shoulder beneath his shirt, feeling the heat from his skin, the movement of his chest as he sucked in a breath.

He reached up to the wide neck of her chemise; one hand went under it, stroking the top of her shoulder and pushing the garment down one arm.

"Time for bed?" he whispered.

CHAPTER 36

$\mathcal{W}$ill awoke to a shaft of sunlight through a gap in the curtains. Beside him, Connie slept in a curl, her back against his arm. Last night had sorely tried his control, curbing his lust, waiting until she was ready. He'd wanted to ensure she enjoyed it as much as he did.

It had been a joy to be the one to introduce her to the pleasures of the marriage bed. Unsure at first, she had soon relaxed and responded to his touch, exploring and touching him in her turn. Watching her reactions as she discovered the ways their bodies differed, and the many things they could do to give each other pleasure, had been more arousing than any of the women he'd toyed with in the past.

The sky had shown the first lightening of dawn by the time they finally turned to sleep. That could not have been long ago, for the sun was still low in the sky.

Connie would not have to see the man in the cellar for another hour or so, he thought, enjoying the way the sunlight glowed on her skin, picking out threads of gold in her hair. Turning onto his side, he raised himself on one elbow and watched what he could see of her face, stroking his hand gently down her back. She stirred, stretched, then stilled; when she turned her face to him her smile was the most beautiful thing he'd ever seen.

He knew he'd pay the price at some point, but he could think of better things to do with the next hour than sleep.

Connie reluctantly left Will in bed, dozing again, and crept into her dressing room. Although sated and relaxed in body, her mind had started to worry over the things to be done that day, and there was nothing for it but to get up and pay her usual early morning visit to the spy.

She paused as she caught sight of the yellow gown, and swallowed a lump in her throat. "Did you think about what would happen before you lay with my father?" she whispered, fingering the fabric of her mother's gown. If it hadn't been for the Fancotts, she could have been divorced, cast off completely, and until now Connie had never understood why her mother had taken such a risk. "If you loved him, I know why you did it."

Blinking away a sudden prickling of tears, she pulled on the muslin gown and pinned the front. She had things to do.

In the cellar, Warren said there'd been no change in the man's condition, and she sent the butler to get his breakfast. The spy's outer clothing was still piled in one corner, and once she had checked he was asleep, she swiftly extracted the dummy packet and tucked it up her sleeve. Then she added an extra drop of laudanum to his tea before rousing him to drink it, wanting him to still be sound asleep when she returned the papers.

"He seems a little more restless," she said to Warren when he returned. "I'll come back in an hour to see how he's getting on."

Warren nodded and settled into the chair.

In her parlour, Connie had the new papers sewn into their covering by the time she heard Barton laying out the breakfast things next door. She stowed the packet beneath the tray in her sewing box, and was tidying away the needles and thread when she heard Will's voice in the next room telling Barton he was no longer needed.

"Good morning, my lady," Will said as she entered, his smile warming her insides. He held a chair for her, then passed coffee and rolls.

Connie blushed as she took a fresh roll. Their fingers hadn't touched, but even his presence at the breakfast table had brought to mind some of the things he'd done in the night. And things she'd done.

"Have you been to see our spy?" Will asked, keeping his voice low.

"Yes." Connie took a deep breath, turning her mind back to the problems they still faced.

"We can get rid of him today, with any luck," Will said. "I'll tell Warren he's been here long enough. You could order Warren to have all the cellar rooms swept out and cleaned, ready for me to inspect tomorrow. Say I'm thinking of restocking with wine."

"So he has a reason to give for getting the spy taken away."

"Yes. I don't know who'll send the message, but as all the staff will hear about it, I'm sure someone will. Sandow doesn't know, I hope, that *I* know the spy is here. With any luck, they'll get him off to France tonight."

Connie went over his plan in her head. It was as good as anything she could think of. "May we go for a walk afterwards? I have been in the house for three days. If you are not too tired, that is."

"I..." He broke off and shook his head. "I would like to, but I don't think it is advisable."

"Sandow?"

"I'm afraid so, yes."

That was a pity; it was frustrating having to stay indoors in such lovely weather.

"We could walk around the gardens, if you wish," Will offered. "Or have a table and chairs set under the trees in the orchard and read."

"I'd like that, thank you."

"Connie, I want to go and watch again tonight, to see if there's any sign of the spy being taken away. I'd hoped to have you to myself all night." His smile made clear exactly what he was thinking of. "But I also want to see for myself that he's gone."

"Best to know he's gone," she agreed. "You won't be away *all* night, will you?" Something made her run her tongue across her lip, and his gaze became intent.

"Temptress," he muttered. "No, I definitely will *not* be out all night."
Good.

He finished his coffee, and set the cup back in the saucer. "Connie, I need to see Archer, then I'm afraid I still have the estate books to look through. It seems to take an age for each farm, there are so many years' worth." He stood and came around the table, laying one hand on her shoulder. "This business will soon be over. Don't worry." He dropped a brief kiss on her forehead, and left the room.

A proper kiss would have been better. It was probably just as well he hadn't; it would not do to return to bed so soon.

Will found Mercury munching hay, not looking any the worse for last night's long ride. Archer appeared as he stroked the animal's neck.

"Archer, come and have a look at this fetlock."

"He seemed happy enough last night, my lord," Archer said, as he hurried over. A worried frown deepened the shadows beneath his eyes.

"He is." Will lowered his voice. "I wanted to talk to you."

"Ah."

Will briefly explained what was to be done with the letters and the spy. "How will we know when the man has gone?" he asked.

Archer thought for a moment, one hand rubbing his face as he suppressed a yawn. "Danny Trasker came back, wanted to help."

"Can a child of that age help?"

"Could be handy for keeping watch, my lord. I'll have a word with him—where he's hiding, he'll see anyone going to the house."

"Good idea. Have you heard any more gossip in the village?"

"Only been to the pub once, my lord," Archer said. "Been keeping watch up here, mostly."

"Thank you, Archer. I won't forget it."

"I did hear more about Sandow," Archer continued. "He's a real nasty character. It won't do to underestimate him. The other two usually with him, Kelly and Hall, well, all the ones I spoke to reckoned Sandow was the main brains there. There ain't many people that like him, but they get a bit of extra from the smuggling, and they're frightened to cross him."

"They talked quite freely to you, did they?"

"One or two, once they were half-sprung, like, now they're used to seeing me down there."

"See if you can find out what goods are in a typical smuggling run, and how much of them. I'll give you more drinking money later. Danny—he might be able to tell you more about the villagers as well, possibly the smuggling."

"I'll ask him, my lord. The last cargo, they got it all sorted that same night, after the redcoats had gone, but Sandow was in a tearing temper."

"About the disruption?"

Archer shook his head. "They didn't know why. They've had run-ins with the preventatives before, all part of the business. Sandow don't care as long as the goods get through."

"So do you think no-one else knows about our spy? Apart from Sandow, that is."

"Likely one or two do, or they guess, but it's not common knowledge."

"Well done, Archer."

"My lord, d'you reckon they'll take the spy off tonight?"

"If they've any sense. If the spying part of Sandow's operation is a secret, they won't want a foreigner hanging around the village for too long. He's late, as well. We should go and watch, to check." Will caught the slight grimace that crossed Archer's face. "Go to bed, man, you look like you need it."

Archer nodded, giving Mercury a final pat before he left.

Will went back to stroking Mercury's neck, then found a brush and started grooming him, even though Archer had done a good job the night before. The rhythmic movement helped him to think.

To take over the smuggling, he needed to persuade the villagers to help get rid of Sandow, and then to throw in their lot with him. Demonstrating how much profit Sandow made compared to the pittance he'd passed on could help with that. Facts—he needed to know how much each run brought in, and how much the villagers made from it. He'd get Archer to find out quantities, then he could use the information he'd got from Pendrick and Nancarrow to work out the profits.

Warren was used to Connie sending him for a break when she called on the spy, so the replacement of the letters went smoothly. She stayed with the man for half an hour, and when Warren returned she passed on the order to clear the cellars.

She spent the next few hours working on her summer gown. Progress was slow, her fingers frequently stilling as memories of last night kept intruding. Will found her there in the early afternoon, and she put her sewing aside eagerly.

"Will you come out to the garden?" he asked.

A table had been set beneath one of the larger apple trees, its leafy canopy providing cool shade. A jug of lemonade and plates of sandwiches and small cakes were laid ready for them.

"This looks lovely. Thank you, Will." She sat in the chair he held for her, a feeling of lightness filling her at being able to share the beauty of the day with her husband. The man she loved.

Will passed the sandwiches, and she filled her plate. "Can we do this often?"

"By all means," Will said, the smile in his eyes making her blush. "If the spy's taken to France tonight, I want to go to Exeter tomorrow, to see Kellet about drawing up my will. Would you like to come with me?"

"Yes, please, I'd love to." Spending the day with him, *and* getting away from the house for a while—what could be better?

"I thought about taking a room at an inn for a couple of nights," he went on. "We can go about Exeter without worrying about Sandow.

You can attend a service in the cathedral on Sunday, if you wish. There are dress shops, bookshops…"

"Oh, Will, that would be wonderful." New things to see together. Away from Ashton Tracey, she might be able to forget about the smugglers for a while.

"Don't say anything to the servants, though. Just pack a bag tomorrow morning. That way no-one can give Sandow notice that we'll be on the road."

She *would* forget about it once they were away from here, if he didn't talk about it.

Will reached across the table, and took her hand in his, his thumb making small circles on her palm. "I'm sorry, Connie. I'm doing my best to keep you safe."

"I know."

"I was thinking—if I've got to be out tonight it would be as well to take a little nap now. Catch up on my sleep a little." He smiled, a wicked curve of the lips with that attractive crinkling next to his eyes. "Do you need a little lie down too?"

She felt her face heat. "Perhaps I do."

Will lay with Connie's head on his shoulder, her arm draped across his chest. A gentle breeze from the open window cooled his heated skin as his breathing slowed, his body settling into relaxed contentment.

After a while, his thoughts returned to the present. As they were returning to the house, Archer had come to report. He'd spotted two people entering the front of the house while Will had been in the orchard with Connie, then three people leaving. Will turned his head to look out of the window. The sky was taking on the purple shades of dusk, but there must still be another couple of hours before dark and the possible departure of their spy.

It suddenly struck Will that a small boat with no obvious cargo would not be seized for smuggling, even if a revenue cutter stopped it. By that argument there was nothing preventing them from putting out in daylight. He might already have missed watching it leave.

He should go now. *Damn.*

"Connie, I need to set off," he said.

"Mmm?" She opened her eyes. "Go to watch?"

"Yes, I'm afraid so."

She sighed, then raised herself on one elbow and leaned over, briefly pressing her lips against his. "Go carefully."

Will stopped abruptly at the edge of the woods, Archer almost running into him from behind. There was something different about their lookout clearing... someone was already there. As he watched, the shape melted into the shadows.

"It's only Danny, my lord," Archer said, keeping his voice low. "I thought they might take the man off right away, so I sent him up." He raised his voice a little. "Danny, it's us."

Will heard a rustle, and Danny appeared on the path in front of them.

"Nothing's gone out, Mr Archer, my lord."

"Well done, lad," Archer said. "We'll take over now. I've left more food in the usual place."

Danny nodded and trotted off into the woods.

"Thank you, Archer. I should have thought of that myself." He'd been too busy wooing his wife. He shook his head, rubbing a hand over his face. This spy business wasn't a game—he had to keep his mind on the matter at hand.

That was easier said than done, sitting here in the dusk. The crescent moon turned the breakers below into lines of lighter grey against a dark sea.

He should take Connie up to Lion Rocks one moonlit night. She'd enjoy watching the moon on the water, and he'd enjoy—

Archer nudged him, pointing to the bay down below. At first, Will couldn't make out what Archer had spotted, but finally a shadow blotted out one line of breakers, then the next.

It was a small boat, agile enough to beat away from the shore in this wind. The shape drew away, soon becoming lost against the black of the sea.

"Back," Will said, and the two men got to their feet.

Will let himself into his bedroom, leaving his coat and boots by the door and untying his neckcloth. He moved quietly, not wanting to wake Connie, and set his candle on the table beside the bed.

The room brightened and he turned. The connecting door was open now, Connie a shadow against the lamplight coming from her room.

"We saw a boat leave," he said. She must still be worried if she'd waited up to find out. "We don't *know* the spy's gone, but it's likely."

"One part of this is finished then." There was relief in her voice.

"Yes." She didn't move. "You must be sleepy," he added, "if you've waited up for me." *Say no...*

"Not too tired," she said, stepping into his room.

CHAPTER 37

Saturday 12th July

"Is this sufficient?" Will asked, hoping Connie would approve. The best bedroom in the Ship Inn had a large double bed and plenty of space for their modest luggage. A small adjoining sitting room had a table where they would be able to eat, and armchairs by the fire.

"Very nice," she said, a mischievous smile on her face as she glanced at the bed.

"Would you care for some refreshments?"

"Only if you would, Will. Can we walk about the streets a little? Even seeing so many shops is new."

"By all means."

Downstairs, he sent a note to Kellet asking for an appointment on Monday morning, and then they set off. He steered her away from Cathedral Green. "You'll have plenty of time to look around there tomorrow when the shops are closed."

Instead, they walked along the High Street, pausing to look into shop windows or to venture down side alleys if they spotted something interesting. Will smiled as she walked straight past a shop selling hats, and two with gowns in their windows, but asked if they could go into the first bookshop they came across.

"Of course. We can shop for new gowns another day."

"Another day? We have all afternoon, do we not?"

He laughed at her confusion. "Yes, but I suspect it will not be easy to extract you from a bookshop once you are inside."

She smiled, giving his arm a squeeze. "You may be right. What do you suggest?"

He guided her back to one of the dress shops, and had a quiet word with the shopkeeper about ready-made nightwear. Connie blushed delightfully when she saw the semi-transparent fabrics and lacy trim, and he noted the way she stroked the delicate fabric.

"I don't need things like this, Will, not when you have to build up the estate and—"

"There's enough for treats, Connie, trust me." He'd discuss the estate revenues when they got home; they could decide together where the money should be spent. *After* she'd bought some new clothes.

"I'd rather have some books."

Will checked that the shopkeeper was out of earshot, and bent close to her ear. "These are a present for me, Connie, not for you."

Her puzzled frown quickly changed to another blush, and without further protest she chose two of the flimsiest garments.

While he was winning, he persuaded her to choose two new hats, and picked out a shawl before insisting that he was hungry, even if she was not, and taking her to an inn for a late lunch.

"What would you like to do next?" Will asked, when Connie declined any further sandwiches or cake.

Shopping, and seemingly being allowed to buy anything she wished, was a great novelty, but the clothing he'd already bought for her seemed extravagant enough.

"Can we walk by the docks?"

"If you promise to wear one of your new chemises later." His wicked smile sent warmth shooting through her.

"Do you want to go back—?"

He shook his head. "No, Connie. Make the most of seeing the city." He reached out one hand to tuck a stray strand of hair behind her ear. "There is also the pleasure of anticipation."

He stood, and held her chair for her as she got up. "Come, let us go and invent outlandish cargoes for the ships on the wharf."

Monday 14th July

Connie regarded the shelves surrounding her with delight. So many books! The library at Ashton Tracey was fairly well stocked, but too many of the volumes were dry agricultural journals, or reports of parliamentary proceedings. This would be a treasure trove of both knowledge and novels. And Will had gone off to see Kellet, so she needn't worry about boring him while she browsed.

Nature books, she thought. She loved the wild flowers in the meadows around Ashton Tracey, but she'd never before had the chance to learn all the proper names. Perhaps a small book on birds, too, so she could carry it in a pocket when they went walking.

Yesterday had been quiet. After attending morning service in the cathedral, Will had arranged for one of the vergers to give her a guided tour. He'd followed them around, paying enough attention to ask some pertinent questions and ushering her before him with little touches. The physical contact highlighted how much things had changed since he had joined her in the cathedral at Salisbury.

"Can I help you, my lady?" An elderly man peered at her over spectacles perched on the end of his nose.

"Do you have any books on church architecture? And on ancient monuments and structures?"

Will pushed open the door to the bookshop, the bell tinkling.

"Just looking," he said, when the owner came bustling over. Connie should be in here somewhere.

This shop was a warren of small interconnected rooms, crammed with bookshelves. He'd enjoy browsing the books himself, but he was conscious that Connie had already been here for an hour while he'd been with Kellet. He walked through the shop, looking in each crowded room as he passed.

The meeting had taken longer than expected, but it was worth waiting while Kellet drafted the document he needed. His Last Will and Testament, signed and witnessed, was now lodged with Kellet, along with instructions to contact the Tregarths if anything happened to him. Getting rid of Sandow was still his priority, but at least now Connie's future was more secure if something went wrong.

He found her in the fifth room he tried, smiling as he saw that she did indeed have her nose in a book. She didn't stir as he approached.

"Ah, there you are," he said.

She gasped, almost dropping the book. "Sorry, I was reading."

"No, really?" He eyed the small pile of books on the floor by her feet. "Is that all you've chosen?"

"It will do for today," she said, smiling, but with one brow raised.

Good, she had stopped apologising for spending money.

"I've finished my business with Kellet," he said. "I have one more appointment, when you have finished here." He bent as he spoke, and picked up the books from the floor.

She looked doubtfully at the book she was holding, so he took it from her, and added it to the pile.

"Where are we going?" she asked, as he offered her his arm and they set off down the street.

"In here." He stopped outside the shop where he'd bought those chemises for her on Saturday. He opened the door and ushered her in.

"I've got enough gowns," she said, although she could not help staring longingly at the rich colours and delicate patterns of the fabrics on display. "I suppose they are out of fashion, though."

"I'm only buying what your father should have given you before we were married," Will said.

"Don't you need the money for the estate?" She kept her voice low, conscious of the shopkeeper standing not far away.

"If you carry on arguing, I'll go through the estate accounts in detail with you when we get home," he whispered back.

"Thank you, I'll enjoy that." She bit her lips as she watched the surprise on his face, his laugh.

"I'll hold you to that," he said. "Now, I've arranged for you to be measured and to choose some fabrics and styles. Mrs Walker will get the gowns part done, then bring them to Ashton Tracey for fitting."

She capitulated—it would be lovely to have new clothing. "Thank you."

"This would look good on you," Will said, fingering a pink satin with sprays of tiny roses embroidered on it. He moved onto bolts of kerseymere in darker colours, touching a rich blue. "This for a riding dress."

Connie had a vision of herself galloping along the cliff-tops, the dark blue skirts of her habit flying in the wind, Will galloping beside her.

"And at least two more gowns, Connie," Will continued. "I'll wait to make sure you don't limit yourself to the cheapest fabrics."

Connie, her mouth already open to protest, closed it again. All the penny-pinching she'd needed in her father's house had become more entrenched than she had realised.

An hour later they had ordered a riding habit, a robe à la française in the rose silk, a dark green redingote, and three open robes of printed cotton, with the underdresses to go with them. Connie had never owned so many garments, let alone having six new ones at once.

"I'm afraid we should set off for home now." Will looked up. The earlier wispy clouds were thickening to sheets of light grey.

"I've had a lovely time, Will, thank you."

He patted her hand where it rested on his arm. "My pleasure, my lady."

Connie watched Will's face as he drove, taking in his concentration as he passed a slow-moving cart on a narrow stretch of road and recalling the feel of those lips on her body.

It wasn't the books safely tucked into a box behind them, or the prospect of new gowns, that fed the happiness she felt; it was the time she'd spent with Will. Their intimacy was part of it, but so was the way they talked together, laughed together. It had all been so... so ordinary. The sort of things that happily married couples might do. Couples who loved each other. She loved him; she hoped he was coming to love her.

"Will, can we do this again sometime?"

His smile as he looked at her warmed her heart. "I think that next time we should go to Salisbury. You can see Stonehenge."

"Yes, please!" She felt a warm glow of pleasure that he'd remembered.

Will noticed a man digging in the formal gardens as they approached the house. He stood as the chaise approached, seeming to inspect both Will and Connie, before touching his hat and resuming his work.

Will helped Connie down by the front door, and drove on round to the stables. Archer, waiting for him, started to back the chaise into the coach house.

"Them men Mr Nancarrow sent came on Saturday," he said. "Tanner and Neilson."

"I saw one of them in the front garden," Will replied.

"That'd be Tanner. Mr Nancarrow told them what they were wanted for."

"Do they seem reliable to you?"

"Me, my lord?" Archer's brows rose. "I... er... as far as I can tell. They don't say much."

"Did you tell them not to speak about why they're here?"

"Yes, my lord, like you said. But don't you want to put off Sandow and his gang from...?" He paused, his hands still on the harness.

"What are you thinking?" Will asked, curious to see if the groom had come to the same conclusion as he had.

"Hiring guards tells folks you've got something to hide."

"Go on," Will said.

"People in the village might wonder why we've brought them in, and Sandow might guess we know more than he thinks."

"That's what I was thinking, yes. So we'll continue to let people think they are just extra gardeners." Will took the bridle while Archer sorted out the rest of the harness. "I'll probably be riding around the farms again in the next few days, but not with Lady Wingrave. Make sure they know to report to you in my absence. Send word if they question your orders."

"I... Yes, my lord."

Will hoped he wasn't giving Archer too much responsibility, but he'd proven himself trustworthy and intelligent so far.

Unfortunately Connie would need to confine herself to the house and gardens for the next few days. He doubted Sandow would try to kill him outright as retaliation for sending the Traskers away. Killing a member of the aristocracy would draw more attention to his operations than the fight with the revenue men. A warning of some kind was more likely, and he'd be safe enough himself if Sandow accosted him. Mounted on Mercury, he could outride any attackers, and he'd take his pistols with him.

He needn't spend all his time on the farms. He'd give Connie the estate accounts, and let her see what she made of them—she wouldn't need his help. Spending some time not doing anything constructive would be enjoyable too.

CHAPTER 38

Wednesday 16th July

Connie slipped the gown on and fastened the front, then stood before the mirror turning to and fro. Not a bad day's work, she thought, smoothing the skirts. Mrs Trasker could have sewn the hem a little more evenly, perhaps, but she doubted anyone would notice a few imperfections. It was only a summer gown for home use, and would do until her new gowns were ready.

"Very nice." Will's voice came from behind her, making her jump.

She twirled, letting him take in her handiwork.

"It suits you well," he added, "although I prefer you without it."

She answered the gleam in his eye with a smile. "Later. How was Knap Farm?"

"I'll tell you over tea."

In the parlour, Connie sipped tea and ate Mrs Curnow's apple cake, listening to Will's account of his morning's trip. After spending much of yesterday at two of the more distant farms, and today's visits, his tour of the estate must be nearly over.

"…good condition, not much to do there. Mrs Knap asked if I'd bring you along next time, although that will have to wait until…"

Connie heard hoof beats and the crunch of wheels on gravel as Will's words tailed off. They crossed to the window to see a post chaise and four pulling up at the bottom of the steps. Two men alighted and stood looking up at the house.

"Tregarth!" Will put his cup down and hurried into the hall.

Connie watched as Barton helped the servant riding at the back of the carriage to unload a couple of valises. Then she checked her hair in the glass over the fireplace, smoothed her gown, and went to greet Will's friend.

"Tregarth. Sir John." Will looked in her direction, encouraging her forward with a smile and a turn of his head. "Gentlemen, may I introduce Lady Wingrave? Connie, my good friend Harry Tregarth, and his father, Sir John."

She dipped a small curtsey, and held out one hand, regarding them with interest. These men would have her future in their hands if anything should happen to Will.

"My lady." Harry Tregarth bowed over her hand. "I am pleased to meet you." His smile was friendly.

"Lady Wingrave." Sir John's gaze was more assessing than his son's. "My apologies for giving you no notice of our visit."

"You are welcome, Sir John." It was too soon to judge, but her initial impressions of them both were promising.

"Are you staying?" Will asked.

"For tonight, at least, if we may," Sir John replied.

"You are welcome, for as long as you wish," Will said. "Warren, refreshments in the library, if you please."

"I will see to the arrangements." Connie knew that it would be up to her to organise rooms, and ensure that dinner was suitable for their guests—her first test as hostess.

"Please join us when you are able, my lady," Will added, the warmth in his eyes lightening his formal words.

Will ushered their guests down the corridor, and Connie went to consult Mrs Curnow.

The cook, after muttering curses at men with no consideration for them as had to provide extra food at only a couple of hours' notice, set to work with a will. Connie took one of the maids with her to help prepare two of the guest rooms.

Will sent Warren away once he'd served the drinks. "What brings you here, Sir John? You made no mention of visiting when I saw you last."

"My visit was a possibility when we last met, not a certainty."

"I was going to visit anyway," Harry Tregarth said. "Apart from anything else, it was time I saw this new wife of yours. Looks like you've done well there."

"I think so." Tregarth could be teasing, but Will chose to take his friend's words at face value. "Did you have a good journey?"

"Not bad, spent a couple of nights on the road. Stopped at the Golden Lion in Shaftesbury last night. Ever been there?"

Will shook his head. "The George and Dragon's better. Good ale."

"No, no…"

Will saw Sir John roll his eyes and get up to browse the book-shelves as Tregarth launched into a comparison of coaching inns he'd patronised recently. Sir John must have come in connection with the spy, but now wasn't the time to discuss that so Will let Tregarth rattle on.

They broke off as the door opened, and all three rose to their feet as Connie entered.

"Sir John, Mr Tregarth, your rooms are prepared should you wish to use them. Dinner will be ready at five."

"Thank you, my lady, for accommodating us so readily."

Will smiled as their two guests left the room. "That was quick work, thank you. Has Mrs Curnow calmed down?"

She gave a little gurgle of laughter. "I think so. Dinner won't be a grand affair, I'm afraid."

Will shrugged. "No matter. Tregarth is happy with whatever is put before him and Sir John… well, if he wanted a formal dinner he should have given us some notice." He took a deep breath. "Connie, Sir John's visit must be something to do with the spy."

"I assumed so," she said. "It is Mr Tregarth who is your close friend, not his father." She brushed her hands down her skirts, and Will noticed traces of dust. "If you'll excuse me, I'll change my gown. The guest rooms were not as dust-free as they should have been."

Hoping she'd done the right thing, Connie had asked Barton to set four places at one end of the long table in the formal dining room. She was relieved to see Will nod in approval when he saw it. He held a chair for her before seating himself opposite.

In spite of Mrs Curnow's mutterings, the cook had managed to produce dishes sweet and savoury, and Warren had chosen what Connie hoped was an appropriate selection of wines from their limited stock.

"How do you like the house, Lady Wingrave?" Tregarth, beside her, spoke with a kindly smile.

"Very much, Mr Tregarth."

"It is rather smaller than Marstone Park."

Connie wondered if this was a criticism, but Tregarth had a twinkle in his eye.

"I always preferred this place when I was invited to spend summer holidays with Will," Tregarth continued. "He wasn't Wingrave then, of course."

"You must visit whenever you wish, Mr Tregarth." Will would enjoy his company, and she rather thought she would, too.

"Yes, do," Will urged from across the table. "We don't stand on ceremony here." He looked towards Warren, standing by the doorway. "Warren, please set out the port on the sideboard and leave us."

Connie heard the clink of bottles and glassware behind her, then the door closed behind the butler.

"So, Sir John, what brings you to Devonshire?" Will asked.

Not the most subtle way Will could have broached the subject, Connie thought, but she too was curious about Sir John's mission.

Sir John glanced at Connie, then took a sip from his wine glass.

"It's a lovely part of the country, Wingrave. Harry wanted to come to see how you were."

"Sir John." Will's voice was calm, but Connie could see annoyance in the tightness of his jaw. Connie's own irritation rose—it seemed Sir John did not trust her.

"I explained how I came into possession of the papers," Will said. "Do you not think that the person who was responsible for both discovering them and replacing them...?"

Sir John's lips twisted into a wry smile as Will's words tailed off. "Very well, Wingrave, if you wish it. I imagine you would relate everything to your wife afterwards in any case."

Connie hoped he would, and Will's nod confirmed it. Her glance flicked to Harry Tregarth, sitting beside her. He must already be in his father's confidence.

"Talbot... Have you been told about Talbot, Lady Wingrave?"

"Yes."

"Good. As I understand it, Talbot always makes use of the best people he can get. Note the word 'people', not 'men'."

Connie relaxed. She had no idea what role she could play in Sir John's, or Talbot's, affairs, but it was satisfying to be included in the discussion.

"First, I have been authorised to tell you—both of you—that the message you found was very valuable. Talbot's department wasn't aware that information of such a nature was being sent to our enemies. He sends his thanks. I am only a messenger here, you understand. These matters are beyond my responsibility in government, nor do I wish to become involved further. However, as you had already spoken to me, and as Harry is known as a friend of yours, Talbot decided that sending me was better than calling on you himself, or summoning you back to London."

Will's eyes met hers, one brow rising. Talking of summoning implied they could make Will obey.

"The thing is, Wingrave," Sir John went on, "Talbot has some idea who may have been responsible, but does not have sufficient information to deal with him, or to know if he is the only one. That is one reason why the papers were returned to be sent on their way. There will, no doubt, be others, and you are in a unique position here to intercept them."

"I discovered those papers purely by chance, Sir John." Connie resisted the temptation to say more, wondering if she had been wrong to interrupt.

"I know." Sir John nodded at her, seeming to have taken no offence. "But Talbot is of the opinion that if you allow the smugglers to use your cellars, one of your men may be able to intercept any further messages."

"How could...? I mean, we cannot plan on the next man being shot," Will said.

"There are ways, Wingrave, but we can go into those later, if you accept Talbot's proposition."

That sounded as if it would involve more than merely letting smugglers use the cellars.

"Go on, Sir John." Will was toying with his wine glass, his interest palpable and the food on his plate forgotten.

"Initially, you would intercept messages, copy them, and send them on."

Initially? "This is not only to identify the traitor, then, is it?" Connie asked.

"Talbot may allow him to continue, my lady, but control what he knows."

"Or send misinformation," Will suggested.

"Possibly, yes. You will not be concerned with the content of the communications, however."

That was just as well. Remembering who knew what about the local smugglers was bad enough; she'd hate to have to keep track of something that could affect the nation's affairs. Whether she wanted to be involved at all was something she'd think about later.

"Misinformation would be discovered eventually, would it not?" Will asked.

"Undoubtedly. However, Talbot may wish to have his own men transported to the continent as well."

"Why here, sir?" Tregarth asked. "Why wouldn't whoever he is send his messages from the Kent or Sussex coast? Much closer to London."

Sir John speared a piece of pie with his fork. "We don't know who he is, Harry. How can we know his reasoning?"

"Then why would Talbot want to use Ashmouth for his own spies, once the traitor has been dealt with?" Will persevered.

"You tell me, Wingrave," Sir John replied. "Excellent pie, this, Lady Wingrave. My compliments to your cook."

Connie had to smile at the irritation on Will's face. It was a good question, though. It had taken Will over a day and a night to reach London, with no stops. It would take at least two days travelling normally, and more in winter. "How long does it take a boat to sail from Devonshire to Kent?"

"It depends on the wind, Lady Wingrave," Tregarth said. "With a westerly wind, possibly similar to the time it takes to ride from here to London."

"I've heard it can take a week or more if the wind's in the wrong direction," Will added. "If the spies have sailed from Brest, or somewhere further south, landing them here rather than the Kent coast could make some journeys quicker."

Using Ashmouth made some sense, then. Not all spies would be going to or from Paris, particularly if Will's guess was correct and the information was intended for the colonies.

"Talbot reasoned something like that," Sir John explained. "Although it is also possible that our traitor lives somewhere near here and just used the smugglers he'd been buying brandy from. And before you ask, Wingrave, I don't know who Talbot suspects."

And probably wouldn't tell them if he did know.

"Well, what do you think, Wingrave?"

Will would want to accept, she was sure. He'd been thwarted in his wish to join the army; this would allow him to do something for their country.

"I will let you know our decision in the morning, Sir John," Will said. He met Connie's eyes, one brow raised, and she smiled, pleased that he had decided to consult her.

"More wine, Sir John?"

CHAPTER 39

*W*ill set the port and glasses on the table. "If you will excuse us, Sir John, Tregarth, we will leave you now. Do make use of the library if you wish."

Shadows were lengthening in the early evening sun, but there was still time to walk in the gardens with Connie. He offered his arm, and they went out onto the terrace, to one of the benches overlooking the parkland. They sat, leaving enough space between them to half turn and face each other.

"You want to do this, don't you?" Connie's expression was hard to read—not outright disapproval, at least.

"It's useful, Connie." A duty, almost, now the task had been offered. It was also more of a challenge than farming. He was enjoying putting the estate in order, but there would be little to do once it was running efficiently.

"Will, I... I was pleased to be given Sir John's confidence, and it *does* feel right to help, if we can. But how safe will it be?"

Will took her hand. "Connie, when this turns into only transporting Talbot's men, it won't be difficult or dangerous at all for us. For the first part—intercepting messages—the danger isn't from the spies."

"Sandow?"

"Yes." He ran a hand through his hair. "The only way to reliably know when a messenger is being carried is if I, or someone I trust, is running the smuggling. I've been finding out about the way it works, and Sandow is cheating the villagers. I could take over."

Her eyes narrowed. "Have you already been thinking about doing that?"

"Sandow has to be got rid of, Connie, you agreed to that."

"That doesn't mean you have to run it." She sighed. "I suppose what Sir John is asking you to do *is* a good reason."

"If I get rid of Sandow, someone else will become the leader, and may be just as bad as him. If I take over, I can try to run it without the violence."

"*Try* to run it without violence? That isn't good enough, Will."

"Connie, I will *not* use Sandow's methods. I'm not sure yet exactly how to go about it, but I'm working on it."

Connie met his gaze for a long moment. "Very well."

"It may involve some bribery," he added. "I can't explain to preventatives like Sullivan what we are about. Better that than another battle where men could get killed." He hated to admit it even to himself, but this proposition gave him a legitimate excuse for something he'd been thinking about doing anyway.

She nodded wordlessly, her gaze on the lowering sun. It was a lot to take in for one evening; he should give her some time.

"Connie, do you want me to leave you to think? I said we'd give Sir John our answer in the morning."

"I would like some time to consider, yes. But Will, if I say no, will you really give up the idea?"

"I would try to persuade you to change your mind," he admitted. "But this is our home—I will not do it if you do not agree." He stood. "I'll join the others."

Alone on the terrace, Connie watched the sun set, turning the sky from dusky blue through pink to purple. It reminded her of summer evenings in the vicarage garden, snatched when her father was away from home. She'd always wished for a loving family, like the Fancotts, but now she realised she'd thought little beyond that bare statement. Mr and Mrs Fancott both had their own goals in life, in addition to bringing up their children and, now, doting on their grandchildren. In their case, it was looking after their parishioners.

Will had a purpose now, in improving the farms, and hopefully in helping her to bring up their children when they came. But once the improvements were made there would not be enough to do to keep him busy. For a man with a taste for adventure, running the estate and bringing up a family would not suffice. He'd need something more; something like this offer of Talbot's.

Her initial reaction had been to refuse; it was too risky. But the current peril was from Sandow. Messengers going to and fro, doing their best to remain unnoticeable—would they really cause additional danger?

This new life was still a little strange to her, but when she'd settled into it properly she would need a purpose of her own, in addition to family. She would never have chosen to be part of his espionage project, but Will needed it as well as wanting it. Her role could be to make sure he considered the welfare of others involved—the villagers, and the servants here at Ashton Tracey. It would be *his* project, but she would encourage him, help him when she could, and accept that it was part of who he was—of who *they* were.

Martha had said it would be well. Connie smiled as she returned indoors. Her friend could never have imagined this.

Connie gently moved Will's arm from her waist and got out of bed. Moving quietly, she pulled on a chemise and robe and sat in the window seat listening to the sounds of the night.

Their lovemaking had been as good as before—better, really, now some of her shyness had gone. She had lost herself in the sensations, the joy of giving pleasure as well as receiving it. Now, though, she envied Will's ability to sleep. Her mind would not rest, turning over the implications of the proposition Sir John had presented.

It would not—could not—be a secret known only to the two of them. The villagers would not be comfortable dealing directly with Will, so that meant someone else would have to be directly involved. Archer, probably.

All the villagers would know. About Archer, at least, and by inference that Will was involved in some way. And if the villagers knew, then all the staff at Ashton Tracey would know too.

"Connie?" Will sat up in the bed, little more than a pale shape in the moonlight.

"I couldn't sleep," she said, pulling her robe tighter around her body.

He threw the sheet back and came over to her, pushing his arms into the sleeves of his banyan. She moved to one end of the window seat, and Will sat down next to her.

"Are you thinking about Sir John's proposition?"

"Yes." She had yet to give him her answer, and now she had more questions. "Will, they want you… us… to do this for a long time. Do you trust your father not to change his mind and sell the place?"

"No, I do not."

"He will find out, about the smuggling at least."

"Not if we're careful."

Connie shook her head. "You can get rid of Mrs Strickland, but she would go straight to your father. If you keep her, eventually Archer will miss a letter from her, or she'll give it to someone else to take to the post. We don't know yet whether anyone else here is in your father's pay, either. Would he regard smuggling as breaking your agreement?"

"Undoubtedly." It was something that had been at the back of Will's mind since the discussion at the dinner table. Trust Connie to have thought of it too.

He put out a hand to stroke her hair. "We'll make a good team, Connie."

He couldn't make out her expression in the dim light, but he heard her sigh.

"Will, I accept that you want... need... to do this, but I don't want you to lose Ashton Tracey over it. That would end your usefulness to Talbot. And you only married me because your father threatened to sell—"

"Connie, stop!"

He shuffled closer, and took her hand. "That was part of the reason, yes. But I realised it was time I settled down. I also did it for my sisters, in a way."

"Your sisters?"

Damn this moonlight; he couldn't see what she was thinking. "My father will arrange their marriages as he did mine. I don't intend to let them be married off to someone they do not care for, and I can do that better with you to help me guide them through society."

"I don't know anything about society." Her words were slow, doubtful.

"Don't worry about that now, Connie. The point I am trying to make is that Ashton Tracey was not the sole reason. And all those reasons are irrelevant now that I know you." He put one arm around her shoulders, feeling the tension in her body. "I would not go back and undo this marriage, Connie."

She relaxed a little.

"Come back to bed," he whispered in her ear.

"Don't try to distract me, Will." She pulled away.

You distract me, woman. He bit his lip against the impulse to say the words.

"I'm not trying to distract you, Connie. I had been thinking the same thing. I have an idea, but I need to think it through first." He put out one hand again. "Come to bed. Just to sleep, if that's what you wish, but I like the feel of you beside me."

She was still for a moment, but then put her hand in his and allowed him to pull her to her feet.

CHAPTER 40

Thursday 17th July

Will and Connie met Sir John in the library before breakfast.

"I take it that your Mr Talbot is not offering payment for my services," Will said, getting straight to the point.

Sir John inclined his head. "Correct. It is assumed that the satisfaction of serving our country is sufficient for men—and women—of our station."

"You are aware, I think, that Ashton Tracey belongs to my father, not to me?"

"I am, yes."

"And that my father has threatened to sell it if I break certain conditions?"

"Yes. Talbot had some enquiries made before deciding on this proposal," Sir John replied. "Reasonable, under the circumstances, I think."

It was, Will had to admit. "The point is that my residence here could be terminated with little notice. Unless, that is, you or Talbot are prepared to lend me enough money to buy the place."

"Go on," Sir John urged.

"It would require some subterfuge," Will continued, "but that should not be an impediment, given the business you are recruiting us for."

"Agreed."

"My idea is that you, or Talbot, agree to sell Ashton Tracey to me if it comes into your possession. One of us can arrange for news to reach my father that I have broken his conditions, at which time he will probably be happy to sell the place at a bargain price to anyone who shows an interest."

"That could work, I suppose." Sir John appeared to be mulling over the suggestion. "And the loan you require would be for this agreed sum—how do you intend to replay it?"

That was the sticky point in Will's plan. "It will naturally be a loan on very favourable terms," he replied. "Low interest, over a long term. The estate revenues will be sufficient to start repayments in a few years, but I should be able to make some profit from the smuggling required by your proposition."

Sir John met his gaze. "I have enough authority to agree to that. Do you accept Talbot's proposition, then?"

Will looked at Connie, wondering what she thought of the idea now. She turned her head towards the window.

"I will discuss it with Lady Wingrave," Will said. "Will you excuse us?"

Once they were alone on the terrace, Connie turned to him. "Will, if Talbot holds the mortgage on this place, he could foreclose at any time and you would be forced to sell. How is that different from being under your father's thumb?"

"I have to assume that Talbot would only make such a decision after rational reflection, not in a fit of pique because he imagines I've flouted some arbitrary decree of his."

She nodded, that thoughtful crease on her brow again. "And I suppose knowing some of his business means you have some hold over him, if things go sour."

"I'm not too sure of that, Connie, given the kind of business Talbot is in. I don't think threatening to disclose his secrets would be a good idea, for us or for the country. I don't know him, but Sir John does, so I have to trust Sir John's judgement in this."

"He won't ask you to do anything else, will he? I mean, could he ask you to become a spy yourself?"

Will smiled, almost laughed.

"I wasn't trying to be amusing." Her voice was sharp.

"I'm sorry, Connie, but it was the idea of me being cool-headed enough to do such a thing." He took a deep breath. "I give you my word not to agree to that, should he ever ask. Will that do?"

Her face softened and she smiled. "Very well."

"Thank you. It would be wise to get something in writing, about the mortgage at least, but we can go into Exeter this morning. Now shall we have breakfast and give Sir John our answer?"

Connie elected not to accompany Will and the Tregarths into Exeter. The cool breeze and thickening clouds reinforced her decision— several hours in the chaise would not be pleasant if it rained.

She started by going over the menus for the coming week with Mrs Curnow, before deciding she needed to confront the house-keeper. Although she'd been glad of the woman's absence at first, it was time she resumed her duties—and performed them properly.

Connie tapped on the door to Mrs Strickland's office.

"Come in, Mary!"

Connie pushed open the door. Mrs Strickland sat at the desk at one side of the room, a pen in her hand.

"What took you so long, girl? I sent for—" Her mouth shut with a snap as she faced Connie, and she hastily turned over the sheet of paper she'd been writing on.

Another letter to the earl?

Connie waited, keeping her gaze on the housekeeper. Mistaking who was knocking was understandable; not apologising for the mistake was insolent.

"I... I'm sorry my lady. I asked that girl to... to come..."

"Never mind, Mrs Strickland." Connie noted the walking stick leaning on the wall by the door. "I'm pleased to see you can get around without your stick now. I think it is time you resumed your duties."

"I... er, yes, if you wish it, my lady."

"Good. I wish you to help the maids clean the two guest rooms used last night. Sir John and his son may not have noticed, but there was far too much dust around, and the windows had not been cleaned in an age. Even rooms under holland covers need some attention."

The housekeeper's lips thinned. "I will see they do a proper job, my lady. If I had been—"

"You misunderstand, Mrs Strickland. We are short staffed, you will *help* them."

The woman finally got to her feet—as she should have done when Connie walked in. "I am a housekeeper, my lady, not—"

"And I am Lady Wingrave, and your employer. *I* had to assist the maids in preparing the guest rooms yesterday."

A red flush appeared on Mrs Strickland's face, but she said nothing more, only giving a curt nod.

Connie turned to leave, almost colliding with the little scullery maid as she dashed into the room.

"Oh, sorry my lady!" The girl's eyes were wide, her mouth round in surprise.

"No matter, Mary. Carry on."

Connie retreated to the parlour, not entirely satisfied with the confrontation, but feeling that she had, at least, come out the winner. It was petty, perhaps, but if she was prepared to help out, there was no reason for the housekeeper to refuse. Even Warren was looking after Will's clothing.

Will—it would be several hours before he returned from Exeter, even if his solicitor could see him straight away. She would write to Martha again, and then go over the household accounts. Once Will had dealt with Sandow, they could take on more staff, and she should start planning for that.

Will watched Kellet's brows rise as he explained the document he wished the solicitor to draw up.

"Most unusual," Kellet said, when Will had finished. "To summarise, you wish me to draw up a mortgage agreement for an undisclosed sum, with a Mr Talbot, using an estate you do not own as security. Is that correct?"

"Yes. To expedite the sale of Ashton Tracey to me, should it come into Talbot's possession. Naturally the document will not be used while the estate still belongs to my father."

"Very well. Can you call back in half an hour?"

"Some refreshments while we wait, gentlemen?" Will asked, once he was outside Kellet's office. The Tregarths accepted.

"This business of getting my father to sell Ashton Tracey..." Will began, as they sat with mugs of ale and dishes of sliced beef and braised vegetables before them. "I'd like to get it over with as soon as possible."

"Did you know Elberton is divorcing his wife?" Harry asked. "We could start a rumour that she's been to see you."

"I did know, yes" Will said. "She's already visited."

"What did your wife have to say about that, Wingrave?" Sir John asked, a forkful of beef halted in mid air.

What business is it of yours?

"Not much. She came while I was out. Connie sent her away with a flea in her ear."

Harry snorted. "I'd like to have seen that."

Sir John ignored his son's comment. "Wingrave, if you have any other secrets, best tell your wife sooner rather than later."

"A man with secrets is susceptible to blackmail. Is that what you mean?" Will asked. "Talbot said that." And he'd already told Connie all his secrets.

"And it is still true," Sir John said. "But in this instance it is advice from a married man. Telling them before they find out for themselves is always the wisest course. Assuming you care what your wife thinks, that is."

"What do you mean by—?"

"Nothing at all, Wingrave. Some men do, some men don't." Sir John pointed his fork at Will. "And some men are too ready to see criticism when it isn't meant."

Will pressed his lips together, the amused curl of Tregarth's mouth not lightening his mood. Sir John hadn't said anything that wasn't true. He took a deep breath. "Thank you for your advice, Sir John, I will endeavour to follow it."

Sir John regarded him with narrowed eyes for a moment, then smiled. "When you grow up, Wingrave, you could be an asset to the government. We need more people interested in the good of the country, not men intent on lining their own pockets. Now, have some more beef, it's excellent."

Will helped himself, not sure whether he'd just been complimented or insulted.

At a sound from the next room, Connie looked up from the seam she was unpicking. A footstep. It wasn't Warren's measured tread—was Will back already? She hadn't heard hoofbeats from the drive.

She jumped to her feet as a man appeared in the doorway, his piercing eyes fixed on her face. She'd seen him before somewhere, in Ashmouth perhaps? He wasn't tall, or broad, but the measured way he closed the door and walked towards her exuded menace.

"Who are you? What do you want?" Her voice rose in pitch as she spoke and she stepped backwards.

Sandow?

She took a deep breath to scream for help, but he closed the remaining space between them, pushing her back against the wall with one hand over her mouth. She flinched, heart racing, trying to turn her head away, but his fingers pinched hard into her cheeks.

Metal flashed before her eyes. A knife.

"Make a sound, and I'll use this," he threatened, his voice still quiet.

She nodded as best she could, and the pressure of his hand relaxed a little. His face drew closer.

"I want that milksop husband of yours to keep his nose out of my business." His quiet voice was more frightening than shouting would have been. "He sent Jenny Trasker away. He crosses me again, on *anything*, and I'll have you instead of her, whatever he thinks."

He let go abruptly, and her knees almost gave way. A sudden tug on her scalp, a flash of the knife, and he held a lock of her hair in one hand.

"This is the only warning you'll get. Next time it'll be your nose, or your throat."

Connie hardly breathed as he crossed the room to a window, then she slid down the wall to sit with her arms wrapped around her knees, shaking.

CHAPTER 41

*W*ill handed Mercury to Stubbs in the stable yard, pleased to have made it home before the rain started. Warren took his hat and coat in the hall.

"Lady Wingrave?" Will asked.

"She was in the parlour earlier, my lord."

Connie wasn't in the main parlour, so he crossed to the door of her sewing room. As he opened the door, a cool gust of air hit him; one window was wide open, the curtains blowing in the breeze. Will strode across the room and slammed the window shut.

"Will?"

He turned, seeing Connie's white face rising from behind a chair, her eyes wide.

"Oh, Will!"

He dropped his satchel of documents and rushed over as she moved towards him and stepped into his arms. "Connie, what is wrong?" He pulled her close, feeling her rapid breaths.

"He came. Here." Her voice was muffled against his waistcoat.

"Who came, Connie?"

"He… he didn't say his name, but it m…must have been S…Sandow."

"Sandow, here? Connie, are you hurt?" He held her away from him so he could see. "Did he lay a finger on you?" Good God, what might he have come back to? A beating—or worse?

She closed her eyes, her chest rising as she took a deep breath. "I'm not hurt. Just frightened."

"Thank God." He wrapped his arms around her again, feeling the tension in her slowly ease. "I shouldn't have left you here alone, Connie," he said into her hair. "I'm so sorry."

It was his job, his role, to protect her, and he'd failed. "Connie, what exactly happened? *When* did this happen?"

"Only a few minutes ago. He went out of the window."

Hell—if he'd been a few minutes earlier he could have caught the bastard.

"He..." She swallowed, and when she spoke again her voice was steadier. "He said if you don't stop interfering in his business, he'll use the knife on my face next time."

"Next time?" He slackened his embrace, putting one hand beneath her chin so she looked into his eyes. "Did he hurt you?"

"He cut off a piece of my hair."

"Damn him." Will strode to the window and pushed up the sash, leaning out to scan the parkland beyond. Sandow was long gone, of course.

Wait—someone was moving near the trees. Will had one leg over the windowsill when he felt a tug on his arm.

"Will, what are you doing?"

"Someone's out there. Let me go, Connie, I'll catch the bastard—"

"And he'll stick his knife into you." She did not relax her grip on his arm as she moved to stand beside him. "That's not him. Too small, and he's coming this way. It looks like Danny."

She was right, of course. Hopefully he would have come to his senses before catching up with Sandow, but going off half-cocked would only get him injured or killed.

"How did he get in, with the new gardeners keeping a lookout? Warren should have been keeping his eyes open too, and Archer." They couldn't *all* be in league with Sandow.

He'd been talking to himself, but Connie answered. "I don't know, but we need to ask some questions."

"You should go to your room, Connie, rest. You've had a shock."

She shook her head. "No, Will. I need to *do* something, not lie there alone and relive it."

Connie sat at the kitchen table, the shaky feeling in her legs gradually subsiding. Will sent Barton to summon the gardeners and stable hands to the kitchens, and Warren to fetch the indoor staff. He sat beside her, one comforting arm around her shoulders and pulling her towards him. Mrs Curnow took a seat, and soon Barton, Mrs Strickland, and the two maids joined them.

At Will's command, Warren set a small glass of brandy in front of Connie, but she only took a small sip, coughing as it stung the back of her throat. Sandow's visit had been terrifying enough, but once he had gone her main fear had been that Will would do something stupid and get himself badly injured, or even killed. That danger seemed to have passed, thankfully.

"My lord!" Danny burst into the room, gasping for breath, his gaze moving from Will to Connie.

"Danny, we're all safe," Connie said.

"I seen him. Sandow, I mean. I'm sorry, I couldn't come and warn you, he was..." The boy gulped, looking close to tears. "I was too frightened to—"

"Danny, you couldn't have stopped him." Will stood up and put a hand on the lad's shoulder. Danny stared at him, then nodded. Looking at the servants, Connie saw puzzlement on all faces. Except, perhaps, on Mrs Strickland's.

Was her confrontation with the housekeeper this morning the reason for Sandow's visit this afternoon?

Clumping footsteps heralded the arrival of Stubbs, Archer, Yatton, and the two new gardeners—the men who were supposed to be keeping watch.

Why hadn't they spotted Sandow?

Will turned to Connie. "Can you explain what happened?"

Connie glanced at the waiting staff. Most of them still appeared confused, but Archer, Warren, and Mrs Strickland were clearly concentrating.

"There's been a man in the house. A stranger. He threatened me with a knife and said Lord Wingrave should stop interfering in his business."

Will looked around at the staff as Connie spoke. Their faces displayed varying degrees of shock and horror, but no-one looked guilty, as far as he could tell.

"It seems too much of a coincidence that this happened at the exact time I arrived home," he said. "Danny, what did you see?"

Danny sniffed, and wiped his nose on his sleeve. "I was in the trees, and I seen Sandow. He was hiding in the hedges and the like in the front of the house."

Damn—one of the new men was supposed to be at the front of the house at all times. Will eyed the gardeners one by one.

"My lord," Tanner said, wringing his cap in his hand. "I was clipping the hedges in front, but she came out and said Lady Wingrave wanted the back garden dug first." Tanner's finger pointed at Mrs Strickland.

"That's a lie," the housekeeper declared. "I do not give the orders for—"

"Enough!" Will raised his voice to cut across her.

Mrs Strickland looked at him, her lips tight and hands clenched.

That looks as much like fear as anger.

"When was this, Danny?" Best get the rest of the story first. "How long before I returned, I mean."

"Dunno exactly. A while. I would have come to tell someone, but he'd have seen me."

That was fair enough—Danny had already come to enough harm at Sandow's hands. "Then what happened?"

"I heard a whistle. Come from near the road, I reckon. When I looked again, Sandow wasn't there. I started up to the house, then I seen him climbing out of a window." The lad sniffed and rubbed his face again. "I lay down so he didn't see me."

Will put his hand on Danny's shoulder again. "Thank you Danny. You did nothing wrong."

The bastard had not only threatened Connie, but flaunted his power by doing it when Will was almost at home.

"Warren, how is it that this man got into the house without anyone noticing?"

"The windows in the parlour were shut, my lord. He must have broken in through one of them, or come in through the front door."

"Archer, go and check the windows."

Archer dashed off, and Will took a deep breath, maintaining his patience with an effort. "Warren, I'm not asking which entrance he used, but why no-one saw him."

"Mrs Strickland was consulting me about linens and crockery, my lord. It was a lengthy discussion." Warren's eyes narrowed as his gaze turned to the housekeeper.

"I was polishing the silver," Barton chipped in.

"The maids were in the kitchen with me, my lord." Mrs Curnow's chin went up, as if challenging Will to blame her.

"As you all should have been, Mrs Curnow," Will confirmed, and her posture relaxed.

Mrs Strickland had been with Warren. As Will looked at the housekeeper, her gaze slid away.

Of course, she *was* the most likely suspect. The statements from Tanner and Warren backed that up. He breathed deeply, controlling his anger. She'd helped Sandow threaten Connie with a knife.

"Barton, Warren, escort Mrs Strickland off the premises. She has ten minutes to—"

Connie's hand on his arm stopped him. "I think locking her in her room would be better, my lord."

Why? He took a deep breath; Connie would have a reason. "Lock her up."

Mrs Strickland, mouth set, got to her feet and marched out. Barton and Warren followed.

Archer returned from his inspection. "No sign of any windows being forced, my lord."

The front door then. Somehow that made it worse.

He felt a touch on his arm, and Connie spoke. "My lord, what would your father do if this man harmed you?" She turned her head away, looking at the assembled servants. Ah, *they* were the intended audience.

"You know how vindictive my father is. I'm his heir, and he'd take revenge. The person—or people—responsible would be tried and hanged. And anyone he even *thinks* may have helped—if they're lucky, they may only get transported."

Widening eyes suggested that his message was getting through.

"He's not above bribing the magistrates and judges, or paying people to give false witness," Will added. He wasn't sure of the latter, but he wouldn't put it past Marstone. "However wealthy Sandow might be through cheating the villagers, my father can outspend him. Marstone has influence in high places, and will win in the end."

He wasn't sure how much help his little speech would be, but it might restrain one or two of the villagers from backing up Sandow. Connie gave a nod when he looked at her. Moving his gaze across the servants, he wondered which of them would talk in the village.

"I expect you all to be vigilant from now on. If any of you see anything suspicious, you tell me. If I am not around, you tell Lady Wingrave, or Archer. Is that clear?"

Nods all round indicated that his message had got through.

"Very well. Archer, Danny, come with me, please." He offered his arm to Connie, and led the small party to the library. A buzz of talk started as the kitchen door swung to behind them.

Connie sank into a chair and took a sip of the brandy that was still in her hand.

Will sat down at his desk and took some papers out of a drawer.

He nodded at the two who had come in with them. "Take a seat." They did so, Archer looking ill at ease and Danny curious.

"Why d'you reckon Sandow came now, my lord?" Archer asked.

"I had a bit of an argument with Mrs Strickland this morning," Connie interjected. "She's only just started going about the house again." And if she'd obeyed Connie's orders, she'd have spent part of the morning with the maids in the guest rooms—plenty of time to find out anything they knew of the past week's goings on.

"That Mary looked frightened when you was talking, my lord," Archer said, his unease disappearing as he became involved in the discussion.

Mary—the scullery maid who'd been waiting on the housekeeper. She could have been sent down to the village with anything Mrs Strickland had found out. If that was right, then the rest of the staff were probably guilty of nothing more than keeping their mouths shut about anything they saw.

Will looked up from the notes he'd been consulting. "Archer, tell me anything new you've found out about the villagers."

Connie rested her head on the back of the chair, watching through half-closed eyes as Archer reported and Danny chipped in with his own opinions.

"Why has no-one got together to fight back?" she asked, when they finished speaking.

Archer shrugged.

"He gives money to whiddlers," Danny stated.

"Informers, I imagine," Will said. "So no-one trusts anyone else?"

"Not enough to go against him. He brings in the smuggling money, too, see." Danny's brow furrowed. "My lord, you said something about cheating, what was that about?"

Will gathered his lists together and started to explain. Connie was surprised at the amount of research he'd done. Danny and Archer both looked a little confused as he went through the calculations, but appeared happy to trust his conclusions. Danny's eyes grew round at Will's estimate of Sandow's profit from a run.

"What I don't know," Will finished, "is how much each villager contributes, and what they get back."

"It's nothing like that, my lord," Danny said. "But Sandow, he can talk to the Frenchies to buy the stuff."

"Je parle français, aussi," Will said.

Connie smiled as Danny scratched his head.

"I suspect the people he buys from speak sufficient English to conduct business," Will added. "They must make a tidy profit, too."

Danny nodded, glancing at Connie and back to Will. "My lord, why are you telling *me* all of this?"

Will leaned back in his chair, steepling his hands in front of his face. "Danny, you are the only person in the village who I *know* will not tell tales to Sandow. I am not going to stand for him threatening Lady Wingrave, or me. Or your family, come to that. Will you help me?"

The boy's shoulders squared as Connie watched, and he sat up straighter in his chair. Connie didn't like the idea of recruiting someone so young into this business, but Danny was already involved.

"What do I have to do, my lord?"

"You and Archer try to talk to a few of the villagers—without Sandow finding out. Once we get rid of Sandow I will take over organising the smuggling, but it will be run *fairly*."

Danny's head tilted to one side. "What if someone don't want to contribute?"

"Then they need not."

"They'll tattle."

"I can probably arrange for the revenue men not to listen." Will looked Danny in the eye. "What I will *not* do is have people beaten up."

Danny looked at Archer, doubt clear in his face. "They won't listen to the likes of us.

That was true, Connie thought. But it seemed Will *had* been thinking this through.

"You two can find out if a few men might back me up. We'll pick a time when Sandow is away and I'll come and talk to them. Once we have a few people on our side, it will be easier to recruit others to help get rid of Sandow."

"Maybe we start with Bill Roberts," Danny said, looking at Archer. "I used to reckon he was sweet on Ma, so he don't like Sandow much."

"Very good. Archer, take him back to the kitchen and get Mrs Curnow to feed him. I'll leave it to you to decide how best to get to talk to the right people."

"Right you are, my lord. C'mon, Danny."

Connie watched Will as he shuffled his papers together and put them away. There must be something more to his plan—Sandow would not let someone take over without a fight. And Will would make that his task; he wouldn't get someone else to fight for him.

She would just have to hope he was careful.

Will pushed the desk drawer closed. Connie still sat in her chair, watching him. What was she thinking?

"Will, don't underestimate him. He's not big, not much taller than me, but—" She broke off, wrapping her arms around her body. "His eyes…"

"I will be careful, I promise you." He went over to her chair, going down on one knee in front of it and taking her hand. "Connie, I'd like you to go to Exeter for a week or two, until this business is sorted out."

"Why?" She pulled her hand back.

"I haven't the men to protect you here, even with the two new ones. Or to Sir John in London, if you want to be sure of being beyond his reach."

"No, Will. I'd be worried sick about *you* all the time."

He let out a breath, surprised at the pleasure her statement gave him. He'd try again to persuade her, but tomorrow would be soon enough.

"Why did you stop me sending Mrs Strickland away?" he asked, turning to other matters.

"She must know something about Sandow and what goes on in the village. I thought we should question her before we decide what to do."

Of course. He should have thought of that himself.

"That's a matter for tomorrow," he said. "Come, let us see what Mrs Curnow can give us for dinner."

"I've made sure everything is locked up," Will said, standing in the doorway that linked their bedrooms. He walked over to where Connie sat in front of her dressing table, brushing her hair.

She met his eyes in the mirror. "You think he might come back?"

He'd said it to reassure her, not to worry her. "No."

Not so soon, at least.

He took the brush from her hand, moving it down the length of her hair in slow strokes. She tilted her head back a little, eyes closed in what he hoped was enjoyment, but there was still that small frown.

"Come to bed?"

"If you wish it."

She didn't sound keen on the idea. Putting the brush down, he moved so he was leaning on the dressing table, facing her. "Connie, I'm a man. I *always* wish it."

Good, that raised a tiny smile.

"But I do not want you—ever—to feel you must agree if you do not want to."

She looked away. "I'm just…" She pressed her lips together. "Will, that man got into the house and no-one saw him, except Danny. He'd been lurking outside—"

"He's gone now, and I'm here. I'll keep you safe, Connie. No-one is going to threaten you again."

"Can you just hold me?"

"Yes." He led her to his own bed, so she'd be free to leave in the night if she wanted to. The sky was not quite dark, and enough light came through the gaps in the curtains to let him see what he was doing. He climbed into bed and patted the space beside him.

She snuggled into him, her head on his shoulder and one arm across his chest. The tension he could feel in her back gradually eased, and a sense of calm spread through him. There were still problems to be solved, but they could wait until later. He wanted her, yes, but that, too, could wait. It was enough for now to have her in his arms.

CHAPTER 42

Friday 18th July

"What are we going to do with Mrs Strickland?" Connie asked as they sat down to breakfast. It was a question Will had struggled with since he awoke.

"What do you suggest?" He poured himself a cup of coffee.

"She won't get another position without a character, so if you offer one she might tell you—"

"Us."

A small curve of her lips told him she was pleased at being included. "Tell *us* what she knows," she finished.

"Good idea. The nearest place she could look for work is Exeter."

"Which is well within reach of Sandow."

"Indeed—so the stage fare to London could be an added inducement."

She smiled, and reached for another slice of toast. He was glad to see her with a better appetite than last night.

After breakfast, Will asked Warren to bring Mrs Strickland to the library. He sat behind his desk, Connie in a chair beside him, with notepaper ready on the blotter.

"My lord?" Mrs Strickland stood with her hands folded in front of her. Remarkably calm, under the circumstances.

"You are leaving my service as of today, Mrs Strickland, without a character." He pushed some coins across the desk. "Two pounds, and that is generous."

Mrs Strickland eyed the coins, her lips thinning, and then fixed her gaze on Will's face. "I've served this household well, Lord Wingrave. You can't just—"

"Oh, I can. Besides, you have your pay from Sandow as well, have you not?"

"He... I mean..."

Will smiled without humour. "At least you are not trying to deny your involvement."

Mrs Strickland looked at the floor.

"Good," Will continued. "I will drive you down to Ashmouth. I'm sure you'll find someone there to help you get to Exeter, or wherever you choose to go." Would her arrival in Ashmouth in the chaise be enough to make Sandow suspect that the housekeeper had given information to Will?

She thought so, for her face paled and her knuckles showed white.

"Or Lady Wingrave can write you a character, and someone will drive you into Exeter."

"That... that would be preferable, my lord."

"I'm sure it would," Will retorted. "There is a price, however. You will tell us everything you have done for Sandow, and everything you know about his business. If your information is worth anything, I will even pay your fare on the stage to London."

Mrs Strickland closed her eyes for a moment. "Yes, my lord."

"Excellent. Lady Wingrave, would you like to start?"

They questioned her for half an hour, Will doing most of the talking and Connie taking notes and interspersing questions now and then.

In the end, they had nothing concrete against Sandow, but a good deal of general information about people and relationships in the village. He'd pass that on to Archer later.

Will even wondered if the housekeeper was glad to be out of her current situation, but any small sympathy he may have had soon withered as it became clear she had willingly taken Sandow's money, and bullied any of the other staff who stood in her way. She had at least confirmed that Warren and the others had done nothing more than look the other way and keep their mouths shut.

"I'll get Stubbs to take her into Exeter in the chaise tomorrow," he said, once Warren had taken the housekeeper away again.

"Do you think she'll go to your father?" Connie asked, gathering her notes into a tidy pile.

"Why would she do that? Oh, to report further on my activities, in hope of some reward?"

"That's what I was thinking, yes."

"She may, but it doesn't matter now. By the time she gets there, Sir John, or one of Talbot's people, will already have told some tale to him." He smiled without humour. "If she thinks Marstone will pay her for information he no longer needs, she's heading for disappointment."

"Not a way to keep your employees happy," she stated, pushing her chair back. "There's nothing else we need to do today, is there?"

"The estate books, still, I'm afraid."

"And household accounts for me," Connie said, turning her gaze to the window. "We could sit in the orchard for a while this afternoon if the weather clears up."

"I'd like that." He enjoyed the sway of her hips as she left, before turning to the ledgers.

Tuesday 22nd July

Peering into the glass as he scraped his razor down one cheek, Will wondered if the good weather would hold today. He was becoming impatient to get this business with Sandow finished.

His second visits to the farms over the last few days had been useful, but he'd missed Connie. He paused, the razor arrested halfway between jaw and bowl. Today's visits could wait—he'd spend the day with his wife instead. Once Sandow had been dealt with, she could come and meet the farmers and their wives with him. She would be at ease with the wives in a way he was not, and could extract information he could not get himself. And he would have the pleasure of her company.

He scraped the last bits of his jaw, and rinsed the soap from his face. If she was to come with him, it would be helpful if she knew more about each farm. They could spend the morning together going over what he'd found so far.

His thoughts turned to Sandow again as he pulled his shirt over his head. Archer had identified a handful of men who might be prepared to stand up to him—if they had someone to spur them into action.

It was nearly mid-day when Archer interrupted their discussion in the library. "My lord, can you come down to the village this afternoon?"

Connie put her finger on the accounts to keep her place.

"What's happened?" Will asked.

"Bill Roberts is ready to talk, and Sandow's been seen riding out of the village."

Connie's chest tightened. Will would go down to the village, but what would happen if Sandow came back?

"Give me ten minutes to change," Will said to Archer. "I'll see you outside."

Archer nodded and left, closing the library door behind him.

"Stay indoors, Connie," Will said. "Lock yourself in your room, if you feel you need to. Sandow's not likely to come here, but with both me and Archer in the village, better to be safe than sorry."

She put a hand on his arm. "Will, don't underestimate him."

He bent forward and kissed her forehead. "I'll be careful, I promise. I made a will, remember? If anything happens to me, Harry

Tregarth and Sir John will look after you—you won't need to have anything to do with your father, or mine."

"That's all right then," she retorted. Martha had said that men were often oblivious to things in front of them, but did Will really not realise she cared for him?

"Connie?"

"Be careful, Will. Please."

He hesitated. "I have to go, Connie."

Connie rubbed her face after he left, wondering if she should go after him and apologise. She loved him—she could not let him go with such a cool farewell.

The clatter of boots on the stairs roused her from her thoughts and she hurried into the hall. "Will!"

He turned in the doorway.

"Come back safely."

His lips curved in a smile that went straight to her heart, then he waved a hand and hurried down the steps to where Archer was waiting.

She stayed in the doorway until the two men were out of sight, glad they had parted on good terms. She had to trust he wouldn't take unnecessary risks and would indeed come back to her safely.

That didn't stop the weight in her chest at the idea he might be hurt. Will hadn't seen the menace in Sandow's eyes.

"My lord?" Archer spoke from behind Will as they walked through the woods.

"What is it, Archer? Changed your mind?"

"No. My lord, if this ends up as a fight…?"

Will stopped, turning to face the groom. "You think it will?"

"Sandow ain't stupid, my lord. He went up the road, but there's no saying whether he's really gone or if he's got wind of something going on. He's bound to know that me and Danny have been talking to folk, even if he hasn't caught us at it yet."

"True enough."

"You think so, too, my lord, else why pistols and a knife?"

Will patted his pocket—the bulge made by the pistols *was* obvious. "Your point, Archer?"

"He won't fight fair, my lord. You shouldn't, either."

"I'm not regarding this as an exercise in pugilism, Archer, but thank you for the warning."

"Kick him in the ballocks if you can, sir. He deserves it."

Will turned and walked on, cringing at the thought of being on the receiving end of such a blow. Doing something like that in the heat of a brawl was one thing; planning on unfair tactics seemed different, wrong.

He recalled the morning in Tothill Fields that had begun all this. Allowing Lord Elberton to take his second shot had been a bloody stupid thing to do—honour be damned. He'd thought he had no-one who depended on him, but his sisters would have been distraught if he'd been killed, and completely unprotected against anything his father might do to them in future.

Now there was even more at stake, Connie above all. And he finally had the chance to do something that would serve his country.

Archer was right—this wasn't an affair of honour. Sandow was a man with no honour.

Will ducked his head under the low cottage door. Inside, the small windows made the light dim, despite the sunshine outside. Seven men were gathered, one sitting at the small table, the others standing around the walls with folded arms. The furniture was basic—only a couple of chairs and a low cupboard, but the stone-flagged floor was clean. Some lengths of wood leaned against the wall in one corner— makeshift clubs, Will guessed.

"Danny, keep watch," Will ordered. The lad nodded and headed back up the street. Archer took up a position by the door to the tiny scullery behind the house, saying something in a low voice to the man nearest to him.

"I'm Bill Roberts, my lord." The seated man rose as he spoke, a brief gesture towards the remaining chair being his only concession to courtesy. He had a less weather-beaten face than the other men—a carpenter, Archer had said.

"Thank you for allowing me to talk to you all." Will sat, and put his hat on the table. "Only seven of you?"

"Only seven of us with no families, my lord."

Sensible, he had to admit, although a bit more support would have been useful. "Let me start by showing you how profitable your free trading is."

"Why're you doing this at all?" A stocky man with dirty blond hair spoke. "You never bin 'ere more'n a few days a time 'til now, then you stick your nose into our business."

Willing to talk, Archer had said. He glanced at his groom, who just shrugged. But it was a fair question.

"Sandow threatened my wife. He beats up boys and women. He likely does the same to other families, or threatens to." He scanned his audience; no-one disagreed.

"Go on, then," the blond one finally said. No 'my lord' there, Will noted. His rank wasn't going to sway anyone in this room, but that was as it should be. Men who had been persuaded by argument and their own interests would be more reliable.

"This is an estimate of the profits from a single run." Will spread his papers out on the table, and went through the explanation he'd given to Archer and Danny a few days before. There was some head scratching, but Roberts and an old man with a beard pulled one of the sheets towards them and talked in low voices.

A sound from Archer's position made him look round, and he glimpsed his groom slipping out of the room, two of the villagers following. He resisted the impulse to go after them—Archer would call for help if he needed it.

"My lord." Roberts pushed Will's calculation towards him, some of the figures amended. "Them's more like the amounts of goods. There's more profit in it than you thought."

The blond man looked over Roberts' shoulder. "That makes it

worse. Sandow's keeping even more to hisself than you said." He turned his head. "Jimmy, come and look at this."

Will moved away, allowing room for the remaining villagers to gather around the table. From the snatches he heard, they were weighing up the risks of defying Sandow against the financial benefits of everyone having a greater share in the profits. There was a chance, of course, that they would decide to manage the smuggling themselves, but the fact that they had let Sandow continue unchallenged for so long showed a lack of initiative.

He moved over to the rear door, curious to see where Archer had got to. A muffled shout and a metallic clatter had him reaching down to check that the knife inside his right boot was loose in its scabbard. If it came to a fight in here, he should not try to use his pistols; there was too great a chance of hitting the wrong men. Talk at the table stopped.

Scuffling, then another metallic clatter followed by a dull thud. The door opened and Archer slipped through, his clothing dishevelled and a red mark down one side of his face. "Two of 'em, my lord. Tied up now. Danny says Sandow is on his way with one more."

"Someone told?" Roberts glared at the other villagers.

"You can worry about that later, Roberts," Will said. The two villagers who had helped Archer came back into the room, and the man nearest the clubs started to pass them round. If Sandow did venture in without checking on the two men he had sent to the back door, nine men might be too many in such a small space.

The silence grew tense, the villagers gripping their clubs and turning towards the door at any small noise. Even Will started when the back door opened, but it was only Danny slipping inside.

"He's coming. Got Kelly with him."

If all the accounts of Sandow's behaviour were true, Will would do the world a favour by shooting him when he walked in, but even with Archer's warning about the man not playing fair, he couldn't bring himself to do that.

The front door opened, and everyone turned in that direction, the villagers' knuckles whitening as they gripped their clubs.

CHAPTER 43

*C*onnie set the preserving jars in a row on the stillroom table, and checked the number of them against an old list. She had to be doing something while Will was away, to stop her mind dwelling on her fears. Unfounded fears, she hoped.

"There's more in another cupboard," Mrs Curnow said, coming into the room.

"I…Thank you." Talk, that's what she needed—to talk to someone. Not about Will, but about something else altogether. "How… how much sugar do we need for making jam?"

"He'll be all right, you'll see," Mrs Curnow said. "What you said about his lordship—Lord Marstone, I mean—I made sure Mary told her mother in the village. Stubbs, too. Sandow's a nasty one, all right, but he's not stupid."

Connie hoped she was right.

⁓

As Connie had said, Sandow was nothing special to look at, but the expression in his eyes sent a shiver of anticipation down Will's spine.

Sandow moved forward into the room, followed by a much larger man. The nearest villagers took a step back.

"If it isn't the little lordling," Sandow sneered, coming to a halt in front of Will.

This was the bastard who had frightened Connie. Will made an effort to calm his breathing. *Don't think about that now. Pretend it's a fencing match. No, a tavern brawl—no need to fight fair.*

He raised one brow and looked Sandow up and down in the best imitation of his father he could manage.

"Sandow, I presume? I believe you met my wife a few days ago."

Sandow stepped forwards, putting his face close to Will's. "Nice piece, she was. Bit too much of a Long Meg for me, but I'll have the pleasure of her if you don't keep your nose out of my business."

Ignore the threat.

Will moved one foot backwards, bracing it on the floor. "I think not." He waited until Sandow opened his mouth to speak again, bent his head and thrust forwards, the top of his head meeting Sandow's nose.

Sandow staggered back, a stream of curses muffled by the hand held to his face. The villagers stared open-mouthed as blood dripped through his fingers and ran down his chin.

Kelly stepped out from behind Sandow as Will steadied himself. Will flung up one arm to block a fist aimed at his face. His return blow landed on Kelly's ear as he dodged out of the way, but then Will froze. A shiny knife blade was waving not six inches from his eyes. The snarl on Kelly's face made it clear that he was only too ready to use it.

"My lord!" That was Archer.

Will spun away from the knife and then staggered sideways as an impact on the side of his head made his ears ring.

Sandow.

He ducked, and Sandow's clawing fingers grazed his head instead of gouging his eyes. He swung, but his fist met only air.

What the hell is everyone else doing?

"Come on you bastards!" Archer's voice rang out again. Will's eyes, focused on Sandow, registered movement at the edge of his vision.

Sandow, too, had a knife. Space, he needed more space. The back of his thighs met the table. Instead of retreating he had to step sideways to dodge Sandow's blade.

He had a knife in his boot. Time—just a second to distract Sandow and give him a chance to reach it.

His hat, on the table.

He reached and swung it towards Sandow's face as the man lunged forwards. Instead of grabbing his own knife, Will caught Sandow's wrist, forcing the man's blade away from his eyes. Sandow's momentum pushed Will backwards until he sprawled on his back on the table with Sandow a heavy weight on top of him.

"No!" A boy's voice, almost a scream.

Sandow's head lurched down towards his own, coming hard into contact with his nose. Will pushed, and to his surprise Sandow rolled off him, flopping to the floor with a groan.

Danny Trasker stood above the prone body, a club in one hand. He raised wide eyes to Will's face. "Have I killed him?"

Will bent forward to see. Sandow's chest was moving. "No, lad."

Sandow's eyelids flickered. Will's fist connected with the man's jaw as he opened his eyes. His head snapped sideways.

Not enough. Sandow was hurt, but still half conscious.

Will stood astride and wound his fists into the front of Sandow's coat, pulling him upright as the man struggled feebly to free himself. If he came round properly someone else would get hurt.

Steadying Sandow with one hand, Will hit him again, as hard as he could. This time Sandow fell to the floor, his head striking one corner of the hearth with a sickening crunch.

One of the villagers pushed past, bending over the prone body. Roberts.

It had taken the villagers long enough to join in, Will thought, cradling his aching hand. But the fight had been quick, and there was scarcely room to move with so many men in such a small space.

Archer and two of the villagers had overpowered Sandow's henchman. The groom stood with one foot on Kelly's back while the other two tied him up.

Will became aware of his nose throbbing, and warmth spreading down his chin. Groping in a pocket for his handkerchief, he pressed it against his nose and bent over to see why Sandow was still unmoving. Roberts had fingers resting against the side of the man's neck.

He looked up at Will. "He's dead."

Will rubbed his free hand in his hair. *Dead?*

He'd never killed a man before.

The villagers stood still, staring at the body. Finally, Danny spoke. "He's really dead?"

Roberts put a hand on the boy's shoulder. "He is. It's over, and you done well, lad. I reckon you saved Lord Wingrave's life."

Danny's eyes focused once more on the still form of Sandow on the floor.

"Danny, can you take a message to the big house for me?" Will asked, his voice muffled by the handkerchief.

The boy nodded, wiping one sleeve across his face.

"Tell Lady Wingrave that Archer and I are safe. I'll be back in an hour or two."

Danny nodded again.

Roberts looked around. "Moore, Porter, go with him."

One of the men put his arm around Danny's shoulders as they ushered him out. Roberts picked up a toppled chair and gestured for Will to sit in it. Will gingerly removed the handkerchief from his nose, but it was still bleeding.

Now he only had a dead body and three prisoners to deal with.

"Could drop the lot of them in the sea," one of the villagers suggested, to murmurs of agreement.

It was tempting, but then one of them might feel justified in doing the same to someone else in the future.

"No." Will said the word with enough force that they all turned and looked at him.

"Sandow assaulted me, and I killed him while defending myself."

316

That had the advantage of being the truth. "The magistrate will accept that story."

Roberts pursed his lips. "All right."

"The other three will be handed over for trial on the same charge of assault." Were there other gang members who would testify in their favour? "The magistrate will take my word for it," he went on. "If necessary I can arrange to have them tried further away than Exeter."

From the mutterings and exchanged glances, not all the men were happy. He could deal with that some other time—his main objective for the evening had been achieved.

"Archer, get the body and the prisoners brought up to Ashton Tracey."

"Right, my lord."

"Roberts, we can discuss the free trading tomorrow. I can offer several advantages in terms of credit, and so on. But if you want me to be involved, I'll have no more violence. Let me know when the rest of the villagers are ready."

"Aye, I'll do that. my lord."

Good. Now all he had to do tonight was to face Connie with a bruised face and bloody nose.

～

By the time Will had been gone for two hours, Connie and Mrs Curnow had progressed to drinking tea and eating cake while the cook reminisced about the days when Lady Marstone had come here every summer.

"She didn't used to entertain, but cooking for them lads kept me busy, right enough. Mind, we had a lot more staff th—"

Connie turned her head at a sound from the scullery and shot to her feet as the door burst open and Danny Trasker dashed in.

Will...?

"His lordship sent me to say he's safe," the lad gasped. "Mr Archer, too."

Connie sank back into her chair, limp with relief, as Mrs Curnow

317

walked across to the open door. Connie drew in a sharp breath at the sight of two men standing there, hats in their hands.

"We were sent up with the lad, mum, to make sure he got here safe."

Mrs Curnow stared at them for a moment, then gave a quick nod. "You want some food?"

"No, thank you, we best be getting back."

They vanished, and Mrs Curnow bustled about, putting the kettle to boil and cutting a large slab of cake. "Sit down, Danny. You'll be wanting something to eat."

"You are not hurt, are you Danny?" Connie asked, as the boy pulled his chair up to the table. Streaks in the dirt on his face looked like tear tracks.

"No, my lady."

Connie resisted the impulse to ask Danny what had happened while he ate. Will was safe, which was all that mattered, and she'd get a more coherent account from him when he returned.

Danny didn't seem to know what to do with himself when he'd finished eating, so Connie suggested he keep watch at the front of the house.

It was nearly an hour before he came dashing back, saying a lot of men and a cart were coming up the drive.

The front door opened, spilling light onto the top of the steps as Will trudged up the drive. "Take them to the stables," he said, and Archer led the horse and cart round the side of the house.

In spite of the pain of his battered nose and bruised face, Will felt energised when he saw Connie silhouetted in the doorway. She was safe now—even if Sandow had more sympathisers in Ashmouth, the rest of the villagers would have the confidence to deal with them without his intervention.

"You're hurt," Connie exclaimed as the light fell on his face.

"A bit bruised, that's all." Her eyes turned to the blood staining his neckcloth and shirt. "Just a bloody nose, Connie, honestly."

"What happened? No, have something to eat first. Do you need bandages or…? That looks like—"

Will took hold of her shoulders and pulled her towards him. "Connie, I'm fine, but I could do with something to drink."

She gazed into his eyes. "I'll get something. Go and sit down."

Five minutes later they sat in the library, Will with a mug of ale in one hand.

"What was in the cart?" Connie asked.

"Three prisoners, and Sandow."

"Sandow…?" Her eyes widened in alarm.

"He won't trouble us any more."

"He's dead? How…?" She took a deep breath. "Not now—you can tell me about it tomorrow. But will there be no more threats, then, to anyone?"

"No. The other three, they'll be tried for assault." He kneaded the back of his neck, now stiff and sore.

"Do you need to do anything else tonight?"

"Not tonight, no. Tomorrow I need to find the local magistrate, get all this mess sorted out legally."

"Pretend you're an upstanding, law-abiding citizen?" Her mouth curved up a little.

"Ha, yes." Ironic, for a future smuggler, but there was no need to break more laws than he had to. He looked down at his coat. "I'll get myself cleaned up, then it's time to retire."

Will stared up at the canopy over the bed, listening to Connie's slow breathing. She'd fallen asleep soon after they curled up together, but his mind still buzzed with the events of the day. Sandow's death was for the best—dead, he couldn't escape from jail, or intimidate juries to return a verdict of not guilty. That was logical, but he heard again the sickening sound as Sandow's head hit the hearth.

Could he have done anything differently? He wasn't sure—too

much had depended on the actions Roberts and the other Ashmouth men had chosen to take.

Archer had done very well. He would make a good go-between for the liaison between Will and the smuggling operation. Danny could be useful, too, when he was older, but the first thing to do for him was to get his family back home.

Connie's breathing changed; she wriggled and snuggled closer to him.

With her in his arms, he was at peace.

CHAPTER 44

ednesday 23rd July
"This has arrived for Lord Wingrave, my lady."
Warren entered and laid a letter on the corner of the desk. "Stubbs brought it down from Ashton St Andrew when he returned from Ottery. Mr Nancarrow said he'd get the Traskers sent home as soon as he could."

"Thank you, Warren."

Will and Archer had set off early to take the three prisoners and Sandow's body to Exeter. He might not be back for hours. She picked up the letter—there was no harm in seeing who it was from.

The frank was a scrawl, but the name looked like Tregarth. Could their plan to get Marstone to sell Ashton Tracey have worked already? It would be good thing, if so. Will could concentrate on his business with Talbot, and on improving the tenant farms. He might have to manage that with no further money from his father—the allowance Marstone had made would certainly stop. A man such as the Earl of Marstone would have great influence, and could surely make their lives difficult in other ways as well, if he chose to.

A shiver of unease ran through her as she remembered telling Will about her true ancestry. Will might not mind, but his father certainly would. She hoped Will would not feel the need to taunt his father with that information.

The sun was slanting low through the windows when Will returned, still covered in dust from the road, and joined Connie in her parlour. "All dealt with," he said. "There'll have to be an inquest on Sandow, and I'll need to be at the assizes when the other three are tried, but the magistrate didn't foresee any difficulties."

"That's good."

Her smile warmed him as he took the letter she held out.

"Sir John?" He broke the seal and unfolded the page, a grin spreading across his face as he read. "Marstone sold Ashton Tracey to one of Sir John's colleagues, and he has signed it over to me, as agreed. Sir John says the documents are being forwarded to Kellet in Exeter. He didn't say how he got Marstone to do so—I'll get the full story out of him next time I see him."

"Does it matter?" Connie asked, her voice sounding rather flat.

"It would amuse me to know. Connie, this is good news—this is our home now, properly. My father cannot take it away." Finally, he would be able to live his life as he wished to. As long as he could keep up the mortgage payments, but between improved rents and some income from smuggling, he should be able to manage that. "Sir John says that Marstone volunteered to come here and ensure the place was ready for its new owner."

"That doesn't sound like... Oh. He means to come and evict you himself?"

"No doubt. And to read the riot act and escort me—us—back to Marstone Park." His father had spied on him and dictated to him for years—the tables would be well and truly turned. "I have to say this will be the first time I'm actually looking forward to meeting him."

Connie didn't look pleased.

"What about you, Connie? Don't you want your father to know he'll not be gaining by selling you off?"

"No, Will. I just want to forget about him. Please don't invite him here on my account."

Getting up, he crossed to her chair and put one hand on her shoulder. "Don't worry. I won't if you don't want me to. Time for bed?"

Friday 25th July

Marstone came two days later. Will had been in the village discussing the possibilities for smuggling, and saw his father's coach as he rode into the stable yard.

"When did he arrive?" he asked, as Archer took Mercury from him.

"A couple of hours, maybe, my lord."

Damn. Had Connie had to entertain him for all that time? He hurried round to the front of the house—he did not want his father to upset her.

Warren awaited him. "His lordship is in the large drawing room, my lord."

"Lady Wingrave?"

"Er, Lady Wingrave was in the kitchen gardens when Lord Marstone arrived. She said she was not at home to visitors."

Will's anxiety lessened. "She is not with him?"

"No, my lord. I understand she is still in the gardens. His lordship was not pleased."

I'll bet he wasn't. Will recalled his father's description of Connie as obedient and knowing her place, and he couldn't help smiling.

"He went so far as to order me to fetch her, my lord."

Will's brows drew together. That was going too far.

Warren cleared his throat. "I'm afraid I resorted to untruths, my lord, and claimed not to know where she was."

"Good man." Will startled Warren by clapping him on the shoulder. He debated whether his father would be more enraged if he took the time to change, or if he presented himself in all his dirt.

Go now. The sooner Marstone was on his way again, the sooner Connie would feel she could come back indoors.

In the drawing room, his father sat by the fireplace, his face set in its usual lines of disapproval.

"A fine time to show yourself, Wingrave. I've been waiting for hours. Hours!"

"That's hardly my fault. I didn't know you were coming." Will sat on the arm of the facing chair, swinging one leg.

"I have been left here alone. Your wife had not the courtesy—"

"*You* had not the courtesy to inform us of your visit." Will took a deep breath. Losing his temper would only satisfy his father that he was winning.

"You should have expected it." The earl's expression smoothed, his lips curving in a cold smile. "After what I heard of your activities."

"What did you hear?"

"You've been dallying with that strumpet again. I told you not to—"

"Is this the talk in town?" He hoped not, for Connie's sake. It would be a few years before they needed to be there to support Theresa and Lizzie, but he didn't want people even thinking about Connie as someone unlucky enough to have an unfaithful husband.

"Your housekeeper informed me," the earl said. "Sir John Tregarth, too—it seems he saw her in Exeter. I warned you, Wingrave, in the most specific terms. I said if you flouted my conditions I would sell this place to pay your debts, and I have done so. You will return with me to Marstone Park. In addition to ensuring your behaviour is appropriate, your wife clearly needs further instruction on the manners expected of a well-born lady."

The earl leaned back in his seat, his mouth now expressing malicious satisfaction.

Will smiled—Connie's true ancestry would wipe the sneer from Marstone's face. His father would be livid. He'd...

What will he do?

His smile faded. Annulment? Will would not countenance such a thing, but that would not stop Marstone trying to make it happen. Although Charters *had* deceived Marstone about Connie's true birth, the Church wouldn't consider that sufficient grounds even if Will applied for an annulment himself. But his father would stir up gossip, scandal. He didn't care about that for himself, but it would be very unpleasant for Connie.

"Well, boy, have you nothing to say?"

Will gazed at his father, seeing the earl's smirk beginning to fade. He could tell his father that Ashton Tracey was now his, and enjoy the earl's defeat.

"What do you want me to say?"

Perhaps his father's bewilderment was sufficient revenge, although he'd only spoken to gain time. What was it Fancott had said—no, quoted? Something like the best revenge was to not be like your enemy.

He'd won, even though his father didn't know it yet. Marstone would find out in due course, but there was enough satisfaction in being free of him, with a useful occupation and a wife he loved. And he'd be more able to help his sisters, when the time came, if he didn't gloat now.

"An apology for your disobedience, at least. You will return—"

"I will vacate the house as soon as the new owner asks me to in person," Will said, now needing no effort to keep his voice calm. "Do you wish for some refreshment before you leave?"

Marstone appeared to be lost for words. Will rang the bell, and asked Warren to ensure the earl's coach was readied for departure.

"You cannot eject me from my own—"

"You sold it," Will reminded him. "I do not want my wife upset by confrontations, so I think it best you leave now."

"Nonsense. You will accompany me—"

"No. I will not upend this household at a moment's notice." *Or ever, not at your command.*

He rang the bell again, ignoring his father's tirade.

"Lord Marstone is leaving now," he said, when Warren reappeared. "Father, I bid you farewell."

He ran Connie to earth in one corner of the kitchen garden, beyond the rows of carrots Stubbs was hoeing. Work on the garden was proceeding much faster now the two extra men no longer had to watch for intruders. Someone had brought a chair and small table for her, and she sat in the shade of a pear tree, concentrating on something in her hands.

Embroidery, he saw, as he got closer, his heart lifting at the sight of her bent head in the dappled shade, and at the ready smile with which she greeted him.

How could he even have contemplated throwing her ancestry in his father's face? He would do nothing to harm her, everything to keep her safe.

Her smile dimmed quickly to concern.

"He's leaving," Will stated.

"You're not angry that I didn't—?"

"Good grief, no. I was worried in case he'd upset you."

She shook her head, but the happy smile did not return. "What will he do now?"

"Connie, all will be well, I promise. Will you walk with me?"

She nodded, sticking her needle into the fabric and tidying her threads into a small box at her feet.

"I thought we could go to Lion Rocks," he said. "I need to get something from my room first."

By the time Will came back outside, Connie was waiting, holding a basket with bottled lemonade and ale, and a slab of cake. Will took it from her, putting something of his own beneath the cloth before holding his elbow out.

She took his arm, wondering what he'd said to the earl. His face looked thoughtful now, not worried as it had been when he joined her in the garden earlier. She'd been expecting triumph, or anger, depending on how their meeting had gone.

"I didn't say much to my father in the end," Will said, before she asked. "I just said we wouldn't be moving out until the new owner asked us to." He looked down at her, his smile gentle. "That's not what you were expecting, I know. I'll explain when we get there."

They walked on, Connie's heart feeling lighter. There might still be trouble from the earl ahead, but Will hadn't made it worse by taunting him. They would face any future problems together.

Once through the band of trees, the waves on the rocks below sounded louder, the cries of the gulls harsher. Connie sat on a rock, the sparkle of sun on the sea still a novelty to her.

Will uncovered the basket, but instead of bringing out the food, he picked up a small box. He opened it and rummaged in its contents, dropping several rings into her lap.

"Your mother's rings?" A bubble of happiness rose inside her. These were a gift. The gowns and things he'd bought for her in Exeter were necessities, he'd said, when she'd tried to thank him.

"Yes. She wanted my wife to have some of her jewels. My sisters have already chosen a few pieces each. These rings—I'd like you to have one, as well as whatever else you like. I've left the other pieces in the house." He reached over to spread them out on her lap. "Which do you prefer?"

They were fine rings, delicate, without the ostentatious gems of her own wedding ring. The prettiest, she thought, was a simple band set with tiny sapphires.

"This one," she said, turning it in her fingers so the gems caught the sunlight. "The colour reminds me of the sea on days like today." She looked directly at him. "They match your eyes, too."

She'd expected—hoped, even—that he'd take that as invitation for a caress or a kiss, but he only smiled briefly before his expression became serious again.

"I like that one too." He took the rings from her and put them in the box, keeping back only the one she had chosen. Rather than give it back to her, he held it in the palm of one hand.

"Connie, before... when we married, I was bored, frustrated with having nothing to do. I resented the way my father tried to control —*did* control my life. When he forced me to wed, I wanted to revenge myself on him."

Connie nodded; she knew that.

"You have made me realise how futile that was. Today, I didn't tell him about your parents for fear of the scandal he might cause. I know I'm no stranger to scandal, but it would be horrible for you. The idea of revenging myself on him didn't seem important any more. As you said about your own father, he can't bother us now. He doesn't even know yet that we will own Ashton Tracey."

"I'm glad, Will." For herself, but for him too, that he'd made that decision.

"Whatever happens in the future, Connie, we'll discuss things, and make decisions between us."

He broke off, glancing away for a moment. When he looked back, his expression was rueful. "I'm making a mess of this, Connie. What I want to say is that whatever my father's motivations were for forcing us to marry, I'm glad he did. You've made me see things more clearly, you're turning me into a better man."

She couldn't take the credit for that, but it was lovely of him to say so. "Will, you did that yourself."

He ignored her words. Instead, he reached out and took her left hand in his, easing off the heavy Marstone wedding ring. Then her breath caught as he picked up the sapphire ring she'd chosen.

"Connie, I love you. Will you take this ring as my pledge for our life together, and my love for you?"

Tears pricked her eyes at his words, at the uncertainty in his face. She'd hoped to hear such words one day, but hadn't really expected to.

"Yes," she managed to say, past the lump in her throat. "Of *our* love for each other."

He slipped the ring onto her finger, and gently pulled her to her feet. "Partners, Connie?" he whispered.

"And lovers."

That kiss was one she would always remember, the sounds of the surf and the gulls fading as her world shrank to the joy of being in his arms.

All would be well.

THE END

Thank you for reading *Sauce for the Gander*; I hope you enjoyed it. If you can spare a few minutes, could you leave a review on Amazon or Goodreads? You only need to write a few words.

～

Sauce for the Gander is Book 1 in the Marstone Series. Each book will be a complete story with no cliffhangers.

Winning Trick is a short novella, an extended epilogue for *Sauce for the Gander*. What happens three years later when Will has to confront his father again?

Winning Trick is available free (on Kindle only), exclusively for members of my mailing list. Sign up via my website at:

www.jaynedavisromance.co.uk

My newsletters will tell you about new releases or special offers. I promise not to bombard you with emails. My website also has details about forthcoming books, and links to my Facebook, Twitter, and Pinterest pages.

ALSO BY JAYNE DAVIS

THE MRS MACKINNONS

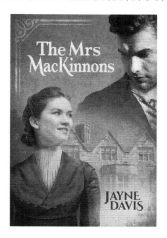

England, 1799

Major Matthew Southam returns from India, hoping to put the trauma of war behind him and forget his past. Instead, he finds a derelict estate and a family who wish he'd died abroad.

Charlotte MacKinnon married without love to avoid her father's unpleasant choice of husband. Now a widow with a young son, she lives in a small Cotswold village with only the money she earns by her writing.

Matthew is haunted by his past, and Charlotte is fearful of her father's renewed meddling in her future. After a disastrous first meeting, can they help each other find happiness?

Available on Kindle and in paperback.